[redacted]

Inheriting the Earth

Photo: Anthea Pokroy

Jill Nudelman

Inheriting the Earth

Jill Nudelman

UKZN PRESS
UNIVERSITY OF KWAZULU-NATAL PRESS

Published in 2012 by University of KwaZulu-Natal Press
Private Bag X01
Scottsville 3209
South Africa
Email: books@ukzn.ac.za
Website: www.ukznpress.co.za

ISBN: 978-1-86914-225-4

Editors: Pippa Jazmine Dyer and Elana Bregin
Layout and design: Patricia Comrie
Proofreader: Nicola Jones
Cover design: MDesign
Author Photograph: Anthea Pokroy

Typeset in 11.5pt Adobe Garamond Pro

Printed and bound by Interpak Books, Pietermaritzburg

We don't inherit the earth from our ancestors,
we borrow it from our children.

(Native American proverb)

Acknowledgements

Acknowledgement must firstly be given to Lara Mallen's Master's thesis entitled *Rock art and identity in the North Eastern Cape Province*. This happy find that I chanced upon while surfing the net enabled me to create a more likely scenario for the diary extracts.

The library notice, 'Bags', was modified from the column 'Library Chatter' appearing in the *Mountain Echo*, December 2006.

A special thanks must go to Andy and the story she told me one day as we pounded the streets of Johannesburg. Without her story, I would never have had mine.

Thanks to Chris Thurman, my supervisor on the MA Creative Writing Course at Wits University. His enthusiasm sustained me when I was floundering in a sea of self-doubt. Gratitude must also be expressed to Leon de Kock and the MA group of 2008/9 for their assiduous readings and constructive criticism.

Thanks to Sam Nudelman, Leigh Nudelman Sussman, Di Michelow-Valle, Ignacio Valle, Debbie and David Lubinsky, and again to Andy for reading the chapters as they rolled off the printer, and for prodding me on when it seemed as if Rose was sleeping the Big Sleep.

To the Writing Group: David Medalie, Maren Bodenstein, Emma Chen, Jean and Ellie Isserow, Liz Gunner, Susie Dinneen, Renos Spanoudes, Damon Garstang and Geoff Sifrin, for their finely tuned ears and valuable comments. Special thanks to Liz for suggesting I send the manuscript to her friend at UKZN Press when I was about to abandon it.

To Michelle Ferrer for penning a synopsis when I couldn't.

To Rob of R. Fischer and Associates for the lowdown on inheritances, wills and last testaments.

To Mark Rosin and Anthony Colegrave for their legal tender.

To Pippa Jazmine Dyer for her vision, skill and the innumerable hours she put in, and to Elana Bregin of UKZN Press for her outstanding editing that she carried out with such boundless patience and flair.

Finally, and with all my love, to Sam and our fab four – Leigh, Craig, Jake and Zach – for their love, humour, support and encouragement.

Prologue

Rose had never driven this far by herself. The journey unravelled in her mind's eye like a reel of grey tape: six-hundred kilometres of unfamiliar road to be conquered. Excited and apprehensive, she whispered a little prayer to the gods of the road and, with both hands clenching the steering wheel, she drove out of the parking garage. There was very little traffic at this time of day as she veered onto the overpass and followed the Killarney bends towards town. From her raised vantage point, she gazed out over Johannesburg. In the distance, Sandton City rose from the urban forest that stretched in a blue haze to the north.

Soon, she reached the unfamiliar section of highway that skirted the city centre, travelling past high-rises, warehouses and factories, partially cleared mine dumps rising tawny out of the landscape. Before long, she was rounding the bends of the massive interchanges on the outskirts of the city sprawl, where working-class suburbia and poorer townships lay side by side in dreary regularity.

Leaving behind the ugly power stations and plantations of electricity pylons somewhere between Alberton and Germiston, she became aware of her sense of relief. It was as if she'd yanked off one of those skull-squeezing Alice bands she'd worn as a child. She felt quite the heroine – the Thelma-Louise of Jo'burg. Where was the sexy mechanic to grind the roof off her car? The Brad Pitt of Boksburg. In her open-top Golf, she would fly in the wake of the wind as she moved away from her past, towards her past, away from her self, towards her self.

The landscape emptied and flattened and she found herself travelling through countryside awash with khakis and olives in the early-morning haze. Clumps of eucalyptus and poplar trees rose soft as felt against the pale sky. Rows of regimented mealie plants spiralled by. A blue-black *sakabula* bird ascended clumsily from a sea of rippling leaves, its long, heavy tail pointing to the ground. Sleek brown cows grazed in green fields. A pair of crows kicked up the red soil at the side of the road as they squabbled over a dead pigeon. Her mind went into trance mode as her car's odometer clocked up kilometre after kilometre in the rising heat.

One blink and she'd passed the dorps of Frankfort, Cornelia, Tweeling, Reitz and Roadside. Signboards warned her that 'Carelessness Kills' and told her to 'Slow Down Now!', or identified the dusty brown riverbeds – the Wilge, Kalk, Hol and Meul – on whose banks willow trees grew with only a promise of water. Koppies rose startlingly out of the veld, their names hinting of their histories and the wildlife that once roamed their slopes – Verkykerskop, Jakkalskop, Leeukop.

The landscape seemed almost devoid of human life. No children waved at her from the side of the road, no labourers on creaky old bicycles trundled by. Only ghosts seemed to traverse the thin topsoil of this terrain – ghosts of those who had perished over aeons of conflict and battle: Boer against British; Boer against Zulu; Zulu against British; Zulu against Basotho. In a country where history had been a disaster, the past came at her from every angle.

The outside temperature was thirty degrees. The Friday-morning traffic had been building up steadily. She noticed her fellow road users were mostly male. They drove with one hand on the steering wheel, elbows jutting out the window, protruding from shirts of starched cotton, faded serge and khaki. Travelling salesmen and farmers, sometimes ferrying women who sat straight-backed beside them, staring straight ahead. Rose shared the road with phantom truck drivers, invisible in their cabins high above the tarmac, and taxi drivers bouncing to the beat that blared from their speakers, while their cramped passengers slumbered. Occasionally, her glance found a female face in profile, focused and serious at the wheel – an expression she recognised as her own. Their eyes would meet fleetingly and Rose would wonder: what was her story? Was she single or somebody's wife? Was she an inveterate lone traveller – or was this journey a first, a rite of passage for her, too?

Thinking how first-world, how civilised the state of the road, Rose moved into the fast lane to overtake a car, a blue Tazz. She returned to the slow lane. A few seconds later, the Tazz moved into the fast lane, overtaking her, now. She felt the driver's eyes on her as he passed. She looked straight ahead. Okay, mister, if it makes you feel better, if you're so insecure about your masculinity – you take the lead.

He had slowed down and was driving abreast of her. She stole a look at him. He leered at her in an unpleasant way and mouthed something she couldn't catch. Then he cut sharply in front of her and slowed again. She slammed on her brakes. God! What was she dealing with here? The Mad Max of the N3?

This is ridiculous. I'm going to lose you now. Hands gripping the steering wheel and mouth set, she moved back into the fast lane and caught the traffic slipstream until she was two or three cars ahead, then returned to the slow lane. But there he was again, driving neck and neck with her, dicing, smirking, playing his silly games. Exasperated, she glared at him though her window: 'Oh, get lost, you idiot!' she said aloud, her voice sounding small and polite to her ears; and with a bravura she didn't feel, she raised the middle finger of her right hand and threw it up for the man to see. A shadow passed over his face. He cut sharply in front of her again, slamming on brakes, slowing to a crawl. She was forced to brake sharply in response. How to get rid of this moron? Shoulders hunched over the steering wheel, mouth dry, she swerved into the fast lane and, stepping on the accelerator, wove through the traffic, keeping a watch on her rearview mirror all the while.

Soon, she couldn't see him any more; and there was the sign for the Harrismith rest-stop. Veering off the highway and speeding recklessly down the off-ramp, she swerved into a parking bay, her breathing heavy, her heart pounding loudly in her ears. Jesus! That was really scary. What an idiot! What game had he been playing? She felt quite weak. With characters like that out there, you had to be so careful as a woman alone. She sat for a few minutes, waiting for her heart to stop its thumping.

Rose rested her head in Livvie's lap and looked up at the ceiling. Livvie's nostrils got in the way. They were scary – like two red caves with thick black hairs poking out.

'Tell me again about my mommy.'

'Your mommy was a beautiful princess.' The woman drew small circles with her fingertips on the child's velvet cheeks.

'What was her name?'

'Ruby. Like the red . . .'

'. . . jewel that princesses wear in their crowns. And why is my name Rose?'

'Because you're as pretty as one.'

'And where did Ruby go?'

'She went away, my darling, to a beautiful place in the sky . . .'

'I want to go there. When can I go?'

'You won't die for a very long time, Rose. I'm your Livvie who loves you and who'll look after you forever.'

Rose and Livvie often spoke about the experience that Rose had had as a baby. Rose insisted she remembered the whole thing – especially how it had ended.

'Impossible,' Livvie always asserted. 'You were just a baby. Less than two years old. Memory only begins at three or four. What you have is a memory of someone else's memory.'

But Rose insisted that she'd woken to feel a woman scooping her up in her arms and wrapping her in a yellow blanket with satin edging. She told Livvie how the woman cradled her in her arms and murmured words of comfort, and how the woman's tears dripped off her chin and into Rose's mouth, which was as expectant as a baby bird's; how, when she'd looked into the woman's eyes, she saw pools of light and warmth, and she felt whole and comforted.

'And I'd been in the room by myself for three days?' she'd ask.

'Mmmm . . .'

'Who was the woman?'

'It was me,' said John indignantly. He had saved Rose after Ruby had died so tragically. 'I picked you up and wrapped you in the blanket.'

'It was the spirit of your mother,' answered Livvie sagely.

Then, when Rose was older: 'Tell me the story of Ruby. What was she like?' she'd ask John and Livvie.

They'd tell her. But after John left, it was just Livvie who replied: 'Your mother Ruby was a free spirit. A beautiful free spirit. She had no roots, no origins. She arrived out of thin air and then she left, leaving no trace. What a tragedy.' She shook her head sadly.

Ruby – beautiful red jewel. Traceless and rootless. She leaves and I'm left with her baggage, Rose thought bitterly.

Then Livvie went, too, dying just as Rose reached her thirtieth birthday. And that was that; her one link . . . gone. The story lay as hard and unyielding as a pebble.

So here was Rose, daughter of the spirit of the air. On her way to find the truth about her origins. She got out the car and walked shakily to the restrooms. They were dark after the glare of the sun. There had been some refurbishment. Instead of basins, a slab of black granite lay like a fallen tombstone. Rose stood in front of the mirror and splashed her face. The water slid surreptitiously into the channel behind the slab. In the weird electric lighting, she couldn't recognise this person who stood in front of her, skin pale yellow, mauve shadows under her eyes, wearing the new clothes she'd bought yesterday – the blue jeans and the white T-shirt with red peonies and green dragons cascading over one shoulder. She took a tortoise-shell clip from her bag and wound her honey-coloured hair up into a twist off her neck. A large black woman in a pink tracksuit emerged from a toilet cubicle – she reminded Rose of Turkish Delight. She came to wash her hands. They smiled at each other's reflections and Rose felt better.

Outside, the concrete blazed white-hot; she felt around in her bag for her sunglasses. Amongst the masses milling about, she recognised some of her fellow road users but Mad Max was, thankfully, nowhere to be seen. Feeling suddenly ravenous, she went into Nando's, bought herself a hot peri-peri double chicken burger, 'slap' chips and a Coke, and sat down on one of the stained concrete benches positioned around a grassy area.

In the hot, steamy air Harrismith's Platberg rose up before her, its shimmering presence reassuring her of her progress. On journeys to the coast with Livvie and John, it had always been the tradition to stop here at Harrismith – the halfway mark, named for the governor of the Cape; the colonial hero in her history books, remembered for his double-quick ride from Cape Town to Grahamstown to warn the British garrison of impending attack by the Xhosas. Rose recalled coming here at a very early age. There used to be ostriches grazing in a fenced-off area. She looked around but couldn't see any. What had happened to them?

Hiding behind her dark glasses, disregarding her fellow diners, she concentrated on the food before her. She felt as if this were someone else's life she was living – someone else holding the burger in both hands and taking large bites. Bits of mayonnaise-covered lettuce and peri-peri sauce oozed out, sticking to the corners of her mouth. She licked them off, enjoying the small fire that burned on her tongue, loving the tempering effect of the chips and Coke. Soon, all was eaten and she wiped her hands on a serviette and resumed her journey.

The landscape was greener and more dramatic now. The road rose like a small intake of breath from the top of Van Reneen's Pass before falling steeply down the escarpment. Deep gulleys grew thick with groves of acacias and spiky aloes dotted the rocky slopes. Clouds were banking above the peaks that lined the distant horizon: the Drakensberg, the Dragon mountains, Barrier of Spears.

The traffic thinned as Rose drove across the valley floor. Dairy farming had stitched together a patchwork of pasture and, in the fields, white cows, like great bovine ghosts, were grazing. She passed kraals and scatterings of poor rural dwellings with mud walls and roofs of tin-sheeting held down with rocks. Three birds flew up and down in an invisible funnel. The temperature cooled as a layer of silver cloud spread across the sky. Rose saw the sign to the Southern Drakensberg.

She motored now along a narrow mountain track, through lovely countryside where the trees were tipped with pink. She hummed along to something familiar playing on her iPod, a classical piece used for a TV ad: da-da dum, da-da dum, de-de de-de dum. Home to mom and something soup, dum dum dum da dum. The landscape was mounded into a series of breasts, full and draped with soft emerald cloth. Rose smiled. Impossible to describe this land in any terms other than the female form. Mother Earth – fecund and receptive, ripe and ready for the human male to claim, name and penetrate.

The cloud had thickened and descended, drifting close to the ground, leaving a fine mist on Rose's windscreen. She switched on her wipers, her headlights already turned on full, but they merely lit a small circle in front of her. The rest of the world was white, like a blank canvas. She slowed down, hugging the mountainside for dear life, her ears and eyes supercharged. She hadn't seen another car since leaving the highway but she felt nervous of encountering one head-on. She sat up very straight and switched off the music. There was not a sound, except for the quiet humming of her engine; not another living soul, save for the goats that romped daintily atop a pile of rocks, and one lone cow tethered near the edge of the road. She felt like the sole survivor in a post-apocalyptic landscape.

As she rounded a bend, her car now climbing again, she encountered a dilapidated truck travelling at funereal pace in front of her. She dogged its darkened outline slowly up the hill. The road soon crested the peak and began its descent. Through her misted windscreen, she saw the truck driver waving his arm, indicating for her to pass. She couldn't see a thing. She had to trust him. She couldn't. She clung to his tail lights, hypnotised by their undulating movement. Around another bend. Again, he indicated that she could pass. Should she take the chance? Could she trust him? She had no faith.

In the valley, the mist lifted temporarily and the road reappeared – a silver snake slithering slowly around the mountainside. Rose accelerated, overtaking the truck, finally throwing off its shackles, flashing her thanks. The driver hooted in acknowledgement. Liberation felt so good. And then she passed the sign to Oberon – just 40 km to go. It was always a thrill finally to see the sign to one's destination.

In no time, she was there – crossing the bridge over the greasy grey waters of the Banqaru River and on to the main road of Oberon, where she was suddenly drawn into the Friday afternoon maelstrom of the little town.

Throngs of people waited about in the fine drizzle, their colourful umbrellas opened like exotic blooms. Taxis stopped without warning in the middle of the road and made U-turns, willy-nilly. Rose passed three blocks of single-storeyed shops, a hotel and a petrol station. She turned right there, as instructed by Brigit, the owner of the B&B where she was headed; and here was the dirt road that would take her straight to it.

The gravel road dropped steeply, crossed a bridge that spanned a fast-flowing stream then climbed again, curving sharply around a hillside.

The landscape was still shrouded in mist, only her immediate surroundings visible, and she drove slowly, anxiously, looking out for the signboard.

Ah – and there it was, at the end of the road: The Chameleon.

The little wooden gate to the property was closed. Rose hopped out the car and, in the fine rain, picked her way through rutted mud to lift the catch, then drove through and parked under a pergola. She looked around. She had arrived.

1

A week after Livvie's wake; Rose stood hesitating, pointing the key like a pistol at the front door of Livvie's apartment in Killarney. Doors, hearts, secrets, truths. Rose exhaled then inserted the key. It was the first time she was entering Livvie's flat since her death.

After the gloom of the corridor, the sudden glare made her squint. Light streamed in through the room's north-facing windows. Time seemed to freeze here, in this space – the flat that she'd grown up in. The weavers' incessant chattering in the plane tree outside ceased abruptly and the buzz of traffic from the M1 grew muted. The world held its breath as a wave of *déjà vu* washed over her. She'd experienced this exact moment before; this total solitude. No other human being here, no animal, not even a pot plant. Livvie always said she didn't want anything that needed feeding and watering. But there were plenty of inanimate objects. What a job awaited Rose! To sort out the left-overs of a life. To make room for her own, now that she was moving in.

Livvie. People often asked if it were short for Olivia. 'You would think so, but my name is actually Livonia – from the Roman goddess, Levanna. She lifted newborn babies up from the ground. God knows what my mother was thinking. She died before I got round to asking her.'

Did Livvie regret not asking her mother those things? Rose certainly mourned all her own unasked questions. Livvie had given up her life of independence to raise a strange child. No biological ties. No legal obligation. Rose didn't think she could do that under any circumstances. So what drove Livvie? Now it was too late to ask. Livvie was gone. And even when Livvie lay dying and they'd both known that time was running out, Rose still couldn't ask. Her questions lay like bits of undigested food in her gut. Oh, how she'd wanted to ask – desperately. But when she tried to expel the words, they lodged in her throat, choking her up, like a stuck fish bone. And her feelings for this woman – she'd so yearned to tell Livvy how much she'd meant to Rose, how grateful she was . . . But she'd known that neither of them had the stomach for such emotional outpourings.

Royal Doulton, Jasperware, Moorcroft. Old-fashioned English ornaments and plenty more of the same. Rose wandered through a drizzle of dust motes, weaving her way through chairs, poufs and ottomans, dressers and display cabinets, occasional tables and coffee tables, marble podiums and wooden pedestals, picking up objects and putting them down again. Things. Memories of death. Rose didn't want them. Livvie had inherited them from her mother, who had inherited them from her mother. Who would inherit them from Rose? Who would she assign to carry out the chores generated by her death? Who would deal with her death certificate, her will, the frozen bank accounts, unpaid bills, redundant furniture and car? A string of tasks as long as the life that had just been lived. Rose had been driving Livvie's car. It was automatic and newer than Rose's old Golf. She had to get rid of one of them. So many things to do. She needed to make a list.

She made her way to the escritoire in search of paper and pen; found herself face to face with the portrait of the witch woman. There was a small copper plaque at the bottom of the frame, engraved with the words, 'The Drakensberg Lady, Sir Philip Geoffrey, 1883'.

The Lady stared past Rose with leonine eyes, her features intense, her skin glowing white. One breast was bared, the other covered in a blood-red blanket that fell from her shoulder. On her head was a turban adorned with brass rings; cowry shells hung from her neck and earlobes, and her arms were draped with plaited leather thongs. In her outstretched hand she held a glinting copper chalice, as if offering it to the presence beyond the viewer's shoulder. What was contained within? Magic muti? Truth serum? As a child, Rose had been terrified by her. She thought she was a queen with magical powers who could look into the place of secrets inside your head, the ones you never told. She smiled now, remembering skipping past when she was feeling naughty, or stopping to stare when she was feeling brave and defiant. Then she could study the bare breast. It was very rude.

The muffled tones of her cell phone pierced her reverie. Marion's name showed up on her screen. Rose wanted to ignore it, but picked up dutifully.

'Darling, how are you doing?' Marion's voice oozed concern.

'I'm fine thanks. Really.' Rose forced her mouth into a smile, trying to sound friendlier than she felt.

'Where are you?'

'In the flat. Trying to sort out some of the stuff. I'm not getting very far.'

'Oh shame. I'd hate to be doing that all alone. I'll come and help you.'

No thanks. You're the last person I need to help me right now, Rose thought, but said instead: 'Actually, I'm . . . er . . . about to go home.'

'Well how about a break on the way? Meet me for a quick coffee. It will do you good to get out. Parque in Norwood. I've just finished my Hypermarket shop.'

Rose hesitated then succumbed, feeling suddenly cheered by the prospect of a caffeine pick-me-up. The job could wait.

She locked the door and left, her heels clicking out a snappy duple-time on the black and white tiles of the corridor.

Marion was sitting on the covered patio, raised above street level with a view of the park. In her cream sweater, she looked like a scoop of ice cream quietly melting in the noon heat. Rose was glad to see her familiar face. One of the nearby tables was occupied by a man in a suit, working on his laptop. He looked up and tried to meet Rose's gaze as she passed but she kept her eyes directed at Marion. Rose bent down to kiss her cheek.

'How's the new grandchild?' she asked, although she already knew the answer.

'Ah . . .' Marion beamed, '. . . just divine. But not so new anymore. He's starting to crawl already.' She leaned forward: 'And so clever! I swear I heard him say "mama" the other day, although he's much too young to be starting to talk. I can't wait to see him again . . . Where's the waiter? He's just standing there like a zombie. Try catch his eye.'

The waiter's vacant stare came into focus. He sidled up to their table.

'What will you have?' Marion asked. 'Something to eat?' She looked at Rose hopefully.

'No, it's too early. Just a coffee,' Rose said to the waiter.

'And a slice of . . . no, I won't. Just a cappuccino for me,' said Marion. 'But I want extra foam – and weak. Weak, not strong,' she reiterated to the waiter's retreating back. She sat back and told Rose: 'Arnold and me are going to the Drakensberg. The Bergsun. Have you ever been there? We went a couple of years ago and it was too wonderful.' Had Marion ever had a bad holiday or a bad experience of any kind?

'That's funny – I was just looking at "The Drakensberg Lady" before I came,' Rose said.

The coffee arrived. 'That was quick for a change. Mm-m-m. Smells good,' Marion pronounced. Her large wooden bangles clunked as she fussed with a sachet of sweetener, trying to pour its contents into the little hole she'd made in the foam.

Rose stirred her coffee absently. 'God, I need this! D'you know the painting I'm talking about?' she persisted.

'Painting?' Marion shook her head. 'Livvie has . . . had so many paintings. I'm not observant when it comes to art.'

'It's this portrait of a woman, called "The Drakensberg Lady". I used to think she had some kind of magical powers . . . when I was little.' She laughed awkwardly. She'd never told that to Livvie. Why was she suddenly confiding in Marion?

Marion had foam on her upper lip. 'Who? Oh, the painting, you mean,' she said vaguely. The bangles clattered as she pushed back her hair. 'Anyway, do you remember the Jacksons? He's a doctor and she's the most fabulous cook. They came with us the last time. We went on a long hike and lost our way. Oh my word! It took us hours to get back to the hotel. You know, people die in those mountains.'

She prattled on then frowned suddenly: 'Was that mine?' She reached for her phone. 'It must be on vibrate. Oh – here's a message . . .' She held the phone at arm's length, squinting at the screen. '. . . from Glynnis. She forgot she had a facial. This afternoon. She's got no babysitter. Why not? Where's the maid?' Marion looked at Rose. 'This new maid of hers! Forever taking time off. Well, I must go. How was the coffee? Mine was delicious!'

2

Rose couldn't face the thought of returning to the flat, so she headed for home – a rented cottage on a large property in Forest Town, near the zoo. The accommodation suited her. She seldom encountered her landlords, a couple who frequently travelled overseas to visit their emigrant children. Ideal landlords, she thought; then again, she made the ideal tenant. She did a direct payment into their bank account unfailingly on the first of every month, never complained about anything, threw no wild parties and didn't keep destructive pets.

The landlords lived in the main house, which was very grand, built with porticos and columns and Spanish plaster and balconies. It had probably been built for a Randlord in the early years of the twentieth century. There had been many additions and improvements over the years, one being the cottage, which now housed Rose. With its own entrance and garden, it was completely private, shielded from the main house and the street by wooden trelises and evergreen hedges. In times like this, when the rambling roses had exploded into baby-pink blooms and the privet proliferated with tiny white flowers, Rose felt like Sleeping Beauty, protected from the outside world by a thicket of thorny trees.

She had moved in here about eight years ago with her boyfriend at the time: Glen. He was no Prince Charming. What had she seen in him? He was a hypochondriac mommy's boy. He had to consult his mother on the most trivial decisions, like what brand of pasta to buy or which colour shirt to wear. His mother . . . she'd have been the proverbial mother-in-law from hell. And he was so unspontaneous – everything planned and formulaic. Even the sex. It was very tame for a first love affair. There was none of that can't-keep-your-hands-off-each-other urgency; no illicit trysts in public spaces. (Did that really happen or was it just something you read about and saw in movies?) Rose needed someone more outgoing – an extrovert, a sensualist, to counter her own reserve and ascetism. When Glen left for a two-year stint in London, she'd shed a tear or two but realised afterwards it was more from relief than regret. And here she was ten years down the line, still in the cottage, almost as inexperienced with men as she had been then.

She drove down Second Avenue under the leafy vault of London plane trees growing at regular intervals along the pavement, past large houses that remained invisible behind their high walls, electric-fence wiring glinting in motes of captured light. There were few cars on the road and the only pedestrian she saw was a Moslem boy in his white tunic and baggy pants on his way to the madrasa.

A mere block away, killer taxis hurtled along Death Bend, and the darkened doorways of muti shops on Louis Botha Avenue were best side-stepped by nervous white girls like her. But here was suburban Johannesburg at its arboreal best.

Her car thrust through the thick, hot air on streets splashed with fallen petals: crimson bougainvillea, violet jacaranda and yellow tipuana. The scene looked like the aftermath of a paintball war, but it wouldn't take long before gardeners armed with noisy blowers blew the petals away. November; she loved this time of the year. Her windows closed, the air conditioner blowing cool, she listened to her iPod. A woman's voice rang out, clear as a bell:

You cannot hypnotise me
So don't give me your stupid line
About how suggestible I am
Don't make your problems . . . mine . . .

Rose saw an elderly black woman walking in the road. She had a blanket wrapped around her middle and was carrying a shabby tog bag. As Rose drove past she materialised in the rearview mirror, motioning slowly, wrist waving like a sea anemone.

She probably wanted a lift to Killarney Mall. Rose thought about stopping but decided the Mall was well within walking distance. Then, she felt sorry for the woman. Her walking looked so laboured. The way she was limping, her shoes were clearly pinching her toes. Rose changed gear and reversed the two-hundred metres, her engine whining petulantly. She watched in her rearview mirror as the woman lolloped towards the car. Finally her face popped up at the passenger window, unexpectedly fraught. Rose saw she was crying, rivulets of tears rolling down her cheeks.

What now? Rose leaned across to unwind the window. The woman scrabbled in her tog bag, then thrust a much-handled official-looking document through the window.

'Please. My husband. My husband,' she gasped. 'He left me in Pietermaritzburg. I don't know where he is now. I have no money.'

Rose glanced at the documents and made them out to be discharge papers from a provincial hospital. She could discern the words '. . . was admitted . . . discharged . . . 2010 . . . observation . . . non-specific . . .'. Why had the woman given her these papers? She passed them back.

'Now I don't know he is alive or dead. Aiieee . . . aiieee,' the woman wailed.

A young black Adonis pulled up on the opposite side of the road and from his white BMW convertible asked Rose if she needed help. She switched off the music. She would have liked to connect, to collaborate with this gallant, but she shook her head: 'No . . . um . . . thanks, but it's okay . . . I think . . .'

The man drove away – as she, too, would have liked to have done at this point, telling herself that it was someone else's problem. But the woman cut such a pathetic figure, she felt obliged to hear her out.

'My son. He is in the hospital. They broke his leg. He has a big cut on his head . . . I need money for my children. My husband he is gone . . . I came to look for him in Johannesburg. I must walk and walk. Look at my knee . . .' She lifted her hem to expose a trickle of blood, so bright and vital against her wrinkled grey skin it made Rose recoil.

'Now, I come to the police but they say they can do nothing. I must go home . . . Aiieee . . .' She wailed again, her mouth a startling rictus. 'But I have no money. I sold my jacket. I have only this.' She gestured to the worn blanket tied around her middle. 'I must go home now . . . and all I've got is this.' She withdrew her green ID book from her bag and opened it to reveal two tattered twenty-rand notes.

So that's what this was all about.

'How much do you need?' Rose asked.

'R275. For the train.'

Rose kept her hands on the steering wheel, looking helplessly at the woman's tears. They made shiny tracks over her brown cheeks, like snail trails. For once, I've actually got enough cash on me, Rose thought. And if this is all true, what a sad story; if it's a scam – well, what a terrible way to earn a living. And her performance was so convincing. Should Rose play the Good Samaritan and take her to the station? It was completely out of her way, a real diversion. But what did she have to do that was so urgent? Still, she hesitated; the woman looked harmless enough, but who knew? Maybe she was a decoy for a gang of hijackers lurking in the bushes.

'Get in.' Rose leaned over to open the door. 'I'll give you the money for the train and take you to the station.' Sucker! But so what? Her generosity wouldn't bankrupt her. It would make her feel good about herself.

The woman got in clumsily and sat sobbing loudly while Rose drove towards the Houghton on-ramp of the M1.

'How can you come to Johannesburg to look for your husband? It's such a big place, where are you going to look?' Rose asked.

'I went to . . .' Rose didn't catch what was said here, '. . . but the woman chased me from there and now, I had to sell my jacket. Aiieee,' she wailed again. 'I sold my three blankets for money . . . My husband must give me money. He's been gone two years now. The police said I must go to the police at my home and put in a Missing Person's. I must go back home.'

'And where is home?'

'Oberon.'

Never heard of the place, Rose thought. She continued her interrogation.

'What were you doing here, in Houghton of all places?'

'I was coming from the Norwood Police Station.'

'And where are you trying to get to?'

'To YMCA in Braamfontein. I must ask some help there,' she answered glibly, between sobs. Her answers came a bit too off-pat, Rose thought.

Tight-lipped drivers clutching hot steering wheels and looking neither left nor right ignored Rose's attempts to move into the middle lane, so she remained in the slow one. Her iPod silenced, she listened to the rise and fall of the sobbing, torn between giving herself over to this tale of woe and remaining sceptical. Finally the sobs subsided and then ceased. The woman took a grubby piece of tissue from her bag and began to wipe her face.

Rose imagined what she might be thinking: Why must the *umlungu* take me to the station? Now I'll have to make my own way back to the northern suburbs for my next victim.

Onto the Queen Elizabeth Bridge and into Simmons Street, where taxis idled in the permanent shade cast by multi-storey parking garages and hulking overpasses. The buildings all looked dreary and depressing, covered in graffiti and grime. Rose couldn't remember when last she ha driven into town. Bree Street was abuzz with activity. Loiterers pedestrians spilled off the pavements, competing for space with car boxes and litter. Expressionless women sat alongside rows of red and orange plastic plates, each displaying a little pile of tomatoes or apples for sale.

Negotiating the traffic, she turned into Rissik Street and shortly afterwards entered the station, at which point she fumbled under her seat to retrieve her handbag. 'I'm sorry for your troubles.' She counted out R275 and handed the notes and coin to the woman. 'I hope you come right.'

'Thank you. God bless you,' the woman said quietly as she alighted from the car.

Rose watched her vanish into the concourse throngs, wrapped in her worn blanket and clutching the shabby tog bag that she'd said held her only possessions in the world.

Heading home, Rose realised she was feeling hungry and wondered what she could eat for lunch. There wasn't much in her fridge. Should she stop at Woollies on the way? Nah, she felt too lazy. Up the hill, the Civic Centre loomed ahead, a concrete monolith – the worst of apartheid architecture. She thought about the accident of birth, the chances of being born at a certain time, in a certain place, to a certain class and a certain race. But these thoughts offered no consolation for the guilt that assailed her at every busy intersection: blind beggars with their tin-holding handlers; ragged street children, glue bottles at the ready; toddlers on traffic islands, watching as their mothers waved weakly at passing motorists. White guilt, bleeding heart. She never had any change for parking machines – she'd given it all to beggars. As she crested the hill, the Constitutional Court came into view and she eased her foot off the accelerator for the downhill run home. Low, grey clouds were gathering in the west.

Immediately she got home, she'd decide which of her possessions to keep and which to get rid of. It wouldn't take long. She hadn't bought much in the way of furniture and decor. Most of it had been donated by Livvie, things she'd wanted to get rid of. The hideous couch with the green upholstery and wooden armrests – that had to go. But her bed, she'd keep. The thought of sleeping in Livvie's bed, the one she'd just died in, was a bit too daunting. Rose wondered who moved furniture. It wasn't really a job for big furniture movers. She needed a man with a bakkie. Where did one find such people? She didn't know. She'd never had to do anything like this by herself before.

But the moment she crossed the threshold into the cottage, her good intentions dissolved. After scraping together some lunch – a sandwich made with the last slice of bread plus the crust, the end of the cheese and some tea – she flopped onto her bed and fell asleep. Outside, rain started to fall, a soft, feminine rain, freeing the fecund scent that lay trapped within the red clay earth as it soaked into the ground.

It drizzled throughout the night. The morning arrived sullenly, demanding socks and jersey – clothing that had lain forgotten in drawers these past few weeks. Armed with black dustbin bags, intentions fortified by good sleep, Rose arrived at Livvie's flat, determined to begin with the worst first – the bedroom.

A leaden light trickled through the windows and she shivered as she entered the room, still redolent with the sweet smell of death. She could see Livvie lying there, waxen, cadaverous, her vitality and humour already consigned to life's outbox.

Rose switched on the light, crossed to the dressing-table and sat down on the stool. Ancient hairbrushes with bristles matted with grey strands; depleted jars of moisturiser; bottles of perfume; smudgy tubes of lipstick; dusty pots of powder – lined up like an arsenal, ready to do battle against the ravages of time and disease. Katrina, Livvie's domestic, must have created this orderly arrangement when she cleaned the flat for the last time.

Rose looked at her face in the mirror. Wide forehead, porcelain pale in the harsh electric light; hair a no-nonsense shoulder-length bob the colour of dark honey. Her eyes, speckled grey and wide-spaced, looked startled – a deer caught in headlights. She picked up a tube of lipstick, slowly smeared it on her lips and tried to smile at her reflection. Siren. Vamp. More like vampire. The crimson lipstick had bled onto her teeth.

Her lips felt heavy with their new veneer. She hardly ever wore make-up. Or jewellery. Her clothes, too, tended towards the conservative side – nothing too fashionable, tight or revealing. She was certainly no fashion plate. She didn't even know what was in fashion. Then again, neither did Livvie. Mind you, that hadn't always been the case. Rose had seen photos of Livvie wearing mod polyester trouser suits and pale lipstick. Who would have thought? She had been much thinner then, and had sported a shiny blonde helmet of hair. But that had been before Rose had entered her life, in the days when Livvie had worked for a large accounting firm in town.

So why had Livvie never returned to the corporate world as Rose grew older and more independent? Instead, she had started her small accountancy practice that she ran from home. Rose knew it satisfied her material needs but wondered whether it had fulfilled her other needs, whatever those had been. And though she had had a large circle of women friends – why had there been no regular men in her life? Of course, John had been around in the early days. He had lived with them in the house in Sandhurst, but in a separate wing. What was the story there? Were he and Livvie never intimate? How did Livvie fulfil her sexual needs? People could ask the same question about me, Rose thought wryly.

John had left for Paris when Rose was about six. Livvie told her that he'd gone when he found out he had cancer, that he'd wanted to die there, in France. Why this was, Rose never found out. Was there someone special in Paris with whom he wanted to spend his dying days? With Livvie's death, all these questions would remain unanswered forever. Questions and question marks; they lay like rocks strewn in her path, always tripping her up.

Rose couldn't believe the junk that had accumulated over the years: an empty tin of hairspray that rattled angrily as she opened the drawer;

a few forlorn hair-curlers; paper-clips; buttons; even an old shopping list. She wiped the surfaces clean, then upended the drawers into the open mouth of black plastic. Clean sweep. It felt so final.

Now tackling the built-in cupboards that occupied the length of the room, she threw open the double doors. A scent of cinnamon and vanilla washed over her like a wave of longing, but when she thrust her nose in deeper, she could smell mustiness and old building.

What was she going to do with all these clothes and shoes? She didn't want any of them. They wouldn't fit her anyway, Livvie had been much bigger than her. She could invite Livvie's friends and ask them to take whatever items of clothing they wanted. Why not a party? There were parties to celebrate all of life's passages – kitchen teas, baby showers, christenings – where, traditionally, the guests brought gifts; so why not a passing-on party, where the guests got to take gifts home?

Wishing she were taller, she balanced on the built-in ledge of the cupboard, gripping the upper shelf tightly with one hand and grabbing at the contents stored there with the other.

Finally it was all laid out on the carpet: containers and hat boxes; packets filled with trinkets and costume jewellery; half-completed knitting; balls of wool; sentimental keepsakes; school reports and certificates.

Then there was a wooden box.

It was beautiful, with mother-of-pearl inlay and curlicues in the corners and around the keyhole. Time had patinated the wood to a burnt umber. Why had Livvie not displayed this amongst her other treasures? And what was in it?

The box was locked.

Burning with curiosity, Rose struggled to think where the key might be. She remembered there had been some keys in the drawers before she'd upended their contents into the black plastic bag. Crap. Stupid. Picking the bag up by the bottom, she shook it. With a clatter the junk landed in a heap on the carpet. She sifted impatiently through the pile, finding several small keys: a flat steel key; a singled-toothed skeleton key; a tiny tubular key; and a rusty one with ornate metal fretwork. Eeny meeny miny mo. Sitting cross-legged on the carpet, she laid out the keys in a row: steel key, skeleton key, tubular key, rusty key. She chose the rusty one. It was almost too easy. The hinged lid opened.

The box was filled with an odd assortment of objects. There was a small plastic bag filled with . . . seeds. Seeds? Old dry seeds. A catalogue of some sort. A folded piece of paper. Two faded Polaroid pictures. A beaded thong of plaited leather. What an anticlimax. What had she been expecting? Rubies and pearls?

The seeds interested her. She picked up the bag and poured a sample onto her palm. Some were round, some winged. She studied their wrinkled brown integuments and delicately ribbed wings. She sniffed them. Odourless. Was there a secret contained within each embryo, perhaps the cure for humanity's ills? Was this a repository of rare seeds, the last of a species? Recently, there had been a large underground storehouse in Iceland built for this very purpose. She hadn't known Livvie was a custodian of the world's bio-diversity. Not bloody likely! Livvie's interest lay with the inanimate. Rose poured the seeds back into the bag.

The leather thong could have been a holiday souvenir. She turned it over in her hands, feeling its light weight, the warm texture of the leather, noticing the symmetrical arrangement of the beads on the plaited strands. The beads were made of brightly coloured glass – red, green and shiny gold ones.

She picked up the two Polaroids. A man and a woman, their over-exposed features flat in the bright sunlight. Who were these people? There was a place and date printed in small square letters in blue ballpoint on the back: *Oberon, Sept. 1981*. Oberon. She'd heard that name for the first time just the other day. The woman she'd picked up – she'd said she came from Oberon. And here it was again. Strange how life offered up these coincidences.

Rose picked up the catalogue and turned it over in her hands. It was from a London auction house. The foiled silver writing on the dove-grey cover read: 'Catalogue of fine paintings from the English Classical Academy of the Late Nineteenth Century. Twenty-three lots. 15th November, 1972, 10.00am.' She flipped through the pages, glancing at the small colour reproductions on auction – landscapes, portraits, interiors.

Then there was the folded piece of paper – a final invoice from Morris Hunter Detective Agency, to John Clemens, 30 June 1986. For 'services rendered in full and final settlement'. Morris Hunter! What a blast from the past. She hadn't heard the name in years. He was the detective that Livvie and John had hired to scour the world for possible relatives of Ruby . . . friends . . . anyone who could claim the baby Rose.

Right at the bottom of the box was something else . . . a small book. Somebody's diary. It looked very old, with a heavy leatherbound cover and brittle, yellowed pages. She was almost afraid to handle it in case it fell to pieces in her hands. Opening it carefully, she saw handwritten entries dated from over a century ago. The writing was neat and slanted. Somebody's family heirloom? What was it doing in Livvie's possession?

Rose wanted to mull over the curious collection of objects further, in her own space. She packed the items carefully back into the box and, carrying it gingerly, like something fragile and marked 'this way up', left for home.

3

In the privet outside Rose's window, a barbet announced his desires to the world, waking her with his loud trilling. Shafts of sunlight filtered into the room through the Venetian blinds, onto Rose's pillow. She threw an arm over her eyes, and drifted.

Her mind wandered to the work that had kept her up till the early hours. She wrote scripts for a production house that produced educational material for TV. Rose's field was the life sciences. It was a freelance position and the job suited her. She seldom had to go into the company's offices, which was an advantage. The less she had to do with the scary head honcho, Charmaine, the better.

Rose had been working on an animated sequence showing the process of cell division: meiosis, mitosis. In the dreamy state between sleep and wakefulness, her brainwaves oscillated in alpha mode, invoking odd images of the process:

chromosomes like dragonflies
float on pond,
then taking flight
alight on spindles.
In frames, flicker apart: chiasmatic separation;
a daughter cell is born haploid, hapless.

Rose laughed in her head, delighted. Remember the words, write them down, she told herself, though she knew that in transcription, their magic would be lost. Then she drifted back to sleep and dreamt the dream again, the one where she had to fight her way through a shady glen. And then she was in the bright, white room. Livvie was there. But she, Rose, was Livvie. Where was Ruby? She had to be found. The baby was coming! She ran from the white room into a double-volume entrance hall and watched herself as she ran with John down a long passageway. Suddenly, the passage stopped. As they retraced their steps to the entrance, John disappeared . . . Rose-Livvie climbed a staircase and ran about this way and that, but there was no way out. Ruby was in labour and she was trapped in the house. Abruptly, she found herself in Livvie's wardrobe, thrashing about to escape its claustrophobic murkiness. Vanilla and cinnamon. Where was the door? She pushed up against something hard and was flung onto the carpet in Livvie's bedroom. There was a morass of junk – boxes, packets, tubes of cosmetics, unidentifiable keys. She scratched through the pile. There was something she needed but she couldn't remember what it was . . .

She woke, sweating, her breath uneven, her pulse racing. Dream-disordered, she sat on the edge of her bed as the last vestiges ebbed away. What was she so desperate to find?

Struggling to open her heavy lids, she staggered to the living area. There was the box. On the kitchen counter just as she'd left it the previous evening. Now fully awake, she picked it up, opened the security gate and stepped outside.

The air was gorgeous and fresh, raising goosebumps on her bare arms. Barefoot, in her floaty chiffon nighty and carrying the box, she was Pandora, the first mortal woman, about to release troubles on an unsuspecting world. She made her way to the bench under the old plane tree, treading softly over rough-hewn railway sleepers, careful to avoid sharp stones. Necklace vines hung down from the Cape Myrtle and brushed against her; bees buzzed, humming paeans to spring; and she could smell the heady scent of the Yesterday-today-and-tomorrow blossoms drifting on the breeze.

Under the plane tree's huge canopy, she knelt amid the exposed roots that snaked thick and tumid in the dark soil and placed the box tenderly on the bench, lining up the objects beside it.

She picked up the photos, angling them to block the stippled light, peering closely at the subjects. The man was wiry, sporting a droopy moustache and a cowboy hat pushed low on his forehead. He faced the lens, his shoulders slanted and hands hanging awkwardly by his sides.

The woman was busty, slim and small, with long, fair hair and a smile that time had not tarnished. She'd dropped her chin a little and turned her shoulders slightly in her T-shirt. Sultry. Showing off her best side.

When Rose placed the photos side by side, she saw that both man and woman had posed in the same spot, trading places to shoot each other, water reflecting through willow leaves behind them. She turned the photos over and re-read the captions, looking closely at the writing, trying to decipher more in the small, neat handwriting: *Oberon, Sept. 1981*. After a time, she put the photos back on the bench, alongside the other objects.

Now she paged through the catalogue, more slowly this time: paintings of ladies in white dresses and picture-hats, at the races or in English country gardens; stern governesses forever keeping watch over Victorian children; odalisques pouting on couches; landscapes of misty isles in azure seas and treed green pastures. One lot had been circled in ballpoint pen. It was titled: 'The Bushmen pay homage to the White Goddess, 1883. Oil on canvas. 2.25m x 1.75m. Artist: Sir Philip Geoffrey.'

Hey! This was the same artist who'd painted 'The Drakensberg Lady'. Rose continued reading: 'Under instruction of the owners, Mr and Mrs Simon Crystal.' The picture featured a woman in three-quarter profile. In a white dress, curls falling from her bonnet, she reclined under a rocky ledge, leaning on one arm, the other extended towards two figures – the Bushmen of the title. They were bending over in front of her, their arms stretched out behind them like wings. The White Goddess. What was she doing in the presence of these Bushmen? Had Livvie been thinking of buying this work? Was that why it was circled in ink?

She replaced the catalogue in the box and returned to the photographs, mulling over them again, turning them over once more to read the inscription at the back: *Oberon, Sept. 1981.* Where exactly was Oberon? What was happening in 1981, in the world, in South Africa? It was five years after the Soweto riots. The country was burning. It was the year before Rose was born – in June 1982. She counted on her fingers. Nine months, in fact! Oberon – the place of her conception? Did all this have to do with her parents? Were these photos clues? How could she make such a leap? Blood rushed to her head and knocked loudly. Hello. Anyone home? She peered at the woman's narrow hips at the edge of the frame. Are you my mother? Is this your box? She felt like the lost little bird from the storybook who asked of everyone and everything, including ducks, chickens, forklifts and boats: 'Are you my mother?'

And the man – was he her father? She peered closely at his shadowy features; his jaw, the slope of his shoulders. But there was no recognition, no familiar traces in the etiolated image.

Rose had never seen a photo of her mother Ruby. And no one knew who her father was. As a child, a family tree had grown in the fertile soil of her imagination – a father who was noble and brave, a scientist, an explorer, a Daddy Warbucks . . . Scarlett Pimpernel . . . James Bond. Or, John. And her mother, Ruby, the fairytale princess who had died and gone to the beautiful place in the sky. Could it be that, instead, her father was this cowboy-hatted hippy dude? And this blonde babe – was this Ruby?

Fury surged in her innards, rising from her gall bladder up into her oesophagus. It was thick and powerful and thrashed about like a trapped serpent in her throat. It tasted bitter. Why had Livvie not shown her these photos? She was livid! Livid with Livvie. She wanted to scream and cry out and pound her fists into concrete. She had always been so desperate to know what Ruby and her father had looked like. If she could have seen these, she would at least have had a hook to hang her fantasies on.

Why, Livvie? Why did you keep this hidden? Were you trying to shield me from disappointment? Did you know something? Did you know that there were no answers to be found in the box? Or had you just forgotten its existence?

But why blame Livvie who'd been nothing but caring and self-sacrificing? She had been the most adoring, adored and supportive person in Rose's life. It was Ruby who had done the unforgivable; Ruby, so unthinking, so unfettered, who'd died without leaving a single connection, not a trace of family member or friend; so unconscious of a past, or a future. It was almost as if she had renounced her humanity. Like an animal, once mating had taken place, there was no further contact with the father. And the natural link between mother and child – even that she'd broken.

Rose wept, her tears quickly disappearing into the thirsty slats of the bench. She remembered an Enid Blyton story about a naughty pixie who, armed with a sharp pair of scissors, had cut people's shadows from their bodies and stolen them clean away. As a small child, she had wished that the pixie would steal the shadows that had darkened her small and secret world.

This anger, this rage – where had it come from? She was normally so placid and docile, accepting that her home situation was different from other people's, not talking about it, just quietly getting on with life. She wiped her eyes and dripping nose on her nighty, burying her face in the chiffon fabric, grateful there was no one around to witness her actions.

As she lifted her head again, the sun's rays, filtering through branches, alighted on some small, pale eggs nestling between the tree roots; the eggs were cracked, their insides empty. Rose lifted the broken shells and held them up to the light where they glowed with milky incandescence. As she turned them this way and that, a shard as sharp as glass penetrated her index finger and a tiny drop of blood oozed out, crimson against her white skin. She sucked at the injury, tasting the blood's charged particles. She lifted the multi-stranded thong and, using her body to hold it in position, tied it onto her wrist; then, picking up the diary, she started to read . . .

25th September 1880

Six weeks have passed since I bade farewell to Papa and Imogen. I remember Papa's parting words, "Goodbye, Goddess". That's what he teasingly calls me on occasion. It's a moniker that has stuck ever since. As a child, I used to go out riding and imagine that I was Diana, Goddess of the Hunt. Now, I have become two-faced Janus instead, looking forward to my adventures with delicious (if somewhat apprehensive) anticipation, and backward as I think of my home with such longing and nostalgia.

I remember strolling through the long grass that grows rank in the south meadow, a few days before embarkation. I had been finalising my plans with Papa when I stepped out for a breath of the sultry August air. Darling Papa. What other father would allow his unmarried daughter to undertake such a journey? Although I must admit that it took many hours of convincing and cajoling before he capitulated. But from that time on, I have had nothing but his blessing and wholehearted support.

Not that I can say the same for dear sister Imogen, who is completely horrified and fears that I have become fodder for the gossip mongers. The talk is that father has been far too indulgent since mother passed away, and that I have run wild as a moor pony. Imogen thinks this unfettered liberty is madness. According to her, I will not survive for one moment in the African wild. Adventures of this sort are the preserve of hardy eccentrics—women with penchants for donning men's clothing, and little prospect of matrimony; certainly not for the likes of one such as I, who has been so cosseted and pampered all my life.

I do suspect Imogen's trepidation has to do more with wagging tongues than genuine fears for my safety. She says that travelling unchaperoned will be my undoing, as on my return—if indeed I do live to return—I shall be doomed to spinsterhood, for no one will want to marry such a wild and untameable hussy.

Imogen, albeit the younger, has always been the more prudent and down-to-earth sister. Now that I have distance on my situation, I cannot help wondering if she is right and this adventure is but a grand folly.

4

Rose opened her laptop hibernating quietly on the table and, in the Google search window, entered: 'Faded Polaroids'.

A list of sites popped up on her screen. Clicking on one at random, she read:

> *Does anyone know if old faded Polaroids can be restored? Have found a couple of pics of my late dad playing in a folk band with some other beardy dudes in the 70s and they are really faded.*

One reader had responded:

> *Photoshop will restore colour – but you'll need to scan them in and fiddle with them.*

Another had said:

> *In short, yes if they aren't totally f*cked.*

Someone else had warned:

> *Don't do it!*

So maybe the photos could be enhanced, but who knew how to fiddle with Photoshop?

The only person Rose could think of was Gary, the IT teacher at the school where she used to teach. Gary with the strange surname. What was it again? Omungri. Their friendship hadn't been that strong to begin with and now she felt awkward to ask him a favour. She hadn't seen him or even given him a thought since she'd left the school two years before. But there was really no one else who could help her. She gnawed at a piece of hard skin at the side of her nail. I'll phone later, she told herself.

She tabbed back to Google, typed 'Oberon' into the search box and pressed enter. Numerous sites appeared. One said:

> *A tourist paradise in the Southern Drakensberg. Nestling at the foot of the peak known as Dragon's Tooth, Oberon is a quaint village famous for its hospitality. Situated near the Lesotho border, it was established in 1848 by a group of Germans fleeing the March Revolution and the resulting turmoil in Germany. Aldous Bergmeier, the leader of the group, named it Alberich after the legendary sorcerer in German folklore, but as more and more English colonised the area, the name changed to Oberon. Bergmeier, who originated from a long line of dairy farmers, recognised that the land around Oberon was ideal for dairy farming. The farm he founded still exists today as the Oberon Dairy Farm and Cheese Factory. It is run by Aldous's third great grandson, Roland Bergmeier. Visitors to Oberon are encouraged to visit the Cheese Factory and sample its world-renowned range of cheeses . . .*

It was strange that she had never visited the Drakensberg. Rose couldn't remember Livvie going there, either. She recalled Livvie leaving her only once, when she was about seven, to visit John in Paris shortly before he died. Other than that, she and Livvie had rarely spent time apart. Even after moving to her own place, Rose would join Livvie for holidays in Cape Town, where Livvie owned a flat in Sea Point. They had gone down for two weeks in February, both of them knowing that this would be their last holiday together. Livvie had been diagnosed a few weeks earlier with cancer of the pancreas and though she still had energy at that stage, she was starting to look frail and her appetite was waning. They went on slow scenic drives around the peninsula, with Rose driving the rental car, and took leisurely walks on the promenade, breathing in the soft, coastal air. Often they did nothing but sit at the window in the lounge, their feet up on the sill, in a comfortable envelope of silence, and watch the sea. Or they spoke about the things that didn't need speaking about; Livvie told her she wanted to redecorate the Sea Point flat.

'I've always hated this carpet,' Livvie said.

Rose agreed, as was her habit.

'And the lounge suite – it's looking really shabby.'

Again, Rose nodded; but she couldn't understand. What would be the point of redecorating? Surely Livvie knew that she wouldn't be around to enjoy the new furnishings for long – or was she in denial? How strange it was to make plans for a future in which she knew she wouldn't take part. It was as if by looking towards the future she could delay the inevitable.

It dawned on Rose that the Sea Point flat was probably hers now, and that she could perhaps take whatever money there was from the estate to fulfil Livvie's last wishes. But without Livvie to do it with, it would be no fun. If she were to go anywhere at this point it wouldn't be to Cape Town but to the Drakensberg – to this Oberon place, to try to trace her biological parents. It was a dream that had lain dormant while Livvie was alive because Rose had always feared it would be too hurtful to pursue it. Now she was free.

She resumed her research, typing in the name 'Philip Geoffrey'. Wikipedia's response was swift:

Philip Geoffrey (1838–1914) was an English painter in the style now known as Classical Academicism. The range of his oeuvre included historical paintings, Greek and Biblical mythology, scenes from exotic locales and portraits.

Life: He was born in Bath, United Kingdom. From 1856–1859 he attended the Royal Academy Schools. In 1859 he left for Paris where he worked with the Rue de la Roche group of artists. On his return to London he exhibited at the British Royal Academy and soon after, was elected a member. He was knighted in . . .

She skipped ahead.

Geoffrey's best-known works include: 'Pandora releases the Keres' (1863), 'Prometheus tied to a rock' (1879), 'Adam rises from the earth' (1888).

So, the 'White Goddess' and 'The Drakensberg Lady' weren't among his best-known works. She tried searching for the paintings on Google, but all that came up was a reference to a 1948 essay by the poet Robert Graves.

Abandoning Geoffrey, Rose typed in the words 'Morris Hunter' and 'Detective Agency' and clicked. Her screen admonished:

Your search – Morris Hunter or Detective Agency – did not match any documents.

Rose gave up. Standing up, she arched her back in a long stretch. This all felt too much like an exercise in futility. She had things to do at the mall, there was nothing edible in her fridge and she wanted to clear Livvie's postbox.

She went to shower. With the water beating down on her head, she closed her eyes and imagined she was in the Drakensberg. She stood in the shadow of Dragon's Tooth, in a mountain dell surrounded by pale sandstone, on which antelope the colours of the earth leapt about. A cascade of clear water fell from the cliffs, enfolding her in a silver cloak. Lifting up her face, she allowed the water to enter her mouth. The hard metallic taste of Johannesburg water brought her back to earth. She stepped out the shower and, shivering, threw on her clothes from the day before.

Since her last visit to the mall, a huge Christmas tree had been erected in the middle of the aisle and garlands of tinsel looped up the escalators and along the moulded ceilings. Where had the year gone? Everyone always said that, when the decorations went up.

The year that Livvie had died. Hard as shell and bitter as a walnut. Another year done with. Rose had always heard old people saying how life passes you by almost before it begins. She was beginning to believe it.

Livvie's postbox yielded the usual accounts, adverts, and charity requests . . . and a collection slip. Crap. A speeding fine. It had to be Rose's. Entering the post office, she joined the long queue of people shuffling slowly forward, their stares fixed on the single teller behind the counter. She wondered how he could carry out his job with such unruffled indifference, seemingly oblivious to the glares and mutters of the impatient customers. Rose would collapse under the strain.

She watched as a woman in overalls walked up to the lottery-ticket seller. She put her hand inside her bra and dextrously extracted her money to pay the vendor. How would this woman's life change if she won a few million rand? And Rose's own? Money brought with it its own problems.

Finally, the worker behind the counter took the slip that Rose tendered and handed her the speeding notification. The whole transaction proceeded in complete silence. There was the photo of her car; no denying it.

Her cell phone rang. 'Hello, is this Ms Clemens?'

The security guard, beady-eyed and wide-girthed, pointed to a sign under the counter that said 'No Cell Phones' and waved his hand in the direction of the door. Bully! I'm going! I'm going!

The voice on the other end continued: 'This is Mr Bleazard's secretary . . . the lawyer dealing with the Howse estate. He needs to make an appointment to see you. Would this Friday work for you? 10.30? Can you come to our offices in Catherine House?'

Rose said that would be fine. She took the escalator to the level above, noticing distractedly the debris that had got trapped between the grooves of the escalator treads. She supposed the lawyer's appointment would be about the will. She dreaded it. Livvie's voice from the dead. It would make her death so final. Livvie's life's finale.

She walked into Exclusive Books and shuffled around the shelves, stopping at the travel section. There were dozens of titles: Guides to Rome, Paris, Madrid, London, New York, Chicago. Nothing on the Drakensberg. Only an *Atlas of National Parks and Reserves in South Africa*.

She zigzagged over to the South African section and saw a coffee-table book: *The Mighty Drakensberg: uKhahlamba, the Barrier of Spears*. Flipping through its glossy pages, she found:

> *Oberon is a picturesque village in the heart of the mountains, providing the ideal destination for the intrepid tourist looking for adventure as well as those craving the peace and serenity that is offered aplenty by these magnificent surroundings . . .*

There was a panoramic shot showing the village at the foot of the peak called Dragon's Tooth. Her wrists straining under the weight, Rose carried the book to the adjoining coffee shop. Sitting at a table, nibbling at a carrot and pecan-nut muffin, she read on:

The area provides archaeologists and anthropologists with a rich source of San hunter-gatherer history. It is a veritable treasure trove of rock paintings.

She looked for any mention of a White Goddess in contact with the Bushmen.

'Er . . . excuse me.'

She looked up. There was a man standing at her table.

'Do you mind if I sit here?' he asked, promptly seating himself without waiting for her reply. 'All the tables are full.'

Rose looked around and saw that they were.

'A beautiful part of the world,' the man said, glancing at the book. 'I go there quite often.'

He was probably around her own age, dressed in a blue shirt and khaki chinos. He had a friendly, open face.

'Actually, I've never been,' Rose said wistfully. 'Where about do you go?'

'Everywhere. I know the Berg well. I was in the Southern region a couple of weeks ago. Hiking. I love it there. It's much less developed than the Central or Northern Berg.'

The Berg. Trendy people called it the Berg – as if it were theirs to abbreviate.

'I've just done a cycle race in the area,' he continued. 'I did it last year as well.'

She sneaked a glance at his lean body. 'It must be strenuous,' she said lamely.

'You're not joking. There's been so much rain this year . . . there was so much mud that I had to carry my bike for most of the way! Up hills, down hills . . . through rivers. But ja.'

Rose smiled, leaning back in her chair.

'Do you know Oberon?' she asked.

'Ja. In fact, I've often stayed there, at a great spot, just outside the village. It's called The Chameleon, if you're ever in the area . . . The owners are friends of mine. They bailed out of city life a couple of years ago and opened a B&B. It's got this really fantastic garden. It's worth staying there just to see it.' His phone rang and he smiled apologetically as he took the call.

'Hello, Anton here. Yep? . . . I'm not in the office at the moment . . . He hasn't got back to me yet . . . I did indicate that if he hadn't signed by . . . yes, yes . . . As I understood it . . .'

Rose's coffee and muffin were finished. Since the man's exchange showed no signs of concluding, she stood up and gave a little wave goodbye. He held up his free hand. Did that mean wait or goodbye? She wasn't sure but wasn't brave enough to find out. Returning *The Mighty Drakensberg* to its place on the display stand, she walked out the shop.

Later, shopping done, she mustered up some courage and phoned the IT teacher. It turned out much better than expected. He was more than willing to help. 'Why not come round now?' he suggested.

She drove west to a yellow facebrick house in Greenside. Her finger hovered for a second on the intercom panel as she read: 'House', 'Maid'. Then she pushed the bell. The gate opened and she drove in.

The garden was untended, yielding only bitter aloes and Red Hot Pokers. Grass roots poked through the fallow soil where there should have been lawn. She walked tentatively down the slastoed path, removing her sunglasses and dropping them into her bag. The sun was sinking behind the gargantuan date palm that soared higher than the roof. Did Gary live in this big old family house by himself?

He opened the door: 'Howzit. Your Facebook status true then? No one snapped you up yet?' He hugged her genially. The house was gloomy in the late afternoon light. Rose was glad to see him.

'I hate to impose. I really appreciate this. You must . . . let me pay you for your time,' she rambled on.

'Don't be ridiculous. It's cool, really. A pleasure. Good to see you, Rose.' She remembered him always wearing the trademark blue T-shirt with the Superman logo emblazoned on the front. He was still wearing it.

They walked past the lounge. From inside it, a TV was blaring. 'My grandparents,' Gary said. 'Come, I'll introduce you.' He led the way.

Two old people sat side by side on La-Z-Boy recliners, their feet up on the extended foot-rests, watching TV. The furniture in the room looked as if it hadn't been upgraded since the 1970s.

'Gran, Grandpa,' Gary shouted, 'this is Rose.'

'Hello,' Rose smiled.

'Rose who?' the old man demanded suspiciously.

'Clemens,' Rose replied.

'Clemens? What sort of name is Clemens?'

'It's a name, Grandpa. From England,' Gary cut in, his tone exasperated.

'England?' the old man repeated. 'Ah.' He nodded his head. 'And what does your father do?'

Gary rolled his eyes. 'Grandpa, Rose has come to work.'

'Ah.' His grandmother nodded her head.

'They all live in the hope that I'll bring home a nice Jewish girl,' Gary told Rose as they left the room.

'So, why don't you bring home a nice Jewish girl?' she asked.

Gary shrugged. 'Maybe I'm not looking for one.'

'Who's all?' she wanted to know.

'Oh, my whole family. My parents, grandparents, aunts, uncles . . . you name it. They feel it's their duty to see me married off. To one of the tribe.'

A tabby snaked around their legs and meowed as they walked on down the passage.

Gary switched the light on and pushed open the door to a room. 'S'cuse the mess. This was my sister's room. I made it my study when she got married,' he said, as if this explained the disorder. 'Sorry . . .' he removed an empty pizza box from a chair and wiped the seat with his sleeve. 'I don't let the maid in here. She moves all my stuff and then I can't find anything.'

The cat had jumped up onto the chair where Rose was about to sit and curled up there, licking its paws.

'Just kick him off,' Gary said, gazing intently at the computer screen and moving the mouse around.

'No, I feel flattered. He likes me. I don't want to hurt his feelings,' Rose said, perching on the edge of the chair.

There were footsteps from down the passage. A plump woman in her fifties stood at the door. She was very well groomed, not a hair out of place, and wore lots of make-up. She was dressed in a mustard twinset and expensive-looking, very tight jeans.

'Oh, hi, Ma.' Gary introduced his mother to Rose, who half rose out of her chair.

The woman addressed her warmly. 'Would you like a cup of tea, doll?' Then in the same breath, she berated her son: 'Gary, how can you bring a girl to this room? Aren't you ashamed of the state it's in?'

'Ma, this is my work. We're working. Rose has come here to work. Not judge the decor.'

'So, let me pay you. It's your work. Come on,' Rose pleaded, when his mother had retreated back down the passage.

'Nah, man. I just said that to get my mother off my back. She drives me mad. Nags me like I'm some teenager.'

Then move out, Rose wanted to say. She wondered why he still lived at home at his age. Odd.

When Rose showed Gary the photos, he shook his head. 'These are totally fucked,' he said. 'Like, who are these hippy dudes?'

'They might be my . . . long-lost parents,' she replied.

'No way! Okay, I'll try my best.'

He positioned the pictures onto the scanner. The images appeared side by side on the computer screen. After much fiddling with the mouse: 'Sorry. This is about the best I can do,' he said apologetically.

They both looked intently at the screen. Rose's heart fluttered.

'Your mother's a babe,' commented Gary.

I'd love to have inherited those boobs, Rose thought, but never said, not wanting to draw attention to her own small ones. Or that blonde mane, and that wide, confident grin. So different from Rose's own smile, always so hesitant and unsure.

'I don't know if she is my mother. She could be,' Rose ventured.

'You look nothing like her,' Gary observed.

'Gee, thanks.'

'No, well, you're gorgeous in a different way, doll. You must take after your old man. This dude.'

'If that's who it is . . .'

They looked at the man's image.

'What's with the hat pushed down so low? Like he's going incognito.' After a period of silence, Gary said: 'So you didn't know your parents? It must be weird, man.'

Rose nodded. 'Or any other family.'

Gary whistled. 'Jesus! Must have its advantages, though. I wish I never knew some of mine!'

'I think you're so lucky to . . .' Rose broke off, then continued: 'I want to try and contact anyone who might have known my mother . . . who was around at the time, before she died. My adoptive parents hired a detective to try and track people down . . . But that was such a long time ago. I wonder if he's around still – the detective, I mean.'

'Phew!' Gary said. 'It's complicated. So your surname . . .?'

'It belongs to John Clemens, the man . . . who adopted me. It caused major confusion when I was at school. He left to go live in Paris when I was still young and Livvie brought me up. She was my guardian. Her surname was Howse. She never actually adopted me. That's why I'm Clemens,' she added as an afterthought.

'Your real mother? What was her name?'

'Ruby Le Grange.'

'Sounds like a porn star from the platteland.'

'It's French Huguenot, I imagine. But it may not even have been her real name.' Rose fell silent for a moment. 'I've never seen any identity documents. Maybe, she gave herself the name. Maybe, she wanted to recreate herself, make a new identity. That detective who was hired – he contacted every Le Grange in the country, but no one had ever heard of a Ruby.'

For a short while, they both looked thoughtfully at the screen. Then Rose asked: 'Where does your surname come from?'

'We think that when my great grandfather arrived here from his *shtetl* in Lithuania, the customs official heard "Omungri". The story goes that my great grandfather thought the man was asking him how he was – not what his name was – so he said, "Oy, I'm hungry". Those must have been among the few words of English he learnt on the boat coming over. So that's what the official wrote on his immigration papers.'

'You're kidding me, right?' Rose said.

Gary shrugged. 'It's a story. But we're the only family that I know of with that name. My great grandfather had seven sons. And two daughters. Probably by the time he was my age. They really knew how to be fruitful in those days.'

'There was no TV.'

Gary laughed. 'Now, you'll find us Omungri's all over the show. I've got a place to stay if I ever find myself in Toronto, San Diego, Sydney, London, or wherever. And we haven't changed; right now, I'm fucking starving.'

'Smells like fish and chips tonight.'

'Not for me. I live my own life. Should we go catch a pizza? I'll put these on disk for you,' he said. 'Here are your originals.'

'Thanks. That's great.' She slipped disk and photos into her bag. 'So, you don't really know what your roots are, either?'

'Roots, shmoots. We're the wandering Jews. My roots? They're here. In this country. Where should we eat?'

26th September 1880

Perhaps you were right, darling Imogen. I am sorely missing the considerable comforts of home and, I hasten to add, my dearly beloveds. I do know that this journey was partly spurred on by my desperate desire to escape my situation—the obligation incumbent upon me to marry and marry soon. Even though not one of the suitors who came to court was worthy of a second glance. It was becoming increasingly intolerable to me, obliged to entertain these sorry specimens and listen politely to their inane banter when all I wanted to do was paint.

It was indeed after one such visit that I formulated my plan. We were in residence at the London townhouse when Lord Locust, as I refer to him, flounced in and with his usual supercilious mien, dropped his gloves, hat and cane into Annie's startled hands and installed himself into Papa's favourite armchair, the one by the fire. There he pontificated about how the potato blight in County Cork has affected the English economy . . . on and on. Well! I could not bear to listen to such dreary verbiage so while Imogen was responding prettily to his conversation, as is her wont, I was at liberty to page through the periodical lying on the occasional table—that most wondrous of publications, The Athenaeum.

This edition featured Bushman rock paintings reproduced by Mark Hutchinson, an artist hired by the Governor-General of Natal for the purpose of copying the rock paintings in the Giant's Castle area. The paintings are so intricate in detail and so intriguing in content that they have imprinted themselves upon my mind. As I turned the pages, I closed my eyes and imagined journeying to that natural gallery, walking along ancient mountain tracks amidst the towering cliffs, where silver ribbons of water tumble from weathered rocks and where, amongst layers of soft yellow sandstone, I could view for myself the marvellous painted antelope and stick-limbed warriors.

The prospect was not as unattainable as one might suppose because Papa's brother, Henry, has for many years been stationed within a few days' journeying from this site, in the tiny hamlet of Oberon. He knows the area well and I knew his presence would make a strong case in my favour. He could provide me with accommodation and any expertise that would be required in the way of suitable guides and other necessary servants. So, to Lord Locust's surprise, I jumped up, advising him over my shoulder that Imogen would show him out, and ran from the room to find Papa.

And here I find myself. After six weeks at sea I can barely wait to disembark. The tedium of life aboard the ship has become unbearable but I suppose this is always the case when one's destination beckons so enticingly within range. When next I write in this journal, I shall hopefully be on terra firma . . .

5

Johannesburg's birdlife was in full throttle: mousebirds in the bushes; a Piet-my-vrou in the tree; querulous louries; weavers, mynahs, mossies and doves singing in unresolved cadences. The soft summer breeze rattled the blinds and the sun glared onto the book Rose was working from. The page was open to an illustration of the map of the human genome, all twenty-four chromosomes exploding outwards in a wheel. Wheels within wheels. Here were the switches that turned life on – and off. A few of the more common genetic disorders were marked: colon cancer on chromosome two; Huntington's chorea on four; Alzheimer's on fourteen; breast cancer on seventeen; hypercholesterolaemia on nineteen.

If she had to draw her own map, what would it look like? She didn't know what her ancestors had been struck down with. Now there were blood tests for some of these diseases, if she were really concerned – but what would she say? Please test me for every genetic marker that exists? What a neurotic! Like Charmaine, her boss. She was quite crazy, whirling around her de luxe offices like a skinny dervish on high heels, barking orders at her sullen staff, cell phone attached to her ear. You had to admire her drive and the success she'd achieved in her business, but Rose was pleased that her job required only a minimum of face-to-face contact with her.

Rose's thoughts strayed from Charmaine to Gary. She mulled over his offer of the night before. When they'd arrived back at his house after supper, he had nonchalantly asked if she wanted to come in for coffee. Was it his intention to bed her, she'd wondered, with his aged grand-parents right there in the next room and his parents across the passage? What had been in his head? Maybe it was only coffee he was offering – but in Rose's view, it was time he moved out anyway. 'Um . . . thanks, but I'd better get home,' she'd answered. 'The Friday deadline looms.'

Dead line. Why had these two words been cobbled together to describe the notion of time running out, when a dead person, whose time *had* run out, was merely described as 'late'?

Dead line, dead lock, dead heat, dead beat. Dead end. That's where the photos had taken her. She needed someone who could positively identify the woman in thc photo as her mother Ruby. Who could she ask? Who of Livvie's friends would have been around at the time Ruby was alive? Livvie's friendship with Marion had begun when Rose started school, long after Ruby had died. But Marion might know of friendships that were older.

Rose phoned her. 'Do you know of anyone I can contact who might have been around at the time of . . . when Ruby was . . . still alive?' she asked.

Silence.

'No, darling. I'm afraid I can't think of anyone. It was long before I met Livvie,' Marion replied.

'Ja, but . . . weren't there maybe some of Livvie's friends from around that time who you might have met?' Rose persisted.

'Hmm. That's a possibility. I'll phone if anyone comes to mind,' Marion eventually replied.

Rose cut the call, feeling despondent.

The khaki-clad gardener passed by her window, his footsteps crunching on the gravel drive. She heard the hosepipe splashing on the metal of her car. A dog barked in the distance. Time passed and absorbed in her work, she only realised its passing when she smelt roasting lamb wafting over from the main house. Late afternoon already. She wondered if Betty and Harry, her landlords, were around. She needed to give them notice. She'd decided that she couldn't go to Oberon until she'd sorted herself out here and moved into Livvie's flat. It was hers now, so why should she continue to pay rent on this place?

She walked around the hedge, head down as she negotiated the path leading up to the main house. The property flattened into a flawless expanse of lawn, interrupted only by the sparkling pool in which no one ever swam. Usually by this time of the year the beds were lined with a glorious riot of impatiens, but a virus had attacked the plants and she'd heard that Johannesburg's gardeners were struggling to find suitable replacements.

Harry and Betty sat on the veranda in the golden afternoon light. Potted hydrangeas in shades of litmus flowered next to stone-clad columns. The couple watched her progress up the path.

'Hiya, Rose. Take a seat. How you doing? What can I offer you to drink?' said Harry genially as she stepped onto the veranda tiles. 'Nathan!' he shouted. His weight made a deep impression in the overstuffed cushions of the couch he was sitting on. His face was florid and his neck hung over the collar of his emerald golf shirt. 'Aaah,' he sighed, stretching both arms out along the back of the couch. 'Best time of the day, this. Best climate in the world.'

The gardener had changed into man-servant mode, the khaki overalls exchanged for a short, white jacket and the floppy hat gone. He stepped onto the verandah, releasing clouds of cooked lamb smell through the open French doors.

'Hi. Fine. Nothing, thanks. Um . . .' She caught Nathan's interrogative eye and amended: 'Water . . . sparkling. Thanks.' She sat down on a white wicker armchair that had no view of the garden. She was dreading to say what she'd come to say, fearful of telling them she was moving out, though she wasn't sure why.

'So,' said Harry, whisky tumbler in hand, 'what can we do for you, young lady?'

'I'm . . . moving into my mother's flat in Killarney,' Rose blurted out. 'So, I've come to give you notice.'

'Oh – that's terrible! You've been such a good tenant,' Betty frowned. Her little drop earrings shook in time to her displeasure. She sat sideways in her chair, legs crossed at the knees, one silver-sandalled foot tapping up and down. She was well preserved for her age. She must have had some body work done. Face, too.

'I'll pay next month's rent, of course. That gives you about six weeks' notice. Is that okay?' Rose asked anxiously.

'Livvie was a lovely lady,' Harry said, his expression doleful. Harry and Betty had known Livvie. It was through that connection that Rose had found the accommodation. They'd all moved in similar circles, although their acquaintanceship with Livvie had been fairly recent. Harry and Betty would probably not have met Ruby. Rose was tempted to ask them, but didn't.

'Don't you know anyone who would want to take the cottage? Someone nice and quiet, like you. I don't want any rowdy students,' Betty said sharply. She took a small sip of the colourless fluid in her glass.

A little boy peeked out from behind the French doors. Rose cocked her head playfully to meet the child's eyes. Betty followed her gaze.

'Oh that's Talita's child,' she said offhandedly.

'What's his name?' Rose asked.

'Pulley.'

'Pulley? That's unusual.'

'No, it's quite a common black name.' Betty spelt it out: 'P-U-L-E.'

'Oh,' Rose said, '*Pule.*'

The child came over to Betty and swung on the arm of the chair. 'No!' Betty reprimanded him sharply. 'Don't swing on the chair. Martha must take him.' She made as if to rise but then sank back again and looked at Rose. 'I don't like to touch him. He's got Aids. We just found out recently,' she told her, *sotto voce* behind her hand.

'Oh my God – that's awful!' Rose exclaimed. 'How old is he?'

'About two,' Betty replied.

The conversation ceased momentarily as Nathan walked out onto the veranda holding a tray. He handed Rose her water.

'You know . . .' Betty shifted her weight in the chair, '. . . he got it from Talita.'

What a dreadful thing, Rose thought. How did a mother live with herself, knowing she'd infected her baby with Aids?

The bubbles of sparkling water pricked her lip. She knew about the terrible statistics, the toll Aids had wreaked on society, but here was its human face. This poor suffering woman. And her child. So tragic.

Betty continued: 'She's supposed to work for me two days a week. She comes in, but after five minutes, she goes back to the room.'

'And I pay her, for these five minutes!' grunted Harry.

There was a short silence. Betty settled back, pursing her red lips. 'You know, one day, oh – a few months ago – she came into the kitchen and I suddenly noticed how thin she'd got. She looked like a walking skeleton. I said to her, "Talita, you look terrible. You must go for an Aids test". And when she gets back, I ask her what the result is, and she says, "Madam, the test was negative". Stupid me but I believed her.' Betty paused to take another delicate sip. 'Then, she went mad . . . crazy. Started washing everything in sight . . . not in my house, of course – I wouldn't have minded if my house got cleaned properly for a change . . .' she gave a tinkling little laugh, '. . . but in the servants' quarters. Walls, floors, cupboards. She went mad with Martha, too, attacking her, smacking her, cutting up Pule's clothes, throwing everything out the window . . . So we took her to the Gen. Then, Martha tells me she's being tested for TB. TB! I got hysterical. I wanted to know if Harry and me were at risk. But it wasn't TB, it was Aids. I got it out of Martha eventually.'

Rose shrugged, a helpless expression on her face. Betty continued unabated: 'I wanted to visit her at the Gen but it's so disgusting there – cockroaches, rats . . . nothing works . . . the lifts, the escalators, everything's been stolen. Healthy people get sick just walking in through those doors. All I can say is, thank God she doesn't have TB otherwise we'd all have had to go for X-rays. And then what!' Betty said.

Then what? Then Betty and Harry would have gone to a sparkling private clinic with state-of-the-art equipment and smiling nurses and had some X-rays taken – which in all likelihood would have been free from all signs of disease. Rose shook her head.

'So now she's on the treatment. I don't think it's doing much, though. Have you seen her? I can't look at her. A walking skeleton!'

'The woman must go back home . . . to the rural area or wherever. I hate this sickness under my roof,' Harry shuddered.

Betty shook her head, earrings trembling: 'Oh no, Harry. I can't tell her to go. I'd feel too bad – for Martha's sake. Martha's worked for us for such a long time.'

So Betty had some compassion after all.

'Then Nathan can bring his family up from Zimbabwe and we'll have a whole location in the backyard!' Harry retorted.

The child, in the meantime, had caught Rose's eye on him. He came over and held onto the arm of her chair, jumping up and down, laughing breathlessly.

Rose laughed, too. 'Hello, Pule.' She stretched towards him to pick him up, aching to feel his weight on her lap but he eluded her grasp and bounded just beyond her reach. Then his face took on a serious expression and he looked at her, appearing to weigh her up, testing her in some way. The spell broke and he ran onto the grass with a skip and a hop.

'He's so cute!' Rose watched him as he ran haphazardly around the garden.

'It's a problem,' Harry said dryly. 'They're all cute at this age.' The ice cubes clinked as he swirled his whisky.

'How's he doing? Is he on treatment?' Rose asked.

'I don't know,' Betty said. 'I must say, I don't like this Aids thing in my house. If I had young children, there's no ways I'd allow this.'

'Where's the child's father?'

'God knows. I doubt Talitha even knows,' Betty said in an exasperated tone. 'Anyway, whoever he is, he's probably dead by now.'

'What can we say – this is Africa,' Harry added, grimacing as he gulped down the last of his whisky.

Martha came out to fetch the boy. She picked him up under his arms, swung him round and put him on her back. At first he yelled in protest but then quietened and craned his head to look at Rose. She smiled and waved.

'Martha, won't you switch off the oven? You can go off then,' Betty told her.

'Yes, Madam. Good night,' she said and disappeared back into the house.

In the pale light, Betty's pink cardigan had merged into the green cushions on which she sat and all tones took on shades of grey. The conversation ambled along desultorily. Rose waited for what seemed like an opportune moment then stood up and said she had to go.

'We're off to our daughter in Toronto in a few days. Nathan can help you with the move,' Betty said.

'That's very kind. Thanks,' said Rose, stepping off the veranda.

'And don't be a stranger, okay?' Harry shouted after her.

Back in front of her computer, Rose stared into its dark screen. What was the life expectancy for a child on anti-retrovirals? She googled 'Life expectancy, Aids, Children' but she couldn't find any helpful answers.

It was time to resume her work on the DNA script. As she opened the document, she heard the gravel crunching outside her window. There was a knock at her door. Who could it be at this time? She didn't feel like interruptions.

'Who's there?' she asked.

'It's me, Miss Rose, Martha. Sorry to worry you.' She stood on the doorstep, surrounded by blue-and-white-striped carrier bags. 'Can you open your gate for me? The driver is coming from home. I give him the food for my children once a month. He usually comes to the big gate but they . . .' she jerked her head towards the main house '. . . went out and double-locked it.'

'Where's home?' Rose asked.

'Ficksburg.'

'Ah . . . where the cherries grow. Who's still living at home?'

'I've got two there still, and my grandchildren from Talita and my other daughter. She's passed away. Last year. I'm trying to get the welfare for her children but the social worker is making a lot of problems. She says I must find the father. Can you believe? Where am I going to find the father? I don't even know the father.'

Rose felt indignant for Martha. Her helplessness. 'Who's looking after them while you're here?' she asked.

'Nobody. My husband's mother is there . . . but she's too old now. She's like a baby, she just lies on the bed all day. She doesn't know anyone anymore. My . . . how do you call her? . . . sister-of-my-husband – she's looking after her. But it's too difficult for her. The children, they're looking after themselves.' She sighed and shrugged her shoulders.

Lost children. Lost to society. Uneducated, unskilled, unemployable. And lost fathers.

The driveway was illuminated by shafts of headlight shining through the wooden slats of the gate.

'Here's the driver. Thanks, Miss Rose. Remember to close the gate.'

6

Catherine House, with its glass cladding, looked like a cube of blue sky brought down to earth. A uniformed security guard pulled the glass door open and checked Rose's name against a list. He pointed her to a dimly lit reception area, where a receptionist with a face like a block of wood ticked her name off in an appointment book. Rose perched on the edge of a sofa, feeling like Country Mouse in her smart frock, handbag on her lap. There was red wallpaper and prints of English hunting scenes on the walls. Magazines were splayed like hands of solitaire on the glass-topped coffee table.

'Hello – Miss Clemens?' She looked up from the highly polished shoes to their owner, a nattily dressed man in his early forties. His right hand was extended. Rose stood up and shook it. It felt solid and cool.

'How do you do. I'm Marshall Bleazard. Please, after you . . .'

Marshall Bleazard. Legal Eagle. Buzzard.

Meekly Rose followed the black suit. They padded silently along the carpeted passage, stopping at a doorway where he indicated that Rose should enter. The room was bright, the street visible through the glass skin of the walls. She could see the traffic below though she couldn't hear it. A large, polished desk dominated the space and there were bookshelves filled with identically bound law tomes lining the walls.

Rose sat down on the chair Bleazard offered, her handbag balanced on her knees, and watched him take his place across the desk. It was empty except for a chrome perpetual-motion desk toy – the type with the hanging balls – and a manila file. She noticed that Bleazard had large pores on his nose. They marred his suave looks a little but Rose decided they were probably necessary as drainage channels for his excessive confidence.

'Would you like anything to drink? Tea? Coffee?' he asked. He was polite and professional.

She shook her head although she could have done with something to drink. Her mouth was dry as a desert but she didn't think she would manage to swallow anything right now. She wondered why she was so nervous, as if she were about to sit for an exam.

'Well, let me begin by offering you my condolences . . .' He allowed a pause for her reply and when none came, said briskly: 'Should we get straight down to business?'

He opened the manila file, sliding reading glasses out of his jacket pocket and slipping them onto his nose. He began reading:

'John Clemens Trust. For the benefit and general welfare of my adopted child, Rose Clemens.'

He frowned at her over his glasses, as if to check she was listening, then continued: 'Firstly, your adoptive father made you the beneficiary of a trust consisting of numerous assets and some cash. Ms Howes, as his common-law wife . . .'

Bla bla bla. What was he saying? Rose had picked up the last bit. She interrupted: 'You mean they were married?'

'Not exactly, but they did live together . . . shared a house. This gave Ms Howes spousal rights. She had usufruct over the immovable trust property, meaning she had right of use over the fixed assets of the trust.'

What? Usufruct? Rose tried to look nonchalant, like this was a word she came across every day.

'For you, the terms were stricter. The trust paid for your education and granted you basic living expenses until you were self-supporting. Mr Clemens stipulated that this was to be kept a secret from you.'

'From me? Why?'

The lawyer shrugged, delicately rubbing thumb and forefinger together. 'Perhaps he wanted to protect you from fortune hunters. Or teach you the value of money. We can only guess at his motivations. I wasn't the lawyer who drew up the trust deed, you understand. I never knew any of the participants involved here.' He looked across at her. 'You have a few years to wait until you inherit. The trust property will only vest on you as beneficiary on your thirty-fifth birthday. It may be that Mr Clemens considered that, by that age, you would have enough maturity and responsibility not to squander the family fortune. On that date, you are entitled to receive assets and capital and the trust can be terminated, if you so wish.'

She nodded, feeling stupid. Shouldn't she be asking questions?

'So, to tell you the assets which comprise the trust property . . .'

Yes – that was a question she had on the tip of her tongue.

'. . . there is a nice property portfolio and a substantial share portfolio. By the way, the trust continues to grow as we speak because the income generated is constantly being reinvested. For each million that accrues, the trust grows by about twelve thousand a month, after tax.'

Each million! How many were there?

Bleazard looked at her with a faintly encouraging smile, as if he guessed some of the turmoil she might be feeling. 'Fortunately, you don't have to worry about any of it. It's all being ably looked after by property agents and a stock-brokerage firm, and overseen by us.'

'God!' was all Rose could say. When she was on a teacher's salary, she could hardly support herself and had been forced to give extra lessons after school. It had been an agony. She and her students had sat side by side at her dining-room table, the students surreptitiously fidgeting with their cell phones and she glancing at her watch. And all the while, there were these millions sitting in a trust fund for her benefit and welfare.

'So that's the Clemens trust. Now to the Howes estate. Livonia was well off in her own right. She made excellent investments through the years, reinvesting dividends, buying offshore, acquiring property. So after the expenses and taxes are paid, you will be entitled to the remaining estate but, again, the will stipulates that you can only get full control at the aforementioned age of thirty-five. In the meantime, the executor is instructed to negotiate a monthly allowance with you and there is provision for certain large expenses that may crop up – such as a car. All to be effected at the discretion of the executor, which is . . . me.' He smiled at her over the top of his reading glasses then, flipping through more documents, noted: 'And there are also, of course, the personal and household assets, such as gold coins, jewellery, paintings, collectables, antiques and so on. You must know that Mr Clemens and Ms Howes each inherited large estates from their own respective families, and since they were both singletons with no offspring of their own, those estates both pass to you, too.'

Rose gulped. She felt stunned. 'I . . . I always knew there was no shortage of money. We lived well, but you would never have thought . . . we didn't live extravagant lives. And we just never discussed money . . . I had no idea . . .'

He wasn't listening to her ramblings, however. 'I'm just waiting for the latest share values from the broker but what I can tell you is, the rentals, share portfolios and other assets . . . they're sizeable.' He sat back in his chair, pocketing his glasses and interlaced his fingers over his chest. A gold watch peeked out from under his dazzling white cuff.

Rose spread her palms to the ceiling in a gesture of complete helplessness and shook her head. Marshall raised his eyebrows. What was he thinking? Poor little rich girl – you're not going to get much sympathy from these quarters!

Rose felt the need to explain. 'I've really got everything I need. I don't want any . . . I've never wanted for anything . . . in the way of . . . material things.' Her cheeks were burning.

The lawyer's expression was non-committal.

'Look, it will take a few months to wind up the estate. Plus, you have the five years to wait it out until you turn thirty-five. If you want, you can forgo the allowance – it can be reinvested. So, in fact, you can ignore your inheritance indefinitely; your life doesn't need to change. My advice is, take some time to digest it all. Mull it over. If you want to discuss the monthly allowance, give me a call.'

A lizard, metallic black, disturbed by Rose's footsteps, darted into the clover that grew in the flower box abutting the building. The midday sun was blinding on the white concrete pavement. Rose scratched in her bag for her sunglasses and cell phone. There was a missed call from Charmaine. She couldn't bear to deal with her right now. And why should she? She was a millionaire! No – multi-millionaire. A multi-million-heiress. She repeated slowly. 'Mull-ti-mil-lion-aire!' The word rolled so easily off her tongue: M-m-m had such zesty flavour; the l-l-l full of allure; and the open ending 'aire', so nonchalant, so blasé.

But here she was, still the same person living the same uneventful life. She should be out and about, enjoying the high life with the rich and famous. Where did one find these people? Did she really want to know?

Her knees were shaky, her mouth dry. Signing the documents, her hands had trembled so much she'd hardly recognised her own signature. Adrenaline. Fight or flight. Stimulation of the autonomic nervous system. Constriction of the capillaries. Rapid pulse. Sweaty palms. She wanted to tell the man she passed on the way to her car: 'Guess what! I've got megabucks, lucre, lolly, spondalucks, boodle, moolah. I am a m-m-m-i-ll-io-nair-r-re!' She wanted to tell somebody. But who? Marion? No. Definitely not. A friend. But she didn't have any real friends. There was a time when Charmaine had tried to befriend her, had made a few friendly overtures, but Rose had fobbed her off. There was no one she could tell.

She had reached William Nichol motorway with its expansive grassy verges and electrified fences. 'Money, money, money, la la la-la.' She hated that song, with its silly lyrics. Now it played over and over in her head. On a whim, she turned left at the top of the hill and found herself in a stream of cars, like salmon swimming towards Hyde Park Corner.

Once in the parking garage, she followed the now predatory currents, circling slowly around and around, searching for empty bays, sniffing out departing shoppers, alert for the winking promise of reverse lights. There were none. She was back at the ramp and circling upwards to the roof. She had never been up here before. It was apparently a well-kept secret because she found a parking space easily, between a Jeep and another 4x4. She squeezed out of her car, holding her door open just a crack, trying not to touch the Jeep's bodywork.

She hadn't been to Hyde Park Corner in years. She passed shoppers, individual and in groups; people who sauntered when they walked, drawled when they spoke and wore clothes with subtly engraved logos on the pockets, like badges of membership to an exclusive club. She, too, could belong if all it took was money.

Music tinkled from the PA system. She rounded a corner and was confronted by a doorway leading into a clothes shop. In her whole life, she had never entered this shop. A girl perched on a stool behind the counter, reading a magazine. 'Shout if you need any help,' she called out then resumed her reading.

Normally, Rose would have felt intimidated by sales ladies in fancy shops but today the girl just looked . . . (she struggled for the word) . . . ordinary?

She ran her hands through the clothes on the rails; weightless fabrics floated through her fingers. A dark-blue chiffon caught her eye. She lifted the hanger from the rail and held up the garment.

'What a beautiful dress,' Rose remarked breathlessly to the shop assistant.

'Try it on.' She hopped off the stool and walked round the counter. 'It will look fantastic on you, with your fabulous body. It's an Elie Tahari, the American designer.'

'I never have occasions to wear dresses like this,' Rose told her apologetically, following her through to a mirror-lined room with fitting booths.

'Come out when you're done,' the assistant said, hanging the dress on a hook in a cubicle.

Rose bunched the dress up, her hands trembling slightly from adrenaline leftovers. She pushed her arms through the armholes and then released the garment, feeling the chiffon drift down over her breasts, her hips, as light as cosmic dust. Midnight blue. It was a change from her usual beiges and creams. She emerged from the cubicle.

'Wow!' The saleslady looked impressed.

Rose laughed, 'Yes – especially with these!' She lifted her foot to display her well-worn baby-doll pumps. 'It's beautiful but it's really not me. I look like something out of *The Great Gatsby*. Anyway, I don't know how anyone can justify spending R20 000 on a dress.' As Rose said these words, she realised that the amount was only a tiny fraction of her worth.

'You'd be surprised!' the girl said.

Rose's cell phone rang. 'Listen, the animator will be emailing you early next week to let you know when you can download the file from the ftp site. Give me your feedback by Wednesday,' Charmaine shouted in her ear.

'So the script was . . .?' Rose started to say but Charmaine had already rung off.

Charming Charmaine. Rose felt relieved, though, that she'd been given some breathing space. Her head was too full to cope with work matters.

The saleslady was back on her stool behind the counter when Rose emerged, the dress hanging limply over her arm like a newly hatched butterfly. Rose handed it over. 'Maybe, if there was a really special occasion . . .' She left the sentence unfinished and walked out the shop, empty-handed.

Driving from the shopping centre, she was pulled along Jan Smuts Avenue by the post-lunch Friday traffic, still completely fixated on her newly revealed fortune. She'd restrained herself from buying the dress but when the estate was wound up, she could buy the whole rail . . . the whole shop if she wanted. She could give in to every extravagant whim that took her fancy. She whooped aloud. Then sneaked a sideways glance at the driver in the next lane, hoping he hadn't caught her in the act.

At the bottom end of Rosebank, the traffic light in front of her changed to red. As she braked, a *Homeless Talk* man materialised at her window, waving his latest edition. 'Sorry,' she mouthed, shrugging her shoulders, 'no change.' She watched in her rearview mirror as the vendor disappeared down the row of idling vehicles. She tried to imagine his life. She couldn't; she had no idea how he lived. How long did it take him to earn R20 000? A lifetime? Never? It wasn't fair. If she had bought something so extravagant, so unnecessary as the dress, it would be burning a hole in her car boot right now. Buy now, pay later, with the currency of guilt. Would she feel better if she gave it all away to charity? Probably not.

The idea of unlimited funds. She had never been one to covet material things, to pamper herself with regular massages or facials or hairdos. But never to have to work another day in her life? Ever? It was beyond her comprehension. And then? What was she to do with herself? Mooch around malls, trying on expensive lifestyles? And when people got to know that she was quite the heiress, would they all clamour for her friendship?

She was no longer the same person she'd been yesterday. She could never be that person again. How strange that money could have this power to change a person's identity. She felt a resurgence of her earlier panic and her hands became clammy on the steering wheel, her pulse racing. Could she share these feelings with anyone? A therapist? No, she would tell no one because who would empathise with her? Hers was such an enviable position, to most people. She could never reveal the source of her anxiety. This surfeit of riches was just too embarrassing. She would have to conceal it. A concealment of who she really was. Who was she?

The taxi behind her hooted. The light had turned green. As she geared to go, her eye was caught by some wooden bed bases balancing against a shop front. A second-hand furniture shop had taken root amidst Union Billiards, Pool and Pond, Adult World and Elite Dry Cleaners. The taxi revved threateningly up her bumper so she turned the corner and pulled into the parking lot across the street.

She parked between two blue-gum trees, their trunks thick as colossi. The car guard, in a fluorescent orange jerkin, hauled himself up from his spot in the shade and came over with a sour expression on his face.

'I'll see you soon,' Rose told him, wondering where she would get the requisite R2 from, since she'd emptied her purse of change.

A short while later, Rose exited from the furniture shop with a spring in her step. Her furniture was sold to the man in the blue dustcoat, who said it was all 'no problem', and that he'd fetch her stuff '*voetstoets*, finish and *klaar*'. She'd accept any price he offered. She'd never been one to haggle. And now especially – what did she care? He promised he'd come round on Monday with his guys and the bakkie. What a win! He'd even move her boxes and swop the beds. By early next week, she would be installed in the flat. How would it feel to be back in her childhood home?

Her phone rang.

'Hi, Marion.'

'Rose! I've got such news for you!'

And I've got such news for you, Rose thought.

'I've just been to a book talk with my friend, Lottie. Do you know her? It was fabulous. They had Joan Collins's sister – Jackie. She must be my age but she looks twenty years younger. Well, so would I if I had her money and could afford all that plastic surgery.' Jeez, Marion, get to the point, thought Rose, sidestepping the seedy characters lounging against street poles and slumped on wooden crates. The pavement was in bad shape; tiles jutted out at odd angles, creating receptacles for the detritus of the pavement loiterers: blackened banana peels, colddrink cans, cigarette butts, plastic bags. She clung to the strap of her handbag, hopping off the kerb and sidling along the road verge.

'. . . So I was sitting next to this woman. You are not going to believe it!' Rose waited. 'And who was it? The sister of the architect who worked with Livvie and John! Just when you ask me about people who might have known your mother, up she pops. Isn't that amazing? Alice Wright – she's the architect. Her sister's name is . . . I forget . . .'

'How did you make the connection?' Rose asked.

'I don't know . . . I think we were talking about people leaving the country and how sad it is that families are separated, living all over the world. Not me, though – I'm so lucky that I still have all my children here.'

Rose had reached her car. The car guard was hovering. As she searched in her bag for her keys, her phone clamped between ear and shoulder, she felt a coin. What was its denomination? She glanced at it – oh darn, R1. Better than nothing. She handed it to the guard, avoiding eye contact.

'Amazing!' Rose said, getting into her car. 'So what now? Did you get an email address or something?'

'No. You're going to faint when you hear this. Alice is arriving this afternoon! I mean, can you believe it? She's been living in Australia for years – now she's coming for a family wedding. I said – well, she absolutely has to see you. She's only here for about ten days, and they're all going to the game reserve after the wedding – like we did, remember? After Glynnis's wedding. We took all our overseas visitors to Kruger.'

Rose sat in her car and looked at the layer of red dust hanging heavy on the western skyline. Finally. Finally a start. Here was someone besides

Livvie and John who had actually met Ruby, who had interacted with her, spoken to her. She had to meet this architect. Could she dare to hope that she'd remember anything? It was all such a long time ago . . .

She remained where she was, waiting for Marion to send the number. But when it came through, Rose could only stare at it, her thumb suspended over the green dial icon. The number faded into nothingness and then there was only black. When should she phone? Tonight? No, she'd let her settle in a bit. Tomorrow. After the weekend. Sooner. Sometime. In between moving. She needed cardboard boxes. This directionless drifting along was making her crazy. She had to get organised and move into the flat already. Only then could she leave for Oberon.

She went into Pick 'n Pay and made her way to the large swing doors marked 'Staff Only'. There was a glass-covered panel on one of the doors but it was so murky that the interior of the storeroom remained obscured. Rose waited for a staff member to emerge. Muzac blared over the speakers; her worst – Christmas carols. There was a nasal announcement for an errant staff member to get back to her till, immediately! Finally, a man in blue overalls appeared. Rose asked if she could have some cardboard boxes. He nodded and told her brusquely to wait.

She stood beside a fridge dedicated to fancy imported ice-cream. It was something she'd been tempted by but never tasted. She pushed the heel of her palm into the hollow below her sternum and realised she was starving. When last had she eaten? She read the price on the small tub: fifty bucks. What a rip-off! She took a tub out of the fridge anyway and went to pay for it. It came with an attached wooden spoon.

The ice-cream was cloyingly sweet. A brown sludge of toffee ran through it. *Dulce de leche*: the sweet of milk. Mother's milk. Pabulum. She returned to the fridge, studying the names of the other flavours. Chocolate-chip cookie. Vanilla honeybee. She became aware of a presence standing next to her.

'Gary!'

'Thought it was you.' He held a box of chocolates gingerly, like it was something hot.

'I'm waiting for some cardboard boxes. I'm moving – to my adopted mother's flat,' Rose told him.

'Cool. Do you need some help?'

'Thanks, but I haven't got much. Just my clothes . . . kitchen stuff . . . books.' She foresaw an opportunity. Vanilla honeybee. Grab it before it disappeared. She blurted out: 'Are you busy tonight? Not to help . . . just to . . . we can . . .' her voice tailed off.

'Sorry, doll. I'm going to my relations in Boksburg. Don't ask. But hey! I'll come tomorrow?'

Rose nodded, a little crestfallen and somewhat regretting her casually bandied invitation. She really didn't want his help – for how, in all practicality, could he be of any? Sorting and packing in the presence of an observer. No thanks. That was way too exposing. And distracting. She needed to think about what to keep and what to discard. She hated having to concentrate on a personal activity while playing the good hostess at the same time. No, she wouldn't phone him. And she'd switch her phone off in case he phoned her. But, no – that would be rude. She would phone him but she'd tell him . . . she didn't know what she'd tell him.

She watched him retreating down the aisle. She should have offered him her ice-cream. Her hunger had waned.

7

Early the next morning, Rose started packing but her phone presented too great a distraction. She eyed it from time to time. She picked it up, about to press the dial button but then stopped herself. She was at a loss as to how she would identify herself. Whose daughter should she say she was? Ruby's? John's? Livvie's? Finally, without more deliberation, she hit the call button.

'Is that . . . Alice?' She was aware of her voice quavering but she couldn't stop it. 'This is Rose . . . um . . .' She didn't know how to proceed so she plunged right in. 'I'd . . . just like to ask you about Ruby Le Grange, my mother . . . what you remember . . . anything. I'd also like to show you a photo . . . if it's her.'

'Rose! Yes, hello . . . I can't believe it! My sister told me you'd be calling. I don't know how helpful I can be but I'll try. I'd love to meet you anyway.'

'You must have lots of family commitments while you're here. I don't want to step on anyone's toes,' Rose said timidly.

'Let me ask my sister what the plans are. She's my diary,' Alice said with a laugh. 'Can you hang on a minute?'

She came back to the phone. 'How about this afternoon? Can you come for tea? From tomorrow, life gets mad.'

Alice's sister lived in a house in Orchards, in a leafy cul-de-sac boomed off and manned by a security guard. Rose pressed the buzzer on the gate. She heard a catch being released and entered the property. The front door was so solid that it swallowed the sound of her knock. She waited. No one came. She pushed tentatively. The door opened and she found herself in an entrance hall with a passage to her right and a lounge to her left.

The furnishings were what could be described as urban African chic: terracotta tiles, brown leather couches, wooden masks and free-standing giraffes. There was no one about. She wasn't expecting a welcoming committee but this was just . . . rude. Should she call out? She tiptoed through to the lounge and waited. Still no one. She made her way onto the patio that faced an emerald square of lawn surrounded by flowering shrubs. Gardenias, fuschias. Oleanders. 'Did you know that they are one of the most poisonous plants in the world?' she asked the brown-grey starlings trilling in the trees.

The seconds ticked by. This waiting alone like a small antelope testing the waters only added to her state of agitation. Was she in the right house? She felt like she was trespassing. Should she phone to say she was here? She'd brought Gary's enhanced copies of the photos with her. What if it wasn't Ruby in the photo? She would be devastated. This was getting ridiculous now. She wanted to call out, 'Coo-ie. Hell-o-o. HEY!' But she didn't have the courage to break the silence.

Finally, she heard footsteps and a woman hurried out onto the patio. She was tall and skinny and wore beige trousers and a white blouson top. Was this Alice or the sister? Rose smiled, about to greet her, when the woman collapsed into a fit of weeping. She covered her face with liver-spotted hands.

The woman hugged Rose tightly, weeping into her shoulder. This had to be Alice, then. She smelt faintly of lemon, lavender. Oh God! What was wrong with her? Rose, wrapped in the stranger's embrace, stood stiffly, unsure of what to do or say. Did she need words of comfort? Rose couldn't think of any so she just timorously patted her back, which felt as bony and delicate as a baby bird's. The woman finally let go of her.

'I'm so sorry. I don't know why I'm feeling so emotional,' she apologised in a choked-up voice. Rose kept silent.

'Apologies that you had to let yourself in. The maid must have opened the gate for you. I think the rest of the household are all napping. I'm so sorry, I can't seem to stop crying. Let's sit down. How are you?' She led Rose to a couch.

'Er . . . fine, thanks,' Rose replied, her voice small and unsure.

Alice went inside to fetch tissues. Rose sat down on a chair that faced out onto the garden.

Presently Alice emerged again, more composed now. 'All this water under the bridge. The years have passed so quickly. It makes me sad just thinking about it. It's been such a long time – thirty years at least.' Rose nodded. 'My family and I, we left for Australia a short while after your mother died, and then . . . I lost touch with everyone. Ruby and I were pregnant at the same time, you know. I have a son a few weeks older than you. You were such a beautiful baby, Rose. You really were a little rosebud,' she smiled, wiping her eyes again. 'You know, don't you, that at the time, no one had any clue about your family. There was no relative, no one who could take you.' Alice's voice trailed off and Rose finally asked the question that had been hovering at the tip of her tongue – the question she'd never dared to ask Livvie; perhaps she'd feared the answer.

'What did Ruby die of, do you know?'

'It was a brain haemorrhage, I think. Something like that. I never knew exactly. I presume there must have been a post-mortem, but I never heard about it. She was too young to die like that – only about thirty, you know,' Alice replied.

My age now, Rose reflected. She wondered whether early death from brain haemorrhage was something carried in the genes.

'I have some photos I'd like show you, if you don't mind,' she said, taking them out her bag. Her heart thumping loudly in her chest, she passed the one of Ruby to Alice.

'Oh dear – I can't see a thing. Hang on. Let me fetch my glasses.'

Ditsy dame, Rose thought as she waited, exasperation rising in her gut.

Alice returned with the glasses perched on her nose and studied the photo.

Come on, come on – talk to me! Rose couldn't bear the suspense.

Finally, Alice exclaimed: 'Amazing! Where did this come from?' Her face softened into a smile. 'Yes, that's Ruby. You can't really see from the photo, but she was lovely. She had a fragility about her. The type of woman I imagine men naturally want to protect. Although . . . she was anything but fragile; tough – and competent. Never let the builders or any of the suppliers get the better of her.'

Rose passed the photo of the man over to Alice. 'And him?' she asked breathlessly.

Peering, Alice shook her head. 'This one's not clear at all . . . and the hat doesn't help.' She turned the photo over. 'Oberon, September 1981,' she read slowly.

'I'm wondering . . . if it could be my father. Look – the two photos are taken in the same spot.'

'Maybe; but to identify him from this . . .' Alice's voice tailed off. 'I've been trying to dredge up all that I remember,' she went on. 'I don't know if it will be too helpful . . .'

'Whatever. Anything.'

'I remember the day John hired your mother. We were on site. It was the first house that he'd bought to renovate. There was knocking and banging and white dust everywhere and I remember that John looked completely overwhelmed. I don't think he'd thought the whole thing through. He hadn't realised how much it would all eat into his time. He was a stockbroker, what did he know about renovating houses? He hadn't hired a construction company or anything, he was doing it all himself. I suppose he still had his clients to deal with at the same time. Markets to play. Whatever it is that stockbrokers do. And this was only the beginning. I told him we needed to think about hiring contractors – roofers, plumbers, electricians, kitchen fitters . . . you know. And then there would be the usual hundreds of choices to be made – paint colours, light fittings, carpets, tiles, appliances, door handles. What he needed was a project manager, someone to coordinate everything, make sure things ran smoothly, run around to the various suppliers. I was just the architect, I couldn't get involved in all that. I had a practice to run. John climbed up on a little pile of rubble and gazed around helplessly. He looked a bit like that teddy bear in the nursery rhyme – the one with blue eyes and curly hair. You know the one I mean?'

Rose nodded, not wanting Alice to stop.

'Just then he sneezed. It must have been the dust and the khakibos, but it was funny – we spoke about it afterwards – because when he recovered, when he opened his eyes, there stood Ruby. She was pointing to a rusty Mazda parked in the street. It looked as if it was held together with pieces of string and chewing gum. She said, "I'm really sorry to worry you but my car just died." She asked to use the phone – to get hold of her boyfriend, she said. We thought we'd wait with her until the boyfriend arrived but then John and I had to go. So we never did get to see him, this boyfriend. Ruby used to speak about him often. When she fell pregnant, we assumed he was the father of her child; but no one ever saw him. We used to rag John, accuse him of being the father, because we all knew how he felt about her. He categorically denied it.' She glanced at Rose. 'It feels funny, talking to you like this – about the father. Your father.'

'No, please,' Rose said quickly. 'Please go on. It's fine. Who's we?'

'All of us. The builder, plumber, electrician, kitchen man . . . other contractors. We were a little team, worked together on quite a few houses. Until Ruby's death. Then the team broke up and we went our separate ways. What a tragedy. She was so young. You were so young.'

'How did she come to work for John?'

'That first day that she rocked up, we chatted a bit while we waited for the boyfriend to arrive. She started asking us questions. She was like that – very friendly, outgoing, bubbly. John told her about his project, that he'd bought this house to renovate and resell on spec, and of his plans to buy more if this one succeeded. I remember her saying, "The country is tearing itself apart. Everyone is doing the chicken run and you stay and fix houses. You have faith!" Something like that. This was the early 80s, remember, when the violence was at its worst. People were leaving the country in their droves. She told us that she and the boyfriend had recently moved up from Durban and that she needed a job. And John employed her. Just like that! I think he was so desperate. He never asked for references, qualifications – nothing. He took a chance and it panned out.'

'And what were her qualifications? Did you ever find out?'

Alice shook her head.

Rose hesitated. 'And her accent? How did she speak? Did she sound . . . educated?' Funny how she'd never wanted to ask Livvie these questions.

Alice shrugged. 'She was English-speaking.'

'A Durban accent?' Rose persisted.

Alice looked vague. 'I don't know. Is there a Durban accent?'

Rose shrugged. 'Didn't she ever talk about her family?'

'Not really. I recall something about the mother moving to England and the father living here . . . Jo'burg, maybe . . . no, I don't remember. It wasn't clear. That's as much as I can tell you.'

'The family must have been so . . . dysfunctional. Losing touch like that,' Rose commented.

They sat in silence for a few moments. Then Rose, in a small voice, asked: 'Do I . . . am I . . . anything like her?'

Alice looked at Rose and shook her head. 'Sorry, darling. I can't see a resemblance. You remind me more of Livvie. Your gestures, the way you speak. I'm so sad I never got to see Livvie again – how we lost touch like that . . .' She sighed.

'I'm thinking of going to Oberon,' Rose said. 'Maybe I'll find out more there. Maybe someone will recognise them . . . the man . . . know who he is.'

'Don't get your hopes up, Rose,' Alice cautioned.

'I can't believe no one ever saw any man in her life,' Rose persisted.

Alice shook her head. 'It's strange, you know,' she said, 'even though we all got on well and worked together for quite some time, our relationship was more professional. We weren't really friends off site. None of us. We didn't feel free to grill Ruby about the man – or men – in her life. John was much closer to her than the rest of us. That's why we thought he might have been the . . . your . . . father. He bought her a bakkie and she even moved into one of the houses he'd renovated. But there again, although there were workmen going in and out while it was being finished off, no one ever saw evidence of a man living there. No suits in the cupboard, no shaving kit in the bathroom. And, of course, at the funeral . . .'

Alice paused to look at Rose, searching for signs of distress before continuing: 'There was a memorial service held in a church, somewhere in Parkhurst or Greenside, that side of town. The church was beautiful – huge, curved wooden beams supporting the ceiling, and beautiful stained-glass windows . . .'

'Yes?' Rose was eager for her to continue.

'All of us were there, all the people who had worked with her on site. Livvie, too. She wasn't part of the team, but she and John were friends and she knew Ruby. And John's parents were also there – did you know them?'

'No, not really. They died when I was very little.'

'And those were the only ones who came. No family. No friends from another life. We all waited in the hope that someone would appear to claim you. But no one did.'

Returning home, Rose felt as exhausted as if she'd run a marathon. She sat down on her couch and kicked off her shoes, enjoying the sting of the sisal rug on her soles. What was she? A candidate for the bastinado, the hair shirt, obligated to pay penance for the sins of her father? And mother. She got up, walked to the fridge and stared at its frugal contents: milk carton, bottle of orange juice, piece of gouda cheese, some salad greens. Nothing appealed, and she was still full anyway from the cake and tea that Alice's sister had served when she'd finally surfaced from her nap.

Rose eyed the pile of books waiting to be packed into the cardboard boxes then transferred her gaze to the rosewood box, an inscrutable presence on her kitchen counter. Inside it, the mysterious clues: catalogue, diary, invoice, seeds and Polaroids. At least she knew now that the one was of Ruby – that was confirmed. And the other revelations . . . it had been disconcerting to hear her paternal origins spoken of in such remote, impersonal terms. Alice had given her more insight into John's character than Ruby's. Rose wished she could have known him better. She'd liked his spontaneity; it was a trait Livvie had taught her to spurn.

There was as much mystery surrounding John as her biological parentage. He must have been a wonderful human being – his sense of responsibility so super-developed that he felt obliged to adopt her, his employee's child. Imagine. It was inconceivable that someone would do such a generous thing. Though, true, he had gone away afterwards, leaving Livvie, literally, holding the baby. He lost points for that. Why had he rushed off to Paris like that, when Rose was only six? Livvie must have known the answer to that; why had she never told Rose? Why had Rose never asked?

She studied Ruby's photo. Alice had called her death 'a tragedy'. It was, of course; to have died at such a young age. Before her life had even properly begun.

What was Rose going to do now? Should she try to make contact with Maurice Hunter? She didn't think so. He had exhausted his leads all those years ago. What more could he tell her that she didn't already know . . . that's if he was even alive still? And the catalogue painting, the diary, the seeds, the thong? What should she do about those?

All she knew for sure was that she couldn't face packing. Why was she putting off the move like this? She was like a piece of chaff borne along on the winds of fate. Drifting. Drifting and dithering. She needed to take control. She needed to get to Oberon.

29th September 1880

We docked in the port of Durban at the break of dawn—and not a moment too soon. Despite my relief and excitement it was with heavy heart that I bade adieu to the delightful S— family who provided such pleasant company, especially Mrs S— whose feminine good sense I shall sorely miss.

Walking down the gangplank, my senses were assailed by the lush verdure of the land, the glittering ocean slapping the sides of the vessel, the shining brown bodies of the stevedores and their many-tongued chatter. Once on terra firma, I was accosted not only by the clammy heat of the tropics but also by Hindoo women in bright saris, eager to sell their wares that ranged from shiny baubles to fragrant curry powders and odiferous fish. The place was teeming with the English arrivals and their relatives.

I was distracted with needing to find Uncle Henry. Since we last saw each other when I was no more than a tot, it was certain that he would no longer recognise me, and I had not the faintest idea of his appearance. I scanned the crowd, looking anxiously between the parasols, bonnets and boaters and there in the distance I noticed a man in a light linen suit and straw boater, twirling a Malacca cane and walking towards me with lively gait. There was no mistaking him. He is so much like Papa although considerably younger and smaller framed, but he has similar features and the same mop of sandy-coloured curls.

"And you must be my niece. How do you do?" he greeted me. Then he bowed low, removing his hat and sweeping it across his body. I asked him how he had recognised me and he told me that I was the spitting image of my mother, which was most intriguing to hear. I was very small indeed when she died and have no recollection of her. Father never mentions her name, perhaps still mourning her loss, even now. I wanted to pursue this avenue of conversation for I am starved for any snippet of information regarding her but I was aware of Uncle's need to depart.

He offered me his hand and we walked along the docks to where my luggage was waiting. The driver had to make several trips back and forth to load my many pieces onto the carriage.

While this was in progress I had time to peruse the wares on sale. I purchased a sackful of the most inexpensive hair adornments, delightful brooches and some bracelets made with lovely red, green and gold glass beads. They are sure to brighten any outfit and perhaps shall come in handy to distribute as gifts. I have such a surfeit that I can well afford to part with a goodly number. After Uncle had made his purchases—fresh foodstuffs, spices and the like—I was introduced to some of Uncle's curious friends and acquaintances. Then we embarked on the long ride to Oberon.

Dusk had crept in while she had sat reading on the couch. Rose switched on the TV and sat staring at its screen, unseeing. This was one of those times when she wished she could drink. But on the few occasions that she had consumed more than a tot or two, she'd felt so toxic the next day that now she hardly ever touched the stuff.

Earlier she'd switched her phone off, not wanting to be interrupted while she was with Alice. She switched it back on to check if Gary had phoned – and was really pleased to see that he had. There was a voicemail message from him: 'Howzit, Rose. What're you up to? Phone me when you get this.'

When had he called? She looked at the time. It was seven now. Should she phone him? She still couldn't face the packing and was bored with her own company. Before she could have second thoughts, she called up his number and hit the dial button.

Half an hour later, Rose opened her door to Gary's big frame on her doorstep. He was armed with a box of pizza and a bottle of tequila.

'You sounded tense. So I brought along a little something to help you relax.'

Rose laughed. 'I was thinking earlier that if I was someone who drank, I would have a drink tonight.'

'Never drink alone,' Gary admonished, looking around for a surface to deposit his burdens onto. 'Do you have shot glasses?'

'No, I don't. I never drink – hate the stuff. Do you need a plate for your pizza?'

'You're sharing it with me. We'll eat out the box. Come on girl, tonight you're breaking out.'

'I'm not hungry . . . okay then,' Rose conceded. 'Give me a drop of tequila . . . but I really mean a drop. I'm not joking when I say I can't take it.'

'You must be like woman in Chinese proverb: "she take liquor – by the ears".'

Rose snorted. 'Here are wine glasses. I've got salt . . . no lemons, though.'

'We don't need that shit,' Gary said, stuffing a segment of pizza into his mouth and pouring the tequila. 'Let's go sit on the couch. What's on TV?'

They sat side by side, distractedly watching a programme where Japanese participants had to undergo some sort of impossible obstacle course. The smell of pizza and hot cardboard filled the room. Rose picked up her glass and took a delicate sip. She made a face.

'You can't drink it like that,' Gary advised. 'You need to *sluk* it back. Like this.' He downed what was in his glass. 'You better eat some pizza – to line your stomach. Here.' He picked up a piece and cradled it to her mouth. Rose bit off a chunk.

'Now go for it,' he told her.

Under his beady stare, she held the bowl of the glass and took a generous swig. The liquid exuded a comforting warmth as it made its way down her gullet, and further down, to her knees. She liked the feeling, so quaffed some more. Her arms and legs felt numb. She took another big swallow and sank back into the couch.

Her mind strayed to the events of the afternoon. She wondered what Alice's son was like, whether there could exist some connection, some bond between them. She regretted not having asked Alice about him – his life, what he did, that sort of thing. She was aware of Gary shifting position and wished he would stop eating and drinking and make his move. C'mon Gary, she willed, opening her eyes.

His gaze was meeting hers. He lifted her legs and swivelled her round so that she lay back on the couch. She closed her eyes and felt his breath, warm and moist, on her neck, her ear, her mouth. He nuzzled her lips with his and raked his fingers through her hair.

'That's nice,' she murmured. His hand moved under her top, to her breast.

'Gary.'

'Mmmm?'

She sat up suddenly. 'I'm feeling very nauseous . . .' Then she added: 'Give me a moment. It'll pass.'

'You need some water.' Gary banged around the kitchen cupboards looking for a glass and finally brought her the water. Rose sipped it slowly.

'How are you feeling?' he asked, after a few minutes.

'Not great.'

'Can I get you something? Do you have anything to settle your stomach?'

'No. Wait a bit. Let's watch some TV. I'll be okay in a while.'

Damn, she thought. She lay back again, resting her legs on Gary's lap. He had a wiry mop of dark-ash hair that, at this moment, she found quite attractive. She watched his profile as he polished off the pizza, and his hands, fiddling with the remote. She was having difficulty focusing. She closed her eyes and, soothed by the drone of the TV, quickly fell asleep.

Light was just beginning to creep into the world when she awoke in her bed. Her mouth felt like the surface of Mars and she had a headache that started in the pit of her brain and radiated out to her eyeballs. She was in her panties and T-shirt. Gary was gone.

When she had the strength to raise herself from the bed, she gulped down some black coffee, then gave herself over to the task she had been avoiding, deciding that packing was the best distraction for her hungover state. It was astounding how much junk she'd collected over the years, despite her diligent tidying and throwing away. It was a depressing activity, this disposal of memories but she didn't want to start her new life encumbered by the past. Fresh start, clean flat. She had yet to deal with Livvie's junk and her hangover was slowing her down.

Her iPod played The Rolling Stones's 'Ruby Tuesday'; Ruby Tuesday, Ruby Le Grange. That couldn't have been her real name. She'd modelled herself on a song. A song and a prayer. What had Ruby been running from? What chains bound her heart? Or was she just a freedom-loving flower child? A throwback to the 1960s; didn't she know that the call for love, peace and happiness had faded into the amorphous *zeitgeist* of the 70s? Durban, the last outpost – of hippiedom. Ruby the flower child who named her lovechild Rose. It could have been worse – Rose could have been a Daffodil or Hyacinth. But perhaps she'd got her mother completely wrong. Alice had painted Ruby as competent and grounded. It didn't sound as if she'd been some flighty airhead. But it didn't matter either way; what mattered was that, like the Ruby in the song, her mother's freedom had come at a cost . . . in this case, to Rose's identity and her relationships with others. Her relationship with Livvie, especially, had suffered in the shadow of Ruby's ghostly presence, perpetually hovering between them.

The sudden insight saddened Rose. She wished she'd understood these things while Livvie was still alive. Now it was time to shake off her anger at Ruby. Time to move on. Who knew what had motivated her mother to do the things she had? Maybe it wasn't for Rose to judge.

The packing went faster than expected and by Monday morning, she was ready to move. She took one final look around the empty cottage, now so alien and forlorn; gave a last glance through the window at the view of rambling roses and thorny thickets. Then she went outside to wait for the removals bakkie to arrive.

8

Rose loved Whitecliff Court, where Livvie's flat was. Someone told her it had been built in the 1920s by an Isidore Epstein to house the dynasty he envisaged, with the parking garage of the present said to have accommodated his stables and carriages. Epstein, entrepreneur extraordinaire newly arrived from New York, had had the grand plan to build a mini-Manhattan in Killarney Johannesburg, complete with art deco finishes and a New York lifestyle.

Killarney may have provided sophisticated city living back then but nowadays the suburb was locked in constant battle with rising crime and grime. The building, however, retained an air of elegance with its wooden-framed windows and pilastered balconies.

Aaron the security guard was at his post, a familiar sight in his black jacket with its epaulettes and badges. He'd been there for so long he was like a fixture.

'I'm sorry about the old lady,' he said to Rose. 'The building's not the same, you know. All the old people are going.'

'Times change, hey Aaron. Things don't stay the same forever.'

'Aai. These new people are not like the old ones,' he told her glumly. 'They're no good. And they bring their no-good friends. The other day, I saw some tsotsis with screwdrivers outside, trying to take the burglar bars off Mrs Segal's bathroom window on the first floor. I ran with my stick and shouted at them. Then they jumped down and ran away. But maybe they'll be back. You must keep your windows shut.'

Rose got into the lift and the old trellis gate closed with a clang. Exiting on the first floor, she walked along the corridor to Number 12. She was fumbling in her bag for the key when a young woman emerged from the neighbouring flat. She wore tight white jeans and carried a large yellow handbag slung over her shoulder, her ears adorned with the biggest hooped earrings Rose had ever seen. Her skin was the colour of black arum lilies.

'Hi,' she said brightly. 'Are you moving in? Joy to have someone my age as a neighbour! This building's full of old people.'

Rose tried to gauge her age. She must have been a good ten years younger than Rose.

'Did you know my mother? Livvie?' Rose asked, conscious of her dusty, dishevelled state. The girl shook her head.

Rose explained: 'This was her flat. She died about a month ago.'

'She died in the flat?' the girl asked with wide eyes.

'Ja.'

'I wouldn't like to live where someone has just died.'

'I'm sure she'd be happy that I'm back. I grew up here. My name's Rose, by the way.'

'Abisola . . . Abi. Gotta go. Call if you need anything. Maybe we could go for a drink later.' She sauntered towards the lift, leaving a trail of floral notes in her wake, her hair hanging stiff and shiny down her back.

It was late afternoon. The light in Livvie's large front room was fading fast, blurring the edges of objects. Rose flopped onto the floral couch by the window, too exhausted to think of unpacking the boxes that the removals people had stacked randomly around the flat. She kicked off her sandals and put her feet up; the parts that had been exposed were grey with dust. Abisola had worn dainty strappy sandals with big glass beads on them. And her toenails were painted electric pink. The colour had looked amazing next to her black skin. Could they be friends? Rose wished she had a circle of close women friends, like Livvie had had. She liked the idea. A circle of friends, like a tambour supporting the fabric of friendship, as they each added their different coloured threads. They would be there for each other, to lend a sympathetic ear or gather in times of loss or celebration.

Could she count Gary as a friend? He had phoned yesterday at noon to find out how she was doing. Rose wasn't sure if she regretted their aborted dalliance or not.

'How's the *babalaas*?' he'd asked.

She'd laughed, feeling embarrassed. Friendship with a man was complicated. It was as if she had entered into some sort of contract with him but had broken it and was now obliged to make good. She had wanted him, on Saturday night, when she was feeling low and vulnerable. She didn't know if she still wanted him now.

'Come for supper next week, when I've settled . . . unpacked. You can take your chances with my culinary skills,' she'd said lightly.

Shadows conspired in the corners of the room. A breeze had sprung up. The plane tree's branches scraped the window pane . . . *interloper*, they hissed. Rose thought of Abi's discomfort about living with the dead. Perhaps Rose would never feel entirely comfortable living here amid the traces of Livvie, always imagining her footsteps, smelling her smell. Yet she didn't want Livvie's memory to fade, either. Her eyes went to 'The Drakensberg Lady' on the wall, shadowed by the gloom of the hour; offering no comfort and no truths, staring with her eyes that looked straight past Rose.

The rosewood box fitted in perfectly with the antique marquetry of the table on which it rested, but Rose's laptop appeared strange on the polished walnut of the dining-room table, surrounded by the cyclopean glare of twelve balloon-backed chairs. She needed to check out the genetics file sent by the animator. Charmaine had asked for feedback by Wednesday. One more episode of the series after this – and then what?

What was it the lawyer had said about a monthly allowance? Should she phone him? She checked her cell phone for the time. She was going to buy herself a Rolex, she decided. No, she wasn't. She didn't like them and she'd never wear one in Johannesburg anyway – too risky. It was 4.45 p.m. Still time to phone.

She gathered her courage and dialed Bleazard's number. The secretary told her he was out. She wasn't sure whether to be relieved or disappointed.

She drifted around the flat, not knowing what to do with herself, walking into her childhood bedroom. Livvie had kept it as a spare bedroom when Rose had moved out. It had been refurbished slightly, but the room still read as a palimpsest of her childhood. There was the pale patch on the carpet where she had spilt the acetone when she was experimenting with nail polish at age fifteen; and the oily marks on the ceiling left by Prestik where she had stuck posters of epicene boy singers.

Her cell phone rang.

'Hello, it's Marshall Bleazard here, returning your call,' came his pompous voice.

'Hello. Um . . . Mr Bleazard . . .' she began.

'Please, call me Marshall.'

'Er . . . you mentioned something . . . about a monthly allowance . . .'

'Yes. You need to come up with an amount and come in to sign the documentation. Phone my secretary tomorrow and make an appointment.'

'And . . . er . . . if I want a new car, how do I do that? I mean, how would I pay?'

'The car dealer would need to send me the invoice. And Rose – can I call you Rose?' He didn't wait for her murmured assent but went on: 'I'd like to take you out to dinner on Saturday night.'

Oh no! What excuse could she make?

'Sure,' she heard herself say. Crap. She couldn't believe she'd accepted.

'Would eight o'clock be alright? I'll pick you up. Where are you staying?'

She told him, feeling dismayed. She would have to phone back tomorrow with an excuse. What could she say? She'd think of something. He was the fortune hunter John had been protecting her from. What a cheek! Surely this was unethical?

No sooner had she ended the call than the landline rang. It was Marion.

'Hello, Rose darling! I'm phoning to find out how the move went. I don't know why you didn't get more help. When I moved I had a whole army of people helping me. Well, I suppose I had collected a lot more in the way of possessions than you. I was more settled, for one thing. And I had a whole family to move. Listen, the girls and me are coming round to you on Saturday afternoon for tea. We'll bring the snacks. You just supply the tea.'

Again Rose acquiesced, and wished she hadn't. Oh God! What a Saturday she was in for. She didn't feel like entertaining Marion and friends – the mother hens clucking and fussing around her. And she didn't know how she was going to sleep a wink in Livvie's bedroom. When the furniture men had removed Livvie's bed, her heart had ached so much that she'd had to sit down. And now her bed sat in its place, her sheets, pillows and duvet heaped in a pile on the naked mattress. And there was still the debris piled on the carpet that she'd created on her last visit – plus all her boxes stacked around the flat . . .

The night passed slowly. For hours she lay awake, inhaling Livvie's musky smell. It crept out from the fibres of the carpet, through the cracks of the wardrobe doors. And the noises – the creaking of the plumbing, the clickety-clack of footsteps in the corridors, the sound of unfamiliar voices. Heavy-duty trucks rumbled on the highway, declutching around the Killarney bends. She imagined their long haul north laden with containers from China, and their return, filled with livestock or fresh produce from Limpopo or Mpumalanga.

2nd October 1880

Oberon is a quaint and charming little village neatly laid out, with a main street running through it where one can find the general dealer, hotel and magisterial offices. Branching off from this are residential streets lined with modest cottages constructed of wood and corrugated iron.

Uncle's dwelling, as the magistrate's abode, is on a much grander scale than the others. Situated on the outskirts of the village, it is built from brick and boasts a drawing room, parlour, morning room and gentleman's study, where I now sit in the glow of the desk-lamp and write this diary.

Considering the remoteness of his station, Uncle's standard of living is most civilised. Although he remains a bachelor, his home is excellently appointed and sparkles under the constant ministrations of his houseman, Abel, and various houseboys. I had hoped that perhaps Uncle had employed a lady's maid for me but as on board the ship, I must perform my own toilette, dressing my hair and managing as best as I can with my stays. My outer garments, I give to one of the boys to wash but I see to my underwear myself, telling myself that this basic style of living builds character.

Hearty meals provided by the aptly named cook, Parsley, have been interesting, to say the least, even appetising...in parts. The vegetable soup at last night's dinner consisted of bits of carrots, beans and glassy potatoes floating about in tepid, salty water. For the next course, we had freshly caught trout fried in butter and some braised beef. Both were delicious, as would have been the accompanying local varieties of spinach and mushroom—had they been thoroughly washed and freed of grit and soil. For dessert we dined on stewed plums which, Uncle informed me, were a gift from Mrs Grindlay, a widow who most likely has her eye on Uncle as a prospective second or third husband, although he seems oblivious to her charms. To these plums were added dollops of cream as good as ever I've tasted and finally some wonderful cheese purchased from Oberon's cheesemaker, Albert Bergmeier. I thought it would be peevish of me to point out the weevils in the Bath Oliver biscuits that were served with the cheese! Uncle, probably hankering for a genuine taste of England, did not seem to notice them and ate the biscuits with relish. I politely declined, deciding not to draw attention to the critters. Had I known, I would have brought fresh supplies of these English comestibles with me.

Yesterday Uncle took me on a walking tour of the village and its surrounds. High up here in the foothills of the Drakensberg, the landscape's beauty is reminiscent of Switzerland's. The air sparkles like champagne and the light has a wonderful quality, its pure sharp colours so different from England's muted tones.

Oberon itself nestles in a valley under the magical Dragon's Tooth, an enormous wedge-shaped boulder that sits atop the mountain peak. The Tooth is a wondrous spectacle, constantly changing colour, depending on the position of the sun. When the day is young, it blushes with a girlish pinky glow. Towards midday it glowers, its complexion a charcoal grey. And at sunset, it assumes a magical golden hue.

The village is surrounded by delicate green pastures where fat sleek cows graze under the watchful eye of farmers who are mostly of German extraction. One can immediately discern this by their cornflower blue eyes, wheat-coloured hair, tall statures and sturdy frames.

I was greeted most cordially by the Oberon inhabitants but couldn't help smiling at the clothes they wear—delightfully charming but hopelessly outmoded. Men in lederhosen and women in shapeless frocks suitable only for the Bavarian Alps certainly do not meet my requisites for sartorial elegance. It wouldn't be amiss to have The Lady's Magazine or La Belle Assemblée sent out here, post-haste. I felt quite the fashion plate in my charming spotted poplin frock and matching parasol and suspect that many envious female eyes were cast in my direction.

First light brought a choir of Hadedas, loud and complaining. Rose went back to sleep. Much later, she was aware of ringing. It took her some time to realise it was the front-door bell. Stumbling out of bed she threw on clothes and went to look through the peephole.

Abisola. Oh God! To entertain half asleep. Blinking hard, she ran her fingers through her hair and opened the door.

'Hi. I brought you something. A welcome gift.' Abisola was holding a cardboard confectionery box sealed with a Pick 'n Pay price-sticker. 'Did I wake you?' she asked disarmingly. Her widely spaced eyes gave her face a look of openness.

'No . . . not at all,' Rose lied. 'Thanks! This is really kind of you.' Rose took the box. 'Is this something to eat? Come in and I'll make some tea.' She led the way to the couch by the window.

'Great view,' commented Abisola. 'Better than mine.'

'What can I get you to drink? I think there's coffee. And tea. Might be some herb tea as well. Sorry, I don't have any milk.'

'Whatever . . . herb tea. I hope you like Danishes.'

Rose never ate them. 'Love them,' she replied enthusiastically, opening the kitchen cupboard where the teas were stored. Everything in its place, all familiar. 'Ginger and lemon or fruity berry?'

'Fruity berry. Are all these things your mother's?'

'Yep. Not my taste, most of them,' Rose said, arranging the pastries on a plate and stacking tea things on a tin tray decorated with a doleful pastel kitten. She made a note to donate the tray to a needy cause.

'I love them! These little glass animals – they're so cute. Especially the hedgehog.' There was a trace of the foreign to her accent.

'Where are you from?' Rose asked, as she put the tray on the coffee table.

'Nigeria. My family's still over there. I'm here studying. I live with my cousin.' She lifted her cup, negotiating its porcelain ear with her long nails, and took a cautious sip. She declined the pastries on offer but Rose felt obliged to tackle a large custard slice.

Abi told Rose about her parents living in the Niger Delta; her siblings; what she was studying; her complaints about the beauty therapy institution where she was studying; her studying habits; her dreams and aspirations; what she cooked for supper; and how her cousin complained about her cooking. Rose heard that he was strict and wouldn't let her have men come around. All the while, her French manicure flashed like new moons at midnight, her hands moving constantly as she spoke.

She never asked Rose a single question about herself or her life, and Rose didn't offer any information. She thought that perhaps it was a cultural thing, that maybe Africans considered it rude to ask. Rose wasn't bored by Abi's monologue. She enjoyed listening to people's stories, always in awe of those who could talk about themselves with such lack of self-consciousness. In any case, she felt that her own life was so dull that there was nothing she could have contributed.

'Hey!' Abi said suddenly. 'Let's go out for drinks tonight. I'll ask my cousin if he can take us. He won't let me go out with just my girl friends. He says it's not safe – girls on their own.'

Rose weighed up the offer. It was too soon. She needed to get to know the neighbours better first. Maybe it wasn't safe for her to go out with them on her own. She hadn't even met the cousin yet. Maybe they were human traffickers. They'd kidnap her and force her into prostitution, or hijack her kidneys. But she was a big girl, wasn't she? She could look after herself. This was her problem right here – people made overtures of friendship but she felt lazy to go out and made excuses. Soon, they stopped trying. Time to take the bull by the horns. 'Okay,' she said with a nonchalance she didn't feel. They agreed on a time and Abi left soon afterwards.

Evening came too quickly, bringing with it the dilemma of what to wear. Rose hunted through her boxes, working the scissors under the tape that sealed each one, finally locating the box she wanted. She yanked out her stone-linen pants and cream silk shirt, upsetting the layers that she had packed so carefully. Despite her efforts, the garments were as crumpled as the cow's horn. Which cow? Where did this memory come from – out of the blue? A chain of events, of cause and effect, that led to the bed, where Livvie read to her from an illustrated *Mother Goose* as her lids grew heavy. The place of her childhood located here, in this flat. The place of her history remembered. It was all so familiar. She knew where everything was, from the tin trays to the brooms to the ironing board, even though these had belonged strictly in Katrina's domain.

But it was her ancient past, her unknowable history, to which she craved admittance; a past that was so frustratingly inaccessible, so removed from her knowing, that she had as much chance of accessing it as she had of penetrating the unconscious.

By nine o'clock, Rose had lost her desire to go out. As per usual, she felt too ensconced in the comfort zone of home. 'Go,' Livvie would command. 'You'll enjoy it once you're there.'

She heard her neighbours' door slam and the crescendo of their footsteps approaching. Despite herself, a frisson of excitement fluttered in her stomach.

'This is my cousin, Obayana,' said Abi as they stood outside Rose's door. How would she remember his name? It was a bit like Pollyanna. Maybe she could call him Oba. Oba and Abi.

He loomed large in the passage, wearing loose trousers and matching tunic in a bold black, brown and white print. His teeth flashed in the dull light of the corridor as he smiled broadly, taking Rose's hand in both of his. A triangle of cocoa-coloured chest peeped from the top of his tunic. A large gold watch gleamed on his wrist.

Abi looked just fabulous in a sequinned T-shirt and black jeans with bits of bling on the back pockets. Rose felt so dowdy next to both of them; she decided she was going on a shopping spree. Tomorrow.

'You'd better watch out for him. He's a real charmer,' Abi warned Rose. Everything about her shone – her hair, her lips, her eyelids. 'And he's married,' she added.

'Ho ho ho,' he laughed heartily.

They went to a club in Rosebank called The White Russian – but there were no whites of any nationality within, only black people. On the way there, Obayana told Rose that he was in the import/export business. She wanted to ask what commodities he traded in but she didn't want to probe too much in case it involved something illicit – ask no questions, hear no lies.

People spilled out onto the pavement from the club's entrance. They stood around in groups, leaning on the bonnets of luxury convertibles that were parked in the adjacent parking lot. They all looked so cool in their designer clothes. A man slid his wallet out of his back pocket with a shimmy of his shoulders, in a move that was pure cool. Rose felt very conscious of her paleness and her dull clothes. She shouldn't have come. A woman with the sleekness of a cat and a feline coldness in her eyes came up to Obayana and embraced him, pushing her breasts up against his chest. He placed a proprietal hand on her buttock.

They jostled their way into the lobby, met by music that throbbed like a heart. Once inside, they found space on a leather couch near the dance floor. Rose was squashed between Obayana and a man wearing dark glasses and leather pants who nodded to Rose as she sat down. She felt heat radiating through the layers of linen and leather from their touching thighs. The monotonous thump of House music vibrated through her shoes. Abi perched briefly on the arm of the couch then disappeared into the smoky haze. Oba looked smoulderingly into Rose's eyes and told her she was beautiful. She wanted to ask him about his wife and children but the music drowned out speech. He ordered her something to drink. When it arrived, the drink was opaque and moved lazily around the glass as she brought it up to her mouth. She took a small sip. It slithered down her throat, smelling of coffee and paint thinners.

'What's this?' she asked.

'This is a White Russian.' Oba grinned at her, his teeth very white.

'Ah.'

There was a DJ on the platform, intermittently lit up by slits of laser light, like barbs of observation. Lissom bodies moved on the dance floor. Rose liked watching them, from the shadows. It was true, black people really could move – at least the ones on this dance floor.

The man on the couch had melted away, leaving the gap to be taken up by Abi. She had reappeared with a group of friends in tow, all bright-eyed, swamping the couch with coltish brown limbs, short skirts and enthusiasm. They were curious, wanting to know Abi's friend, showering her with solicitousness. 'How are you doing?' 'Do you need anything?' 'Are you fresh?' 'Are you cool?' Their lips were like ripe black plums, thick with re-applied lip-gloss. They accompanied Rose to the toilet, telling her that black men were not to be trusted.

The girls pulled Rose onto the dance floor and cleared a space for themselves amid the moving mass of bodies. They moved unselfconsciously and she, shadowing their moves, became an indispensable part of their circle. The White Russian helped her let go of her reserve. She closed her eyes and submitted to the thump thump vibrating through her shoes.

Obayana drove home very fast. Abi sat relaxed in the back seat, eyes closed, bobbing to the beat that thumped through the car's speakers. Rose pushed her foot down, braking vicariously as the car bounced in the ruts of the road. She wondered if Oba's hand on her thigh was just normal African friendliness or if she should read it as incipient foreplay.

Obayana walked her to her door and waited while Rose, her keys at the ready, unlocked it.

'Well, thanks,' she said brightly, turning round to face him. He put his arms around her waist and breathed into her ear that he wanted her, had to have her, taste her honey. She smelled the alcohol on his breath. And some sort of cologne, a bit peppery – like nasturtiums. Now what? She didn't want to offend him, didn't want him to think her racist, but this man was just too . . . different; not to mention married.

'Look, I'm really tired. I hardly slept last night. I've got work to do tomorrow and I need to wake up early.' Her words spilt one into the other.

'Tomorrow night, I'm coming for you. No excuses. I won't take no for an answer.' He laughed, 'Ho ho ho' and strolled jauntily into his flat.

A sex pest – living next door. What did he think? That for the price of a drink he had bought himself a night of passion? He couldn't think much of her if he imagined she came this cheap.

For a long time Rose lay awake, hearing the throb of the music in her bones. She thought about Obayana and his promise – or was it a threat? Tomorrow night, when he came, she would make sure she was not at home. She would go out. Somewhere. Anywhere. But there was the night after that. And the one after that. And the next. She couldn't go out every night, could she?

And then there was the Saturday teatime arrangement with Marion and the mother hens. Although they meant well, the last thing she wanted right now was them clucking in her space. And her date with Mr Sleazard Bleazard on Saturday night. What a weekend she was in for! When would she learn to say no?

If only she could run away from it all. All of it. The money included. This inheritance was making her mad. But where would she go to?

Suddenly she knew; Oberon. She would go to Oberon. Just like that she had decided. The Berg was calling her. What was the name of the B&B that the guy in Exclusives had mentioned? The Lizard? The Gecko? She thought for a few moments; no, The Chameleon.

It was late but there was no time to lose. She had to act before the momentum of the moment was lost. She leapt out of bed and scurried down the darkened passage to her computer on the dining-room table. She opened it, blinking from the sudden glare, and googled 'The Chameleon, Oberon'.

It looked wonderful on the website – the rooms, the garden, everything completely charming. The contact details listed the proprietors, Hank and Brigit Lieber. She composed a quick email to them and, before she could be assailed by second thoughts, pressed the send button and went back to bed.

9

Rose had read on The Chameleon's website that the cottages had been converted from an old stable, which had sounded quaint and romantic; but the building in reality was disappointingly nondescript. There was nothing particularly charming or welcoming about the block of plastered concrete with its tin roof. Everywhere appeared deserted. Freezing in her T-shirt and exhausted after her long journey, Rose carried her bags from the car onto the veranda. She was wondering what to do next, whether to phone the proprietor, this Brigit Lieber, and tell her she'd arrived, when a woman appeared.

'Hello, I'm Brigit.' She extended her hand for a very brief handshake. 'How was the journey?' She spoke in quiet tones, a plain woman, a few years older than Rose, big-boned with short, mousy hair. She wore a pastel sweater of the kind that her mother's generation might have worn, a shapeless denim mid-length skirt and moccasins.

'It was . . . fine. Thanks. Gee! It's really cold.' Rose rubbed her bare arms and shivered.

'We needed the rain. It was unbearably hot earlier. Well, here's the key to your cottage. You're in this one.' She pointed to the door of one of the semi-detached units. 'We don't have other guests at the moment. Hank and I are right over there.' She indicated a house obscured by thick shrubbery about fifty metres away. 'Breakfast is served in the main house from eight to ten. If you need to get going early, we can pack a picnic basket for you.' She gestured into the darkening mist: 'You can wander around the property as you like. It goes right down to the river in that direction, and on the other side nearly to the top of the mountain. There's a fence between us and the neighbours so you don't need to worry about trespassing. Let me know if you need anything – extra blankets or whatever.' She paused. 'You're really shivering. I won't keep you. Go inside and get warm.'

'Just one thing . . . can I get Internet access?' Rose asked.

'You'll have to come inside the house, to our office. We charge R30 an hour.'

Rose agreed readily although it really wasn't great. She hated working in other people's space. She'd feel rushed to finish and vacate.

'One more thing – where would you recommend I go for supper? Somewhere casual,' she asked.

'The pub at the Oberon Hotel is really nice. The food's good there. Or, The Olive Branch. That's good, too.' Brigit smiled thinly. 'Well, see you in the morning.'

Rose opened the door and dragged her bags into the cottage. The room was warm, a welcoming fire quietly ablaze. Along one wall was a built-in kitchen with fitted stove, fridge and sink.

On a coffee table lay a tray with a small decanter of sherry, a glass, two *lebkuchen* on a little hand-painted plate and a spray of pale-blue hydrangea. Magazines like *Getaway, Country Life* and *Your Health* were neatly arranged on an occasional table.

Rose wheeled her case down a small passageway, past a dressing table and mirror built into a niche, to a bedroom with a double bed that was dressed in crisp white percale, with a scatter of bolstered cushions.

In the en-suite bathroom, Brigit had supplied thick white waffle-weave towels, Charlotte Rhys soaps and creams, as well as scented candles – something Rose never used.

She lit the candles, ran a bath and, in a haze of vanilla, slid into the water, arms all goosebumpy with pleasure. There, she languished, every now and then stretching out a foot and with a dextrous big toe running in more hot water.

Later, she threw another log on the fire and sat in her bath towel at the dressing table in the rosy glow of the candlelight and embers. She dried her hair with the supplied hairdryer, another thoughtful touch provided by Brigit. She barely recognised her soft, golden reflection in the mirror. 'Who are you?' she asked, her grey irises glinting as they caught the candles' flickering light. And she felt such an intense flutter of anticipation that it seemed as if a host of butterflies had taken flight in her stomach.

By the time she was dressed, it was seven o'clock. Rose turned on the TV. DSTV, disappointingly, yielded only Supersport channels. She would really rather not go out, but she had to eat.

She eyed the sherry and, feeling sophisticated and independent, poured some of the golden liquid into the glass. Closing her eyes, she drank a libation to the god of travellers who had delivered her safely from the Mad Maxes of the road and out of the mist into this haven.

The sherry tasted delicious, even for one as teetotal as Rose. Ensconced in comfort, she wondered how she would ever drag herself back into her car and to the village. She took another careful sip. Before long the glass was drained and she felt completely relaxed. This frightened her because she realised how easy it would be to start drinking. Addictive behaviour was definitely an inherited trait.

The alcohol made it easier for her to get back into her car and drive the five kilometres along the dirt road, in the black of the rural night, to the centre of town. The Oberon pub sounded like a good idea. She put the Polaroid copies in her handbag; there were sure to be locals and oldtimers to ask her questions of.

The Oberon Hotel was quaint and shabby. Large, leaded windows framed a narrow doorway, which led into a small reception area. There was an abundance of wood-panelling, furniture, exposed ceiling beams. It had that old hotel smell from years of accumulated cooking smells, rancid fat, stale beer, and dust balls accumulated in all available nooks and crannies. The floorboards creaked uncertainly as she walked down the passage that led to the pub.

Rose hesitated in the doorway and cast her eyes around the gloomy room. She had expected to see more people on a Friday night but only one of the tables was occupied, by a family group munching big hamburgers. She was relieved. It made it easier for her to slip in unnoticed and make her way to the bar, a large, wooden-pen-like affair that occupied the centre of the room. Arranged around it were half a dozen table-and-chair sets hewn from railway sleepers – all very rustic.

Choosing a stool in the shadows, she sat straight-backed, hands resting on the bar's sweaty surface, and looked around. There were large black-and-white photographs of fishermen displaying freshly caught trout and of the hotel and village, taken back in the early days. The fast-changing images of MTV flashed from a TV suspended from the ceiling. Rose never watched the channel, didn't know the hottest hits nor cared who sang them. She read the subtitles: someone called Lil Wayne was on.

A bartender-cum-waitress paced about the confines of the bar. Rose tried to catch her eye but she kept disappearing behind columns. Two middle-aged black men in white lounge shirts came in and sat down on Rose's right. It was nice to see racial mixing in places like this. They wouldn't have been allowed in here in the days when her mother was in the area, busy being impregnated. But even today, the country was still so segregated. When Rose attended cultural events like concerts or theatre, she always noticed how white the audiences were. And if she were to attend black events, like soccer in Soweto or an R&B concert, she'd probably feel like a single grain of rice in the meat stew.

A group of three men and two women entered the pub amidst much jollity. They all seemed to be wearing khaki clothing, brogue-type shoes and had what looked like DIY haircuts. Rowdy and dowdy. They sat at a table across the way where Rose could watch them from the corner of her eye.

The All-American Rejects were on the screen now. Strange how all these people seemed to be singing remixes of classic rock. When Britney Spears appeared and started singing Deep Purple's 'Smoke on the Water' in a deep bass voice, Rose realised that the TV sound had been switched off and what she was hearing was a CD playing in the background. The barperson took the black men's order. Rose felt a little peeved; she'd been there first. Finally, the woman stood before her. Her whole mien was unhelpful. Rose wanted to ask what her problem was but requested a menu instead.

A man wearing faded jeans and a leather jacket came in. He removed the jacket to reveal a faded T-shirt and sat down at the opposite side of the bar, illuminated by the halo of light cast by the overhead lamp. Rose's vision of him was slightly impeded by a column, which was a good thing; otherwise he might have been aware of the intensity of her gaze. He was quite striking, with his craggy features and rangy body. He had the fit, outdoorsy look of a hiker or mountaineer.

The bartender took the money from the beer drinkers and dawdled over to her till where she stood, apparently sorting out all the change in her drawer. Eventually she came over to Rose again. Miraculous. Rose ordered a Greek salad. 'Is it possible to get the dressing on the side, please?' she asked, and feeling very daring: 'And can I get a glass of red wine?' The woman nodded amiably and Rose decided that she wasn't so bad, just short on waitressing skills.

The two black men sat nursing their beers. She thought about asking them if they had always lived in the area and whether they recognised the subjects in her photos. But she felt shy of intruding herself into their personal space.

A woman in maroon overalls emerged from a doorway next to the bar, carrying Rose's glass of wine. Rose took a sip and caught a snatch of the conversation from the rowdy-dowdies to her right:

'They're called dolerite dykes.'

'Sounds like a lesbo group.'

'Ha ha ha.' They all shared in the joke.

'Lesbo; I've never heard that term.'

'I got it from a *South Park* episode. That's where I get most of my information from.'

'Ha ha ha.'

'I've shown some of the episodes in class. To illustrate . . . oh, I don't know . . . satire, stereotyping, hypocrisy, the concept of monopolies . . .'

'Haven't you had complaints from parents? It's age-restricted – over eighteen, isn't it?'

'I'm waiting to get into trouble with the powers that be.'

Teachers. The waitress slapped a greasy plastic place mat down in front of Rose, followed by serviette-swaddled cutlery, a side plate and an arts-and-craftsy wire container with grubby bottles of condiments and salad dressings.

The hiker-mountaineer was slowly sipping his beer; a Hansa, Rose noted. She examined him furtively as he sat staring intently at some invisible horizon. The Camel Man. She wondered if he were resident in the area. How old could he be? Mid to late thirties? She calculated: even if he were towards the upper end, he could only have been seven or eight years old at most when the photos were taken. Maybe it was worth a shot to ask him anyway; but he looked so distant and, again, she felt intimidated to approach.

Her Greek salad arrived. It was really good, especially the feta. Perhaps it came from Oberon's Cheese Factory. The Camel man was now eating a steak. He ate slowly, chewing deliberately and concentrating on his food. There was a loud guffaw from the school teachers. Rose turned her head, smiling. Their merriment was infectious. One of the women in the group caught her smile and returned it; a game of badminton – shuttlecock smiles.

Rose waited for her bill and a coffee, that she now regretted ordering. It was taking too long and she felt like such a spare part sitting all alone at the bar.

'Come join us,' a voice said at her shoulder. It was the smiling woman from the rowdy table across the way. Rose hesitated. She felt awkward at the prospect of joining such a tightly knit group, but more awkward to refuse. She nodded and slid off her stool, grateful to be relieved of her isolation, moved by the woman's kindness.

There was a shifting of seats and beer mugs to make room for her. Introductions were done. Rose repeated the names in her head, trying to memorise them. Four out of the five were local school teachers and the fifth was an old friend visiting from London for a few weeks. They were thrilled to hear that her background was in teaching as well.

'I thought I recognised that mad glint in your eye!' cried the man called Steve, who was married to the smiling Megan.

'We're ordering another round. What will you have?' Ronald asked, boyish, with dark, tousled hair and dishevelled khaki clothes. Dark-brown puppy eyes. Rose refused the beer he offered. 'I'm waiting for coffee,' she told him.

'That's no good. You've got to have alcohol if you're going to cope with us,' he joked.

Rose laughed. 'I'll cope.' But more beer arrived and Rose felt obliged to partake.

'Ooh – I love this song!' Megan gushed, as Procol Harum's 'Whiter Shade of Pale' seeped from the speakers. 'Da da dum dum,' they all sang, not sure of the words. Rose couldn't join in – even bolstered by the beer. She stretched her mouth into a grin but it felt fixed and fake.

The bartender was totting up on her cash register. They were the only customers who remained. Steve shouted to her: 'Hi – can you turn the music up?' They listened for the next number. Pink Floyd's vocalist advised them they didn't need no education.

'I go with that!' cried Steve, rising from the table. He started to dance, chin thrust forward, shoulders jerking from side to side on his stocky frame. The others followed suit. Megan held her hand out to Rose and she allowed herself to become part of the rollicking group.

The alcohol had blurred the edges of her reserve but even so, dancing was difficult for her. It felt so forced as she went along with them, dancing round the tables, holding waists in a Conga line, regrouping, randomly connecting then separating again, like molecules in space.

Kind Megan, to have drawn her into the group, but Rose preferred to be an observer instead of a participant, choosing to live life from the margins rather than in the centre. She wasn't used to such concentrated sociability. It wasn't in her nature. Nature. Nurture. Nonsense – it was her choice. Friendships needed nurturing and effort, energy and obligation, if they were to be maintained. It all depended on one's priorities. The song changed, the tempo quickened. They linked arms and cavorted round the tables. Clockwise, anti-clockwise. The bartender sat on her stool, eyeing them with a steely glare. 'Last round,' she announced. They staggered back to their chairs, sweating and laughing.

'Wasn't this the best fun?' Megan cried, beaming at Rose, who nodded enthusiastically but wasn't quite as sure.

'Beers for everyone,' Steve called out.

When their breathing had returned to normal, Megan suggested to Max, the UK visitor, that 'Rose should join us tomorrow'. Then, addressing Rose: 'We're going on a trip up the Sani Pass.'

Max agreed: 'Absolutely. She must come. The more the merrier!'

Rose held back, not wanting to intrude. 'Um . . . I've got some research to do in the village tomorrow. It's quite urgent.'

'Tomorrow night then,' Megan persisted. 'We've got a booking at the best restaurant in the area – Leighton Manor. We've never been before so it's a real treat. I'm sure it won't be a problem to change the booking for one more.'

Driving back to The Chameleon in the pale glimmer of her headlights, Rose thought about her evening. Her newfound friends were a cheerful bunch. They'd set out to have a good time and by golly they made sure they had one. It was better than being miserable and complaining. She wondered whether she'd overstepped any social boundaries, said anything stupid. It embarrassed her to think of herself sitting among these strangers, inveigling her way into their lives.

Why had Megan wanted her to join them again tomorrow, seeming almost insistent – even extending the invitation to supper? Maybe Megan's super-friendliness had the others groaning into their beers – 'Oh God, there goes Megan again, befriending every waif and stray that comes into town'. Or, just maybe, people were attracted to Rose and actually wanted to befriend her. Could that be possible? Then why was it that she had no friends? Was it because of her habit of refusing invitations, of always pulling back from overtures of friendship? It just seemed too exhausting to have to keep up the patter, ooze with charm, maintain the good impressions; so much easier to be on her own. After a while people gave up. Who could blame them? No, she wouldn't refuse the supper invitation. She'd go.

Rose was grateful for the separate entrance to the cottages when she returned, after midnight. She slipped between the crackling sheets of the strange bed and fell asleep listening to the low rhythms of frog music.

10

7th October 1880

The preparations for my travels to Giant's Castle are nearly complete. I have met my mount, Dolly—a dear little bay of about 14 hands high. She is one of those sure-footed mountain ponies, good tempered and docile, so unlike my Zeus who awaits my return to merry olde England.

Uncle Henry has hired two Basotho bearers, telling me that he prefers them to the Zulu tribe whom he says are treacherous and will murder you in your bed if you don't watch out! I'm also going to be accompanied by his houseman and occasional translator, Abel, a most respectful soul whom he trusts to keep this headstrong lass out of trouble. I'm not sure how Uncle will do without him. He is a real asset, being half Bushman and half Basotho, speaking both tongues fluently, as well as reasonable Zulu and English. He also has a smattering of the Boer language, which is a dialect of Dutch. His Western-style manners are most delightful and quaint.

The village where we are headed is Patilweng so that Abel may visit his relatives. I can barely wait to see the Giant's Castle paintings, although I do not mind stopping over in Patilweng for a few days as this will allow me to study the Bushman ways and perhaps afford insights into their art. Abel's mother is a Bushman, born there. When she was a young child, she was captured by British soldiers and given to a farmer's wife as her kitchen maid. I think this practice wickedly unjust and told Uncle so. He replied that the Bushmen have brought it upon themselves with their incessant cattle raiding and thieving ways. In retaliation, the British commanders shot many of the men and captured the women and children, who were then taken to colonial farms as servants and labourers. Uncle's answer does not temper the cruelty inherent in the practice.

However, I am most grateful to Uncle Henry for the trouble he has taken to ensure my safe passage, although he is most disapproving. He warned me of the dangers lurking in the hinterland. He paints a bleak picture of a country plagued by marauding bands of cattle raiders and horse thieves. In addition, relations with both the Zulu and Basotho tribes are fraught. Last year, our British troops suffered an ignominious defeat at the hands of the Zulu warriors and tensions simmer as the colonial government plans reprisal attacks. The Basotho chiefs in the area are rebellious and recently, one withstood an eight-month siege until finally his men were killed by British soldiers. There is even a rumour that King Letsie is planning to take up arms against her Imperial Majesty. But I told Uncle Henry that nothing will scupper my plans... although at times, I must secretly admit to feeling rather afraid of travelling in this wild country. However, when I cast my eye over the serene landscape and meet its delightful inhabitants, I feel sure that I shall survive this excursion.

Who switched the light on? Light was streaming into the room . . . through a skylight in the ceiling. God! What time is it? was Rose's first thought as she woke. Who puts a skylight in a bedroom? was her second. She turned onto her stomach, burrowing her head under the pillow and tried to return to the comfort of dreams; but it was useless. She got out of bed, slid her feet into slipslops and padded to the lounge, pulling back the curtain to look out the window.

Pine trees towered in the cloudless sky. Birds alighted on the uppermost branches in slow motion. In the distance, the basalt face of Dragon's Tooth blushed pale pink in the dawn light. Rose walked out onto the dewy grass, into a morning as still as an antelope in a clearing.

A shriek rent the quiet, high and urgent, rising and falling away, like the call of a wild cat, only more pronounced. The scream came again – an injunction, a summons for her to partake of the delights of the Berg. From round the corner strolled the screamer – a peacock, dragging his long tail behind him. He stopped, jerked his head from side to side and, catching sight of her, turned to face Rose.

They stood very still, eyeing each other – duellists at dawn. With languorous aplomb, he opened his tail, the turquoise jewels in their silver caskets turned to brilliance by the early rays of the sun. And she, Rose, became an Indian princess in a hillside palace for a moment, until he slowly dropped his tail and began to preen, contorting his neck awkwardly and pulling violently at his plumage with an ugly, rasping sound. He gave another of his high-pitched, hysterical mewls, looked at her disdainfully, and continued on his way.

She followed him through the shrubbery to a courtyard of paving stone alternating with blue, spiky mondo grass. There the peacock stopped, at an open door that showed a view of kitchen, evidently the customary source of his breakfast. Rose continued around to the front of the house, treading a path of white pebble-stones that led to a low retaining wall. Beyond it were five stone steps descending to a large, sunken area. Rose perched on the wall to admire this garden in the mountains, but instead of feeling peace and serenity, she was assailed by a mild discomfort. What brought it about, she couldn't understand. Maybe it was the ordered wildness of the place, or the smell of the wild mingling with the tang of pine, rose and orange.

Her eyes were drawn to pots of neatly shaped conifers and orange-tree topiaries standing among metal trellises overgrown with plumbago and purple morning-glory, their tendrils trailing chaotically into sunny places carpeted with marigolds and nasturtiums, whose bronze and copper petals threw golden, spicy notes into the air. Strelitzias, stems pious and unbending, poked their heads into places where they didn't belong, and those beloveds of English country gardens, bluebells, foxgloves and hollyhocks, grew rampant amongst indigenous heaths and heathers. A pumpkin vine crept stealthily over purple groundcovers, golden shrubs and other things she couldn't name.

In dark, cool corners, arum lilies proudly bore their shining, waxy chalices amidst herbs that huddled above the dark loam soil, the tender, luscious foliage reduced to lacy skeletons by the insatiable chomping of snails. While in the deeper earth, earthworms tunnelled blindly, carving out secret places from rank, decaying matter. In the middle of the garden, a pond shone black, like used motor oil, and in its centre a concrete fish issued a thin, silver ribbon of water into the air.

Rose got up and followed the steps down to where the pebble path resumed. It led her now past an avenue of iceberg roses, branches heavy with papery blooms. Half closing her lids and breathing deeply of the piquant scent, she stumbled over something. Oops – clumsy. She'd been so entranced, she'd forgotten to watch her step. Looking down, she was startled to see a pair of feet, bare and brown and cracked at the heels.

'Oh! Sorry!' she apologised.

The feet's owner appeared, emerging from the hedge like a wild hog disturbed from its foraging. He sat back on his haunches, a trowel in one hand.

'Well, hello!' he said. His eyes looked her up and down admiringly. She shrank back from his gaze, suddenly aware of her bare legs emerging from pyjama shorts. 'Look what the gods have delivered!' he announced, standing up and wiping his hands on his shorts. He took her hand: 'Hank,' he smiled. 'Welcome to my garden of earthly delights.'

His smile was dazzling. The mountain sun had tanned his skin to a burnished copper. He was tall and meaty, looking like he would run to middle-aged spread in a couple of years. But for now, what a specimen! A speci-man? And this was the mousy Brigit's husband?

Bolder now, Rose returned his smile. 'Hank? Sounds American.'

'My actual name is Heinryk. I got the nickname Hank at school – you know, first-team rugby and all that. I was Hank the Tank, prop of note.'

Hank the Hunk, more like.

'You?' he asked.

'Er . . . Rose. I'm staying at the cottages.'

'Rose – by any other name would smell as sweet. Here, smell this.' He stooped to take up a handful of dark soil and, standing close to her, held it under her nose. 'Fantastic, hey? Can you smell?'

Rose sniffed deeply, aware of his proximity and the warmth emitted by his hand against her face. 'Smell what?' She glanced up at him through eyelashes that all but fluttered.

'Sex. And death. You can smell it in the soil.' He crumbled his handful, letting it fall through his fingers and scatter on the ground. She became aware of the rich, loamy smell.

'My garden – it's pulsing with sex and death. Sex and death,' he repeated, snapping a blood-red rose off a woody stem. 'This flower . . .' He stroked the swollen receptacle at the base of the bloom, '. . . here's the female sex organ, swelling with life. All this fertility and abundance growing off death and decay. Here,' he said, gazing at her with a twinkle in his grey-blue eyes, 'this is for you. A rose for Rose.'

'Thanks.' She blushed, taking the flower from him carefully. There were many large thorns to avoid.

'So, Rose.' He stood with his hands on his hips, looking at her as if she were a female sex organ. 'How did you like waking up communing with the gods?'

The fluttering of her heart seemed to have thwarted her powers of comprehension.

'Sorry?' she said.

'The skylight. I put it in the bedroom so that there's a window to the gods.'

'Er . . . ja . . . great idea!'

Sex appeal. This man oozed it from every pore. Best to get away from him. She felt quite unsettled. 'Well, I'm . . . um . . . going for a walk,' she stammered.

'Be sure to pass through the portal. Read the words on the rusted plate.' He closed his eyes and intoned: '"He who enters this portal will partake of the fruits borne of Nature and will be nurtured by the Goddess of Truth . . ."'

The man spoke in riddles. What did that mean?

'Okay,' Rose said brightly.

He nodded, a smile playing around his lips. She felt his eyes on her until she rounded the hedge, where she paused to catch her breath. Through a foliaged archway, she could see the blue-green of the distant slopes. Heartbreak Hank. Their encounter had left her feeling quite weak at the knees.

At the edge of the garden, the property sloped steeply down to the river. Rose walked through the concrete archway of the portal and paused to take in the inscription on the rusty plate, which read as Hank had quoted it. She continued on down steps that had been carved out of the mountainside. Bees reeled around the wild mountain flora, drunk on the sweet medicinal scents. Ribbons of water trickled into secret pools and the grass was alive with cicadas, trilling from indiscernible locations. The air was heating up, steam rising from the earth. She felt hot. Flustered. Droplets of sweat mobilised in her armpits, readying themselves to roll down her sides.

When she reached the river, she looked upstream to where it curved around the bend of the mountain. The sun's reflections skittered across the water's surface like salmon catching the currents. Rose scooped up water in both hands. She splashed her face, then poured the river directly into her mouth, tasting its pure, clean essence that arose from a source deep within the heart of the mountain. She felt an urge to lie down on the bank and immerse her whole head in the water, to feel the river's currents tugging at her scalp and fish nibbling on her hair . . . a river goddess. But the thought of wet hair dripping down her neck as she made her way back to the cottage was less inviting.

Brigit greeted Rose as she entered the breakfast room. 'It's going to be another sweltering day. I hope you were comfortable last night.'

'Yes . . . absolutely. Everything was great. Thanks for the welcoming sherry and the fire. You have the most fantastic place. Paradise.'

'Thanks.' Brigit smiled and directed Rose to a chair. 'There's Continental breakfast, which you can help yourself to. Or Happiness can make you a cooked breakfast.'

'I'll just help myself, thanks.' She went to the yellowwood dresser and took a carton of yoghurt and some cut pineapple and melon.

'Bring the madam fresh coffee,' Brigit instructed the woman called Happiness, then hastened from the room.

'The madam'. The term made Rose cringe. It was so redolent of the bad old past; but she wasn't going to judge Brigit for it. She'd said it so naturally. Political correctness hadn't reached these parts yet, even in 2012.

Happiness brought the coffee then hovered, barefooted, at Rose's elbow. There had been two pairs of worn-down pumps placed neatly alongside the mat outside the door. When Rose first saw them, she'd wondered if she were expected to remove her shoes, too, like she was about to enter a temple.

Rose told Happiness: 'You don't need to worry about me. I've got everything I need.' Happiness nodded, her demeanour passive, her face expressionless. She moved away and stood against the wall, leaning back on her hands. Her presence made Rose feel uncomfortable. She would have preferred to be left alone.

A boy of about four ran into the room making a roaring noise, his arms outstretched. He stopped his activity to inspect Rose.

'Hello,' Rose said. 'You're a big aeroplane. Where are you off to, Mr Aeroplane?'

'My daddy's a pilot.' The boy spread his arms again and wheeled out the back door, where the peacock stood pecking at crumbs.

A harassed domestic worker entered, bearing a pale-skinned toddler secured to her back with a towel, African-style. The child was pulling away from the restraint, trying to get a better view of her surroundings.

'*Haai*, Jamie. Don't run away . . .' the woman called to the four-year-old. She saw Rose: 'Hello, ma'am.' Hissing at the peacock to 'Go!', she stepped into one of the pairs of shoes, crossed the courtyard and disappeared from view.

Brigit re-emerged, shouting after the childminder: 'Stay in the garden. Don't let Jamie go into the long grass.' She turned to Rose: 'Snakes,' she said.

'Snakes! I took a walk down there this morning. I didn't think about snakes.'

'Adults move quietly and calmly. They mostly keep to the paths where the grass is kept short. Jamie runs and jumps around everywhere, off the paths and in the snakes' territory. They're very territorial. They only strike when they feel threatened. We lost a dog recently to snakebite – we were very upset. You need to respect them and tread with care.'

Well, that's comforting, thought Rose; though she'd never considered natural threats to be as threatening as man-made ones.

The peacock continued to stand at the back door, stock still. 'Shame. I feel sorry for your peacock. He must be lonely. He needs a partner,' Rose observed.

'I don't want any more.' Brigit was replacing the lids on the large cereal jars. 'We inherited him from the previous owners. And a whole flock of guinea fowl, too. There are only a few of those left now. Most have been taken by birds of prey.'

'So, dangers lurk in paradise,' Rose quipped. Then she asked: 'Have you always lived here?'

'No. I'm from Durban originally. Hank was born here in Oberon, but his family moved to Durban when he started high school. That's where we met. Can I get you more coffee?'

'I'm fine, thanks. When did you move here?'

'A few years ago. When I was pregnant with Jamie. We wanted our children to have this rural childhood but I suppose we'll have to rethink when they get to high-school age.'

'It seems like an idyllic life for children. Aside from the snakes, of course,' Rose smiled. 'Idyllic for adults, too.'

'Oh it's not so easy financially. We all have to do a variety of jobs to survive. Hank hires out his services as a pilot – he has a small plane. He takes tourists for flips in the Berg and sometimes he's hired by farmers tracking stock thieves. We also have an interest in a dairy farm. It's the same for everyone round here. Friends of ours . . . he fixes tractors during the week and is a mountain guide over weekends, and his wife is an illustrator who runs a small nursery growing irises. In addition to the B&B, I also run a small animal welfare NGO. We work mainly in the black areas, educating the community how to care better for their livestock and other animals. We also get called out to act against cases of abuse sometimes.' She paused and then asked: 'What do you do, Rose? You said something about research.'

'Well actually, my job is writing educational scripts for TV. But my research here in Oberon is . . . personal. There are things I need to find out about my . . . origins. Can I maybe start with you?'

'I've got a few minutes,' Brigit said.

'Then I'll just ask you . . .' Rose reached in her handbag for the enhanced copies of the photos. 'I'm trying to identify these people. The photos were taken in Oberon in September 1981.'

Brigit gave a cursory glance at each. 'That's over thirty years ago. How old would these people be today?'

'If they were in their . . . say, early thirties in the photos, then they'd be in their sixties today.'

Brigit looked doubtful. 'I don't know who they are. The photos aren't too good, are they? You can hardly see the man's face.'

Rose nodded grimly. 'Who would be the best people to ask, do you think? Like locals, or oldtimers who've lived here forever.'

'You could start with Roland Bergmeier at Oberon Cheeses. You'll find him on the road to Heimat. Or his neighbour, old Thomas Bretton. He owns the big cattle farm on the neighbouring property.'

'Hold on.' Rose scrabbled for her handbag under the chair. 'Let me get my notebook or I'll never remember . . .'

'There's also Denton Dalbert at Lakeside Farm. It's about ten, fifteen kilometres along the Valley Road. The Dalberts have roots that go back to the original settlers. And ask Hank, too. His family also goes back to the year dot. He's popped out to the dairy farm. I don't think he'll be long.'

'Thanks a lot. And . . . aside from the snakes, is it safe here? Can I walk alone?'

'Yes. The locals are very friendly. You can greet them with a *sawubona* and they'll greet you back.'

'I saw lots of . . . locals in the village when I arrived. Where do they all live? Is there a township in the area?'

'No, there's no actual township or location close to Oberon, though there are lots of black villages scattered around. And there's quite a big informal settlement near Heimat. But it's very rural here. Most of the workers live on the farms.' Brigit walked towards the door as she spoke. 'Well, good luck. Let me know how you get on. See you later.'

In the sunlight, it was a bright new world. On her left, the mountain rose in smooth, verdant planes and to her right, through a curtain of pine trees, the terrain fell away to the river. There were smallholdings dotted with houses and assorted farm buildings. And a farm school, sponsored by a big dairy cooperative; big business doing its corporate social responsibility thing. She'd love to become involved somehow, to fund a project – but what? It required an energy she didn't possess.

The school was silent now on this Saturday morning, and lifeless as a tomb. A man walked his Alsatians along the road, their low-slung bodies sashaying obediently to the tug of the leashes. Their owner waved at Rose as she passed. In a pasture, a cowherd whistled a mournful refrain and flicked his switch back and forth amidst a heaving mass of cattle. Now, nearing the village, Rose could see the bare rock formation of Dragon's Tooth erupting from the mountain top, like a canine tooth in profile, glistening dirty pink in the sun.

The mountain looked directly onto the village of Oberon, which nestled in the valley and crept a little way up the slopes. The village bustled with Saturday-morning shoppers, but there were also the ever-present loiterers standing about aimlessly or sitting on the edges of the pavements, feet resting on the national road.

Rose slowed to allow a bakkie that was pulling out of a gateway to enter the flow of traffic. It had the words 'Oberon Security' written on its body. So, Oberon was not as crime-free as Brigit had made out.

Brigit. Rose would love to be friends with her. She was down-to-earth and sensible, although a real plain Jane with her clumpy build and pale complexion. She and Hank made such an incongruous couple. Did she know what a flirt he was? Rose felt a little guilty that she had let him unsettle her mettle.

She travelled now towards Heimat, along an oak-lined avenue that ranged through a broad valley theatrically encircled by mountains. She decided to follow Brigit's advice and start with Roland Bergmeier at Oberon Dairy Farm and Cheese Factory.

Arriving, she entered a shop lined with refrigerated shelves displaying an array of cheeses. There were tables stacked with bottles of preserves, pickled walnuts and packets of biltong, and a sign on the wall that read: 'Wine and cheese are like friends, best enjoyed when they are old.'

Old wine, old cheese, old friends. Shouldn't it have said 'friendships' instead of 'friends'? Whatever – Rose had neither. Neither old friends nor old friendships.

'Be with you now,' the saleswoman called out, following a dumpy customer around the shelves as she made her selections.

The dumpy customer was saying: 'We're at our wits' end, I tell you! It feels like we're being targeted. Ja, well – what can you do?'

'What do the police say? Are they on top of it?'

'Never! They're absolutely useless. We've reported it but I bet you they don't even come to take a statement or do fingerprints or anything. Been there, done this . . . you know what I mean. They just never even bother to pitch.' The woman continued to rattle off her frustrations. 'I tell you, I don't think I can take another one of these incidents.'

'Shame. It's terrible. Didn't the alarm go off?'

'I'm not sure. No one heard it. We'll have to upgrade the system. Listen, I must get going . . . check on what's happening at the restaurant.' They walked to the counter where the cheese lady started tallying up the purchases. The transaction complete, the customer went on her way.

'Shame. They have a restaurant in town and they've just had their umpteenth break-in in the eight months since they opened,' the cheese lady told Rose. 'This time, they broke the glass of the counter and threw food around. What for, is anybody's guess. Who knows what makes the minds of these criminals tick.'

'That's awful! The place looks so peaceful. It's hard to believe things like this happen here,' said Rose.

The cheese lady nodded. 'Especially since they moved down here from Jo'burg to get away from the crime. At least no one's been hurt in any of these incidents.' Both she and Rose sighed, shaking their heads. 'So,' she said, adopting a lighter tone. 'How can I help you?'

'Um . . .' Rose floundered. She didn't know how to begin. Her mission suddenly seemed an exercise in futility. What did the past matter, when the present carried so much more weight?

The cheese lady's friendliness was encouraging, 'Would you like to see how our cheeses are made?' she asked. 'I can take you through the factory.'

'Yes, I would, but . . .' Rose hesitated then pressed on, '. . . can I just ask you first – I'm trying to identify the people in these photos . . .' She held them out to the cheese lady. 'They were taken in Oberon, in 1981.'

'1981?' The cheese lady shook her head. 'I didn't live here then. I'm from 'Maritzburg, originally. A lot of us living here now moved from other places.'

'Someone suggested I ask Roland Meierberg.'

'Berg*meier*. He's in the factory. Come, I'll take you to him.'

She led Rose though a doorway into a maze of huge, stainless steel vats. The room that housed them was dark and chilly. Maybe her mother Ruby had stood in this very spot, thought Rose. Could the memory of a person linger in the air, in the spaces of a room? Could Rose smell her presence if she breathed in deeply enough?

'Mr Bergmeier,' the woman called out. The cheesemaker, a man in his sixties, looked up from studying a temperature gauge on one of the vats.

'This lady wants to identify the people in these pictures. She thought you might be able to help.'

'Hello, I'm Rose Clemens.' Rose was about to extend her hand and explain her mission but he made no eye contact with her. He stood with a scowl on his face, holding what looked like a giant metal syringe poised for insertion into the vat. So Rose just held out the photo of the man for him to see, watching his face for reaction, hoping he wouldn't linger over the photo in self-recognition; she definitely didn't want this surly man to be her father! But he merely glanced at it then grunted, with a barely discernable shake of his head.

'Well, thanks anyway,' Rose said. The cheese lady shrugged her shoulders and led Rose back to the shop.

'So much for that,' the cheese lady commented. 'Maybe you should ask his sons. No, on second thoughts, they're probably too young.'

'Does he have a wife? Perhaps I could ask her.'

'It's his second wife and she's not from here. The first wife died a couple of years ago.'

The cheese lady paused, then said: 'Can I ask why you're trying to identify these people?' She laughed. 'There goes my curiosity getting the better of me. My husband always warns me that curiosity killed the cat.'

Rose hesitated then decided it might not be a bad idea to divulge her purpose. Why shouldn't people know she was trying to trace her biological parents? It sounded like news spread quickly here. Her quest would precede her and ease her way. It would mean she wouldn't have to explain herself each time she interviewed someone.

'No, it's fine,' she reassured the other woman. 'I was adopted when I was young, and I recently found these photos in my . . . adopted mother's home after she died. I think they might be of my parents.'

She was aware that she was not telling the absolute truth – that the woman in the photo had, undeniably, been identified as her mother, Ruby Le Grange. But it seemed too complicated to explain. 'The date on the photos – it's the month of my conception. That's what made me make the link. I may be completely wrong but Oberon seems like a good place to start.'

'My goodness! What a story! Let's think. Who else could you ask?'

Rose took out her notebook and stood poised to write.

'I don't really know who else there is,' the woman said disappointingly, after a silence. 'I can only suggest Thomas Bretton next door. I'm Cathy, by the way. If I think of anyone else, I'll let you know. Where are you staying?'

As Rose drove out of the Cheese Factory, she mused that most people here, like the helpful Cathy, would probably be sympathetic to her cause; reunions with long-lost relatives always got public interest going. Unless the public was Roland Bergmeier, of course. What was his case anyway? He obviously preferred the company of cheese.

She continued along the road, following the wire fencing that she assumed was the boundary of Thomas Bretton's farm. Brigit had referred to him as the Cheese Factory's neighbour. Pine trees grew thick and black beyond the fencing, screening the property from passing traffic. Before long Rose came to an open gate that led onto a dirt road. She turned in and followed the road, which curved then stopped abruptly at the edge of the trees.

She emerged from her car to gaze upon a large field where dozens of ochre-coloured cattle grazed, their bodies steaming in the mid-morning sun. A distance away, across the field, she spied a farmhouse. Apparently, the only way to reach it was through the field. There were calves as well as cows in the field, and larger specimens that could have been adolescent bulls. She knew nothing about these beasts. Were they dangerous? Some had the beginnings of horns. But they seemed placid enough.

Rose ploughed into the field of emerald green. At first, she stuck to the path that wound through the tall grass and reeds but the path quickly petered out, giving way to muddy marshland. As the going grew wetter, she veered from the straight line that would have led her directly to the farmhouse, forced to zigzag to avoid the large, black puddles seeping up from an abundant water table. At every turn her way was hampered, either by puddles or beasts – all twitching tails and shuddering flanks, looking at this interloper from under their bovine lids with surly expressions. The sun beat down on the top of her head and the humidity made her breathless. Flies buzzed about her ears, fresh from their forays into piles of steaming dung. Wading through wetland. Fun in the fen. She looked up and saw a man across the field, standing by the farmhouse. He was leaning on a walking stick and waving his hat at her.

'Hiya,' he shouted. 'Come this way.'

Rose walked in the direction he indicated and soon found herself on firmer ground, the marsh giving way to kikuyu grass and then a slastoed path. The bottom of her jeans and her hiking shoes were black with mud.

'Were you looking for me?' the man's cultured voice called out to her.

'Phew,' Rose panted, melodramatically fanning her face with her hands. 'Thanks. Are you Mr Bretton?'

'Yep. That's me.' His dog, a large Boerbul, sniffed at Rose's muddied feet. This dog better not dare sniff my crotch! she thought.

'It's my lucky day when such a pretty young lady comes looking for me,' Bretton chuckled, ushering her towards the veranda. He was old but spry and very dapper in his cream-coloured chinos, white shirt and Panama hat.

'The gate you came through – it should have been closed. My worker in his brilliance left it open for my cattle to wander out into the road. You should have taken the second entrance. It would have led you straight here.'

They reached the veranda. 'Come and have a seat,' he invited; then, 'Dora!' he shouted. He threw his hat onto an old chair and indicated to Rose to take one of the two shabby wickers that were angled towards each other for easy conversation. He sat down, the dog flopping at his feet.

'I'm Rose Clemens.' She leaned forward to shake his hand.

'What can I offer you to drink, Rose Clemens? Something cold? How about homemade lemon juice?' Dora the maid appeared at the door.

Rose was sweating and her face burning from her trudge through the field. She needed to remember to wear a hat the next time she went out in the heat of the day. She'd have to buy one. 'Something cold would be excellent.'

The farmer asked what he could do for her and Rose showed him the photos and briefly told her story.

'Well, it's neither of my sons, that much I can see even with my cataracts. But he does have the Oberon look.'

'What's that?'

'It's the look of the forefathers of this town. I think they were all related somewhere down the line. I suppose you'd call it an Aryan look, although that description has fallen foul of modern-day sensibilities. You know – blue-eyed and blond-haired. But it also fits Scandinavian . . . Dutch . . . English, too, come to think of it. I fear I've become too fanciful in my dotage.' He wheezed a chuckle.

In what way was he being fanciful? By suggesting that the person in the photo had the Oberon look – or that there was even such a thing as the Oberon look? Bretton's cheese-making neighbour certainly didn't conform to any such 'look', real or perceived.

'Roland Bergmeier – he's original Oberon stock, isn't he? But he's quite . . . swarthy,' she noted.

'Yes, but his mother was an import. Greek, I think. She was murdered a few years ago. In the retirement village where she was staying, in the Midlands. By young thugs. Bloody animals.'

'How terrible! I noticed your security wasn't very tight. Aren't you worried about crime?'

'We've formed a Community Watch to prevent farm attacks. We haven't had any. Yet. But I'm philosophical. Let them come, I say. They can have what they want.' He leaned forward, hands resting on his thighs: 'You know, I read an article in the newspaper about farm attacks. It seems like there's a whole organised crime system to force farmers – white farmers – off their land. The foot soldiers do the dirty work – they commit murder and mayhem on the farms for the leaders, the generals. Then these kingpins move in and take over the farms. And the government does nothing. These politicians! It suits them, you see. Less land to redistribute. They think they're gods, meting out farms that have been in families for generations. So here we are, the white farmers, between the devil and the deep blue sea.'

'Have there been land claims here?'

'Yes, there have been a few successful ones by black farmers. But they have no knowledge of commercial farming. They let the land go to rack and ruin . . . and if they bother to farm it at all, they revert to subsistence farming. It's going to ruin the country. We'll go the way of our northern neighbour, Zimbabwe.' He jerked his thumb over his shoulder. 'But I can't worry. I'll be dead by then. My chest.' He patted his chest and coughed a few times, as if in confirmation.

They sat in silence for a few moments. This generation was so unable to adjust to the changes, Rose was thinking. His profound pessimism, too, was typical. But perhaps his views about the country were realistic. Was Rose optimistic about the country's future? She didn't want to think about it.

Bretton asked: 'How's the lemon juice?'

'Delicious. Life gives you lemons and you make lemon juice.'

He chuckled. 'Now, back to your business: no, I don't recognise the man in the photo at all. Or the woman. My children would be the ones to ask but they all live overseas now. None of them wanted to farm this land and they left the country years ago. Let me think; who were their contemporaries?' He drummed his fingers on the arm of his chair. 'You've obviously met my neighbour, Bergmeier. I'm sure he wasn't much help,' he grunted. 'Then there are the Dalbert twins. Dariel's gone, but Denton's still here. And Robert Lieber . . .'

'Lieber? I'm staying at the Lieber's place – Hank and Brigit.'

'No no, Heinryk . . . Hank . . . is much too young. He was a real *laat lammetjie*. Robert's his brother. He'd be the right age but he lives in Durban now, I think.' He reeled off a few more names then fell silent.

Rose thanked him and stood up to leave. The dog stood up, too.

'I'll direct you to your car. You don't need to go back the roundabout way you came. It's been a pleasure,' he smiled. 'You must come and visit me again, Rose.'

Driving back to Oberon, Rose thought about Thomas Bretton's reference to the Oberon look. Did it exist? Was it only men who displayed its traits or did Rose manifest them as well? She was fair . . . ish and grey-eyed. Or was she, now, being fanciful in her desperation to find her roots?

Passing a shop-lined square, she spotted The Olive Branch, the other restaurant Brigit had recommended. It was nearly lunchtime so she pulled into the parking lot.

The restaurant's hand-painted sign dangled lopsidedly from a pole attached to the wall. There was a glazier busy replacing a broken panel of glass in the door, and the counter had been taped up with brown paper. The restaurant owner turned out to be the dumpy customer whom Rose had seen earlier in the cheese shop, though she didn't seem to recognise Rose. So – it was business as usual, despite the break-in.

The owner apologised for the disorder, explaining that they'd had some trouble. 'Where would you like to sit?' she asked. Rose looked around. The restaurant was relatively small but it extended into a second section beyond a glass divider, and then into a third. It was hot inside. Ceiling fans turned lazily, barely stirring the torpid air. Rose chose to sit near the front door so as to catch any breeze that entered.

She put in her order for toasted cheese and, while she waited for it to be delivered, studied the photos on the walls: black-and-white prints of Drakensberg landscapes, all for sale, judging by the price tags stuck in their corners. Who was the photographer? She decided she liked the work. Maybe she would buy one or two to start replacing some of Livvie's pictures – though not 'The Drakensberg Lady', of course. And so would begin her real ownership of the flat.

Gazing around, she was surprised to see the variety of goods on offer on the shelves: tins of Spanish olives; Italian tomatoes; German sauerkraut; Dutch wafer biscuits; Italian pasta; Greek olive oils; and Australian liquorice, red and black. In the further reaches of the restaurant, books replaced the comestibles; food for the mind. Restaurant, photo gallery, purveyor of fancy foods and bookshop – another example of financial need fostering enterprise. Rose couldn't wait to inspect the titles – but only after the toasted cheese; she was famished.

Within arm's reach, lay a pile of tabloid-sized newspapers on a low cane table: *The Mountain Mouthpiece*. Rose picked up a copy and paged through it. Adverts and religious notices; the opening of the refurbished Spar; a letter bemoaning the rampant local development; an article on wildlife in the Berg; entertainment for the upcoming Christmas season; photos of the recent mountain marathon.

She became aware of loud talk from the group at the only other occupied table. They were young and chattering excitedly to the owner in Afrikaans. Rose was interested to know what they were saying but their words emerged like machine-gun salvos, too rapid and idiomatic for her to follow with ease. One of the group was telling a hiking horror story: 'We started walking round in circles and found ourselves back at the place we'd started from. Ja! It was really scary. We were that lost. And there was lightning.'

'*Ja-nee*,' said the owner. 'You need to be careful of getting lost out there. And watch out for lightning! People think the Highveld is dangerous but more people die in these mountains from lightning than on the Highveld. People should know not to hike when it's lightning. Ja. That's the way it goes.' She began another hiking anecdote but it was long and complicated and Rose lost the plot. She resumed her perusal of *The Mountain Mouthpiece*.

A young waitress deposited her toasted cheese on the table. Then the owner came to Rose's table to ask how Rose was doing. Her English was as fluent as her Afrikaans. She wanted to know if Rose had done any hiking and where she was staying.

'At The Chameleon,' Rose replied.

'Oh – Brigit and Hank Lieber.'

'Do you know them?'

'Everybody knows everybody here. And their business. Ja-no, even us, though we're quite new here. We moved down from Jo'burg about a year ago. We had an HR placements business there. But *ag*, you know what, I said "life's too short", so we moved here. To live out our dream in the mountains. We love it. My husband does the cooking. He learnt how to cook when he lived in the south of Spain for a while.' So that explained the Gipsey Kings seeping out from the speakers. 'Is he the photographer?' Rose asked, indicating the wall prints.

'Ja – he is. Good, isn't he.' She glowed with pride.

'They're great.' Rose hesitated then said: 'I was in the Cheese Factory this morning and I couldn't help overhearing your . . . about your break-in.'

'Ja, we've been having some trouble lately.' The owner's expression turned downcast but she was more than willing to talk. 'You know, since we opened here ten months ago, we've been burgled or broken into at least six times,' she informed Rose. 'They've buggered up the counter, damaged the outside signage, smashed the door panels, broken windows – even destroyed some of the furniture.'

'That's really awful. What do the police say?'

The woman expelled air from her pursed lips. 'Pah! I tell you – they are complete idiots. They don't have a clue what they're doing. We don't even wait for them to come and take fingerprints anymore, we lose out on too much business. We have to close the shop, and we wait and wait but they just never pitch. But anyway, they're useless. And these are white cops, you know, not some illiterate black bunch.'

Rose squirmed inwardly at the woman's choice of words. She wondered why people imagined that just because you shared the same skin colour, you automatically shared their viewpoints. She continued chewing her toasted cheese, regretting now that she'd opened the conversation.

'They say it could be young blacks coming over the border from Lesotho, but I can't understand it. They hardly seem to take anything. It's more about damaging things, causing trouble. Ja-no – so why do they do it? Well, I'll tell you one thing, we're not going to be scared off. We're not giving up.'

'Shame. Well I hope you get to the bottom of it,' Rose said, pushing her empty plate aside. Catching the waitress's eye, she signalled for the bill.

'Pop in around lunchtime tomorrow if you're not doing anything,' the woman said, as Rose went over to the till to pay. 'There's a crowd that always comes on a Sunday. Ja, they're great fun.'

11

10th October 1880

We left the magistrate's abode under a bright blue sky—I, Abel, the two bearers and the horses loaded up to the hilt with provisions. Bidding Uncle goodbye I held back my tears, feeling most apprehensive and cursing my folly. Whatever motivated me to undertake such a perilous endeavour, I asked myself. But as the journey progressed and with Abel as my guide, I began to relax and enjoy it.

Abel is a font of homespun knowledge. From time to time he pointed out species of tree and wildflower, calling them by their native names. For the rest, we rode along in silence. Familiar by now with the extreme heat of the country, I had discarded my riding habit in favour of khaki trousers held up by braces, a man's shirt and sturdy veldskoene that appear de rigueur for male travellers in these parts. If Shakespeare's heroines can clothe themselves in men's garb then so too can I! To complete the outfit I threw on a large white bonnet and my most elegant pair of lady's riding gloves. How my outlandish tout-ensemble would amuse you, Imogen. For now, I revel in the freedom these clothes have to offer although I haven't forsaken feminine dress just yet, having packed frothy gowns as well as corsets and petticoats, which I will don upon reaching my destination.

I have stipulated to Abel that my feminine sex is no reason for special treatment. My horsemanship is as good as any gentleman's and I am a fine shot with a rifle—all thanks to Papa for choosing me as his honorary son. In this regard, he had Hobson's choice. Imogen would not have succeeded in this role. She is a most delicate creature.

The mountains are magnificent. The light constantly amazes me, its palette filled with clear blues and greens, with not a trace of the muddy, the mossy or the grey—so unlike the English landscape. We stop from time to time so that I can sketch the surroundings but I am afraid that I fail most dismally to capture the sublime beauty of my subject.

Although the land is for the most part wild and empty, we are reminded of the presence of men by the horse and cattle tracks that we follow. These led us past the remotest of the colonial farms, and the Berlin Evangelical Mission Station. Shortly thereafter we set up camp, where we have bivouacked overnight. Our maps indicate that we are somewhere on the frontier between the Basotholand Protectorate and Natal.

At about five o'clock, Rose received a call from Megan to say that they had changed their dinner booking to include her and she should meet them at the Oberon Hotel in an hour. No later, if they were to catch the sunset. These were spectacular here and she should bring a camera if she had one.

Rose arrived with ten minutes to spare but the other five were already waiting, Steve, Megan and Max, the English tourist, in one car, and Ronald and Petra in the other. They all greeted her warmly.

Steve told her to hop in the back and the two cars left in convoy.

'Look how amazing the Tooth looks in this light,' Max said. Rose looked out the window. The peak glowed a pearly grey in the diminishing sunlight. 'It's magical how it changes with the light,' he went on.

'When you live here, you don't even notice the scenery any more. You forget just how magical it is. Unless there's a tourist with you, and then you start seeing it through different eyes,' Steve put in.

'Like the mountains – I take them for granted most of the time but when I think about them, they are magical – so ancient and huge, you feel like an ant next to them,' said Megan, waxing poetic.

'Are you all from here – born and bred?' Rose asked. They were driving along another tree-lined avenue, the sun dropping behind the mountains to their left.

'Not at all,' Megan answered. 'I've only lived here for two years. I moved here when we got married. Steve's been here the longest. Isn't that right, Steve?' She deferred to her husband.

'I suppose. I've been here for about seven years. Ronald and Petra – I'm not sure. But they certainly aren't from here.'

The restaurant was situated about ten kilometres from the village in the opposite direction to Heimat along the Valley Road. It was part of a luxury lodge started by another recent transplant from Johannesburg – so Rose had read in *The Mountain Mouthpiece*. A solid brick of a woman, dressed all in black – black shirt, black pants, black Crocs – ushered them into the lodge through a luxuriously furnished lounge and onto the patio.

'This is so larney,' Ronald declared.

'Quick, before the sun goes down,' Megan said.

'Where's the waiter?' That was Steve.

'Spectacular view!' Max raved.

How could Rose have thought them rowdy and dowdy last night when they'd first entered the pub? They were nothing but gentility. And they'd all dressed for the occasion. The khaki had been replaced with chinos and golf shirts in the case of the men, and black trousers with silky blouses for the women. The men had plastered down their hair with wet combs and the women had teased theirs up a little. They smiled and waited patiently while a waiter dragged heavy cast-iron chairs about the patio. Well versed in the guests' viewing requirements, he positioned the seats carefully in a row, as if the group was about to watch a movie. Even now, with the day's heat over, the air felt very warm as they settled down to soak in the view, making desultory conversation and sipping lazily on long drinks. Then the sun sank slowly behind the slopes and the lake to their left mirrored the colours of the sky. Megan, Max and Ronald whipped out cameras and clicked unrestrainedly. Rose had never been interested in taking photos.

The rooms of the lodge were situated beyond the patio to the right, separated by a grassed area. A young couple emerged from one of the rooms and approached the patio. They were holding hands and the woman was visibly pregnant. She wore jeans and a tight T-shirt, which surprised Rose. When did pregnant women start flaunting their bumps? Not so long ago, expectant women walked around in tent dresses to hide their pregnancy. She wondered what she would do if she ever found herself in that condition. Would she dare to be so revealing? She wanted to know if Megan had children but felt too shy to ask. She also wanted to know whether Ronald and Petra were an item.

Clouds changed from grey to mauve, and the mountains from mint to purple. Another group of guests arrived, sitting at a table behind the group, in a narrow section of patio alongside the reception buildings. Who could be so blasé about the view that they spurned front-row seats?

The woman in black emerged onto the patio and hovered around the new arrivals. 'Is this a view or what!' she exclaimed. 'I thought you said no one interesting was joining you, just the boys . . . but you never said the boys were these two handsome okes!

Rose turned her head, curious. The two 'okes' were blond, broad-shouldered and sporty-looking. At a glance, the group was a nuclear family – mother, father and their two sons.

'I wish I may, I wish I might . . . there's the first star,' Megan observed.

'Venus. It's not a star, it's a planet,' Steve corrected.

'Yes, sir,' Megan retorted.

The sky's cobalt dome rolled around towards the horizon. A flock of geese honked forlornly as they flew home to roost. Frogs croaked by the lake and crickets tap-tapped like an assortment of metronomes.

There was a radiant burst of orange on the horizon, then darkness fell and with that came the hungry hordes of mosquitoes. They all slapped madly as the pests burrowed into scalps and down cleavages.

'I'm being bitten from here to China,' the pregnant woman whined. 'Let's go inside.'

'Maybe we should, too,' Steve suggested.

Rose and her companions were shown to a well-appointed table, all starched white linen, heavy silver and cut crystal. An oil candle in the centre threw pools of light onto the men's shaven faces and accentuated the touches of colour on the women's lids and lips.

The nuclear family entered the room: the elegant mother, her dark hair coiffured, and the father and two sons, all three of them fair-haired and golden-skinned. Did these men have the Oberon look? Rose had a great view of their table. One of the sons pulled out the chair for his mother and they all sat down with straight backs and elbows off the table.

'Those two are hot, don't you think?' Petra, who was seated next to Rose, observed. 'I'll take the one on the left, you can have the one on the right.'

Rose laughed. 'So are you and Ronald not an item, then?'

'Nah. Just friends. I think he's got his eye on you, Rose.'

Rose looked across the table at Ronald who was studying the wine list. He seemed nice enough.

'Are we all drinking white? What about this bottle for 60 bucks? Or this – a wooded prize-winning Chardonnay for R240?' He grinned, looking round the table to see their reactions. 'Okay – let's settle for this one at R85. Is that okay with everyone?'

Order whatever you want. The most expensive. No problem, I'll pay, Rose could have said. Would she appear a more attractive proposition if he knew her worth? Teachers' salaries were a joke. It was such unmitigated pleasure to spend without mentally tallying up a running balance. But as far as relationships went, her riches were problematic. The inequality of wealth was sure to complicate a relationship. She would never cede control of her finances to a romantic partner – but to keep the money a secret? Such a lack of trust would make for a very shaky foundation.

'How was the trip up Sani Pass today?' Petra asked.

'Great,' Max replied. 'You should do it, Rose. It's truly beautiful up there. And fascinating. A real eye-opener. I was interested to see the total lack of trees; I suppose they've all been cut down for fuel.'

'No, it's the climate zone,' Steve told him. 'Freezing winters, arid summers, high altitude, poor soils . . . it's been grassland for millennia. You're right, though, there is a lack of fuel but that has to do with poverty.'

'I remember that from the time I did the trip – the poverty is pretty grim up there,' said Petra. 'Those naked kids crawling around among the goat droppings . . . and the ultra-skinny dogs . . .' She shuddered. 'It's real survival of the fittest, isn't it?'

'Did you read those population stats in the leaflet?' Max asked Megan. 'They hand out a leaflet on the bus,' he told Rose. 'It gives information about the country . . . statistics, that sort of thing. The numbers in the 20–40 age group are quite drastically low compared to the others. The ravages of Aids, I suppose.'

'I confess I didn't enjoy the tour so much,' Megan said. 'I was freezing up there the whole time! And that thing in the hut with the homemade beer . . . It made me feel uncomfortable, drinking out of the same tin mug as all the other tourists. And the local people participating in the tour, acting out their lives for us – they looked so sour, like it wasn't a pleasure.'

'Well, it should be. It's probably the only money they earn,' Steve remarked, chewing on a piece of bread from the napkin-lined basket.

'It reminds me of when we were in Kenya,' Rose began, and then she was sorry. 'When we were in Kenya.' It sounded so . . . boastful . . . colonial. She had no choice but to continue now. 'There was something similar there, like a . . . I suppose you'd call it a living museum. It was in a park in Mombasa and we walked around to sort-of stations, where the various tribesmen and women actually lived, in their tribal huts, wearing their tribal clothes and doing their tribal thing. There were about thirty of them, all from different tribes. One young man . . . beautiful. But he was just about the last living member of his tribe, staying all alone in this weird artificial environment . . . it was so sad.'

Megan lifted the mood. 'How was Mombasa? I've heard it's a fantastic holiday destination. I've never travelled anywhere in Africa.'

'Oh I suppose that's because Africa starts on the other side of the Limpopo!' her husband noted acerbically. 'Anyway, you have. You went to Lesotho today. You even needed a passport.'

His wife giggled, reddening slightly. 'Oops. You know what I mean.'

'Should we order?' Ronald asked.

Rose glanced at the family across the way, decorously sipping their wine, their backs still ramrod straight.

'You mentioned something about research, Rose. What research are you doing?' Petra asked.

'I'm trying to trace my relatives,' she told them.

'Family tree stuff?' Megan wanted to know.

'Not quite . . . My mother died when I was young, about eighteen months old.'

'That's so sad! What did she die of?' Megan clucked sympathetically.

'It must have been from a brain haemorrhage. Something like that, but I'm not sure. It was completely sudden and unexpected, apparently. She was probably about the same age I am now when she died. No one knew who her family were or how to track them down. And no one knew who my father was. A detective was hired to try to trace my family, so that someone could claim me – but he was unsuccessful. Unclaimed baggage – that's me. Lucky no one sold me to defray expenses.' She laughed but no one joined in. The expressions on their faces showed shock, discomfort, dismay. Incredulity from Steve.

'God!' Megan exclaimed. 'So who brought you up?'

'My mother was working for someone at the time. A man named John Clemens. He adopted me.'

'He and his wife?'

'Just him. He wasn't married.'

'He was single?' That was Steve. Rose nodded.

'Could *you* do that as a single man?' Steve asked Max who shook his head vehemently. 'Could you?' he asked Ronald who shook his head, too.

'John was pretty amazing,' Rose said. 'He had a really good heart. He was living with a woman at the time – Livvie. They weren't . . . lovers or anything. At least I don't think they were; I lived in the house with them and they stayed in separate sections. I do remember that clearly.' Why, she wondered, was she telling them this detail? 'Anyway, he left for Paris when I was about six and Livvie brought me up. She never legally adopted me, but she was like a real mother to me. She died recently. It's been hard. I miss her.' Rose hadn't been thinking very much of Livvie in these strange surroundings but now she felt her sadness return.

'What happened to the man in Paris?' Max wanted to know.

'He died, too. About a year after he got there.'

'What was his story? What did he die of?'

Rose shrugged. 'Cancer, I think.'

'Was he from there? Did he have family there?' Ronald asked.

'I don't know. Livvie and I never really spoke about him. I think we each held back thinking that it would be too upsetting for the other. We had this . . . code of silence. Funny.' Funny, too, how it was sometimes easier talking to complete strangers than to loved ones. Was that why she was opening up like this now?

'Maybe he had a lover in Paris and when he knew he was dying he wanted to spend what time he had left with her,' Steve hypothesised.

'Or him,' retorted Max.

'Maybe,' Rose agreed. 'I've often thought it might have been something like that. Anyway, I found these two photos when I was tidying up my foster mother's flat after she died and it's definitely my biological mother in this one. That's been verified by someone who knew her at the time.' She passed Ruby's picture around.

'She's gorgeous!' was the general consensus.

Steve turned the photo over: 'Oberon, September 1981.'

'Yep. I was born nine months later.'

'Hmmm – so that's what brings you here.'

'And this one might be my father. But his face, his features are impossible to identify.'

They scrutinised the second photo. 'Yes. Impossible!' They were unanimous.

Rose told them where her enquiries in Oberon had taken her thus far. At some stage, the food arrived – seared salmon on a bed of mashed turnips; duck in raspberry *jus*; rare ostrich steak with a pepper crust; almond-stuffed chicken breast in a citrus reduction. It may have been the best cuisine in the Oberon area but they didn't notice.

'Don't you think this looks like Randall?' Megan tilted the photo towards the light of the candle. 'He's the principal of the local primary school,' she explained to Rose.

'Randall with a love child? I think not. The man is gay!' Petra said.

'Ja, and I can't exactly imagine him as a hot young stud,' Ronald chortled.

'Anyway, he's not from here.' Steve the rationalist doused their imaginings. 'No, I can't believe this story. It's impossible that your mother would have had no proper ID with her. Surely this man John needed to see her ID when he employed her? And what about her death certificate?' He stabbed at a piece of the rare ostrich and forked it into his mouth.

'Maybe she did have ID documents, but I've never seen them,' Rose said. 'I'm sure the detective would have exhausted that avenue, contacted Home Affairs for birth certificates and things . . .' Rose hadn't thought of this till now but it was probably the first thing Hunter did. She scooped up some of the wasabi-tinted mash with her fork. 'The other thing I found, in the same box as the photos, was this picture . . .' She unfolded the enlarged copy she'd had done of the catalogue picture. 'The name of this painting is "The Bushmen pay homage to the White Goddess". It's Victorian – done by an English artist, Sir Philip Geoffrey. There might be some connection to my mother but I can't imagine what. And there were also these.' She showed them the unusually beaded leather thong on her wrist, and the seeds she kept in a plastic bag in her handbag. 'It's like they're clues of some kind, but clues to what?'

They pored over the artefacts, offering their theories.

'The man was married and had a fling with your mother. Your mother was sentimental and kept the things you found as mementos.'

'That's why he put on the hat. He didn't want anyone to recognise him.' Everyone laughed at that. 'And when she told him she was pregnant, he denied he'd had anything to do with it.'

'She never told him because she didn't want to ruin his life. She was so self-sacrificing.'

'No, she didn't want a man in her life. She liked her independence. Early 80s, remember. She was a feminist. Back then, women needed men like fish needed bicycles.'

Their hilarity continued. They were so responsive, so engaged with her story.

Ronald stuck his fork into the breast of duck. 'What do you think about this painting? Quite intriguing, don't you think? I mean, a Victorian Englishwoman alone among the Bushmen, in that day and age.'

'Probably just a figment of the artist's imagination,' Max put in.

'Should we be calling them that? Bushmen?' said Petra. 'Isn't it an un-PC word nowadays?'

'Bushmen, Khoi, San – take your pick,' said Steve. 'This year the politically correct term is Bushmen. Last year it was San. Next year it will be who knows?' He took a thoughtful sip of his wine. 'Maybe there really was a white woman living among the Drakensberg Bushmen; it's possible. We know they did have contact with white visitors. White figures even appear in their rock art. Until recently they were thought to be representations of Europeans, but some experts now dispute that. Haven't you heard of that painting, the "White Lady of Brandberg"? You should look it up, Rose, it would interest you.'

Ronald leaned forward to examine Rose's wrist adornment. 'The thong is definitely African, I'd say. Maybe it's Bushman, but the glass beads are unusual. They're usually made from bone, shell or seed – though I'm no expert. There's a Bushman rock-art museum somewhere around here . . . part of the Bergsun Hotel, if I remember. I've never been, but I hear it's worth a visit.'

'I've heard it isn't – more for Japanese, American and German tourists,' Megan said. 'Sounds completely Disneyesque. They've evidently recreated rock art on artificial rocks. What a joke! Why artificial rocks – when there are millions of natural rocks all around here.'

'All the same, it might be worth visiting since you're in the area,' Steve said.

'What about Wits University? Haven't they got good research facilities for this kind of thing? Maybe when you get back . . .' Petra suggested.

Rose nodded. She had never held such a captive audience before. What had happened to her habitual reserve? Her usual tendency was to keep herself tightly enfolded – a shy bud enclosing a secret core. But now, in the sunshine of this company and watered by the alcohol, the petals had unfolded to reveal something of her heart.

They wanted coffee. Their waiter was standing straight up against the wall between two life-sized wooden carvings of colonial-style black serving-men. The waiter's arms hung stiffly by his sides and he wore a solemn expression. He was clearly well aware of the response his pose elicited. Rose's group didn't disappoint him. They laughed and Megan, Max and Ronald whipped out their cameras, moving further and further back to fit the scene in their frames, until they were almost on top of the nuclear family's table.

'Sorry,' they apologised. There was some shared laughter and a conversation was struck up. Before long, the father was accompanying

Megan, Max and Ronald back to their table. People were really friendly in these small places, Rose observed, probably because they were so hungry for new faces and new stories and so bored by the same old tired ones.

The boys' mother smiled vaguely from her seat. With the passing of the evening, she had progressively lost her poise and now sat slouched over a glass of wine, elbows on the table.

Introductions were made at Rose's table: 'Denton Dalbert,' the father said genially. 'I'm from Lakeside Farm, a few kilometres down this road. You'll see the sign.' His voice resonated with charm and elite Midlands education. 'You must come and spend some time there. There's a lake and a garden that's open to the public. Definitely worth a visit.' No wonder they all knew each other, Rose thought. Oberon was so small that sooner or later you were bound to bump into the whole community.

'Oh yes, we've been to Lakeside,' responded Megan. 'We had a picnic there last year. It is a beautiful spot. Maybe we should take Max and Rose.' From her vantage point across the table, Rose surreptitiously scrutinised Denton Dalbert, gazing intently at the shape of his jaw, the slope of his shoulders. He was the right age and he had the right look. Could it be him . . .?

Their eyes met – green on grey – and Rose looked away. Suddenly, her mood changed; the bubble burst, and she couldn't believe her naiveté. How could she have divulged her story, exposed herself as she had? If Dalbert lingered long enough at their table, it was only a matter of time before someone asked him for his help in identifying the photos. And if it turned out to be him? He was obviously well off, with his extensive Lakeside property. He would think she wanted a stake in his life. She did! She wanted to claim her rightful share . . . but only of his heart and his family tree, not his wealth. How would she persuade him that she wasn't just a gold digger? Drop hints that she was quite the heiress and didn't need anyone's money? She didn't think so.

Denton Dalbert went back to his family and Rose's group parted company soon afterwards.

'How long are you here for?' Megan asked Rose as they said their goodbyes.

'I'm not sure. Probably at least another week or so.' She felt she'd become subdued and hoped they wouldn't read it as a cooling off.

'That was a lovely evening. Let's do something again next week then – or on the weekend. A hike somewhere,' Petra smiled.

Ronald offered to take Rose back to the Oberon Hotel where her car was parked and the other four left in Steve's car.

'How about a drink?' he said, as they arrived back at her car. Rose hesitated; should she? Shouldn't she? She was tempted but decided against it. Tonight she'd gulped down an excess of human interaction and sociability and she needed time by herself to digest it all.

'I need bed – I'm exhausted,' she said. 'I got up with the birds this morning. Literally! There's a skylight in the ceiling and it lets the light in. It's going to wake me up every morning at dawn.'

'There's lots of accommodation in Oberon. You should move. You could move into my place, in fact. I have a spare room,' he smiled charmingly.

She laughed lightly. 'I'll try one more night and see how it goes. I could always get those eyeshade thingies they give you on planes. But thanks anyway.' She stood, feeling awkward. Should she kiss him goodnight? A peck on the cheek? She held back; next time.

In bed, tired as she was, she couldn't sleep. She lay watching the moonlit clouds scudding across the skylight. Her insomnia held a magnifying glass to her emotions, so that she felt ever more hopeless, helpless, regretful. Her story had monopolised the conversation the entire evening. It was like she'd suddenly found her voice and the words just tumbled uncontrollably out of her mouth. She'd got drunk on the sound of her own words. And the wine, of course. And just what was she doing here anyway? There were no real leads, nothing concrete to go on. What was her plan? She didn't have one. She was just floundering around like a landed trout.

She had been such an idiot, telling her story everywhere – to that Cathy woman at the Cheese Factory and then again tonight. Why was she so sure that the Polaroid man was her father, or even that her father came from around here? Maybe Ruby had only been holidaying here and the man in the photo was some arbitrary person, his meeting with her mother nothing more than a random encounter between two strangers. If she showed the photo to, say, Denton Dalbert or any other man fitting the bill and he said, 'Hey! Yes! That's me! Where did you get this from?' – then what? What if he *was* her father? So what?

Or – if, one day, she did find her father, destitute, forgotten in an old age home somewhere? What then? Would she feel responsible for him? Yes – she probably would, because that was how Livvie had brought her up. But not for any other reason. She might share fifty per cent of his genes, but DNA molecules were not the building blocks of father-daughter relationships – they did not code for instant love and affection. The truth was that she might dislike him . . . scorn what he stood for . . . eschew his values. When this was the case with natural parents, filial duty and shared history forged bonds of care and commitment. In her case, there were none. No bonds. Ruby had broken them all.

12

In the morning, despite her nocturnal misgivings, Rose decided to take a drive out to Lakeview Farm. Happiness waited on Rose while she ate breakfast. Neither Brigit nor Hank was around. It was already 10.30 a.m. Were they the churchgoing sort? Happiness hovered against the wall like a shadow in her blue overalls and bare feet.

'I've got everything I need, thanks.' Rose cradled the coffee mug in both hands, enjoying the sensation of hot steam on her face. 'You don't have to wait here. You can go if you've got things to do.'

'Miss Brigit told me to wait,' Happiness said tersely. 'I'm going home today. I've got off.'

'I'm nearly finished.' Rose gulped down the coffee. 'Do you live nearby?'

'No, madam. I live far away. In the mountains.'

'How long does it take you to get home?'

'Three hours with the taxi. There is a quicker way but then I must cross the river and walk a long way to my home. Sometimes, when the river is very full, the boys stand in the water with the truck tyre and then you must sit in the tyre and they pull you across the river. But it is bad. Everything gets wet. You have to put your handbag and your shoes in the plastic. And you must pay money to the boys. I got the call that my child is sick.'

Oh God! What did Rose have to go and ask for? Now not only did she feel guilty that Happiness had to wait for her but she felt bad about how hard it was for her to get home and the fact that her child was sick.

'Who's looking after the child? Did they tell you what's wrong? Is there a doctor you can take the child to?'

'There is the clinic. But you must pay and I can't afford until the end of the month.'

'Let me give you something. How much does it cost? Is a hundred enough?' Rose whipped a note out her purse.

Happiness nodded. 'Yes, madam. Thank you. You help me a lot. I pay you back.'

'No, no!' Rose gestured as if to sweep away the debt. 'And please phone me and let me know how the child is. Do you have a phone?' Happiness nodded. 'Here's my number.' She scribbled it down. 'Put it into your phone. Do a "Please call me" – okay?'

'Yes, madam. Thank you.'

Breakfast completed, it didn't take Rose long to get organised. Very soon she was driving through the gates of Lakeview Farm. Opening up before her was a vista of lake and lawn, with huge old trees dotted around and benches positioned strategically beneath them. Someone had carefully spaced new hydrangea bushes along the perimeter fence; this time next year would bring a stunning display of pink and blue blooms. The owners of the farm displayed true generosity in sharing their property with the public this way.

Rose wished she would spot one of the Denton Dalberts strolling around but there was not a soul. She was alone, wandering lonely as Wordsworth's cloud under grey skies. Lakeview had the feeling of the Lake District in England that she had visited as a child.

She walked down to the edge of the lake and watched ducks drift between trailing willow branches and dragonflies dart above the water's surface. Extending far into the green-grey water was a log bird hide. Up the hill, on the other side of the lake, stood a building with a large patio under rustic beams. She supposed the hostess, the elegant mother, entertained here – the Lady of Lakeview; who had looked, last night, like she bore the demands of her position heavy on her shoulders. Rose wandered over to investigate but the building was locked, the shutters closed, the kitchen hatches down.

She walked back to the lake along a wooden walkway that meandered through towering pines. Where the path met the lake, there was a white metal box on a stand. Rose opened its hinged door. Inside, someone had placed a visitors' book, with a pencil attached by a piece of string. She took the book out and flipped through it, her eye alighting on the last entry, dated a few days earlier. It read:

> *I've brought my teenage American children to see where I spent my childhood years. This lovely place brings back many happy memories. It's as well tended and as beautiful as I remember. Thank you.*

If the writer's children were old enough to appreciate their father's childhood stomping ground, then this park had been created and open to the public for at least thirty years – for as long as Rose had been alive.

She raced to the other side of the lake and up the hill. Was this the setting that had provided the backdrop for the Polaroids? Taking the photos from her handbag, she held them up against the landscape. They could have been taken here – or not. The background lacked any defining reference points; only willow trees and lake were visible. Rose longed to show them to Denton Dalbert but the road leading up to the private regions of the farm looked too unwelcoming. Giant oaks loomed, inimical, on either side: no visitors beyond this point. When had the visitors' books been started? Would they be available for her scrutiny? Then do it, she urged herself. Brave the oaks and ask at the farmhouse. But she didn't have the nerve. Her diffidence and passivity were generating nothing but dead ends and frustration.

So maybe, then, she mustn't actively try to find answers. Just imbibe the atmosphere. Enjoy the setting. Live the life, she told herself. Don't lose hope. There's nothing urgent waiting for you in Johannesburg . . .

She returned to her car and drove back past Bergmeier Cheeses and the cultured Mr Bretton's place towards the village of Heimat; along roads she felt certain Ruby, too, must have travelled on. She saw a National Heritage sign pointing the way to the Lutheran Church. Perhaps her mother had even visited that church; she made a mental note to visit it at a later stage.

It might be that in sunshine and amid the weekday bustle, Heimat exuded charm and quaintness, but on this dreary Sunday it was just miserable and depressing. The village centre consisted of a two-storey brick building tenanted by a Legal Aid office, deserted like everything else. Opposite the building was a derelict cottage that had been converted into a coffee-shop and pub. Whimsically named Swallows in the Field, it perched above the field in question, a huge green area that stretched away into the distance. The coffee-shop doors were shut and the windows barred. There was no sign of any swallows. Rose passed a few ramshackle houses set back from the road and pulled into a filling station. A taxi discharged its passengers in the forecourt.

'*Sanibonani, mkhulu*,' the woman attendant filling Rose's car said in greeting to a grey-haired man who had emerged from the taxi. The greeting of respect. '*Ninjani*?'

'*Saphila*,' the man replied, not slowing in his resolute plodding that would carry him to his home far and away. His poverty was palpable. It added to the general dreariness of the place and intensified Rose's melancholic mood.

Fine rain speckled her windscreen and she decided to return to the B&B. This afternoon would be a good time to begin on the final animation episode for Charmaine.

Driving through Oberon she remembered the owner of The Olive Branch telling her about the 'fun' crowd that came there on a Sunday.

The prospect of light banter lifted her spirits. On impulse, she turned into the parking area.

The bookshelves at the back of the restaurant were what drew her automatically as she walked in and she headed straight for them. It was an oddly eclectic selection: self-help, child care, cookery, stargazing, children's picture books, South Africa in photographs, Buddhism, astrology, Tarot and I Ching. Then, to her excitement, on one of the shelves she found a whole collection of books on rock art: *Discovering Southern African Rock Art*; *Bushman Art and the Drakensberg*; *Capturing the Spoor*; *Images of Mystery*; *Unconquerable Spirit*. Fab-u-lous! Which to buy, which to buy?

Two men sat with their backs to Rose, lounging in the deep couches. She couldn't help eavesdropping.

'. . . it was the absolute pits. Three days without water,' one of the men was saying. 'I tried phoning the manager at the municipality but he'd taken his phone off the hook. A Mr Xaba. Completely useless.'

'Ja, this incompetence! I heard it was one of the pumps. Peter Hein took it upon himself to find the problem and fix it.'

'But they need to do something about the shortage of water in any case. Everytime there's an event in the area, we run out of water. And it can only get worse with all this development.'

'Did you go to the meeting about that development on the Heimat road?'

'No. You?'

'No, but I hear it was an absolute fiasco. The enviro consultants are totally in the pockets of the developers. And as for them – they just slip something to the corrupt officials at the Department and Bob's your aunty!'

'Well what can you expect? This is Africa.'

The dumpy owner entered the space.

'Hey, Elmarie. Heard about the latest break-in. Terrible.'

'Ja. We're so fed up, Corrie and me.'

'How is Corrie?'

'Ja-no – he's fine. He's busy in the kitchen making fabulous paella. I recommend it.'

'Let's order a jug of sangria then. How about it?' the man suggested to his friend.

Elmarie spotted Rose. 'How are you doing? What can I get for you?'

Rose held up her hand. 'Nothing for the moment, thanks, I'm fine.'

To her slight irritation, the men turned to ogle her before continuing with their conversation.

'It must be criminals from across the border. They should never have closed down the Commando Units.'

'The Community Watch has been good. They were there in minutes after the Mollers had their break-in.'

My gosh, Rose thought, if this was Elmarie's idea of a fun crowd, she must lead an agonisingly dreary life.

She decided that she needed all the books. To hell with the extravagance. She had to make two trips to the counter to carry them all.

Rose asked where the toilet was and was given a key on a large wooden key ring, which she held gingerly, imagining the many unwashed hands that had clutched it on their way back from the toilet.

The small shopping centre consisted of a tourist office, estate agent, hardware, health shop, pharmacy and a store dedicated to the sale of fishing tackle. Rose continued down the passage to the back of the development, which was dark and dreary, the walls here left unpainted, remaining as bare concrete. Next to the toilets was a corrugated metal door with a sign that said: 'Dr S. Mnuse. MBChB (Medunsa)'. It was unexpected to find a doctor's surgery here, and with such an unprepossessing entrance.

On her way back, she caught sight of the strikingly rugged mountaineer she had seen in the pub. He was leaving the pharmacy carrying a large carton. It was amazing how the same faces kept popping up again and again. She wondered what was in the box, what he could need in such large quantity from a pharmacy. He was such an ascetic type with that far-off look in his eyes – like a prophet whose gaze into an apocalyptic future blinded him to the paltriness of the present. What would you talk about with a man like this? Maybe looks were deceiving and he was really as approachable as a used-car salesman, but somehow she didn't think so.

Rose spent a productive afternoon in the cottage, finishing the draft of the last episode in the animation series. In the early evening, she thought she would check her emails, make some payments and do an Internet search for data she needed. The books she'd bought sat in a pile on the kist at the foot of her bed. Each time she looked at them, she felt excited at the thought of tucking into them. But the right moment hadn't yet presented itself.

Although the rain had stopped and the mist had lifted, clouds still skittered across a nervous sky. She trod lightly through the shrubbery in the mint-fresh air, holding her laptop out in front of her like a tray. Brigit's white Volvo was parked under the canopy but the bakkie that she'd seen the previous morning was missing. She hoped one of her hosts, at least, was home.

The peacock met her in the courtyard and accompanied her to the back door. She knocked softly; Brigit opened. Her face was pale and deep lines were etched like parentheses around her mouth. Excited baby shrieks came from within but in the background the moans of the older child were audible.

'Oh, Brigit, it seems I've caught you at a bad time. I was going to ask if I could use the Internet.'

'It's fine. Come in,' Brigit answered. 'Go through. The office is past the kitchen and then to your left. There's a secured Internet connection. The password's "Lieber".'

The baby was sitting in a high chair, banging a spoon on the tray.

'Jamie's running a high temperature. He's very miserable,' Brigit told Rose as she resumed feeding the baby.

'Oh, shame,' Rose sympathised. 'Is there anything I can do?' she offered, although she secretly doubted she could contribute much in the way of child care.

'Thanks but I'll go to him in a minute. I just need to finish feeding the baby first and put her to sleep.' She seemed quite calm as she said it. Rose would be frantic. Imagine being responsible for these two lives! Rose had never had so much as a hamster to take care of. Where was Hank to help?

She walked through the kitchen and looked down the darkened passage, from where sounds of wailing emerged with growing volume. She wished she were bold enough to take action – to go to the child and placate him. But she feared her unfamiliar presence might upset him further. She also worried that her well-intended actions might unwittingly overstep the guest/proprietor boundaries.

'I'm coming, Jamie,' yelled Brigit.

Rose sat at the oak desk in the study, feeling very much the trespasser in this most private of spaces. She looked round the excessively neat room with its alphabetically arranged lever-arch files and stationery stored in a desk organiser. Even the pale-green deskpad was free from doodles.

Brigit's harassed footsteps sounded from down the passage. The boy's crying ceased and there was the whooshing of bath water. A little later, Brigit walked into the office.

'Rose, can I ask . . . do you have any plans for tonight?'

Rose looked up from her computer. 'No. Why?'

Brigit seemed oddly hesitant. 'I have a big favour to ask. This is such bad timing. Both Happiness and Thuli are off and Hank's out chasing stock thieves – he's away for the night. I have to take Jamie to the doctor. He seems to be struggling to breathe. The doctor said I must bring him in now . . . Jemma's sleeping. Can I ask you to stay . . . in the house . . .

until I get back? I'm so sorry – but I'm quite desperate. I can't leave her alone. I shouldn't be long. The doctor's just down the road.'

'Sure,' Rose said. 'It's fine, really. I've got lots of work to do here. I saw the doctor's surgery while I was at the shopping centre today; Dr Mnuse, isn't it?'

Brigit looked puzzled. 'Who? No, Dr van der Merwe. He practises from his house just down the road. Anyway, please help yourself to . . . whatever . . . in the kitchen if you're hungry or thirsty. You can watch TV in the lounge.'

'What should I do if the baby wakes up?'

'I'm sure she won't – I won't be long,' Brigit repeated. 'Here's my cell-phone number if you need to get hold of me.' She scribbled onto a pale-green piece of paper, then carrying the bundled-up Jamie, was gone.

The Internet connection was mind-numbingly slow. Rose's eye fell on the Reservations book sitting squarely next to the phone. Feeling guilty but unable to resist, she opened it and rifled through its pages. The Chameleon was clearly quite a going concern, enjoying high occupancy rates. Many of the visitors came from overseas – UK, Germany, Canada . . . even further afield, like Norway and Brazil. She wondered if the guy she'd met in Exclusive's was in the book but she didn't know what his name was. She came to her own name, neatly pencilled into Cottage 1 column until Friday. There followed a hiatus but from mid-December, both cottages were reserved. She shut the book and placed it back exactly in its former position.

It felt quite surreal to be sitting there, a stranger in a strange place, alone, with just the hum of the fridge to break the profound silence of the night. Feeling restless, she walked down the passage and into Jemma's darkened room, where she peered into the cot. There was Jemma surrounded by fluffy animals and dolls, in a pink babygrow, asleep on her tummy, fists clenched like seashells. The soft and tender smell of baby powder wafted to Rose's nostrils and for some reason she thought about Happiness's child. She hadn't phoned Rose as she'd promised. Was that a good sign or bad? She reached into the cot and touched the perfect curve of the baby's cheek, cool and smooth as butter. The baby breathed raggedly in through her mouth and Rose snatched her hand away, terrified that she'd disturbed her. She had no idea what she'd do with her if she woke.

She tiptoed out the room and began a tour of the house – to pass the time, she told herself. Like the study, it was organised and uncluttered. Jamie's room was done in blues and greens, with matching curtains and duvet cover. His toys were stored according to type in boxes and jars, the wooden puzzle pieces in their slots, the books ordered by height on the bookshelf. Next door was Jemma's room. And beyond it, further down the passage, was the main bedroom; Rose couldn't resist.

If the Corinthian plenitude of the garden was Hank's creation, then the fastidious austerity of the bedroom had to be Brigit's doing. The room was monochromatic, furnished in creams and beiges. It was dominated by the double bed, which looked too smooth and flat to imagine anything happening between the sheets. But then again, could one ever imagine it? There were no books or magazines on the bedside tables, no straggling wires from cell-phone chargers. The one feature that she attributed to Hank was the signature skylight in the ceiling. There was a bathroom en suite and a dressing room; but, feeling too much the snoop, she gave these only a cursory glance and went back to the study.

Some time later, the landline rang. It was Brigit.

'Jamie's having an asthma attack. He has to be admitted to the Kokstad hospital overnight. I can't get hold of Hank – he's out of cell range. I'm going to phone a friend to come in. But can I ask you . . . to wait until she gets there?'

'Don't worry your friend. I'm fine here. I can sleep on the couch,' Rose told her.

'Absolutely not. I don't expect you to do that,' Brigit said adamantly.

'I really don't mind. It's silly to call your friend out. I'm here. I insist.'

'I can't ask you to do this. You're a guest.'

'It's fine, really it is.' Rose added: 'Please, I want to help.'

She heard Brigit hesitate on the other end, and she understood. Only in a desperate situation would a mother leave her child with a complete stranger. But who was the friend Brigit wanted to ask? Perhaps Brigit's friends, like Rose's, could never really be classified as close enough to call on in a crisis. Maybe that's what had attracted Rose to Brigit; she recognised a fellow lone traveller in time and space. 'Okay,' Brigit conceded. 'If you're sure. Thuli will be in at six tomorrow so she'll take over from you then. There's a spare bed in Jemma's room. Sleep there. You'll be more comfortable than on the couch.' There followed a barrage of instructions: bottles . . . teats . . . formula . . . nappies . . . wipes . . . dummies . . . porridge . . . favourite toy . . . Rose felt weak from the responsibility she had just taken on. How could she blithely walk onto the stage of this domestic drama that was busy playing out? She didn't have the script.

'Yes, sure, right,' she answered glibly.

She couldn't work anymore. Her anxiety made her edgy. She drifted to the kitchen and opened the humming fridge. It was stacked with Tupperware containers and mysterious packages wrapped in tin foil; nothing to tempt Rose except a red apple offered up by the bottom drawer.

She looked for a torch to light her way back to the cottage. She needed her toothbrush and something to read. But she couldn't find a torch in any of the places where she felt strange eyes were permitted to pry. So she stumbled in the dark through the shrubbery, all too conscious of snakes and other dangers that might waylay her passage.

Safely back in the Liebers' house, she again stole a glance at the baby who slept so innocently, unaware of life's pitfalls. She slid into the spare bed, book in hand. But before she'd reached the end of the first page, her eyes had closed and she was asleep.

Much later, she woke with a start, befuddled and disorientated. It took her a few minutes to realise where she was and that the fearsome noise shattering the rural night was the sound of the baby crying. She switched on the bedside lamp to see Jemma standing up, holding the bars of the cot. The baby stopped crying and watched with interest as Rose staggered towards her. But when Rose lifted her out, she started to scream. Rose held the little body tight against her own, cupping the back of her head and joggling her.

'Sh-sh-sh. Sh-sh-sh,' she comforted, but the baby pulled away, her body rigid. Rose bounced her against her chest, pacing round the room, then walked down the passage to the lounge. She turned the baby around and showed her the pale, pastoral landscapes on the walls, telling her to 'look at the horsey and the cow'.

'What does the cow say?' Rose asked in a baby voice. 'It says moo moo.' For a second, there was silence then the wailing began once more.

'There now, there now,' she told her, but the child was inconsolable. Rose wanted to cry, too. The baby would make herself sick. What should Rose do?

As she held her tight, rocking her and patting her bottom, she caught an eye-punishing whiff of ammonia and became aware of the child's soggy nether regions; so that was the trouble. She walked back to the baby's room and pinned her down on the compactum, looking round for nappies. In a flash, Jemma had wriggled out from under Rose's hand and turned over to a crawling position.

'Oh please, Jemma,' Rose begged. She picked her up under the arms and deposited her unceremoniously on the floor. Jemma tottered over to a toy box, plonked down on her bottom and began chewing on a plastic block. Through tear-darkened lashes she watched Rose poke around in drawers and containers in search of nappies and wipes. Her crying had stopped.

'Poor baby,' Rose sympathised. 'Mommy will be back soon, before you know it. Let's change the yucky nappy.' Rose sat cross-legged on the floor, gave a quick wipe at Jemma's nose then tugged at the feet of the babygrow. The child obligingly rolled onto her back and from there it was easy, Jemma quietly gnawing on the block, never taking her eyes off Rose. Rose scrabbled for the dummy that had rolled under the cot, picked up the baby and sat on the armchair next to the cot. She offered her the dummy, which the baby stuffed into her mouth and proceeded to suck noisily, jaw muscles working furiously against Rose's breast. Rose bent her neck towards the baby's crown and breathed in deeply. The smell of baby. With each inhalation she breathed in the smell and the fine wispy hair tickled her nostrils. It was irresistible, that smell, like a drug, a comforter, something delicious. She couldn't stop. Her eyelids grew heavy.

This age of dependency. Now she had a reference point from which to imagine and recall. Memories recollected in tranquillity . . . of Livvie telling her the tale of Rose's resurrection. It had been three days since Ruby last appeared at work. John broke through the door and there was Ruby and there was Rose, alone – all alone – at this age of dependency. Rose herself didn't remember. What she had was only the memory of someone else's recollection and the overflow of imagination. Livvie – or John (that argument had never been settled) – picked Rose up off the floor after three days. Ruby didn't rise. She remained cold in the bed but Rose rose, lifted off the ground by Livvie. Or John. Alone, all alone, all allele, dominant and recessive, receding, mother. And father.

Carrying Jemma close against her chest, Rose lurched to the bed and crawled in, still sniffing at the baby's head. And there they slept, until the first light crept through the skylight and the peacock mewled his lonely mewl and the pigeons rose from the top of the pines.

Rose held onto the bars of her cot and surveyed the room in the pale early-morning light. Climbing over the bars, first one leg then the other, she landed on hands and knees next to her bottle. She picked it up and clamped its teat between her teeth.

Now what was this that lay so yellow and soft in her cot? Her blanket, with its delicious satin edging – so satisfying when rubbed against the nose. She tugged at it through the bars. It resisted until . . . victory! The blanket was free and she brought it to her nostrils and sniffed in its baked-bread fragrance. Surprise! The white rabbit appeared. This, too, she dragged through the bars.

She tottered on her bandy legs swaddled in towelling pink, clutching her white rabbit under her arm, yellow blanket trailing obediently behind; across the narrow divide that separated her cot from her mother's bed. The bottle sighed gently, bouncing on her chest as she walked.

Where was Mama? Here she was. Sometimes Mama disappeared. Pouf! Out of sight. It was as if Rose's very self had been wrenched in two. Terrifying. But here she was, Mama, somewhere under the big mound of cream duvet.

The rising sunlight filtered through the pale fabric of the curtains, illuminating her mother's shape curled at the edge of the double bed. Blanket and rabbit forgotten, Rose laid a dimpled hand on the mound. It did not move.

She pulled herself onto the bed with tight fists; awaiting her was the mouth that sang the Patter Cake song and the eyes that promised Mama-Rosie together forever. She lifted the duvet and – peek-a-boo! Laughed to see her mother's face. The bottle fell out of her mouth with a plop. 'Mama,' she chuckled delightedly.

Her mother's face remained unmoving. No sounds emerged from her mouth, no smiles from her eyes.

The baby solemnly studied the face; so still. She touched the cheek. Grabbed the lips, her small fingers grasping at the pale-pink flesh. Busy hands, babbling mouth. Mamamama, dadadada. She probed the unknown cavities of her mother's nostrils, index finger like a miniature antenna. Her face was intense with concentration. Mama did not move so she lay down alongside her and, finding the bottle within her reach, picked it up and once more started sucking on the teat. Pah! All she got was stale, rubbery air and she spat it out her mouth in disgust.

She became aware of something nasty that enveloped her, breathing fire on her bottom region; another fire was gnawing at her middle. She gave a moan – I'm wet, I'm hungry, I'm thirsty. But 'mumum mum mama' and then 'waaa-aaaa' were the only sounds that came from her mouth. She flung herself across her mother's body, onto the wide expanse of bed and wailed, her face reddening, legs flailing. Still her mother lay unmoving, unmoved, as still as a leaf curled up at the edge of the bed. On and on Rose screamed. Her cries turned to sobs and then to whimpers; finally she quietened. Her little body thoroughly spent, she sucked her thumb and dozed off.

The telephone rang but then it stopped. Cars swished past, pigeons sang a threnody in the pines. Somewhere in the neighbourhood, a mealie-seller cried, 'Mea-lies!'

Later, when the sun reached its peak and the air hung turbid as glycerine, the child awoke. She lay restfully on her back and watched the play of light and shadow on the ceiling.

The telephone rang again. She slid off the bed, lifted the too-large receiver clumsily with both hands and held it to her face. 'Hu yo.' But the ringing had already stopped and all she heard was the drone of the engaged signal. Dropping the receiver, she began to push the buttons on the dial but the activity ceased as she became more and more aware of her aching middle and her throat, dry as sand.

She moaned intermittently, walking around the room. The press studs on the underside of her babygro had come undone, liberating her nappy, which now hung loosely between her creased thighs, filling the air with acrid fumes.

She toddled to the door of the cupboard, which had been left slightly ajar. She opened it and saw that she was not alone; there was another baby. The baby's cheeks were flushed, its hair as wispy as the morning breeze. Smiling, Rose reached out to touch the baby. The baby reached out to touch her, its hands as cold as glass. Bump. Both babies fell backwards.

Rose became aware that the thing she was sitting on was the source of her discomfort. To remove it, she had to undo the tapes but these were obscured by her belly. She looked down to see what her fingers were doing. Finally, success. She stood up triumphantly, releasing a little stream of brown pebbles onto the carpet, and toddled resolutely over the threshold of the room, her bare bottom deliciously free; down the passage, across the new-laid floors, to the kitchen shining with promise in the midday light.

Rose had often explored the exciting things within her reach, offered up by the cupboards in this room, while her mother prepared their meals. The first cupboard housed the sunset-coloured Tupperware bowls stacked cleverly in a tower; in the next, the pots and pans that Rose had banged with a spoon, which made her mother laugh and block her ears; in another, packets, boxes, cartons and tins. She crawled around, scuttling on her bare bottom, opening and closing doors. She found a red plastic lid that she immediately put into her mouth. Too tasteless. Then she tried biting on a pot. Too hard. She spied a wrapped cylinder and recalled how Mama often pulled, as if by magic, a biscuit from inside the blue packaging, and that it was sweet and satisfying. Brow furrowed, she extracted a biscuit and gnawed on it.

Tiring of this, she tottered to the kitchen table, where she scrambled up onto one of the chairs and then onto the table top. There was a bowl of shiny apples by her foot; Rose reached in and took one, biting at its unyielding redness with her new white teeth. The fruit released a tantalising trickle of sweetness but its skin proved too tough to penetrate.

Losing interest, she climbed off the table and went back to her discarded biscuit.

Rose pottered around the house, wandering in and out of half-furnished rooms, and then back to the bedroom she shared with her mother. At times, she moaned and whimpered but mostly she lay quietly on her back, watching the shadows play catches on the ceiling. And so time ticked out its mournful dirge.

The light faded and the air cooled. Objects darkened and tiny goosebumps rippled across Rose's baby skin. Unnamed creatures emerged from their hiding places under the bed and behind the door and skulked stealthily around the room. Rose climbed back onto the bed and crept under the duvet where her mother lay so strangely still. When she touched her, she was met with deathly cold. Rose cried, her sobs rending the air. Finally, she quietened and drifted off into a restless sleep.

By the next morning, her mother still had not woken. Rose slid off the bed but her knees buckled and she crumpled in the narrow aisle between cot and bed. There she lay, drifting between periods of restless sleep and fretful wakefulness, listless and parched, sucking her thumb and clutching her yellow blanket to her nose.

13

There was knocking at the back door. Rose, with Jemma on her hip, opened to admit the barefoot Thuli.

'*Haai!*' Thuli exclaimed, her eyes wide. 'Where's the missus?' The baby stretched out chubby arms towards Thuli. The landline was ringing. Rose, zombie-like from lack of sleep, handed the baby over and went to pick up the receiver.

'Rose, it's Brigit. How's everything?'

'Fine, just fine. Jemma's fine and Thuli's just arrived. How's Jamie?'

'Much better, thanks. We're just waiting for the doctor to see him, then we'll be home. Thuli can take over from you now. Can I have a word with her? And Rose . . . thank you so much for everything.'

Thuli secured Jemma to her back with a towel and a giant safety pin and took the phone.

'Yes, madam . . . yes . . . yes.' She nodded her head a few more times, then replaced the receiver and began fetching jars of cereal, yoghurts, juices, muffins, plates and cutlery from the kitchen and arranging them on the dresser in the breakfast room.

Rose dragged her feet back to the cottage. She felt like she was unravelling from tiredness, like she could sleep for a hundred years. But when she crawled under the duvet and closed her burning eyes, she found she was struggling to push the loose ends of herself back inside her body. It was no good fighting the restlessness.

She went outside, past Hank's garden, and veered onto the path that led down to the river, beating her way through the bushy undergrowth to the cantilevered wooden platform she had spied on her previous visit. She stretched out on her back, crushing pine needles that released their aromatic scents. Her bare feet dangled over the jetty edge above the water and the sun shone through her closed lids. She flung an arm over her face, listening to the coloratura trills of birds and crickets – divas of the veld – and felt the sun's heat intensify as the earth slowly turned on its axis.

How had she survived on her own for three days after her mother died when she was no older than Jemma? But survive she had – so why even think about it? For a long time she lay there, trying not to think at all, until she felt a shadow pass over her. She sat up and there stood Hank, bearing a silver tray laden with coffee, orange juice, croissants, a hunk of cheese, nectarines and a parfait glass filled with layers of yoghurt, fruit and muesli. He crouched down and deposited the tray beside her.

'Oh! Thanks! Thanks so much. This is very kind of you,' she stammered.

Hank put his right hand to his heart: 'It's nothing next to your kindness, Rose. We owe you big time for last night. Really. Thanks a lot.' He looked sheepish as he said it. It made her feel oddly tender towards him.

'It was nothing, truly.'

'Listen. We're having a braai tonight. Just some mates coming round. Join us? About 6.30.'

How to refuse? 'Er . . . okay. Thanks,' Rose said. This was very awkward. She wouldn't know anyone there. But she could leave early. Make an excuse about the mountain air.

'Is Brigit home?' she asked.

'She's on her way,' he told her. 'Don't worry about the tray, I'll send Thuli to fetch it later.' He stood up, caressed her with his smile and was gone.

Cross-legged, she picnicked on the platform. The air was hot and still. Below her, the river wound its way through the cleft between two mountain slopes. A big Pied Crow alighted on the branch above her head and cawed loudly. She cut the cheese into smaller chunks and lined them up on the platform, thinking of the Aesop's fable crow.

'Don't listen to that smarmy fox when he tells you you have a great voice,' she warned the bird. She picked up the tray and made for the house.

Brigit was drinking coffee at the table in the breakfast room while Hank pottered around in the kitchen.

'Ah, Rose. You didn't need to,' he said, entering the breakfast room and relieving her of the tray. 'Let me make you some coffee.'

'No, thanks. I've already had some . . .' Her voice trailed away. She felt nauseous, fragile from sleep deprivation.

'Come on. I've just brewed a full pot. Take a seat.'

'Oh, okay, ' she said and sat reluctantly.

She felt awkward being in the midst of the Liebers' domestic realm and guilty about snooping around their house last night. It was the first time she was seeing husband and wife together. How did they interact? She remembered Livvie and John's fond and easy familiarity with each other. But then, perhaps it was easier to stay fond of each other when you didn't share a bed . . . or a bathroom.

'How's Jamie doing?' Rose asked Brigit, who was sitting opposite her. Brigit looked even paler this morning than she had last night. Her unbrushed hair created an aura around her head. Rose wondered how she was going to have the energy to host a braai, even if only for a couple of mates. And whose mates were they? Hank's? Or mutual friends?

'Turns out it wasn't just asthma but bronchitis. The hospital gave me a nebuliser for him so I can nebulise him at home. He's breathing much better now.'

'Happiness told me her child was sick as well. Have you heard anything?' Rose asked.

Brigit expelled air dismissively. 'I'm sure she would have let us know if the news was bad. Listen, I can't thank you enough for last night. I still feel terrible that you had to step in and carry the can like that.'

Rose smiled and shook her head. The sun crept in through a side window and warmed her back pleasantly. Hank entered the room with the coffee. He set the tray down and then took the seat next to Brigit. 'It's going to be another scorcher today. What have you got planned, Rose?'

'Rose has been making contact with the locals,' Brigit cut in, pouring milk into Hank's coffee and passing it to him. 'She's trying to identify someone in a photo from long ago. Why don't you show it to Hank?' she suggested.

The folder with the Polaroid copies was in the cottage. Rose went across to fetch it. The chances of Hank recognising the man were slim, but it was worth a shot. How much older was Hank's older brother who lived in Durban? Could he be a potential father? Imagine! Hank would be her uncle.

Hank studied the photo closely. 'He reminds me of someone. There's something familiar about him . . .' he frowned.

'Do you have any idea who it might be?' Rose asked.

'Dunno. Must think about it.' He scratched his shaven pate.

'What about these things? They were in the box with the photos. Any idea what they could be about?' Rose showed Hank and Brigit the beaded wrist thong, the seeds, the blown-up catalogue picture and the diary, explaining how she came by them.

Brigit, absently sipping her coffee, volunteered: 'You could ask the librarian at the Oberon Library. She might know something.'

'I've heard there's a rock-art museum at the Bergsun Hotel. Have you ever been?' Rose asked.

'Nah. You know what it's like when you live in a place. You always think you'll get round to visiting these things but you never do.' Hank gulped down his coffee and stood up energetically. 'Well, better get going. Enoch's waiting for me at the farm. See you later. Do you need anything from town?' he asked Brigit. She shook her head and he strode out, tanned calves bulging over the rims of his hiking boots. No goodbye kiss then? Maybe they weren't into little acts of affection when they parted company.

Silence descended on the two women. Smiling, Rose said: 'Your Jemma's just the sweetest little thing. I have to admit she gave me a bit of a hard time at one stage but then she settled beautifully.'

'She mostly sleeps through. I really am grateful that you were there . . . it hasn't been easy, with Hank away so much. I sometimes feel like a single mom.'

'It must be hard on your own. You said Hank was away chasing stock thieves?'

'Yes. With the Farm Watch.'

'Did they catch anyone?'

'I don't ask anymore. It's such a losing battle. They leave in the dead of night, going into the most remote areas, never knowing what lies in wait for them. And if they do find the cattle, they have to drive them back across the border . . . and before long, the cattle are gone again. I don't know what the answer is. Anyway,' she shrugged, 'it's a job. Hank gets paid quite well for it.'

'What happens to the thieves? Are they never brought to book?'

Again the shrug. 'The police are so badly resourced – on both sides of the border. Each village has a local constabulary but the area is so huge, it's impossible to patrol . . . or control. Anyway, all the farmers want is to get their cattle back. For the thieves to get caught and charged, that would be too much to ask.'

Rose shook her head in sympathy. 'Talking about cattle . . .' she smiled, 'I hope Hank told you that I'm coming to your braai tonight? He invited me.'

Brigit nodded. 'Of course. We'd love you to join us. It's the least we can do, to offer you a meal.'

'Can I help with anything? You must be exhausted.'

'No, it's fine. Thanks. Everything's mostly done. Thuli's here to help make the salads and Hank does the braaiing.' She paused. 'Listen, if you're not busy tomorrow, let's go to the museum at the Bergsun. I've always wanted to go and it would be nice to do it together.'

'Great! I'd love that.' Rose stood up, thrilled. She took Brigit's invitation as an overture of friendship. It was something she would never have had the confidence to initiate.

'Well, see you later. We can make arrangements then.'

Rose drove slowly down the main street in search of the library. On the corner, a signpost painted in official green pointed to a block of shops. She parked and walked along the surprisingly litter-free length of pavement, passing electrical supplies, horse tackle, a Wimpy Bar, camping gear, a hardware store and an Absa bank. But no library.

In the camping shop, she asked directions from the young assistant, who pointed her down a side street. On her way out she spotted a stand weighed down with hats and made a mental note to return.

Rose found the library and entered the small, neon-lit room. The librarian was standing behind the wooden desk that dominated the space, nattering away in animated tones to a customer. Rose waited for their conversation to end, distracting herself meanwhile by shuffling along the shelves and scanning the titles of the mainly light reading matter: romances, thrillers, crime. There was a whole shelf dedicated to audio books, also of the same lightweight material. She returned to the desk, hoping the librarian would notice her but she was still engrossed in her conversation.

The other woman was saying: 'I bumped her in the street and she asked me when I was getting divorced. Where does she get her information from? She knows I'm getting divorced before I do!'

The librarian shook her head. 'That's the problem with living here. Everyone knows your business.'

'But I'm not getting divorced!'

'She's trouble. Don't go near her.'

Rose wandered over to a green felt notice board. She read:

Bags!
Keep library items in the plastic bags that are issued. Keep them clean and undamaged. Bring back dirty or damaged items and you WILL pay. If you lose the plastic bag, you WILL replace it.
By order.

Scary! There was a poster for The Mountain Minstrels who were giving a concert on the following Saturday night, singing their own songs and doing impersonations of Elvis. Rose went back to the desk and hovered there, certain that the librarian must be aware of her. But she continued to ignore Rose, who stood shifting her weight from one foot to the other, inwardly fuming but trying not to let her annoyance show. Just tell me that you'll be with me in a minute – or ten – and all will be forgiven, she thought. But simply to ignore her like this – it was so rude.

Finally, the other woman said: 'Listen, I better get going. The boss goes mad if I'm late.'

She left at last and the librarian looked at Rose with raised eyebrows.

'Hello,' Rose smiled sweetly, the joints of her jaw straining with the effort. 'I wonder if you can help me?'

'That depends. I close early on a Monday. In fact, I'm already closed.'

'I just want to ask . . . I've got these things and I'm trying to trace where they come from . . .' She showed the packet of seeds, the catalogue painting and the thong. 'I know it's a long shot but would you happen to know . . . anything about them?'

The woman looked exasperated. 'What do you think I am? An encyclopedia?'

Rose persevered: 'I just thought you might have an idea . . . it's possible they originate from this area . . .'

She broke off, intimidated by the woman's steely glare, then soldiered on bravely: 'What about these photos? Do you perhaps recognise the people in them?'

'No, listen, lovey. I need to go. I don't have a clue what any of this is.'

'Okay . . . um . . . well I'm also doing some research on the San and I was wondering if you had any material on them?'

'I don't get much budget for non-fiction. I'm a just small local library, you know,' she snapped. 'I do have some books,' she said grudgingly, 'but unless you're a resident of Oberon, you aren't allowed to borrow. I've had too much material disappearing. You can only use them here in the library.' She emerged from behind her desk, looking sour.

Rose followed her billowy floral pants to a bottom shelf in a dark corner. It really was a paltry selection. The collection she'd bought at The Olive Branch was more comprehensive.

'Er . . . thanks. I think I'll come back another day, when there's more time,' she said, though her intention was never to set foot in this library again.

'Where are you from?' the librarian asked.

'Jo'burg.'

The woman's demeanour changed unexpectedly to chatty friendliness. 'Did you see the TV series on San rock art on SABC1 a few weeks ago? I'd love a copy. Maybe you could make enquiries for me when you get home,' she wheedled.

A regular Jekyl and Hyde. Rose nodded obligingly. 'Sure. And by the way . . . um . . . I'm also trying to find information on this.' She held out the catalogue picture. 'Have you ever come across it? It's by an English artist – Sir Philip Geoffrey. I'm trying to find out what the source of inspiration for this painting could be. Do you know of any stories or myths about a white goddess in these parts?'

'Hmmm.' The librarian peered at the painting and slowly read out the title: '"The Bushmen pay homage to the White Goddess". No, I've never heard of anything like this. It's kind of fascinating, though. How long are you here for?'

'I'm not sure . . . probably a few more days.'

'Leave me your email address. I'll let you know if I find anything. You know,' she said thoughtfully, 'there is a village near here somewhere whose inhabitants are supposed to be descendants of the Bushmen. I think it's across the border, in Lesotho.'

'Wow! I'd love to visit there.'

'From what I'm told, it's a real godforsaken place. Not exactly a sought-after tourist destination, but it might be interesting for you to go there,' she said chattily.

'Are there any rock-art sites around here, do you know?' Rose asked.

The woman nodded. 'There are probably thousands of them in these mountains, but not many people know where they are. The conservationists keep them a secret – you aren't allowed to visit them unless you go with a proper guide.'

'To protect them from vandalism, I suppose.'

'Yes. But also, the dust from people's feet sticks to the art and causes it to fade. I did one of those tours once – we had to hike seven hours there and seven hours back. I nearly died.'

'So was it amazing, what you saw?'

'Ja – it was pretty amazing.'

'I'm also . . . um . . . doing research on the inhabitants of Oberon. Do you perhaps have any records of the original settlers, or even the more recent farmers? Anything on the history of the area?'

The woman shook her head and walked back to the desk, talking to Rose over her shoulder. 'Like I said, we're a small library. You can see the type of customers we get by what's on the shelves; they're not the most intellectual bunch. In fact, they're a bunch of morons. It would be a good project though – to start an historical archive of the area. Certificates, photos, old letters, that sort of thing. I don't think the farmers round here would give up their family records too easily, though – too many skeletons,' she chuckled.

Rose went on her way. Outside the camping shop, a skinny woman in her forties stood smoking a cigarette. She was dressed in stovepipe jeans and a midriff top. A belly ring was embedded in the slack skin around her navel and her jet-black hair lay lank over her shoulders. She squinted with each deep draw she took, her heavily mascara'd lashes coming together like inky sea creatures. Her eyes followed Rose as she entered the shop.

Rose headed for the hat stand. Its offerings were limited to fuddy-duddy styles, mostly in khaki. The scrawny young assistant sidled up to her and asked if she needed help. His pierced eyebrow looked incongruous under his thick, greasy fringe. Rose shook her head. She tried on a floppy denim number and ducked down to look in the small mirror attached to a nearby column.

'That looks good on you, love.' The skinny woman, now *sans* cigarette, had entered the shop.

Rose tried on a khaki cap. 'And this one?'

'Also nice. Yes – I think I prefer it.'

'Okay, I'll take it.' Rose wasn't going to agonise over a hat.

The woman walked to the till. 'Are you here on holiday?'

'Yep.' It was easier to give the short answer. But then she felt compelled to add: 'I'm also here doing some research . . . on rock art. I've just been to the library to see if they had anything.'

'So, you met the witch of Oberon, did you? She's on her own again. Husband number three's just left her and can't say I blame him, either. He was having an affair with the doctor's secretary. But that's over now because she's gone back to her husband. Where are you staying?'

'At The Chameleon.'

'Oh, the Liebers. That Hank; he's always running to the black areas. I think he must have a black wife and a whole bunch of little black Hanks running around somewhere.'

Really? Had Brigit heard this story? Had Hank? You had to watch what you said in front of this woman.

'I don't know how Brigit puts up with him,' she went on. 'If he was my husband I would have told him to go jump long ago. My beaut's in hospital. He's just had a bypass. And now he wants to emigrate to England. I told him, if you go, you go by yourself. I'm not going to that shithole where it gets dark at three in the afternoon. What does he think? That the English are just waiting for him? He'll sit on his fat arse all day and drive me barmy. As for this assistant he's hired!' She jerked her head at the assistant, who was standing looking glumly out the door. 'Know what he says to me this morning? Will I make him some tea. I said, "Listen sonny, if you want tea, you can ask your mother to make it for you." I ask you! Who the hell does he think he is?'

Rose nodded, wide-eyed. These small-town people just loved opening up to strangers. 'Well, thanks,' she said, taking her parcel. 'I hope your husband gets well soon.' She turned to go.

On the other side of the plate-glass frontage, a man stood looking at the hiking boots on display. He was short and stocky, with arms like a gorilla and a surly, scowling face. Why did he look so familiar?

'That man looking in . . . do you know him?' she asked the store owner.

The woman peered through the window.

'Ugh. He's one of those Ritters. William, I think.'

Rose was still trying to place him. Where did she know him from? 'Are they local?'

'Ja, they're local. But you don't want to have too much to do with them. Scumbags – the whole lot of them.'

Oh, God! The highway – Mad Max! William Ritter. She wondered if he would remember her . . . his mad dicing. Was he about to enter the shop or only window shopping? She moved nervously into the shadows. What would she do if he walked in?

The man was now peering through the window into the shop. Rose held her breath in case he spotted her, but to her relief he moved on. The skinny woman came round from behind the counter and went to stand in the doorway, another cigarette in hand. Rose followed and they both watched Mad Max lumbering off down the street. She was bound to meet him again. There was no avoiding people in this little town. But so what if she did meet him? He probably wouldn't even recognise her, she decided. To someone like him, women were not individuals – just objects to bully around.

11th October 1880

The medicine man was waiting to greet us upon our arrival in Patilweng. Abel had sent word of our coming via one of the bearers, a diminutive wizened old man with a yellow cast to his skin. He was clad in nothing but a loin cloth and beaded bracelets, with legs so thin they resembled pins. He welcomed us in his pidgin English. When we bestowed on him the parcels of maize, sorghum and tobacco we had brought, he broke into a wide toothless smile, his face collapsing into a sea of wrinkles. He appears to me to be the chief here but when I enquired of Abel whether this is so, he informed me that there is no chief.

Patilweng is situated along the banks of the Banqaru River. The village is very small, consisting of no more than 35 people, including the children. Clearly, there has been some intermarriage with the native Zulu and Basotho tribes. According to my unschooled observations, the villagers of more unadulterated Bushman stock tend towards tawnier skins, flatter faces and smaller statures than those with a greater proportion of native blood, who display browner skins, rounder eyes and burlier physiques. Despite the mixing of the blood and doubtless because of the isolation of the village, many of the old customs survive here, and the villagers speak a language akin to the ancient Bushman tongue. Their speech resounds with a range of musical clicks and clucks and it is so very strange to my ears that I can barely believe it is used to convey language. It is almost as if the speakers have little percussion instruments attached to their palates which allow them to click away in prestissimo tempo. I find it most cheerful and amusing and cannot help smiling when I hear it.

The villagers are not unused to visitors but were most surprised to see a white lady. They came out en masse to greet our caravan, the women unashamedly bare-breasted, dressed in nothing but beaded aprons and large necklaces of shell and seed, giggling when I addressed them. Of course, they didn't comprehend a word I said but Abel translated and I hope that they heard from my tone that I was friendly. There were some with babes tied to their torsos by a length of animal hide so positioned that the babes could suckle whenever the desire overtook them. Older children romped around naked and everyone appeared very carefree and happy. This despite the troubles that beset them. For in fact they are a persecuted people, squeezed from all sides by inimical forces and forced to abandon their natural nomadic life to settle here.

My spontaneous purchases on the day of my arrival came in for good use, as I had guessed they would. After my address to the villagers, the women presented me with a beautifully decorated gourd, bracelets, and a necklace crafted from plaited leather and adorned with shells. I in turn distributed the hair clips, beaded bracelets and sparkly brooches that I had bought from the Hindoo women at the harbour. At first I thought to give only to the women and girls, but when a little boy stood in front of me with large expectant eyes and outstretched hand, he and his small friends too became the recipients of some bits and bobs.

Soon thereafter I was shown to my accommodation, which compared to the villagers' quarters is the finest that such temporary living affords. My sleeping arrangements and my toilette area are most adequate and although there are no bathing facilities, the sheeting screen and watering can that Abel has rigged for my shower are a tribute to human ingenuity. I even enjoy warm water!

14

The mouthwatering smell of braaiing meat assailed Rose's nostrils as she stepped out her cottage door and headed towards the Liebers' place. The heat had turned vicious as the day lengthened and although freshly showered she already felt sticky in her floaty chiffon top and pants. A woman's laugh shrilled through the sunset calm. Rose yearned to dig her heels into the sand like a resistant dog but Hank's summons was a leash around her neck.

He stood on the terrace brandishing a two-pronged fork, every now and then poking at the braai and causing the flames to leap like dancing dragons.

'This fire's too hot,' he pronounced.

The men standing round the braai nodded sagely, their faces ruddy in the firelight, beers in hand. The raw meat soaked up marinade in a bowl alongside glass bottles filled with red-hot spices.

On the patio, the women sat round the table, dipping their hands into bowls of chips and scooping up gobbets of taramasalata, hummus and guacamole from hand-painted pottery.

'Rose! Let me introduce you . . . what can I get you to drink?' Hank was all attentiveness.

'Wine's fine, thanks. Where's Brigit?' Rose asked.

'Just putting the children to bed.'

Rose spotted Elmarie from The Olive Branch and gave an awkward wave: 'Hi, Elmarie. I'm Rose. We met at your restaurant.' She took a gulp from the wine glass someone had thrust in her hand. The wine was sour and made her mouth pucker.

'Yes, I remember you,' Elmarie nodded. 'That's my husband, Corrie, at the drinks table.' Corrie, the chef at The Olive Branch, Rose recalled. He was a little man with a handle-bar moustache, a mix between Sancho Panza and Manuel from *Faulty Towers*.

'I'm Lola Gerber. My husband's Montrose, over there in the blue shirt.'

'Lola and Montrose own the Oberon Hotel and pub,' Elmarie told Rose.

'I had a fun time there on Friday night,' Rose said, as she sat down at the table of women. 'Are you . . . both from around here?'

Lola nodded. 'Montrose's grandfather started the hotel.'

Montrose had the look. Should Rose whip out her Polaroids, pass them around and tell her story? She didn't think so. Not tonight.

'Howzit man, Tim. Help yourself to a drink,' Hank greeted the neighbour with the Alsatians. He'd left his dogs at home tonight.

One of the braai maestros slowly poured beer onto the burning wood. It protested loudly and released a cloud of white smoke into the air. The skies were darkening into evening, the place filling up.

Rose felt all at sea, unmoored, adrift, as she listened to the sounds of female voices bobbing up and down on either side of her, their words made incoherent by her disconnectedness. People stood around in groups and pairs or wandered into the garden, pebbles crunching as they trod the paths. She looked deeply into her drained glass. Pop songs from the 80s played.

Brigit and Thuli appeared, carrying platters of pale potatoes, green salad, grated carrot and pineapple, coleslaw and rolls.

Rose asked: 'Can I help with anything?'

'Everything's organised, thanks,' Brigit replied.

An ever-changing group of men hovered round the braai. They came and went, to refill, refuel, fulfil the demands of husbandly attentiveness or flirt with other men's wives. Someone thrust another glass of wine into her hand. Hank, wearing his trademark shorts, put a glistening coil of boerewors on the braai. The meat spat and sizzled, its smell hanging over the guests like a tangible thing. Gaseous gastronomy – one could already taste the burnt offerings. Platters of cooked meat made their way to squatting trivets on the table. Thuli brought out bowls of steaming pap and gravy. Men and women congregated round the table, eager for their chance with the serving spoons.

'The meat's too raw,' pronounced one of the spinster sisters, Pru or Cissy Frockian. They sat side by side, demurely sipping Coke Zeros, their skinny necks protruding from high collars.

'Put it back on the braai,' came the suggestion.

'I like my meat raw,' Hank proclaimed.

'People eat cooked food. Animals eat raw food. That's what separates us from animals,' retorted an Englishman with a greasy comb-over and goitrous eyes. He wore a blue blazer with brass buttons but in concession to South African informality, he'd left his tie at home.

'I'm an animal,' roared Hank, lunging between the two sisters from behind. He put his arms around their shoulders, bending his face close to theirs, which made them giggle into their hands.

'Are you locals? Or from out of town?' Rose asked the sisters.

'We're Oberoners, born and bred.'

'Did you ever know a Ruby Le Grange?' Her question was met with blank stares.

'Go get yourself a piece of steak, Brigit. You look like you could do with a good helping of meat,' remarked Elmarie.

'I'm a vegetarian,' Brigit told her.

'Are you on holiday here?' Rose asked the Englishman.

'Sort of. An extended holiday. I'm writing a novel.'

'Oh.' Rose was impressed. 'Is it your first?'

'Oh no. I'm a published author.'

'Will we appear in your book?' Sissy, or Pru, asked archly.

'I do love your accent. Everything you say sounds so important,' giggled the other sister.

'Can you believe some of the accents you hear on radio and TV these days? They're a joke,' someone commented.

'De -TER- mined and cir-CUM-stance.'

'In-a-VET-able. Hilarious.'

'There's a newsreader who lisps. I mean, this AA or BEE or whatever is all very well but this is just ridiculous.'

'You better get used to it. It's not going to get any better.'

'I love this time of the year,' said the neighbour with the Alsatians. 'Give me these Dog Days, anytime.'

'Actually there's no such thing as Dog Days in the southern hemisphere,' the Englishman told him.

'Why not? I thought it referred to the longest days of summer.'

'No. Dog Days are when you can see Sirius, the Dog Star. In the northern skies, it happens in summer, when the sun and the earth are in closest proximity. But in the southern hemisphere, the Dog Star can always be seen, in the night sky,' the Englishman corrected. They all walked to the edge of the deck and looked at the sky.

'There's Sirius – next to Orion.' He pointed up at the sky. 'See the three stars of Orion's belt? And that's his dagger, over there.'

The stargazers lifted their eyes to the heavens. 'Yes – I see it,' said one.

A newcomer wandered onto the deck. Rose recognised the ascetic mountaineer from the Oberon Hotel. Now here he was again. He stood at the edge of the crowd, lean and gaunt in his faded jeans, looking skywards, a drink in his hand. Was it fanatical zeal that gave his face its haunted look? Rose went to stand next to him.

'Hello. I'm Rose Clemens.' The wine had given her courage.

'Wim Metheus,' he said with a European accent.

'Where are you from?'

'The Netherlands.' Dutch courage, then.

'I saw you in the Hotel pub on Friday night. I thought you looked like a hiker.' He'd had too much midday sun. His skin was ruddy and leathery.

'Yes, I do hike.'

'For a living?'

'No. I run an Aids haven. For terminally ill patients.'

'How long have you been doing it?'

'A couple of years.'

'It must be hard, facing death on a daily basis.'

'Ja, ja.'

'Are you a medical person or involved from the management side?'

'I'm a doctor.'

'I'd like to see what you're doing there. Maybe I could visit some time?'

'Ja, ja. You're always welcome.'

He glanced at her sideways. She'd run out of conversation; smiling vaguely, she walked away and left him to his drink.

She wandered back to the main table, where she encountered the neighbour with the Alsatians. He had the right look. And he was the right age.

Her glass was brimming with wine – again. Her tongue felt thick. 'I saw you walking your dogs the other day. I'm Rose. I'm staying at the cottages.'

'He-mm,' he mumbled through a full mouth, and held up a hand in greeting.

Did you ever know a Ruby Le Grange? She couldn't bring herself to ask the question.

She reached over for a roll and tore off tissue-like pieces that dissolved on her tongue like Eucharist wafer.

Words oozed like tar from the mouths of the men sitting round the table.

'All the new developments. That huge trout-fishing monstrosity on old Tucker's land is a real eyesore. How they got it passed is a mystery.'

'It's not such a mystery.'

'Everyone wants their share of the Berg, don't you know? Ever since the white man arrived, it's been a competition.'

The first man continued: 'It's about exploiting Africa. Always has been. That's what colonialism was all about – the West trying to lay their hands on Africa's resources. Imposing their Western-style democracy . . . Why should Western-style democracy be good for Africans? Benevolent dictatorship – that's the answer for Africa.'

'There are many dictators in Africa. The problem is finding a benevolent one. The chief has always been in charge – that's the leadership style they're used to. The chief can do anything because he's accountable to no one. He's the chief.'

'Africa has its unique problems. Now the Chinese are trying to get their hands on Africa's riches. Good luck to them, I say. Fuck with Africa and you get fucked.'

'The white man's new burden – living with Afropessimism.'

'It's corruption that's going to cause this country to go the way of the rest of Africa.'

'And crime.'

'And incompetence. The place is falling to pieces because all the skilled people have left.'

'You mean all the white people have left.'

'You South Africans are so obsessed with race.' It was the Englishman who spoke now. The mood had turned as sour as the wine.

Rose felt defensive. No, we're not obsessed with race, she wanted to say. But then she thought, maybe it's true – yes, we probably are obsessed, but what can you expect? How can we forget the past so soon, considering where we've come from? You can't just sweep 300 years under the carpet.

'That's rich. Us, obsessed? You Brits are the biggest racists under the sun.'

Someone else had felt as defensive as she had.

'Under what sun? There's no sun in England.' There was derisive laughter.

The conversation mellowed again as dregs were drained and glasses freshly filled.

Rose found herself standing next to a small, round man with a pink complexion that extended all the way over his bald head to the folds at the back of his neck. He was wearing cream chinos and a tank top. 'My laptop was stolen out my car this week. I don't know what the universe is trying to tell me. I so need a hug, Maureen!' Maureen turned out to be the skinny woman with the belly ring, from the camping shop. She was dressed tonight in a strappy purple number that displayed her crêpey chest and the wrinkled skin around her axilla. She encircled the little man in her arms: 'Poor baby!' she gushed.

'Ooh, I love you. You're such a *kugel*!' he cried.

'Hello, love,' Maureen said when she saw Rose. 'How's the hat? Jem, come meet – er – what's your name?'

'Rose.'

'Hello, doll.' Jem swanned over and air-kissed Rose on both cheeks. 'You are gorgeous. I just love your outfit. Oh, there's Corrie. Have you tasted her cooking? It's divine. Totally beyondo.'

'*Her* cooking?'

'What difference? We're all gods . . . goddesses . . . he, she – it's immaterial. Am I too much for you? Just tell me – am I too much for you, darling? This weather is completely O.T.T., isn't it?' Jem wiped his forehead with the back of his hand. 'I hear you're looking for your long-lost father here,' he said. So, the word had spread. And Maureen was the catchment area for gossip. 'Do you think anyone will come clean and claim you?'

'I just want to know my roots. I don't need anything from anyone,' said Rose. 'I've inherited my adoptive parents' estates.' Her tongue flapped loosely in her mouth. She had partaken too liberally of Bacchus's fruits.

Jem closed his eyes and raised his forefinger in the air: 'If you want to know your roots, you have to be uprooted. But if you uproot a tree to know its roots, you kill the tree. You need to listen to Universe. Universe has brought you here for a purpose.'

'Oh! Come dance with me, Jem!' Maureen pulled him onto the deck, closing her eyes and rolling her hips.

Food and alcohol flowed boundlessly and the guests mingled, drawn irresistibly to each other, their appetites heightened by the spicy scents of nasturtium and marigold that rose from the dark garden, and the meat-permeated smoke that hung over them. They flirted, dancing on the deck, wafting down the garden paths and around the pond, where the gushing fountain doused the noise of their carousing. They found private places of knowledge and danger.

'Great party, hey? Hank knows how to throw a good one,' a man said to Rose as she waited for the guest loo. He propped himself against the wall with one hand and held a drink in the other.

'Are you from here?' Rose asked him.

He shook his head. 'Durban. I've got a holiday home here.'

Later, the place emptied out and meat lay forgotten, burnt to a cinder on the braai. White smoke, perfumed with charred bones and red spices, rose up into the ether to the realms of the gods, inviting them to partake of the feast. The moon hovered in the north-west. Brigit had long since gone to bed. Someone had changed the music from Hits of the 90s, and now Latin rhythms slid out from the CD player. The man from Durban caught hold of Rose, saying, 'Let's dance, Foxy Lady,' and whirled her round the deck to the torrid beat of Buena Vista Social Club, surreptitiously brushing his hand against her breast. Rose extricated herself and went to sit on the low stone wall. The stones had retained warmth from the day's heat, and it permeated pleasantly through the thin chiffon of her clothing. Her head slowly spinning in time with the galaxies, she picked out Orion, with his belt and dagger, and Betelgeuse, and Sirius, the Dogstar. She thought about the vast distance travelled by starlight before it entered the eyes, heart and imagination of the lonely dwellers on earth, and it made her sad.

'Rose is getting ready to take to the stars.' Hank had come up behind her.

'You gave me a fright,' Rose said.

'Apologies. You looked so far away.'

'This music makes me yearn for something.'

'What are you yearning for, lovely girl?'

'I don't know; love . . . recognition . . . to be able to play a musical instrument.' She laughed wistfully.

'I know what you're yearning for.'

He draped an arm casually over her shoulders and walked with her past the hot, spicy beds and the cold, wet ones; along paths where the smell of sex and death rose pungently in the cool night air and the moonlight shone white on the pebbles and burnished the leaves to silver. They continued past the gurgling fountain and through the archway with its rusted sign that said: 'He who enters this portal will partake of the fruits borne of Nature and will be nurtured by the Goddess of Truth.'

Rose stopped in her tracks and asked: 'Where is this Goddess of Truth? I want her nurturing!'

'Ah, she's here. Somewhere in these mountains. You'll find her when you're ready.'

'And the fruits?'

'They grow from the seeds of promise. Like the ones you're wearing here. On your wrist.' He brought her thong with its bright-coloured beads to his lips and kissed the inside of her wrist, making a spot that burnt white-hot. Rose trembled and her knees went weak; they walked on together into the wilderness where the path ended abruptly.

'Brigit told me to watch out for snakes,' she told him.

Hank laughed. 'And especially for me!'

They stood on the wooden platform, watching the river run metallic in the moonlight, and heard the hoot of an owl and the flurry of its wings as it took off. And all the while, the sounds of the night mingled with the Latin rhythms that trickled down to where they stood. Hank turned towards Rose and held her, ballroom fashion, moving her slowly round the small deck. She leaned her weight into his body and smelled his male smell and the acrid scent of the charred meat that had seeped into his clothes, and felt his breath, warm and moist, on her hair. A silent moan built in her throat; her blood quickened and the heat of it rose to her skin.

The music stopped. She pulled herself away, suddenly sober, suddenly shy. 'Thanks for the dance.' She mock-curtsied, her light laugh belying the heaviness she felt in her heart. 'I suppose I'd better get going . . . Brigit and I are going to the museum tomorrow and . . . we're wanting to make an early start.'

Later, as Rose lay in bed, she found herself wishing . . . yearning . . . that something more had taken place. What had Hank wanted from her? Was he just being gallant, playing the attentive knight to her lonely damsel? She deeply regretted pulling back. Rose, the shrinking violet. Pathetic.

She replayed the scene over and over in her head, her breathing quickening as she imagined how it should have ended . . . Hank kissing her, his hands moving up over her shoulders and down her back . . . over her top, then under it . . . over her breasts, her ribcage, past her waist . . . his hands feeling the contours of her body, one hand roving over her belly, then moving further down to explore the heat between her thighs . . . and the two of them sinking to the pine-covered slats . . . But that's where her imagination failed her. The music stopped, the dance ended and all that remained was a blanket of darkness under her lids that finally became the blankness of dreamless sleep.

15

Rose woke early, feeling surprisingly intact despite the shortage of sleep and the excess of alcohol. She was eager to get going on the excursion to the museum but when she called round at the Liebers, Brigit cancelled the trip.

'Rose, I'm sorry,' she told her. 'I got a call earlier – someone complaining about the bad treatment of a donkey in Mamphis. It's a black settlement near Heimat.' She looked at Rose over her shoulder. 'I might be able to do the museum later in the day but I really can't say how long this will all take.' Dressed in khaki pants and a home-knitted sweater, she was busy hauling out plastic containers, five-litre drums, wire cages and other assorted equipment from under a tarpaulin and stacking them alongside the bakkie. A young black man worked alongside her, loading up the back of the bakkie.

Rose was disappointed but didn't show it. 'Oh . . . okay. Well, have a good day,' she said. She started walking back to the cottage through the dew-damp foliage, thinking to herself that maybe it was just as well that she wasn't going. Snake in the grass – that was her. She was feeling a little guilt-ridden this morning, about her and Hank's little samba number on the deck; in the cold light of day, her hanky-panky fantasy seemed pathetic.

'Rose!' Brigit called, 'wait!'

Rose stopped.

'Why don't you come along to Mamphis with us?'

Rose hesitated; she hadn't actually done anything wrong . . . had she? 'Okay,' she said. 'As long as . . . I won't be in your way, will I?'

'Not at all. Hop in. We'll be leaving in a few minutes. This is Michael, my helper and translator.' Michael and Rose did the three-part handshake: shake, clasp, shake, with Michael positioning his left palm under his right elbow, in the respectful way.

The air was cool, the sky overcast as they drove out of Oberon on the Heimat road. Rose sat up front with Brigit, Michael in the back of the double-cab.

Brigit drove confidently along the country roads. 'You were asking where black people live? You'll see now. Many of them stay in villages like the one where we're going. It's a pretty basic sort of life.'

'And middle-class black people? What about them? Do they live in Oberon itself?' 'They'. Rose squirmed, realising they had excluded Michael completely from their conversation.

'I don't know, to be honest.'

'Where do you live, Michael?' Rose turned round to look at him, hoping her question would downplay her *faux pas*.

'I stay in Oberon, in the back of someone's place.'

'Well, there you go,' said Brigit easily.

The bakkie's odometer rolled over and the signs of human activity diminished as the fences and cultivated pockets of pine and eucalyptus gave way to increasingly wild and rocky terrain. Gulleys and gorges had been rudely gouged out by nature's extremes. The land fell away dramatically, now to the right, now to the left of the road. Peaks rose so steeply that they were only visible if Rose craned her head, bird-like, to look up and pressed her nose to the window. As on her journey down to Oberon, she felt as if she had been deposited back in time. The ribbon of road ahead and the electric power lines above were all that linked the travellers to the present.

Rose could see Brigit's profile from the corner of her eye. She looked serious, her mouth set in a firm line. Can she sense my feelings about

Hank? Rose wondered. They walked on parallel paths, Brigit and Hank. But, no – that wasn't fair. How could Rose know that?

She couldn't get him out of her mind this morning. He lingered there, coiled and ready to spring to the forefront of her thoughts whenever there was a gap. Hank. He was one of those men who just loved women, who made you feel beautiful and brilliant, laughed appreciatively at your every quip, undressed you with his eyes and stroked your ego. Brigit must know that. She had also succumbed to his charms, once. Surely she must see how he flirts? thought Rose. She knows how I feel and she pities me. She's been through it all so many times before. She wouldn't have invited me today if she felt threatened.

'Here we are,' Brigit said as they rounded a bend. Two rondavels appeared and Brigit slowed and pulled up on the road verge, the bakkie groaning and squealing as its tyres negotiated the unevenness of the course.

The village of Mamphis sprawled before them. Rose was surprised to see its extent. It spread all the way down to the river and up again on the other side, as far as the eye could see. Adobe dwellings and various indeterminate structures showed between the vegetation that grew lush in the valley. Here and there a tin roof flashed like an SOS. Human life was stirring among the dwellings; women ambled along the paths, some carrying water drums on their heads and children on their backs, their clothing bright in the muted, misty landscape.

They drove on again, along dirt roads carved out of the mountainside. Brigit swerved to avoid black water that stagnated in ruts and chickens that hopped and fluttered across the path at the rumble of their engine. She drove slowly, giving pedestrians time to move aside. Through her open window, she greeted them: '*Sanibona.*' Some responded amicably but others looked at her expressionlessly.

As they drove, Brigit explained to Rose that her NGO focused mainly on education and training, imparting information to help communities take better care of their animals. But sometimes people called them in when they saw animals being mistreated. She and Michael were well known here and trusted by many of the villagers.

'But we have to watch out – the other animal welfare agencies don't like us stepping on their turf,' she said. 'We had to be very careful with our name . . . we call ourselves PAW – Protecting Animals' Wellbeing. We do try to avoid competing for funding with the established animal welfare agencies, but the funding pot is limited and when we hold our fundraisers in the surrounding towns we're often vying for the same donors.'

Rose wondered how one went about applying for funding. And did Brigit pay herself a salary? She must. How much did she pay herself? Who assessed what her worth was? Rose felt quite ignorant about how it all worked.

She decided she'd make a generous donation to Brigit's cause as soon as she could access her bank account. Anonymously, of course.

'I don't want to diminish what the other organisations do,' Brigit continued. 'They do a fantastic job, but I think there's room for everyone. It's a pity some people feel so threatened by us. We're such a puny operation compared with the some of the others. It's sad how politics always comes into play.'

'Even when people are trying to do good,' Rose said.

'Absolutely. And there's never enough that can be done.'

Rose was awed by Brigit; she was such a go-getter. That energy of hers – how did one even start something like this? She gazed out the window, reading a handwritten sign that hung above the opening of a corrugated iron shack: 'VEGETABLES HAIRBRAIDING CELLPHONE CALLS – R3'.

There was a stall next to the shack made from warped planks and crooked poles. Tomatoes, potatoes and cabbages were piled high on the makeshift counter. Nearby, goats and chickens foraged for scraps and discarded vegetables. A thick black electrical cable looped between counter and the bonnet of a battered lime-green Mazda that looked as if it had taken root in the long grass. A woman wearing a bright orange turban stood inside the stall. She spoke animatedly on a cell phone and waved distractedly as they passed.

Brigit slowly followed the curving road. 'Okay, we need to find the donkey and his driver. He's the local 'moving' man – you know, if you have furniture or something heavy to move, you hire him. His poor old animal is apparently a bag of bones, sores all over.'

Ugh. Rose didn't feel like being exposed to the suffering of the donkey. Or to suffering of any sort, for that matter. She could remain in the bakkie, looking straight ahead. But avoiding truths because they were too ugly to confront was the worst kind of self-indulgence. What would happen if everyone hid behind their tender-heartedness? She wanted to make a difference, but without sullying her sensitive soul. She watched a scrawny grey dog trot alongside them, his head slung low. He veered into the grass and disappeared.

A woman sat at the side of road, large and solid, crouching alongside a gas-cooker that balanced on a sturdy piece of cardboard raised off the ground with bricks at each corner.

Michael tapped Brigit on the shoulder. 'Let's ask this aunty if she's seen him.'

Brigit stopped the bakkie and Michael hopped out.

He was agile and lean; nice-looking. He loped over to the woman, who was busy frying clumps of dough that she broke off from a solid grey mass and dropped into a fryer. The pieces of dough bobbed merrily in the bubbling oil, releasing oily steam into the air.

Rose watched as the woman and Michael chatted agreeably. Presently, Michael returned holding three doughnuts – glistening, oil-laden spheres coated in crystals of sugar. Michael gestured for Rose to open her window and take his offering. The doughnut was hot in her hand; she closed her eyes, breathing in its fresh, doughy fragrance and sank her teeth into the crispy crust. It was delicious.

‘She said she hasn’t seen him today, so maybe we should pass by his house and ask there,’ Michael said. He pointed in the direction of the river: ‘It’s right down in the valley.’

They drove down the mountain towards the river, where the mist continued to hover as if concealing a secret.

‘I think it’s this one.’ Michael indicated a rondavel. Brigit stopped and the three of them alighted. There were sounds of hysterical barking coming from the back. On a hard-swept yard, a tawny dog tied to a stump broke into a fresh frenzy of barking at their approach, slavering at the mouth, pulling on his chain, jumping up on his hind legs. He was thin and mangy, his ears gnawed ragged by flies. The place stank with his faeces that lay a chain’s length away, causing great excitement for a swarm of bluebottle flies. Brigit shook her head in disgust.

Michael walked back to the bakkie and returned carrying a plastic ice-cream container filled with water. He placed it on the ground, within the dog’s reach. The animal sniffed at it suspiciously then began to lap thirstily.

‘We’ve learnt to carry our own water with us,’ Brigit explained to Rose. ‘The only public tap is miles away. There’s the river, but that’s pretty dirty and a long walk. Most of these people don’t know about regular water for their animals. We’re trying to change that.’

The doorway to the hut was open. The entrance was low and they had to duck to enter. Rose had never been inside a hut like this, made entirely from baked earth: an adobe abode. Her eyes had to adjust to its darkness, her nose to the earthy, yeasty smells of wood, smoke and fermenting milk. The interior was very cool, quite chilly, in fact. The floors were made of hardened dung. In the centre, there was a pile of white ashes in a hearth and, at knee-height around the walls, a continuous bench fashioned from clay. On this structure, Rose saw a woman lying. She was bundled up in a grey blanket, curled up in a foetal position. She twisted her head to look at the newcomers, her eyes big and blank in her gaunt face. She seemed so pathetic that Rose could barely look at her.

'Ask her where the donkey man is,' Brigit said brusquely.

Michael translated. The woman made no response but continued to stare at them.

'Can you see any water in here?' Brigit's voice was sharp.

They looked around the hut. There was not much to see, save for a stack of cardboard suitcases and a few clay vessels on a shelf. Brigit turned to Rose: 'You see how it is here. There's probably not enough water in the place for this woman's needs, let alone the dog's.'

Michael left the hut, carrying one of the clay vessels and returned with it, now filled. He went to the woman, raised her into a sitting position and put the vessel to her lips. She sipped slowly, and when she'd had enough, he lowered her, placing the clay jug on the floor next to her.

The three of them walked in silence back to the car. The cloud cover of earlier had dissipated and the sun shone brightly. Rose shrugged off her cardigan before getting back into the bakkie. Brigit re-ignited the engine and drove slowly down the road. How can you worry about dogs when the people here are so needy? Rose wanted to ask, but stopped herself. She worried that her words would sound too critical of someone she desired to befriend.

'Don't you ever feel like stepping in to help these poor people?' she said instead.

Brigit responded: 'There are lots of people doing things with the community. My thing is to help animals, to alleviate animal suffering.'

They came to a clearing amid the jumble of dwellings. A queue of women, bearing all manner of containers in their arms and on their heads, snaked into the road. They stood patiently in the hot sun, many with babies on their backs, waiting their turn at the tap. Small, dusty children wove in and out between the women's legs or occupied themselves with sticks or whatever else the hardscrabble environment offered up in the way of play material. The very little ones were half naked, wearing only faded vests that stretched tightly across their pot bellies.

Brigit turned to Michael. 'Won't you fill that extra ten-litre drum?' she said. 'We may as well take advantage while the water's available.' She said to Rose: 'This area seems to be one of the last in the country to benefit from the government's social upliftment programmes. No piped water, no electricity, no housing.'

'Why is that, do you think?' Rose asked.

Brigit shrugged. 'I couldn't say. It could be that it's too far off the beaten track, so it falls under the radar. Or politics, maybe. But I'm just guessing.'

Michael took the drum and went to stand in the queue of women and children. He greeted them with his disarming, charming smile and they made room for him obligingly. It wasn't long before he returned.

Brigit turned the bakkie around and started back towards the hut. The village was fully awake now. Men, young and old, had emerged into the sunlight to gather, loiter and laugh or sit, smoking, on big drums that had once contained sunflower-seed oil or paraffin. Some wore leather jackets and loafers and spoke on cell phones, while others were shabbily dressed in faded pants and patched shirts. School children moved in leisurely packs towards the school, skinny legs poking out of black gymslips or grey shorts. To Rose's surprise, many of the kids spoke on cell phones, too. It was amazing how the technology had filtered through to even the most impoverished areas.

As they rounded a bend in the road, they saw the donkeyman's outline on the horizon. He sat high atop his wagon, which was piled with a huge load of sticks; firewood from the forest. Brigit sped up to him as if he might suddenly vanish, braking sharply, so that donkey and bakkie stood nose to nose. She and Michael alighted.

Rose stayed where she was, watching Brigit address the man, her manner belligerent. I actually can't bear to witness this, thought Rose.

But then her curiosity got the better of her and she got out, too, leaning against the bakkie, her folded arms meant to convey that she was an outsider, an impartial observer.

'*Sawubona*, Missus.' The man dismounted slowly from the rickety wagon, using his stick to steady himself. He was old and decrepit, with a sparse, white beard. He wore a shapeless felt hat and what looked like a potato sack, with holes cut out for the neck and arms. His bare legs protruded from the sack, skinny and dusty. Sackcloth and ashes: what might he have to repent?

The sun was now intense and burning Rose's crown. She wished she'd brought her newly purchased hat. She poked around in her bag for her tortoise-shell hair-clip and clipped her hair up.

'We got a complaint about you . . . how you treat this animal.' Brigit laid her hand on the beast's rump. He stood patiently, his back curving from the weight of age and too many heavy loads. Michael translated Brigit's words.

'No, Missus. I treat *imbongolo* well,' the man replied in English. He tapped the animal on its rump with his stick as he spoke. The donkey didn't react.

'He says he treats it well,' Michael told Brigit.

'Yes, I heard him,' Brigit replied irritably.

Brigit pointed to the suppurating sores on the beast's bony back. Rose averted her gaze, feeling her stomach turn over. 'No, look here . . .' Brigit's metal spectacle frames glinted fiercely in the sun. 'These are very bad. They're infected.' She turned to Michael: 'I think maybe we should ask the vet to take a look.'

An old couple came shuffling by, dressed as if for church. The man wore a baggy blue suit, shiny with age and the woman a blue dress with a starched white Peter Pan collar. They stopped to hear what was going on.

Michael was applying disinfectant to the angry wounds with cotton wool. Three schoolgirls walking arm in arm had sauntered up and stood looking on, leaning on each other and giggling. A middle-aged woman, deciding this was as good a place to rest as any, had deposited her cabbage-filled bags and was watching the proceedings with interest.

'These sores are very bad. If you don't treat them with this medicine we're giving you, your donkey will die – do you understand?' said Brigit, while Michael translated. He demonstrated how to apply first the disinfectant and then the ointment, explaining all the while the consequences of neglect.

'It's the white man's medicine. Don't trust it. It will kill your donkey.' The speaker of these words sported a headband and bracelets made of animal skins, and a faded green T-shirt with a picture of Bob Marley. He, like the donkeyman, spoke in English, presumably for Brigit's benefit. 'The white witch wants to kill your donkey.'

'These people believe in traditional treatments, not Western medicine,' Michael commented to Rose.

'That's a lie, old man,' cried another. 'The white medicine works. I know. I gave it to my sick goat and he lives still.'

Brigit directed another severe look at the donkeyman from behind her glasses. 'This animal needs to rest – he won't get better otherwise.'

'No, Missus! How must I eat if the donkey doesn't work?' He leant on his stick sullenly and shook his head.

By now a small crowd had gathered to witness the proceedings.

Brigit turned to Rose. 'This animal should be put out to pasture at its age but since it's the donkeyman's livelihood, it'll work until it drops.'

Rose nodded uncomfortably. Brigit's bossy tone was making her cringe.

'Look –' Brigit said to the donkeyman, 'I'm coming back in a week to check if these sores are healing. If the animal is not better when I come back, I'm going to call the police. They'll take the animal to the hospital and you'll have to pay a big fine.'

Michael translated and a woman from the crowd repeated: 'Ja, you'll pay the fine!'

'You can come to me for the loan, old man,' a dapper man in a tan suit offered smoothly, giving the schoolgirls a sideways glance.

Brigit stood with legs astride and arms folded over her chest, glaring fiercely at the donkeyman. 'Why's he so thin? You don't feed him enough. You must feed your donkey.'

'He must go to jail. He killed his wife because he didn't want to feed her and now he's killing his donkey.'

'What must he do? He's a poor man. We're all poor men. We can't take food away from the people to give to our animals.'

'And your dog! Tied up in your yard. Why doesn't he have water?' Brigit ranted on.

'No, Missus. I give him water.'

'It's cruel to keep him tied up in the sun all day with no water to drink. How would you like that? To be tied up in the hot sun with no water?'

'No Missus, I'm a man. He's a dog.' The donkey man cackled, exposing his toothless gums.

The crowd laughed, too. 'Tie him up in the yard, like a dog. Ja – tie him up.'

'He says his dog is only a dog,' Michael translated needlessly.

'But the dog is a living thing, like you. He gets thirsty. He needs water to drink. And shade. You can't keep him in the hot sun all day like that. You must build a shelter for him. I will give you a piece of shade cloth and poles.'

'*Eish*. Now we must build a house for the dog,' someone jeered.

'We all want the cloth. We all want to build the dog houses,' someone else called.

'They all want shade cloth now,' Michael said.

Brigit raised her voice to address the crowd. 'Isn't that right? If you've got a dog – any animal – you need to look after it. Animals must always have clean water to drink. Just like people. And they can't be left all day tied up in the hot sun. It's cruel.'

Yes. Yes. No. No. Some agreed, others dissented. Their voices rose in dissonance.

'When I come back next week, I'm going to check on your dog, too, that he's got water and shade.'

Brigit got back into the bakkie, Rose and Michael following, and the crowd started dispersing. The donkeyman remained standing beside his donkey, looking surly.

'The onlookers seemed very interested in the whole drama,' Rose remarked as they drove away.

'That's our *modus operandi*. It's all very informal. Michael comes in and visits, talking to the chicken sellers and goat owners or whoever, pointing out cruel practices and explaining how they can look after their livestock better.'

Rose wondered how these people viewed Brigit, her intrusiveness, her whiteness. It seemed as if they didn't take her as seriously as she would have liked. Rose felt sorry for her. 'Do they listen?' she asked.

'It's slow – a battle – but it has its rewards. We do see changes in attitudes. And when we come across abuse, we threaten prosecution. You heard, with the donkey man. And we carry out the threat, too, if they continue to treat their animals badly.'

'These people's lives are so hard. Maybe their suffering hardens them. They have such problems of their own that they can't worry too much about their animals,' Rose said tentatively.

'I don't feel guilty about them being prosecuted. It's my job to make sure the animals are well looked after. It's what I do and I'm comfortable with it. I can't let poverty be an excuse for the abuse of animals. Would you let their hardship be an excuse for woman or child abuse?'

'That's true.' Rose hesitated then said: 'Is it not maybe a cultural thing?'

'Absolutely not! You can't paint abuse as an "African thing". Cruelty to animals is a world-wide phenomenon. I go into the black areas because that's my job but don't think that cruelty to animals doesn't happen in the white areas – it does. There's just as much barbaric treatment of animals by whites as there is by blacks.'

Rose nodded her head placatingly. It sounded as if Brigit had had to justify her stance many times before. She spoke vehemently, almost defensively. For Rose, it was all so new. She'd never thought about any of these issues. Once again, it struck her what a sheltered existence she'd been leading, comfortably shielded from exposure to realities that weren't so pleasant to confront. Time to get real, she told herself. You're living in Africa; no – you're living in the world. Time to take off those rose-coloured spectacles!

Soon, they were on their way back to Oberon. Rose stifled a yawn, wondering if Brigit still intended taking her to the museum. She hoped not. She felt quite drained from the morning's events and not in the mood for more outings.

'Do you mind if we don't do the museum trip today?' Brigit asked, as if reading her mind. 'It'll be late by the time we get back and I have so much to do still.'

'No, that's fine,' Rose said in relief. 'We can do it another day.' She couldn't wait to flop onto her bed and read. Maybe she would go on her own tomorrow.

Checking her cell phone, she saw there was an sms from Ronald: *Hi Rose – Irish pub night in Heimat. Live singer. Come along. Meet at Oberon Hotel 6.15. Ron.*

Come along. Sounded like something casual, a group activity – not a date or anything. Should she go? She felt much too weary to think about it. She held the decision over for later.

When Rose returned to her cottage, the door was open and the worn-down pumps placed neatly side by side next to the mat. The red stoep shone like cattle hide in the skittering sunlight. Entering the cottage, Rose found Happiness on her hands and knees, wiping the floor.

'Hello, Happiness. How's your child?' Rose asked, sidling past her.

'She's much better,' Happiness answered. Sitting back on her haunches, she slowly immersed a cloth in a bucket and slowly wrung it out. Then she resumed her slow, circular wiping.

'That's good.' Rose sank down on the couch in the living area, now pleasantly cool in the shaded light that filtered through the small, fussily dressed window. The tortoise-shell clip was biting into her scalp. She took it off and shook out her hair. Relief. She picked up a *Getaway* magazine and flipped through it without interest: 'Bushwhacking in Botswana'; 'Discover the Karoo'. How long would the floor-wiping take? Rose was desperate for Happiness to leave. The soft, yielding duvet beckoned like a Siren – but she didn't want Happiness to witness her bedding down in broad daylight. It would make her feel too guilty.

She thought about Ronald's invitation, wondering if she should accept. She didn't feel like going out at the moment but she might, just later.

Happiness lingered in the kitchen, wiping in the same slow-motion way the surfaces of the counter, fridge, microwave and sink area, humming tunelessly as she worked.

Oh, come on! I haven't touched anything in there – it's all spotless, Rose wanted to say.

'What was wrong with your child?' she asked instead.

'Sangoma told me it was her blood. There was something bad in the blood. She gave me something to clean the blood.'

God. A traditional healer cleaning the blood. It sounded ominous.

Happiness moved towards Rose and started tidying around her, neatening the cushions on the couch where Rose sat, straightening the magazines, spraying cleaning fluid here and there and wiping the table, the glass ashtray, the silver tray, the almost empty bottle of sherry. There was something mesmerising about the way she wiped. Round and round – as if she were performing some magical ritual. And her continuous humming – like an ancient incantation. It really irritated Rose.

Still she lingered, standing right in front of Rose. What now? Rose thought. Does she want to clean under my feet? She prepared to lift them up.

'Sangoma had a dream about you . . . about the white woman in the place I'm working,' Happiness finally said.

Rose looked up: 'Really? What does that mean?' She gave a nervous giggle.

'It means your ancestors have a message for you. You must come to see sangoma. She wants to see you.'

Charlatan. She'd dreamt up the ancestor story for the gullible white woman who doles out hundred rand notes.

'Where is she?'

'In my village. You must come with me next time. I'll take you to her.'

Rose's interest was piqued. She was keen to go. She wanted to see a sangoma at work. She would try to keep an open mind. And who knew? Maybe the woman had answers for her.

'When will you go, do you think?'

'I'll ask when my next "off" is. I will tell you, then you'll come with me.' Happiness collected up her cleaning equipment and left.

Finally. Rose kicked off her shoes and collapsed on her bed. It felt chilly in the room so she slipped in under the duvet. Looking up at the blue square of skylight above her head, she thought about what information her ancestors might have to tell her. Turning onto her side, she soon fell asleep.

13th October 1880

The villagers here are exceedingly hospitable. They invite me to share their meals but thus far I have politely refused, as the menu requires a hardiness of constitution that I do not possess. In addition to the small antelope such as duiker and steenbuck that roam these parts, the plat du jour frequently features porcupine, mongoose, tortoise, snake, monkey and insect—in fact anything and everything that grows, crawls, hops and slithers.

Fortunately, dear Uncle forgot none of the perquisites demanded by civilised living. Thank goodness for the provisions we brought along! Now I do not even notice the weevils in the biscuits and crunch away at them as happily as the villagers, who are fascinated by my English fare. They especially enjoy the items prepared with refined flour and white sugar, such as the scones that Abel whips up.

I have been learning a little of the Bushman way of life, which is not as burdensome as in days of yore, when the only meat eaten was that which was hunted by bow and arrow. These days the villagers also keep cattle and goats, which they resort to slaughtering when game is scarce. Their diet is supplemented by things of the veldt, which it is the women's task to gather. They also cultivate maize which they grind into flour and cook into a type of porridge, eaten by scooping it up with the fingers. This last I have dared to sample, finding it somewhat insipid for my taste.

The men are adept at handcraft. They use stone tools to fashion spear tips and are skilled at carving out beads and other adornments from the bones left over from their repast. Mention must be made that the glass beads, mined from the trinkets that I brought along, have newly found their way onto the leather thongs used for bracelets, necklaces and anklets.

These villagers are a sociable people who delight in communal storytelling around the fire. As I sit writing this at the small table set up in my tent, night has fallen, and I can hear the babble and the appreciative laughter that the stories evoke among both tellers and audience.

16

Rose arrived punctually at the arranged meeting point at the hotel parking lot, to find Ronald already there, with Petra in the front seat of his car. So, it wasn't a date then. Rose was relieved.

It was a mission to fold herself into the back of his car. It was an old two-door coupé and she had to bend and twist her limbs awkwardly to avoid the thick, black oil that glistened around the door catch.

As they drove down the main street in the light of dusk, Heimat appeared no more charming or lively than on Rose's previous visit. At Swallows in the Field coffee-shop and pub, several cars were parked at odd angles on the sloping verge, testifying to some human activity, at least. And, unlike on her previous visit, the field that formerly had been inert as Astroturf was now aquiver with thousands of swallows fluttering above it. They streamed about the cottage in a constant draught of restless activity, as if there were a swallow metropolis under the eaves.

The pub was full and noisy. A singer sat on a barstool in the corner. She wore a granny-print dress and had long, wavy hair that brushed against her guitar as she sang, haunting folk melodies in a voice as sweet as honey. Was that why it was billed as an Irish evening?

Tables, chairs and couches had been crammed haphazardly into the small space. Rose and friends found room on a couch.

'What will you have?' asked the waitress, a pixie of a girl with short, spiky hair.

'You'll have to have a Guinness, seeing it's an Irish night,' Ronald said.

Rose nodded amiably, inspecting the customers in the murky light. They all looked very ethno-bongo: bearded men in Madiba shirts and sandals; blowsy women in print dresses and African beads.

'Where did all these people pop up from? The village looked so deserted when we drove through,' Rose said.

'From around, I suppose.' Petra scanned the crowd in the dim room. 'Oh, this is fun – we have the Cult of the Goddess here tonight.' She looked fresh and crisp in her jeans and white shirt, brown hair tied back to accentuate her round face. A nice face, Rose thought: regular features, clear skin and well-shaped eyes.

'What's the "Cult of the Goddess"?' Rose asked with interest, thinking of the White Goddess.

'New Age garbage,' Ronald said.

'But what are they? Like a coven of witches or something?'

'Nothing like that. It's just what I call this bunch. I always avoid them if I can,' Petra said dismissively.

'So what's been happening since we last saw you, Rose?' Ronald asked, changing the subject. He took a long swig of his Guinness.

'Not much. I went with Brigit Lieber to Mamphis this morning. Do you know that she runs an NGO called PAW, to do with animal welfare?'

Ronald and Petra shook their heads. Rose continued: 'I think she's doing amazing work, despite all the obstacles she faces. Like – she's always having to justify her position. People ask her why she pays so much attention to animals when the people are so poor and needy.'

'I agree with them. People's needs *are* more important,' Ronald said firmly.

Deep down, Rose thought he was right, but she still couldn't help feeling irked that he failed to see the value in Brigit's work.

'I think it's important that animals are taken care of, too,' Petra responded. 'Isn't that supposed to be the sign of a humane and civilised society?'

'Hitler took great care of his dogs. He had a dog called Blondi that slept in his bed,' Ronald said.

'Is this seat taken?' A large woman in a flowing dress, with hair like a wheat field, floated up to them. Rose bounced a little in her seat as the woman sat down heavily next to her.

'Hi, I'm Sue,' she said, smiling at Rose.

'Rose . . . and this is Petra. And Ronald.'

But the woman's attention was elsewhere. 'Hello, girlfriend – I just love your cardigan,' she greeted a skinny woman walking past. The cardigan was very pretty – a hand-knitted creation in soft limes and pinks, very designer. Girlfriend pulled up a chair and sat down, too. Soon, a circle of women had gathered around the couch. Ronald, nonplussed to be the only male, gravitated to the bar.

Rose and Petra eavesdropped as the women nattered on about their children's various achievements and their specialised diets; whether Montessori or home schooling was the way to go; the advantages of home birthing, and where to find a doula.

'What's a doula?' Rose whispered to Petra, who shrugged her shoulders.

'There's a great organic food market in Cottam that sells homemade wooden toys. I don't believe in plastic, it causes cancer,' one woman said.

'Beth refuses to play with wooden toys. She's such a girlie girl, although she loves the horses.' This was Girlfriend speaking. She emphasised the word 'loves', stretching it out like toffee. Turning to Rose and Petra, she told them: 'We breed horses. Me and my man.'

She looked quite horsey herself. 'Where are you from?' Rose asked.

'Cape Town. Both of us are. I met my hub at a meeting . . . we were both into struggle politics in a big way. He walked into the room and I said, "I'm going to marry you".' She laughed, displaying lots of gum. 'Well, actually, we're still not married but we do live together. With our daughter, Beth. We have such a deep relationship, we don't need a piece of paper to seal our bond. Every night we sit on the edge of our bed and say what's made us sad, what's made us glad, what's made us bad, and what's made us mad today. It's like this totally safe space where we can talk about our feelings without fear of judgement.'

'Before my wedding, I'm going to do a womanhood celebration, with my girlfriends. We're all going to the field and we're going to hold hands and say what it means to be a woman,' another of the group pronounced, her eyes shining.

Girlfriend said: 'I'll say, to be a woman is to change the world for the better. We're going to make it, like, a female space. Long live girl-power!' She raised her fist in the air.

'I'll say, to be a woman is to know the Power of the Goddess,' the wheatfield woman called Sue proclaimed in a loud and resonant voice. 'What would you say?' she asked Rose.

'God . . . you've put me on the spot. To be a woman . . . er . . .' Rose felt obliged to come up with something. 'Er . . . to be a woman is to be a . . . er . . . is to nurture life.' She felt relieved that she'd said something, even if it was trite.

'What would you say?' Sue turned to Petra, who had been determinedly keeping a low profile. Petra smiled with feigned sweetness but said nothing.

'What exactly is the Power of the Goddess?' Rose wanted to know.

'What it says. We are all Goddesses. I am Gaia – Earth Goddess. We worship the great Goddesses – like Athena, Aphrodite, Demeter. We believe that each of us has the Goddess within. You, too, Rose. You need to find your inner Goddess so that your inner Truth can be revealed,' Sue proclaimed.

Did Hank know these women? Hank with his rusty plaque that cited the Goddess of Truth? Did he also belong to the Cult of the Goddess? Rose laughed to herself at the thought. If they weren't already acquainted, she'd have to introduce him to these women.

Hank. She looked at the door, suddenly wishing he'd walk through it. He'd see her and come and sit next to her, his thigh brushing against hers, and she'd feel its heat and without any words she would stand up and he would follow her and they would exit the bar into the dark of the night . . .

'Who would you model yourself on?' Sue was asking Rose.

'Er . . . Pandora?' she said uncertainly.

'Well I suppose you could be her. Pandora was originally an all-giving Goddess – until some male chauvinist decided she was actually mortal and must be blamed for all the troubles in the world. But you look more like you could be Artemis, the Virgin Goddess, the Huntress who is also friend to all small creatures.' She turned her back on Rose, who was thinking: Wow! That was quite insightful . . . though the huntress bit, she wasn't so sure about.

Sue addressed the others: 'So what time are we meeting tomorrow?'

'Didn't we say 8.00? After we finish with children?' Girlfriend replied.

Sue explained to Rose: 'We're going to stand in this field outside here to stop the planes from taking off. There's a landing strip on it.' She waved her hand in the vague direction of the field. 'But there are two thousand swallows that nest in that field, and the noise of the planes is stressing them out. We've spoken nicely to the farmer to please move his landing strip but he refuses, so now is the time for action.'

'But won't you also be disturbing the poor swallows? Standing all over their field like that?' Petra asked with a guileless expression.

Sue looked at her witheringly and stood up: 'Well, must have an early night.' And she flounced out the door.

On the way home Rose and Petra related the conversation to Ronald.

'They take themselves so seriously, those women. I just can't stand their holier-than-thou attitudes,' Petra said. 'And they've worked on themselves so much. In fact, they are just so into themselves. Did any of them ask you one question about yourself, Rose? They think they're these, like, domestic goddesses but really they're just domestic drudges – like their great grandmothers. What's changed?'

Rose felt bad. Had she asked Petra one question about herself? Now she couldn't. It would be too obvious. Next time, though. Next time she would definitely ask her about herself. She'd make a point of inviting her somewhere just so that she could ask her questions. But not tonight.

14th October 1880

Today I accompanied some of the women as they gathered plants in the veldt. I was given a kaross apron to tie around my waist, wherein I was to place leaves, berries and bulbs. I came under the supervision of three young ones who took me under their wings. I pointed to myself and slowly articulated my name. Then I gestured to each of them in turn, saying, 'What...is...your...name?' I had to repeat this a few times before they laughed and pointed to themselves, sounding their names. I heard the first two as Kantla and Bey. I will call them Katy and Beth. The last name proffered was very long and I only managed to catch the first two or three syllables—Conquo—Conquolo. So I have named her Connie.

It fell upon my three new friends, Katy, Beth and Connie to point out the nutritious plant species to me. Whenever I was about to gather one of the inedible varieties they would shake their heads most emphatically.

We pulled water-roots from the shady banks of a river and gathered wild spinach growing in abundance in a patch of sunlight, which we plucked by the handful. There was also bitter melon in season and a type of fruit growing upon a tree, its sighting causing much excited chatter. After a time, I left them to their task and found a rock on which to settle and sketch.

We returned in the late afternoon to find a ragtag band of men arrived with ponies and cattle in tow. They are a filthy lot of ruffians and rogues, representing the wide spectrum of race that exists in this country: Boer, Bushman, native, half-caste and Hottentot. Their skin tones range from yellow to tawny to brown to chocolate and it is difficult to classify them. What business they can have in Patilweng I cannot imagine.

The leader of the group is a man called Hannes Lieber, of Boer extraction. He is a swarthy, bearded giant of a man—possibly the lowest class of white man I have ever had the misfortune to meet. His men leered at us rudely as we passed their encampment, which I am unhappy to report they have set up in close proximity to mine! Most distressing.

I heard one of them make an unspeakable comment, whereupon I picked up the hem of my gown and with as much dignity as I could muster, stalked into my tent. The effect was somewhat lost as I had to bend low upon entering its doorway.

She was becoming accustomed to the light flooding the room at dawn and the peacock's mewls piercing her dreams. She rose later these days, so that by the time she was ready to make her way to the main house, it was nearly eight.

On the patch of lawn outside her cottage, she lingered to watch some Hadedas gracefully settling at the top of the pine, honking loudly. The voices of the Lieber children wafted from the house on the fresh morning breeze. Rose had decided that today she was going to visit the museum, come what may. If Brigit was unavailable, she would go alone.

Happiness stood on duty in her bare feet when Rose entered the breakfast room.

'Do you want eggs?' Happiness asked, bringing her a pot of coffee.

'No, don't worry, thanks. Is Brigit around?'

'No. She went out this morning. Early.'

Rose helped herself to coffee. 'Did you ask her when you can go off again?'

'No. She will tell me.'

Rose thought it a little unfair that Brigit did not inform her staff in advance as to when they could go off.

The metallic jangle of the phone interrupted her thoughts.

Happiness answered then called out: 'Mr Hank!'

Rose's stomach gave a little lurch as she heard his footsteps approaching down the passage.

'Morning, morning. Morning, Rose.'

She watched his back view as he spoke on the phone, nodding and shaking his head intermittently. It was the first time she had seen him wearing long pants; his legs rose like pillars from his brogues to his buttocks, which formed two solid mounds under the khaki. Next time I'm not going to withdraw from his advances, Rose thought. Why had she held back? Was she a slave to some puritanical streak . . . or just committed to common decency . . . the sanctity of marriage? In this day and age, wasn't that naïve? She wasn't experienced enough to judge. The rhythms of human interaction played around her but she didn't know its rules.

Finishing his call, Hank helped himself to coffee and sat down heavily on the chair opposite her. 'Bang go my plans for today. I had some tourists booked to do a flip of the Berg but they've cancelled. Husband has gippo guts.'

'That could be a bit awkward in a small plane,' Rose smiled. She looked down at the pattern of toast crumbs on her plate. Say it, she told herself. Have the guts. Say it now.

'Why don't you take me instead?' she asked casually. 'I'd love to see the Berg from the air. You could add your . . . fee . . . to my account.'

'Great idea! Do you have a warm jacket? It's freezing in the cockpit,' Hank said.

15th October 1880

It seems I have misjudged my neighbours. Abel informed me that these men are traders. They linger here a while, resting their cattle before moving on. "And what do they trade?" I asked in my ignorance. "Cattle and horses," he answered. "But what can the villagers possibly have to trade in return?" I pursued. He told me that they provide grazing and a place to kraal the stock and hide out till the heat dies down.

It transpires that the men are stock raiders, outlaws, on the run from the Mounted Rifles and Commandos that have been set up to curtail these activities. I was alarmed, assuming the inevitable character traits that go with such activities and wanting nothing whatsoever to do with this band of outlaws.

However, when Mr Lieber paid a call on me the other night, I was led to change my opinion of him. He is in fact most charming—what you might call a rough diamond. Bowing with mock courtesy, he invited me to accompany him and his men on a hunt tomorrow. I hesitated before assenting, wondering what English society would think of my gadding about unchaperoned through the countryside with these bandits. Would I be safe? Would my virtue remain intact? I met his long steely look with a steady gaze and decided I could look after myself.

They drove along the now familiar Heimat Road. The bakkie smelt of hot car seats and damp carpets. Rose tried focusing on the passing scenery but the intimacy created by the confines of the vehicle heightened her self-consciousness. She was aware of his maleness, his hand smoothly working the gear stick, the blond arm hairs glistening in the sun; of his khaki-clad kneecaps pushing against the steering column, and the pulse beating in his broad, ruddy neck. Now why had she begun to hyper-ventilate? Her fingers were clenched in her palms and black and silver spots danced disconcertingly in front of her eyes. Panic attack. She cupped her hands over her mouth and breathed deeply into them.

'What's wrong, Rosy? Cold hands?'

'I just remembered – I'm scared of small planes.'

He took her hand and smiled reassuringly. 'Don't worry. With me at the controls, there's nothing to fear.'

Her skin was melting under his touch. She had to breathe. In. Out. In. Out. He let go of her hand to change gears for a bend.

The silence was uncomfortable. Rose scoured her head for conversation.

'I met these women last night who model themselves on Greek goddesses. This goddess thing seems popular in these parts.'

'What goddess thing?' He sounded perplexed.

'You know, like your Goddess of Truth on that archway plaque. The goddess women I met at Swallows of the Field – they really believe in all that stuff. Do you know them?'

He laughed. 'You're the only goddess I know. The plaque came with the house when we bought it.'

The Goddess of Truth. When you were a child, the truth was all there was but even then it sometimes took your breath away when you were ordered to tell it. Be true to yourself. Was there only one truth to live by? Rose wished life were that simple. She asked Hank: 'What would you say the truth is – for you?' What a silly question. The last of the bon vivants, that was her. Gamely, Hank tried to answer her:

'My truth? Hell . . . er . . . you've caught me unawares. Maybe, eat, drink and be merry for tomorrow we die? No; here it is . . . The Goddess of Truth nurtures those who sow the seeds of promise.'

Approaching Heimat, they turned off onto a dirt road that ran alongside Swallows of the Field, following the perimeter of the field for what felt like miles and miles. Finally, the metallic glint of steel hangars came into view and Hank explained: 'I park my plane on this farm. The farmer has a runway, so this is where we take off from.'

A small plane was parked on the apron, the name *Icarus* written in italics on the side.

'Oh God! Who named this plane? I hope it's not prophetic,' Rose laughed nervously.

'Not me. When I bought the plane, it came with the name.' It seemed like everything came ready-named for Hank. What would he have named it, if he'd had to? The Goddess of Truth? Brigit of the Skies? Somehow, she didn't think so.

'Well, climb in.' He opened the door, pulled down the steps and guided her up with a firm hand in the small of her back.

The sun shone through the window of the cockpit, making diamonds and rainbows on the flawed glass. As the noise of the engines whirred louder and louder, Rose's nervousness mounted, blood pounding in her head. Then they were taxiing down the runway, the green field flashing past them.

'What the fu . . .?'

Through the plane's windscreen, they saw women running towards them, hair streaming wildly and loose garments flapping behind them. They were wielding poles, brooms, garden rakes, pitchforks and other implements. Hank slammed on the brakes, causing the small plane to pirouette in a full circle before coming to rest with its nose facing the angry mob.

After a second or two of stunned silence, Rose recovered. 'Here are the goddesses I was telling you about, Hank. Coming to nurture you with their seeds of promise.'

'Their truth, maybe but not mine. I wanna get this baby up in the air.'

He climbed from the cockpit with Rose following. She felt embarrassed to see the women. She should have remembered their planned sit-in.

'Ladies, ladies.' Hank faced the pack smilingly. 'Please, I need to take off.'

'Uh uh. Not gonna happen.' Gaia, aka Sue, stood determinedly on the runway, hands on hips, her large breasts thrust forward like a diving board. The others ranged about her like a pack of poodles bristling for a fight.

'Come now, ladies, let's be reasonable.' Hank was charm itself but Gaia and the other Goddesses were unmoved.

'We've told the farmer that this runway has to stop operating, the planes are disturbing the swallows.'

'Swallows? I don't see any swallows.'

'That's because you've scared them off.'

Hank looked at Rose who looked away, hoping the women wouldn't recognise her.

'I could call the cops,' Hank threatened. The Goddesses response to this was to seat themselves on the runway.

Hank shrugged in defeat. 'Let's go have some coffee,' he suggested. 'There's that place called Swallows that we passed on the way here.'

'I think that's their headquarters,' Rose said. 'Isn't there anywhere else?'

Hank scratched his head, then shook it: 'Not that I can think of.'

'You know where I'd really like to go . . .' Rose said suddenly. She'd remembered the Lutheran Church down the road. This would be as good a time as any to investigate it, if Hank had no objections. When she suggested it, he was his usual obliging self.

'Good idea,' he said. 'I haven't been there since I was a kid. I wouldn't mind having a look-see.'

They parked on the church property, which was surrounded by hectares of green pasture, and walked along the short path that led to the church building. In appearance this was small and unimpressive – a plain rectangle with a pitched tin roof. But according to the National Heritage information board, the building was a valuable and unusual structure, due to the fact that it was constructed entirely from yellowwood. A small brick portico led to the heavy front door, where a bronze plaque read:

Lutheran Chapel of the Holy Spirit.
Building erected in 1874. Church restored in 1990.
Financed by Pine Paper Company Limited.

The door was unlocked. Entering, they were met with the eerie light that flooded the chapel. It filtered through the leaded windows and seeped through the wooden walls with a luteous tinge that illuminated one's every flaw and failing for God's scrutiny.

It was cool in the interior, and drearily Spartan, reminding Rose of a Victorian school room with its pews – also of yellowwood – arranged in banks of two. There were no soft furnishings and no ornamentation. Walking down the aisle to where the pulpit stood uncovered and unadorned, she picked up an old, well-thumbed Bible. Rose wasn't one to believe that the verse chanced upon when opening a Bible at random held some deep significance but she flipped it open anyway . . .

To everything there is a season,
a time for every purpose under the sun . . .
a time to plant and a time to pluck up that which is planted . . .

The passage was quite beautiful but didn't exactly pave a path to epiphany. Putting the Bible down, she continued her exploration of the room. Along the back wall was a large, wooden chest of the kind used for storing treasure or one's trousseau. Rose expected it to be locked but when she tried the lid it lifted freely. Either the pastor was a trusting sort or he considered the chest contained nothing of value; but for Rose the contents were precious enough. Leather-bound journals. She lifted the uppermost one and leafed through its pages: columns of names, dates and parentage, handwritten neatly in faded blue ink.

'What are you looking for?' Hank asked, coming to join her.

She'd almost forgotten him. 'I don't know, to be honest. Look – records of christenings, marriages and deaths. Maybe I'll find my mother's name here. She was probably born around the early 1950s. It's a long shot, but you never know . . . My father could be here too . . . but even if I found his name, I wouldn't know it.'

Hank nodded. 'I'll leave you to it.'

Rose sat down on one of the pews and scanned down the lists of names. She checked through the 1950s, the decade before that and the one after. But there was nothing, no name that sparked a memory or struck a chord of something once remembered but since forgotten. She stood up, put the books back in the chest and wandered to the window. There was Hank, hazy through the flawed glass. He was bending over, studying something that she couldn't see, his shaven pate gleaming in the sunlight. It reminded her of their first meeting, with him on his hands and knees, sniffing the soil; the gardener who could make her bloom. Or deflower her. He had prepared the soil and was ready to sow his seed. Sex and death. She watched him in this garden of weeds and bones, of memories engraved in stone yet forever forgotten. And she felt again that unnamed longing stir deep in her heart.

Emerging from the chapel, she walked around to the graveyard, zigzagging her way between birch saplings and clumps of khakibos that had taken root haphazardly amongst the graves. Everywhere, the grass grew pale and lank. Beneath the oldest graves lay the remains of German pioneers and later British settlers. The tombstones leaned like old men and some were stained with a black liquid that ran down over the inscriptions like inky tears:

Peace perfect peace.
She came from afar and never wanted to leave.
He served this community with love and devotion.

A glass jar that had once held hasty flower pickings brought by a visitor lay moss-stained and forgotten on a plinth.

In the newer section, between the likes of Alexander Nicholson, Elizabeth Young and Gerald Wilson, rested the Zulu dead: Sibusiso Dube, Fikile Mabena and Nomusa Shabangu.

So, there was no separation of races in this graveyard, even at the height of the apartheid folly.

Lala ngoxolo
Tata wethu

Through a brick arch, there was a monument inscribed:

In loving and grateful memory of the glorious dead who made the supreme sacrifice in the Great War.

A long list of the fallen young men – sons, brothers and husbands – had been engraved on its stone pedestal. But where were the names of the Oberon inhabitants of German descent? Interred in prisoner-of-war camps a thousand miles away.

Saddest of all, in Rose's view, was the single gravestone erected for three siblings: James who died at two in 1885; John who died at ten months in 1891; and Mary who died aged four in 1892.

Suffer the little children to come unto me.

'Any luck?' Hank asked her as she walked back to join him.

She shook her head. She was aware of her shoulders drooping under the tragedy of the past and her yearnings of the present.

She felt Hank glance at her. 'Don't lose hope. There'll be graveyards like this in every little village in the area: Garten, Cottam, Oberon, Pennock . . . you could check them all out.'

'That makes it even worse!' she groaned. 'I don't even know what I'm looking for. I *am* losing hope.'

'Hope is what keeps our hearts beating. Don't forget the seeds of hope you wear on your wrist.'

'I thought you said they were seeds of promise . . . or of truth.' She lifted her hand up to eye level, looking at the thong's leather, darkening with wear. She wished he would take hold of her wrist and bring it to his lips again as he had before. Then her guilty discomfiture returned and she knew suddenly that she couldn't do it – couldn't betray Brigit for a few moments of gratification . . . and a lifetime of guilt.

'Yeah, well – whatever. Hope, truth; truth, hope – it's all the same. This is all too philosophical for me,' he laughed. They had reached the car. Left to stand in the heat of the day, it felt like an oven inside. Rose sat gingerly, the hot seat searing through her lightweight clothes. Hank wound the window down energetically and reversed out of the church grounds.

Soon they were on their way back to the airstrip. Hopefully, the protesters would have gone by now. Back to the demands of children and husbands and houses and home-running; domestic goddesses whose commitment to their causes could only ever be a part-time devotion.

Rose looked out her window at the fields of lucerne flashing by. They were so bright, so bursting with green that they looked plastic. Make hay while the sun shines – for Denton Dalbert's dairy cows. Why hadn't she called him yet? Maybe she didn't want to confront the truth after all. They weren't seeds of hope and truth that she wore, but seeds of doubt. And her quest here was merely a delaying tactic for the new life that awaited her in Jo'burg. It felt too much like adulthood, that new life. Entirely on her own, with all her new money and the responsibilities that came with it. That's why she was avoiding it.

She glanced at Hank's profile; Hank the prop, the tank, the hunk, the gardener, with his green fingers and seedy intentions. Hesitantly, she said to him: 'If I give you some real seeds, would you try to grow them for me? I doubt they're viable – they must be long past their shelf life by now but you never know . . .'

'Sure,' he replied obligingly.

The thought of Hank nurturing her seeds was oddly thrilling. It was a way of growing their acquaintanceship, of nurturing their association without a crossing of boundaries she might come to regret later.

His phone rang. 'Yep? . . . Uh huh . . .' His tone was serious. 'How bad is he? . . . Have you called an ambulance? . . . Uh huh . . . okay . . . well just keep him calm until . . . Ja, I'll be there as soon as I can . . .'

He cut the call and glanced at her, his expression grave. 'That was Enoch, my farm manager. There's been an accident – a tractor toppled and one of the guys landed up underneath it.'

'That's terrible! Is he okay?'

'He's alive. That's all I know.' He swung the car around and glanced at her. 'Sorry about the trip, Rose.'

'That's okay. Just as well we weren't already up in the air,' Rose said.

Hank nodded absently. 'I'll make it up to you. Another time.'

Rose said nothing, feeling vexed. Always this suspension, this deferment, this waiting for the perfect moment that never materialised.

Perhaps the Goddess of Truth was trying to tell her something.

16th October 1880

While the men were readying the horses for the hunt, I stood on the plain watching the swallows swoop and dive. A Hottentot man who went by the amusingly English name of William Plommer approached me and gallantly offered to teach me to shoot with bow and arrow. I'm afraid I laughed in a rather self-satisfied way, delighted at the opportunity to show off my marksmanship. I raised the bow he had placed in my hand and took aim. Success! A swallow landed with a thump at his feet. My would-be intructor shook his head in awe. To bring down one of these birds is no small achievement for even the most accomplished archer, because of the speed and height at which these creatures fly.

The medicine man happened to be standing nearby on the edge of the plain looking anxiously to the eastern skies, as is his wont, searching, no doubt, for rain. Upon hearing the commotion, he made his way towards us and spying the small mound of dead swallow on the ground, he became furious. In menacing tones he warned me of the sorcerer spirit who resides within every bird and who enters the heart of the one who slays it. He continued that I had best beware as I have enraged the spirits that roam these ancestral lands, and as the slayer of the sparrow, I now walk with an angry spirit in my body.

Apparently the Basotho chiefs have asked the medicine man to make rain, a service for which he is paid in advance in cattle. A fortnight ago he was given two head to add to his herd. But thus far no rain has fallen. The persistent drought casts the medicine man's power in a poor light and if the rain continues to stay away, it could lead to his downfall. Abel tells me that, increasingly, he blames my presence for the gods' displeasure.

I feel a deep discomfort at his angry threat, and though I tell myself that the English spirits watching over me are more powerful than his Bushmen variety, I am not altogether convinced of this.

This unpleasant confrontation aside, the hunting expedition was most successful. I confess I found the group's admiration for my adroitness with rifle and bow to be most satisfying. The hunt produced some half dozen carcasses, which were given to the villagers to prepare for trading. This they do with the farmers downstream, earning the clan some much needed bartering currency.

In the night, a feast was held. My three friends and I had great fun adorning ourselves with Hindoo trinket and Bushman ornament alike.

After indulging to the point of gluttony, we sat around the fire under the glorious stars and the raiders regaled us with entrancing tales of great daring and near escape. These rogues are most amusing company, albeit the bane of British, Boer and Basotho farmer and pursued all the way from Griqualand in the south to the Natal highlands in the north.

The night proceeded with much revelry. Countless ceremonial toasts were drunk from copper chalices abrim with the raiders' hard liquor as well as the beer brewed by the villagers. Pipes filled with honey-flavoured tobacco mixed with a pungent-smelling weed were passed around for smoking by all. The dancing, singing and carousing continued long into the night, until one by one the revellers collapsed in a drunken heap.

I too partook, the effects of which have rendered me quite insensate. I too danced around the fire and felt myself transported to a place of such beauty and tranquility that I thought I walked in Elysian Fields.

At some late hour, I vaguely recall Mr Lieber helping me to my accommodation. He has an animal magnetism that is positively ensnaring.

17

17th October 1880

This morning I awoke at first light to the sound of the raiders preparing to depart. I was still feeling very poorly, having spent the greater part of yesterday being indisposed, my mouth most dreadfully parched and my head pounding. To aid my recovery, Abel prepared a potion from bulbs and leaves for me, which tasted ghastly. Thereafter, I took to my bed again until Phoebus's winged chariot was high in the sky. Now it is night and I sit at my small table in the flickering candlelight, too weary to write and too restless to sleep. The wick burns low and I breathe in the rarefied air, as cool and sweet as atop Mount Olympus, and listen to the sounds of the night. A nightjar clatters, a baboon barks and a jackal bays with so plaintive a cry that it tears my heart asunder.

Writing this diary allows me to unburden myself of my desperate urge to share my experiences with another fellow being. Though my words are intended for my eyes only, as a reminder of my travels, I am mindful that, whereas spoken words blow away on the winds of time, this paper might carry enough permanence to fall into malicious hands. Thus I write with circumspection. In these judgmental times an injudicious act, even though no fault of one's own, can bring shame upon one's entire family.

Rose stood at the entrance to The Museum of Bushman Culture and Rock Art, waiting for her eyes to adjust to the dark. She hadn't known what to expect but presumed there'd be glass display cabinets and large dioramas, like those she'd seen in New York's Museum of Natural History. She wondered if they still existed, those terrible tableaus of fur-draped mannequins in wild wigs squatting over perspex fires, and moth-eaten woolly mammoths staring glassily into air-conditioned wastelands.

From its ponderous title, she'd imagined the rock-art museum standing out like a blight on the landscape – but it didn't. It had been cleverly hidden in the thick vegetation that grew on the periphery of the Bergsun property. From the approach, all that was visible were two discreet ticket boxes and the short, covered walkway that led to the museum.

Inside was shadowy and vast, a cavern cast from a thousand tons of tinted concrete. There were reproductions of San art on the walls, cleverly illuminated by hidden lighting. Water trickled down the rocky walls, sliding into black ponds. The sharp chlorine smell of them took her back to Sunday afternoons spent around pools in suburban gardens.

She hovered alone in the silence with only the invisible San for company. So much for the promised experts on hand to answer all her questions! The cashier had told her to wait for the film so she waited, shored up by the semi-darkness of the cavern. There was a flicker of light on the rock wall in front of her and the crackle of a soundtrack. She walked further into the chamber and sat down on one of the benches, lifting her chin to experience the full effect of the huge screen that curved around the walls.

The title rolled on: *The secret of the rocks: the art of the San*, accompanied by pounding African rhythms: pan pipes, marimbas and tom-toms. Had anyone other than the ancient Bushmen ever heard the real Bushman music? The small groups remaining in the Kalahari desert – did they still play the old, old music? A sunlit panorama of the Drakensberg lit up the screen and the male narrator began speaking, in a voice typical of South African documentaries: deep, well-articulated and resonant, with a barely there black lilt:

> *The mighty Drakensberg, uKhahlamba, was once home to the San people, the first people to inhabit southern Africa. For ten thousand years, they lived as members of a well-organised and harmonious society. There was no need for chiefs or leaders and all lived peaceably together, hunting game and gathering plants, sharing the land and its wealth, settling where food was plentiful, moving on as it became scarce.*

The camera pans to a rocky ledge that falls away precipitously to the distant valley floor. Here a Bushman walks, his limbs fluid as water. Under the ledge, another squats, his brow wrinkled as he nurses the wisps of smoke newly birthed by his whirling sticks. A woman on her knees pounds a root with a stone. From the unseen speakers come the irregular clicks of a language virtually extinct now, spoken only by the dead.

> *But this peaceful and ordered way of life was to come to an end. By the end of the eighteenth century, colonial farmers had settled into the areas inhabited by the San. They wiped out the game and destroyed the veld foods. Dispossessed of their lands and denied its resources, the San were forced to raid the farms to survive. Their existence was increasingly threatened as they were driven out of the areas they inhabited, mercilessly hunted like vermin or enslaved as cheap labour by the farmers. Sadly, today there are no surviving communities of Drakensberg San. Only their traces remain in the rock paintings. Some of these have withstood the ravages of time, providing a precious record of San lives, their rituals and customs.*

The camera zooms in on the rocks.

Considering the roughness of the rock surface, these paintings are remarkably fine in their detail and delicate colouring. Note the folds of skin around the animals' necks, the expressiveness of the postures, the twisting horns of these elands, all rendered with skillful shading and economy of line.

It was true, the detail was remarkable.

But these paintings give us more than visual beauty, they open up the world of the San to us. This hunter here waits in anticipation of the hunt, his quiver slung over his shoulder, his bow carried aloft. We can see clearly the arrow with its arrow head that separates from the shaft on impact, and the triple curves of the bow that endow the instrument with greater speed and accuracy. This image depicts a woman with a digging stick, the bulb at its base helping to ease its passage through the soil.

To have this record of their lives, their technology – it was something precious . . .

Pictures of women gathering or preparing plants are relatively rare in San art. This is surprising when one considers that a large part of the San diet came from women's contributions. Equally mysterious is that many of the animals depicted in these images did not form part of the diet, nor were they resident in the areas where the San lived. Ethnographers and other experts have postulated that the art represents something more than a literal portrayal of San life. As researchers delve deeper, they increasingly have come to view the art as having profound religious significance, connected to the most important religious San ritual: the Great Dance.

On the rock screen, under darkening skies, women sit around a fire, singing and clapping, while men shuffle around the outer edges of the circle.

It is thought that the Great Dance lies at the heart of much San art. During this dance, the shamans of the clan go into a trance-state in order to enter the spirit world. In this way they commune with the dead and petition their gods for rain, to heal the sick, bring the antelope herds, or chase away evil spirits.

The dance becomes wilder. Some of the dancers lie on the ground, their bodies buffed to a sweaty sheen. Others reel and sway, doubled over, arms stretched out behind their backs like wings. Some of the women also lie recumbent, moaning. The camera cuts away to the art again:

Look at these long lines emerging from the top of the head of this man here, from the back of his neck and between his shoulder blades. Our modern-day scientists believe that these lines symbolise the spirit as it leaves the body, and that the man is the shaman of the clan, asking his god for the potency needed to perform religious and spiritual duties. See how he staggers, his arms stretched out behind him, his body doubled over in pain as the potency boils in his abdomen . . .

The narrator went on to point out a few more fine examples. Rose's thoughts wandered off in multiple directions. She came back to hear the narrator saying:

. . . by painting the visions that appeared to them while in a trance state, the shamans harnessed the supernatural power needed to change aspects of their real world. For example, when white colonisers arrived in the area, their images – men on horseback armed with rifles –

were incorporated into the art. It is thought that this was done not as a literal record of historical events, but in order for the invaders to be rendered harmless by the shamans' powers.

Hmmm, now that was interesting . . .

A particularly fascinating example is the painting discovered in a remote cave in the Patilweng region by anthropologist Arnold Fitzgibbons in 2008. The work in question had been superimposed over earlier paintings and shows the figure of a white woman seen in profile, floating with her arms outstretched. In contrast to the older brush-painted art, this example appears to have been crudely drawn on with a finger. Nonetheless it is not hard to see that the figure wears a Victorian bustle dress and wide-brimmed bonnet . . .

Attention fully restored, Rose sat up. A white woman? What was the narrator saying?

A clue to the age of the painting is the white pigment used, since this pigment is more enduring than the colours derived from the earth. Estimations are that the white lady was painted in the late nineteenth or early twentieth century. Foam and blood stream from her nose, represented by the thick white and red lines, as if she's in her death throes. Two shamanic figures appear above her. Their posture is one of deep supplication to their gods, their arms outstretched behind them as they wait to fuse with the potency that will be released at the moment of her death. Fitzgibbons believes the painting represents a real Victorian woman travelling in the area and her encounter with the San. He conjectures that she may have embodied some sort of power for the shaman and that the painting was his attempt to harness the potency released on her death. Whether this was a real death or merely symbolic is open to speculation. Whatever one believes, what is certain is that if this woman was indeed an English traveller in the region at the speculated time, her sojourn, in all probability, was with one of the last surviving San groups in the Drakensberg area . . .

The voice spoke on for a while longer, but Rose didn't hear the rest. The camera cut to another panorama of the Drakensberg; the closing credits rolled. Then the scene faded and the lights came back on.

Rose sat unmoving on the bench, her thoughts racing so much she barely remembered to breathe. Was this white Victorian woman somehow connected to the White Goddess in Sir Philip Geoffrey's painting? There were just too many similarities. Painted in pigment from bird guano on a cave rock or done in incandescent oils on a canvas – were they one and the same painting? Who *was* this woman? Could she possibly be the same woman whose diary Rose had found in the box? And if so, what was her role in Rose's parentage?

For a long time she sat on in the silent cavern. What to do with this now? How to make the connections? Where to begin? It was so frustrating!

She traipsed the short distance back to the Bergsun and sank into a bucket chair on the veranda, gazing out at the view of treetops and bushes. From here the museum was hardly visible. The chair's raffia prickled uncomfortably against her back. She needed to run this whole thing by someone; someone who could help her make sense of it all. What she needed was a friend. Not Brigit; she was too busy with her children, her life – and anyway, she'd never shown much interest in Rose's story.

Petra. She'd ask Petra to join her at The Olive Branch. She typed a short sms then sat back tensely, waiting for the reply, sucking at her orange juice and watching as it rose, pastel orange, through the straw. After a few minutes, Petra's answer came: *Would love to. Let's do supper. How's 6.30?*

Feeling intensely relieved, Rose paid for her orange juice and headed home to change.

Arriving back at The Chameleon, she saw that Volvo and bakkie were parked in the carport, side by side; both Hank and Brigit were home, then. She was burning to check the Internet. Surely in that super-stocked pantry of information there would be something about a white Victorian lady encountering Drakensberg Bushmen? But she didn't want to use the connection in Brigit's office. No. Not Brigit's office. Rose didn't know why she felt so strongly about that; maybe she was still harbouring guilt over her desire for panky with Hank.

It occurred to her that the books she'd bought might give her the answers she needed. She made a beeline for them, scattering the pile on the bed and kneeling alongside; riffling through this one and that, haphazardly. Words danced before her eyes: trance, dance, shamans, fish, mermaids, blood, potency, eland, rain bull, dots, spots, flickerings, bees, ladders. But nothing at all about a Victorian lady who'd got herself immortalised on rock by a Bushman shaman.

19th October 1880

While exploring my surrounds yesterday, I descried a vista so picturesque that I ordered one of the bearers to set up my easel and paints there and then. I could see Dolly and the other horses grazing peacefully in the pastures surrounding the encampment. To the left and right, maize was ripening in small plots of green and directly in front of me, I gazed upon the rock face rising grandiose into the hazy sky.

The medicine man could not contain his excitement when he saw me at my toil. His eyes burning feverishly, he questioned me about my equipment, touching my brushes and even dipping his finger into my water colours. Then he picked up a brush, my best squirrel, brushed it against his cheek and put it in his mouth, whereupon he withdrew it and admired its fine point. I would have preferred to donate the brush to him after that but I need it—it's my finest! So I merely dipped it into the water and pretended I never saw his uncouth gesture.

In his quaint English he informed me that he too paints, as did his ancestors. He said there are as many paintings in the mountains as once there were great eland roaming this land. The importance of these paintings is such that they give strength to the hunter's arrow, entice the rain bull from the sky, deflect arrows of sickness, appease spirits-of-the-dead and convey messages to the clan members now scattered to the four corners of this land. When I inquired exactly where these paintings were to be found, I was startled by the medicine man's response. His copious wrinkles, so delightfully pronounced when he smiled, deepened forbiddingly around his eyes and he hissed close to my ear—"These paintings are secret and you are forbidden to find them. They hold the potency of the Great God. You may never look upon them, you may never even touch them. If you dare to disobey this, the string connecting the Great God to his people will break and the people will be forced to leave these lands, never to return."

His fierceness restrained me from questioning him further. Although I wish no harm to these gentle people, this is the very purpose of my visit—I am compelled to find these paintings.

Walking into The Olive Branch, Rose paused for a moment to test the air before deciding to sit on the veranda. A creeper with dark succulent leaves fell from the eaves and spilled to the floor. There were wrought-iron tables and chairs with curlicues – heavy enough to thwart burglars from spiriting them away in the dead of night. None of the tables was occupied; it was too early for supper and too late for tea.

'Can I get you something to drink?' the young waitress asked, bringing a fragrant flurry of curry with her from the kitchen. She deposited a menu on the table.

'I'm expecting a friend.' It was important for the waitress to know that Rose wasn't going to be sitting there alone. 'Um . . . okay . . . I'll have a . . .' She looked at the drinks listed on the menu, '. . . cider. Savannah Light.' She'd try it, why not? She'd never had one of those before. 'Sorry . . .' She'd wanted to ask if she could get an Internet connection here but the waitress was gone.

The traffic from the main road hissed by steadily. The waitress brought the cider, which rolled sharp and clean over Rose's tongue. Adult apple juice; she liked its kick. A woman was yelling to her friend across the road. What a pair of lungs! She was disturbing the peace. Rose wished she'd shut up already; so call a policeman. She craned her head to look at the woman. She reminded Rose of someone . . . that laboured gait, the threadbare blanket wrapped around her waist . . . Wasn't this the pathetic person in search of her husband whom Rose had picked up in Killarney and driven to the station? No, surely not! But . . . could it be her?

She half rose from her seat to get a better look but there was Petra coming through the door; short, compact and chunky in her button-down shirt with a pale, diamond pattern, and jeans. No-nonsense sandals on her feet and no discipline issues in her classroom, Rose was sure.

She waved to attract Petra's attention. Now hold back on telling her about your discovery, she reminded herself as Petra came over. Ask her questions about herself first.

They kissed, mwa mwa, like old friends.

'This is a real treat. I really needed to get out this evening,' Petra said, sitting down opposite Rose. 'I've just had some great news . . .'

Elmarie appeared at their table, depositing a second menu. 'Hello, ladies. Nice to see you. What can I get you?' she asked Petra.

'I'll have the same as Rose, thanks. I heard about the Ritters. You must be so relieved,' Petra said. Elmarie turned to shout the order to the waitress inside. 'You can say that again,' she nodded, turning back to Petra. 'So, ja, can you believe it. There must be real bad blood in that family. The father was the same in his day. And the grandfather. Ja-no, it's such a relief to know that the break-ins and vandalising are over now.'

'You mean the Ritters were responsible?' Rose asked incredulously.

Elmarie nodded. 'Turns out they were trying to scare us off. One of the brothers' wives owns the Score Board down the road. They decided we were too much of a threat . . . well you know, when we opened, their business did fall off, I heard. And not surprising – it's really grotty in there. So that all explains why the police were so slack the whole time.'

'Why?' Rose asked.

'Because the Ritter whose wife has the Score Board, he's a policeman. So he just sabotaged the investigation . . . made sure the fingerprints guys never came, that files went missing . . . you know. But ja, what can you do, hey?' Elmarie sighed.

'That's really frightening! I mean, that the whole of Oberon police force should be in cahoots to get you out of business. I can't actually believe that,' Rose said.

'Ag, not all of them, not the whole force. Well, you know, the way we found out was that this Ritter got one of his colleagues fired, and this guy decided to spill the beans in revenge. He came to see us and told us everything.'

'Well it's good that you know who's behind it now,' Petra said. 'Better criminals that you can put a face to than faceless tsotsis from across the border.'

'Ja, I suppose,' Elmarie shrugged.

'I had this weird experience with one of the Ritters on the way down here,' Rose said. 'He started dicing with me on the highway . . . cutting me off . . . it was pretty scary. And then up he pops in Oberon.' She shivered. 'I got the fright of my life when I saw him here.' She looked at the two women, feeling embarrassed by her disclosure. The experience sounded so puny in the telling.

Petra shook her head. 'Well I hope they all sit in jail for a long time – and that more files don't get lost or witnesses threatened or whatever.'

'Ag, we're not pressing charges. It's not worth it. Too much time and trouble. I don't want to have to get involved with it all and what-not, you know. And they won't be worrying us anymore.' Elmarie stepped aside to allow the waitress to deposit Petra's cider. 'I told Corrie we'd get over this – he was about ready to pack up and go back to Jo'burg. Now he's pleased we stuck it out. But I can tell you – we went through hell. And it's not finished yet. Now we're fighting with the insurance company. We didn't even claim for the smaller losses but they still want to raise our premiums to hell. But, ja, what can you do, hey? That's the way it goes.'

Rose and Petra made sympathetic noises.

'So, what can I get you to eat? Should I give you a few minutes?' She left them without waiting for an answer.

Turning her head, Rose saw a familiar figure walk onto the veranda, laden with shopping bags.

'Oh . . . it's Michael,' she said in surprise. She greeted him as he went past their table, making his way to the couch placed along the back wall.

'Michael works with Brigit at her animal welfare NGO,' Rose told Petra. 'Do you think I should have invited him to join us?' she asked.

'You could have. I wouldn't have minded.'

'It's too late now, I'd feel funny.'

'Next time. What should we eat?'

They studied their menus.

'What were you going to tell me? You said you had good news,' Rose said, closing her menu.

'Yes. I applied for a scholarship, in London, and I got it!' Petra's eyes shone in the veranda's diminishing light.

'Congratulations! What kind of scholarship?'

'To study at the University of London. I'll be doing my Master's in History.'

Just as Rose finds a friend, her friend becomes history, thought Rose wryly. But she was happy for Petra all the same. And impressed. She must be really smart, to win that kind of scholarship.

'That's really wonderful. When are you going?' she asked.

'Soon. The course only starts in September, but I want to get settled and start reading for it in the meantime. The resources there are much better than here – the collections they've got are so fantastic. For my field anyway.'

'What is your field?'

'I'm looking at white identity in a postcolonial context – the sense of belonging, or not belonging . . . the idea of rootedness . . .'

'But how fantastic for you.'

Petra nodded. 'It'll be hard to leave my family, though. I'll miss them a lot.'

'Your parents . . .?'

'They're in Durban. And I've got a sister there as well. She's married with kids. I try to get down whenever I can, to see my nieces.'

'Where will you stay in London?' Maybe she was asking too many questions now.

'I've got friends over there. I can always board with them to begin with. And Max said I can stay with him if I'm stuck. Then I'll look for a place of my own.'

'You're lucky to have friends in London,' Rose said.

'You'll soon have one, too! You'll have to come visit when I get a place.'

Rose was touched. Petra meant it genuinely, she could tell. Maybe she would go for a visit, why not?

They sat in easy silence, sipping their ciders. A breeze, pleasant as a friend's greeting, blew through the veranda. Michael was still on the couch, flipping through a magazine and nursing a beer.

‘I came across something amazing today,’ Rose said presently. She told Petra about her visit to the rock-art museum, about the film with its unexpected revelations.

‘What do you think the chances are that this Victorian lady in the rock painting could be the same as the one in the catalogue painting I showed you . . . the White Goddess? And that she’s the same lady who wrote the diary that I found in my foster mother’s belongings?’ she asked in a breathless rush.

There was a silence.

‘It’s possible, I suppose.’ But Petra sounded unsure. ‘You’d need to do a lot more research, though, have something more solid to go on, if you want to join the dots.’

She saw Rose’s disappointment. ‘But I do think you’re on the right track. So don’t worry, evidence is bound to turn up sooner or later.’

Or never. ‘What I’d really like to do is visit some of the rock-art sites – especially that one that they spoke about in the film,’ Rose said. ‘But I’m sure only the select few can go there.’

‘Not necessarily. A lot of them will be off-limits to the public but you can probably organise something. Get permission . . . join a tour . . . find a guide . . . I don’t know.’

Rose saw Michael stand up and gather his bags, beer glass empty. She smiled at him as he brushed past their table again; here was her opportunity. ‘Do you want to join us, Michael? We’re just about to order some supper. Do you know Petra?’

Petra and Michael nodded in greeting.

‘Thanks. But I’ve got to get home. I’ve got someone coming round later.’ He smiled disarmingly. Cagey. Rose wondered if the ‘someone’ was work or pleasure.

A thought occurred to her. ‘Michael, before you go . . . maybe you can help. Do you know any guides who could take me to rock-art sites around here? Maybe a friend who knows the area?’

Michael shook his head. 'Sorry, no. I don't know anyone.' His look grew thoughtful. 'But I do know where some of the sites are. There's one I can take you to, if you like,' he offered hesitantly. 'Maybe tomorrow . . .' He shifted bags from one hand to the other. 'I need to deliver something to my father – his place is right near to where the paintings are. You can come with me, if you don't mind . . . if you're not in a hurry. My mother . . . once we're there she won't let us leave quickly. And I have to make another delivery also . . .'

'I don't mind at all,' Rose said. 'That would be lovely. I'd enjoy seeing more of the area. And I'd like to meet your parents. Thanks.'

'Let's meet here, then, outside The Olive Branch. Make it nine o'clock. Bring your passport – we'll be crossing the border. And wear comfortable shoes,' he added.

20th October 1880

I returned to my tent after my unpleasant encounter with the medicine man and sat at my table to gather my thoughts. My cogitations were interrupted by the strains of women's voices chattering outside. Through the opening, I saw Katy, Beth and Connie sitting on the ground, apparently waiting for me to appear. When they spied me, they became bashful, giggling into their hands.

I invited them into my humble abode. They were fascinated by all my possessions viz. my rosewood tea-box, china cup and saucer, tea strainer and writing equipment—and most especially my mirror. When first they caught sight of their reflections, there was much consternation. Beth even screamed with fright! But after a while they forgot their manners and became a little too self-assured, pushing and shoving each other in their eagerness to view themselves. Most unladylike! I scolded them and ordered them into a queue, allotting each a few moments to gaze upon herself.

Since then, at odd times during the day, girls and women (and sometimes men and boys too) arrive at my tent to gaze upon themselves in my mirror. Beth is particularly vain, visiting frequently. She is a handsome girl, more native than Bushman with her chocolate complexion and doe-like eyes, and taller in stature than the others.

I have become very fond of Connie. She is so taken with my tresses, forever touching and stroking them, that I have decided to allow her to help me with my coiffeur. I am teaching her how to brush and pin up my hair, and also how to tie my corsets and make my tea. She is most willing and a quick learner and I am sure she would make a fine lady's maid. I have given her one of my gowns since, now that we are in such close proximity, I prefer her to be more modestly attired. It is a white gown, of which I have several. When choosing the items of clothing to bring on this journey, I opted for garments made of lighter fabrics such as voiles, muslins and moirés, and largely white in colour, this being more suitable for these hot climes.

Beth and Katy were most upset that they too had not been given gowns. I remedied the situation by giving one to each of them. I have enough to last me for the duration of my sojourn here and don't mind parting with one or two since I am sure that by the time I return to London they will be outmoded.

Sometimes though, performing what one thinks is a good deed has unforeseen consequences. Earlier I was forced to stop writing as there was an altercation taking place outside my tent. Women's voices, shrill with anger and agitation, shattered the bucolic peace. I was forced to investigate and upon looking outside, discovered Beth and one of the older women scuffling in the dirt in the most indecorous manner. It needed no translation to know what was taking place, since the other woman was trying to pull the gown off Beth's back.

"Stop!" I bawled, my voice so raucous that the pair froze. They sat up in the dirt and looked at me in surprise. The gown was badly ripped, one sleeve hanging by a thread.

The scenario called for Solomonic wisdom. Since I cannot donate any more of my gowns, I have decided the women must rotate the dresses amongst themselves. There would need to be some sort of roster system but since none can write, how would they remember whose turn it was to wear the dress? Perhaps I could teach them to write.

As I was cogitating on this idea, the medicine man happened past. It was obvious that he was reprimanding the women. He clicked away furiously at them, then yanked off the brooches they had attached to their aprons, casting them to the ground and stamping upon them in a terrible temper. He accused me of encouraging the people to shun the old Bushman ways and lamented the trouble my arrival has brought to his ancestral lands. He said that the spirits are angry, and this is the reason that the eland's blood no longer wets the ground and the rain does not fall. Then he went on his way, shaking his head and mumbling under his breath. I do fear that I am causing some upheaval amongst this little community.

Later, I mended the tear on Beth's dress so that it looks almost as good as new. The dresses are too big and too long, especially for Connie and Katy, except for the waistlines, where the clasps are unable to fasten. Despite this and the lack of bustles and petticoats, the girls assume a most comely appearance and an air of civilised gentility when wearing them. The axiom that clothes maketh the man—or woman—is so very true.

There is still the problem of the woman who covets a dress. She continues to cast noxious glances at Beth. And the medicine man slinks around, sending his evil eye in my direction and muttering curses under his breath. I try to ignore him as far as possible but his presence makes me feel increasingly uncomfortable.

18

Rose leant against her car and watched from behind her sunglasses the movement of shoppers coming and going. In this high altitude the early-morning sun was strong, ricocheting off the paving, catching the back of her neck and shoulders. Her sunblock was in the cubby hole. She got back into the car and dotted the cream on her exposed bits. The smell filled the car. Evocative. She liked the word; evocative. Evocations. Of what? She adjusted her rearview mirror and looked into her own eyes. Were her secrets and desires still safely tucked away behind their grey irises?

In the distance, there was a rumbling noise, growing steadily louder. A quad bike came into view. God – they were such noisy things. The bike turned into the parking lot and drove towards her car. Michael.

'Hope you don't mind my wheels,' he grinned. 'I borrowed it from the Liebers' farm. Brigit lends it to me when I need to visit my folks.'

Rose looked dubiously at the bike and the wide seat she had to straddle.

He handed her a helmet. 'Hope you've got a jacket. It can be cool where we're going.'

'Got one.' She patted her backpack.

'Can I help you with the strap?' He fiddled under her chin. 'How does that feel?' Actually, it felt very nice. She mounted the pillion and held Michael lightly around his waist. A woman in a tracksuit and high-heeled sandals walked by, her black patent handbag swinging at her shoulder. She stared curiously.

The bike roared through the town like an amplified lawnmower, attracting hostile looks from the sour and old, and covetous glances from the young and young at heart. Now on the open road, their speed increased as Michael opened the throttle. Rose slipped her hands over the hoodie he wore and tightened her grip around his waist. Instant intimacy. His body felt taut as he balanced on the seat.

Soon they were driving along the Valley Road, passing Leighton Manor and Lakeview Farm. Was Rose ever going to phone Denton Dalbert to ask about the Visitors' Books? Why the procrastination? Maybe she was just tired of dead ends and disappointments. As time passed, trails grew colder and leads got fainter. Why should she succeed where Detective Maurice Hunter had failed?

They turned onto a sand road and started to climb, the bike shuddering over deep furrows and beds of rocky scree. The roadside foliage grew more rampant, encroaching onto the road and hampering their passage. Now and again they had to duck to avoid low-hanging branches. Up hill, down dale and through gulleys they went, bouncing around hairpin bends that sloped precipitously away to nothing. Rose's head, which was feeling not quite her own under the heavy helmet, bounced, too.

They stopped and Michael got off and passed her a colddrink from a cubby hole under the seat.

'Are you okay?' he asked. She nodded, glad to stretch her legs and dismounted, too, her head wobbling from the weight of the helmet.

'In about half an hour we'll be in Lesotho. This is a short-cut – through the back door. After that, it's quick. My parents live quite close to the border.' He'd taken off his helmet and was thirstily downing his Coke.

'So I don't need my passport, then?'

'It's for just in case we get stopped. I can't afford to pay your bail,' he laughed.

'Right.' She smiled and cautiously drank some Coke; then, mindful of how it would joggle around in her stomach as they juddered along, she poured the rest onto the road. It fizzed on the surface for a few seconds before the pale soil drank it greedily, leaving only a dark patch on the sand.

They clambered back on the bike. Michael turned off the rutted path onto a smoother sand road, which climbed steadily, the vegetation thinning until they were riding along a pass that offered long vistas of valleys reaching into the distance. They came to a narrow opening between two rocks, only wide enough to admit one car at a time. There was a blackened copper plaque that read: 'Gabriel's Gate'.

Spread before them, surrounded by a mauve ring of mountains, was a valley all ashimmer in the morning heat. God's own land. From their elevated position, the terrain seemed to undulate like a choppy sea. Tiny settlements were scattered across it, clinging tentatively to the peaks and troughs of the valley floor. Michael switched off the engine. The air felt cooler and fresher here than in Oberon. Rose listened as she put on her jacket: silence, except for her own inhalations and exhalations, amplified by the bubble of the helmet.

They went on again, following the road that descended steeply into the valley. From close-up Rose could see that the land was eroded and arid, hardly arable, dotted here and there with a balding pine tree or a clump of wattles. Michael turned onto a side road. They had come to one of the small settlements Rose had seen from above, little clusters of dwellings scattered around the slopes. Some of them were traditional mud-and-thatch rondavels, others constructed from concrete blocks, with corrugated metal roofing and steel window frames. The noise of the bike brought people out from their houses.

'*Haai*,' they shouted. Michael slowed down to greet them. There was much hand-shaking and back-slapping. Were they congratulating him on his white girlfriend, Rose wondered? What did they think of her sitting behind him, holding onto him for dear life? She loosened her grip and tried to create some space between their bodies.

His father's house was a Western-style bungalow with an entrance porch and a tiled roof, situated at the far end of the village. Shiny diamond-mesh fencing encircled the property, which was much larger than the neighbours' – about half an acre of pale, mown grass. The same fencing continued along to enclose an adjacent field, where mealies grew green and tall.

Michael parked in the shade of the house. It was a relief to remove the helmet; Rose's head felt strangely light without it. His parents came out to meet them, his mother short and matronly, wearing a dress made of brown *shweshwe*, the panels artfully arranged, and his father in brown trousers and short-sleeved shirt. Michael introduced them as 'my parents'. Rose wondered how she was going to address them, since she didn't know his surname: Mr and Mrs? He told them she was a tourist interested in the rock art.

Mr, exuding affability and good cheer, ushered them into the lounge. There was wall-to-wall carpeting, speckled like eggshells, and a brown draylon lounge suite. Rose sat opposite a wooden wall unit with a TV and small ceramic ornaments displayed in its compartments. The room looked like it had been deposited straight from the pages of a Joshua Doore furniture catalogue.

Mrs brought out a tray from the kitchen and poured the tea. They spoke English for Rose's benefit but every now and then a Sesotho word coloured the conversation like a bright thread of cotton weaving through white cloth.

'How do you like Lesotho?' Mr asked Rose.

'It's very beautiful.'

'But very poor,' sighed Mrs. 'There's a lot of suffering here.'

Mrs passed around a plate of assorted biscuits arranged on a paper doily. Rose, her cup and saucer balanced precariously on her thighs, took a lemon cream. She remembered how, as a child, she used to prise them carefully apart, scrape off the cream with her bottom teeth and then eat the two halves. She hadn't had one in years.

'What do you think of my new fence?' Mr asked his son.

Michael nodded his approval. 'Very nice.'

'I put it up to keep my cattle safe at night,' Mr told Rose. 'Otherwise, they stray. They're my wealth. I have twenty head. I'm a rich man.' He laughed, throwing his head back and showing his teeth.

Rose was surprised at the ease with which he spoke of his wealth. Among her circle, it was so not done. Maybe he was just teasing her.

'I earned my money working on the mines of the Witwatersrand,' Mr was saying. 'My eldest son is working there now. But Michael didn't want to work on the mines. He likes to study.'

'I didn't know that.' Rose turned to Michael. 'What are you studying?'

'Community development.'

'Where?'

'They run distance courses at the University of Lesotho.' Abruptly Michael stood up. 'We need to go if you want time to see the rock art,' he said.

'But you've just got here! You must stay for lunch. I'm making lunch for you.' Mrs took the cup and saucer from Rose.

'I'm taking Rose to see the rock paintings.'

'But you won't see your brother and sister if you go!'

'Not today, Ma.'

'You must return for lunch, then. I'm cooking your favourite.' Rose wondered what that was.

'Mama, we won't have time. We're coming back to fetch the bike and then we must go straight away to Tjhetjhella Morao. I have a delivery to make and I don't want to get back after dark.' He spoke very respectfully.

'Come, then. I have something for you to take with you.'

Michael followed his mother into the kitchen and after a few minutes emerged carrying two paper bags. 'Snacks.' He held them up for Rose to see.

Rose smiled. 'Thank you so much,' she said to Mrs.

Mr followed them out. Michael fetched a package from the bike's cubby hole and handed it to his father. 'Deworming muti for the cattle,' he told Rose. They waved goodbye to Mr and Mrs.

The road they walked along criss-crossed communal grazing lands, where the dwellings grew more scattered then gradually petered out. Up against a concrete house, geraniums grew, as red and unexpected as a fresh wound. A dog chained to its kennel slept in the shade, its ribs like a set of samurai swords.

'Do people here look after their dogs?' Rose asked.

He shook his head. 'It's the same everywhere.'

'You could start your own animal welfare society.'

'My plan is to start a proper developmental agency here and bring all the projects in the valley under one umbrella. Get them all working cooperatively so each is not duplicating what the other is doing. Once I'm qualified, I want to do that. There are so many upliftment programmes going on here: Aids projects, adult education, women's empowerment groups, school feeding schemes, sports clinics . . . Clowns without Frontiers . . .'

'But no animal welfare.'

'There's a horse NGO but no dog welfare, no. The Basotho are funny that way. Unless they earn money from their dogs, they're not going to bother to take proper care of them. They don't give them meat to eat, just feed them on pap.'

'They're not funny, just poor,' said Rose. 'They probably don't even have meat for themselves.' Rose was quite surprised at his generalisations. She knew that if she repeated his observations in certain circles she'd be shut down sharply.

'And they just let the dogs breed,' Michael went on. 'They don't care. There are no vets around here to do the spaying and neutering anyway. They all leave and go where the money is.' The road curved around a small field of mealies. 'And you'll never see a cat,' he continued.

'Why's that?'

'Because they've all been made into hats! There's no small game remaining in all of Lesotho. A fur hat is a thing every man wants to own.'

As they walked past a homestead, a young woman joined them. She was petite and jaunty. 'Hello. Where are you going?'

'To the waterfall, to see the rock paintings,' Michael replied. Rose eyed the woman, wondering if she was considering joining them for their excursion and hoping not. What a bore it would be to have this . . . person tagging along with them.

She addressed Rose: 'Where are you from?'

'South Africa. Johannesburg.'

'Do you have a job for me? I can clean your house.'

'Sorry, I don't.'

'I want to come to Johannesburg.'

'Leave your family and friends? Johannesburg's very different to here,' Rose replied curtly, thinking: Egoli – place of gold. Bright lights. Big city. That difference is what attracts you.

After a while, to Rose's relief, the woman left them and they continued on their way. Michael pointed out the crèche and the primary school. As they passed, they could hear the children's voices rising clear and sweet in the quiet air. Some stopped what they were doing to wave. Michael told her that the schools here loved receiving visitors but that she'd be expected to dig into her pockets and give them a donation.

'I don't mind,' she said earnestly.

He laughed. 'Another time we'll go.'

Rose asked about the standard of education in the country. Michael told her it was good and that the literacy rate was very high – almost a hundred per cent.

'All kids must go to primary school – it's compulsory; but not high school. In fact,' he said, 'girls go further than boys. The boys must herd the cattle, so they fall behind and drop out.' He pointed to a building in the distance. 'There's the high school where my brother and sister go. I also went there.'

They had come to the edge of the village. The path fell steeply down a ravine. Michael reached out his hand to steady Rose and she took it, even though she was rock-steady. His hand was dry and warm and she clasped it tightly as she jumped off a rocky ledge onto a wide bed of unyielding material that shone smooth and white in the late morning sun. It looked like a river of marzipan. Michael told her it was once molten magma that had bubbled up from the core of the earth, forcing its way through fissures and faults, flowing up banks and around bends, filling hollows and flattening humps, then cooling off and finally hardening into this natural pathway.

They came across a young herder sitting on a rock, trying to hit an invisible marker with stones. Two large orange dogs slept at his feet, looking well fed and docile, their coats glossy, while four big cattle browsed at the edges of a dry river bed. Rose and Michael crossed there and began the climb up a steep, wooded trail. Rose followed Michael's lead, using the same hollows in the rock that he used to gain a foothold, pulling herself up by the same branches that he'd held. Her legs felt like jelly and her breathing came raggedly. Unfit. She needed to start some exercise. How much longer to go now? She stopped and looked upwards to where mountain ended and sky began. Was that where they were headed? The climb looked gruelling. The return trip will be easier, she consoled herself.

Michael was moving steadily ahead of her. She liked him. She thought him beautiful, with his sensitive face and sculpted body. Would she sleep with him, though? She'd worry about Aids. Was that being racist? Would she be less worried about sleeping with a white man she didn't know? She wondered if he found her attractive, too. She couldn't tell; she couldn't read the signs.

Suddenly, they were at the top, walking along a level track on a grassy plateau. The view was breathtaking, the basalt crags of the Malutis stretching around them forever. The name Maluti meant 'The Range' in Sesotho, Michael told her.

To one side, the plateau dropped vertically, exposing a rock face of bare basalt, its edge notched by a skein of water that spilt over the sheer lip, shining like a barb of light as it plunged down the rock face. They zigzagged downwards until they reached the deeply shaded pool where the waterfall came to rest.

'Drink. This is the sweetest water you'll ever taste,' Michael said. He was right. Afterwards, they sat side by side on the flat, pale rocks. Rose leaned back on her hands, listening to the susurration of the waterfall. She lifted her face to the pale sky, closed her eyes and fantasised about Michael kissing her, his mouth tasting fresh and sweet from the water he'd just drunk. But she wasn't going to initiate anything; rejection would be too unbearable.

'Are you okay? Should we carry on?' he asked.

'Yep.' Quickly she opened her eyes and jumped up. 'Let's carry on.'

They followed the river for a while and once again started to climb, hugging the rock face that was no longer basalt black but pale shale, thick with shrub. Rounding a bend they saw, tucked in the mountainside, a shallow depression shielded by a large, overhanging rock. And there it was – the art they had come to see.

Rose felt breathless, struck with reverence and awe. There was something in the air here, something transcendent and holy. The rock surface teemed with figures, animal and human, layer superimposed upon layer, rendered in ochres and reds. In one section was what looked like a strange harlequin with collar and tricornered hat . . . a leaping man with legs like threads and arms aloft . . . an eland emerging from the rock . . . It was hard to make the figures out clearly. They were all so faded, the rock surface so crowded with them.

She stared for a long time at the complexity that was there then said in a whisper to Michael: 'These white figures over here . . . what do you think?' They were grouped together in one corner, slighter more defined in their white pigment than the rest; a small someone sitting with elbows on knees . . . large ears . . . or was it an antelope's head? Beneath it, a figure of a man looking so abject he seemed about to collapse. His head lolled . . . there was a slackness in his legs . . . red lines like blood emerging from his torso. Other white figures lying prone . . . one in a puddle of red . . .

For the first time, Rose was sorry she didn't own a camera. She glanced at Michael, who merely shrugged in response to her question. Rose hesitated then said: 'Have you ever come across a painting of a white woman in Victorian-style dress on any of these rocks, Michael?'

He shook his head. From his backpack, he took out the paper bags that his mother had given him and handed one to Rose. She took it hesitantly, feeling it sacrilegious, somehow, to eat in front of the paintings. Walking on a little way, she sat down on a flat-topped rock with her back to the art, gazing at the deep gorge that dropped away at her feet and the mountains that rose on the other side, wrapped in a silence so profound it made your ears feel redundant.

She was interested to see what Michael's mother had packed: a peanut-butter sandwich on homemade bread; a box of Liquifruit; a small chocolate bar; and a red apple.

'My mother – look!' said Michael, coming to join her. 'She's given us school lunch. This is what I took to high school. Every single day. Except for the chocolate bar; that was for special treats only.' He laughed.

'It's so kind of her. I haven't eaten a peanut-butter sandwich since . . . I left school. Yum! It's delicious.'

Swallowing, she told Michael: 'I got given more or less the same school lunch as you. Except for the apple – I never ate them. I'm still not fond of them. Do you want mine?' she asked, holding it out on the palm of her hand.

Michael grinned. 'I'll swap you something for your apple.'

'Okay, what?'

He looked around. 'This magic pebble. If you rub it between your hands, it will give you great wisdom.'

They swopped the apple for the stone. 'Let's hope you're right about the stone,' Rose said, smiling wistfully.

He placed her apple in his backpack. 'I'll keep your apple for later. Maybe there'll be a hungry child.' Standing up, he asked: 'Are you ready to go?'

She nodded and lightly touching his forearm, said: 'Thank you. This was fantastic, really. I don't have the words . . .'

Walking back to the rock face she stood close up to it, looking attentively at the paintings, trying to imprint their details on her memory. Then rejoining Michael, she threaded her arms through her backpack and they began the long hike back to the village.

Helmet on and astride the bike once more, Michael told Rose that they were heading for Tjhetjhella Morao, an Aids hospice in the area, to deliver some drugs.

Aids hospice? Rose's thoughts did a quantum leap; the mountaineer doctor – didn't he run an Aids hospice somewhere here? Could it be the same one?

They passed back through the opening in the rocks called Gabriel's Gate and travelled south this time, into flatter terrain, where the air felt warmer.

Turning off onto a narrow track, they started climbing once more, the land becoming less inhabited the hillier it grew. Finally, in what seemed like the middle of an infinite nothingness, they saw the haven cutting into the side of a slope – a white single-storey building with a few outhouses around it.

They entered the gates and pulled up alongside the main building. Rose dismounted and removed her helmet.

'What does the name mean?' she asked Michael who was busy unpacking the cubby hole.

'It means something like . . . "retreating". I can't translate exactly.'

A nurse in uniform, all shining brass badges and epaulettes, emerged from the building. She introduced herself as Maud Khoali, the matron, telling Rose that she'd come out of retirement to run the hospice. She didn't find it easy, living so far away from civilisation.

'There's no shop nearby, no cell-phone reception . . . electricity only runs for a few hours a day, when the generator's on and, worst of all, there's never enough water. We pump it up but there's not enough for our needs.'

Rose wondered about the choice of location. The place must have been expensive to build – having to haul materials such a distance. And the problem of getting in supplies . . . who would choose to build a hospice so far off the beaten track? Someone who himself needed refuge, she thought, in retreat from the world of human connection and communication.

They entered a small reception area with wall-to-wall linoleum, a built-in desk and a row of steel-framed chairs. There was a distinctive odour pervading the place, a strong smell of disinfectant – but also something else, sweet and ghastly. The smell of death? It brought back memories of Livvie's closing days with such vividness that nausea welled up in Rose's throat. She wanted to run out the door and gulp down some fresh air. But she controlled herself, as always. Bursting heart, swelling heart. It was Ruby who followed her heart; Rose kept hers firmly where it belonged.

'Would you like to see round the clinic?' Maud was saying. 'We have about thirty patients at the moment. They're all full-blown cases. Some, we give ARVs, if we think they've got a chance. There've been one or two miracles – they start the treatment and they get better, so we send them home. But for most, it's too late. The drugs are very strong. If you give them to such sick people . . .' She shook her head. 'The body must be strong enough to cope with these drugs.'

Maud escorted Rose through a labyrinth of small rooms, each occupied by three or four people who looked to be in the final stages of the disease. It was devastating to see them. They were stick thin and hollowed out, some so close to death that Rose could almost see the Grim Reaper hovering about their beds. She smiled like she was some sort of Florence Nightingale. What a fraud! She felt like a voyeur, merely satisfying her own morbid curiosity. And all the while that unbearable smell . . .

'The patient in this bed . . .' Maud pointed at empty sheets, '. . . she died yesterday. She woke up and said "Oh, Thursday seems like a good day to die" – and she did.'

Rose was glad when they left the ward. They came to a partially closed door.

'That's Dr Metheus's office. Would you like to meet him?' asked Maud.

Rose wasn't sure. What would she say to him? Hello, you're doing a wonderful job.

Maud knocked on the door and they entered an office lined with metal shelves overflowing with files, papers, medical books and equipment. Rose saw monitors on the floor, a baby scale sitting beside them. The desk, too, was chaotic, inboxes and outboxes equally overflowing.

Dr Metheus, in white coat, frowned up from his laptop, his blue eyes all the more piercing in his sunburnt face – like he could see into Rose's soul and beyond. He was all hard angles; the Camel Man.

He stood up when he saw her and came round the desk to shake her hand, which was embarrassingly hot and clammy against his cool, dry one. She felt herself blush.

'Rose Clemens,' she told him.

He nodded. 'I remember. Maud has shown you around?'

'Yes. This facility is . . .' Her voice petered out embarrassingly.

'Do you want something to drink, my dear?' Maud asked her.

'Um . . .'

'Can we have some tea, Maud,' the doctor asked in his terse way.

He escorted Rose down the linoleum passage onto a veranda where patients wrapped in bright blankets and seated on a motley collection of chairs took in the warmth of the sun. Maud brought the tea and Michael joined them. They sat looking out at the view beyond the low stone wall, to a quilt of hills and shadows.

Rose listened as business was discussed: the problem of shortages, in the form of medicines, staff, finances, equipment; an upcoming reportback meeting with the community . . . She observed how Michael and Maud deferred to Wim in all these matters when a decision was needed.

Rose wondered what drove a man like him to live this lonely life so far from home. What had he left behind in Europe? She was fascinated by people who could uproot themselves as he had done and resettle in a culture that was so alien. Difference always presented itself as a barrier to her. And for him? Was he indifferent to whether someone was European, African, black, white, rich, poor, educated, uneducated? Did he relate to all in much the same way? Or not? She had noticed at the party that he didn't seem to engage much with the other guests. Maybe they just weren't his type . . . or was it that he was simply too intense for light social intercourse, driven by some overdeveloped sense of responsibility to humans in need? Was this his need?

'Rose is interested in rock art,' Michael was saying. 'I took her to the place by the waterfall.'

Wim gestured towards the hills. 'There's also that place at the bottom there.'

Rose blurted out: 'Have you ever seen . . . anywhere around here . . . a painting of a white figure . . . a woman, dressed in Victorian clothing? I saw it in the film they showed at the Bergsun museum.'

They all shook their heads.

'I've never been to the museum,' Maud said. 'Is it worth going?'

'I thought so. It was . . . helpful to me,' Rose replied. Wim looked at her, waiting for her to explain but she didn't. Instead, she offered: 'The site we saw today, it was difficult to make out too much. A lot of the time I wasn't sure what I was looking at.'

'They mostly are like that, the rock-art sites. The ones you see in books – they've all been photographically enhanced,' Wim told her.

They chatted for a while longer, then Michael stood up: 'We'd better get going. We don't want to be driving back in the dark.'

Wim accompanied them to the bike and stood watching as they climbed on. Michael turned the ignition key, revved a few times and they were off. As they passed through the gate, Rose turned her head, cumbersome in the helmet. Wim was still standing there. She raised a hand in leave-taking and he slowly mirrrored her gesture, disappearing from sight as they took the bend.

When they arrived back in Oberon, Michael deposited Rose at her car. Impulsively she ventured: 'Michael . . . I'm going back to Jo'burg soon. Do you have an email address? Are you on Facebook? Let's keep in touch.'

She offered him her hand and they did the three-part handshake: shake, clasp, shake. Then she drove along the darkening roads of Oberon, back to The Chameleon.

The air had cooled with the coming of night and Rose shivered as she got out the car to open the gate. The cottages stood in darkness. Fumbling to insert her key in the lock, Rose heard rustling in the bushes. 'Who's there?' She whirled around.

Happiness emerged out of the dark bushes. It was the first time that Rose had seen her out of her work clothes. In her servant mode, subservient and subsumed by overalls, she was an ageless, faceless presence whose problems Rose didn't want to hear about. But now, in the navy skirt and pink sweater, Happiness took on a personality. It was an amazing transformation.

The clothes, despite the probability that they were Brigit's cast-offs, revealed the woman; her sagging breasts and rolling stomach told of her age and stage of life, and the relatively narrow hips conjured up the young girl she had once been. Her hair, normally covered by a doek, was combed out and neatly clipped and she'd drawn in eyebrows with a black pencil – presumably they were intended to add glamour but they just made her look stern.

'I am going off,' she said simply.

'Are you leaving now? Going to your village?' It looked that way, but Rose hoped not. She was far too exhausted to trek to Happiness's village tonight. The sangoma who had dreamt up her ancestors would just have to wait.

'Tomorrow. I'm catching the taxi.' Relief. Maybe Happiness had a hot date tonight – all dressed up like this.

Rose remembered the long story about getting to Happiness's village. 'Should we go in my car? Would it be easier?' she offered.

'Yes. That will be easier. Much quicker.'

'What time? 9.00? 10.00?'

'9.00 is good,' Happiness nodded, and disappeared into the bushes the same way she'd come.

19

The next morning Rose, with Happiness in the passenger seat, travelled back along the roads that she and Michael had traversed the previous day. But instead of veering off onto the narrow bike track, they turned off a few kilometres further north and followed the Elands' Way signposts.

'What language do you speak?' Rose wanted to know.

'Sesotho,' Happiness told her.

'What's your Sesotho name?'

'Quonqholotsane.'

Rose tasted it: 'Quon-qho-lot-sane.' Click click tsk in her mouth. 'What does it mean?'

'I don't know. I'm named for my ancestors. People say it's very old. From the Bushman language.'

'Are you from the Bushmen?' Rose asked hesitantly.

A nod. 'Before, our grandparents and parents didn't want to talk about it but now the white people come and tell us this.'

'White people came and told you?'

'Yes. They come from the university. They sometimes come with cameras and exercise books. They ask questions. They say it's important that we must know these things.'

'What things?' Rose demanded.

'That we come from the Bushmen, and our customs.'

'Your customs? Are they different from other people's around here?'

'I don't know.' Happiness shrugged her shoulders.

Rose glanced sideways at Happiness. She was small-boned and her skin did have a slightly yellow cast to it. So was it true, were Happiness and her people descended from the Drakensberg San? Was her village the one off the beaten track that the librarian had mentioned? The anticipation was almost too much. Rose felt a shiver run up her spine. A strange feeling overcame her, a feeling of intense expectation, as if she were about to uncover all of life's mysteries; but the feeling dissipated as quickly as it had come.

The road wound its way up the mountains, ending in a parking area surrounded by palisade fencing. Within was a prefab cabin that housed a Parks Board office, with a large sign attached to the wall that read: *It is compulsory for all hikers intending to use the hiking trails to visit the office before starting out.*

They entered the cabin, where Happiness and the Parks Board Officer greeted each other like long-lost friends, launching into a long and animated conversation. The officer, without breaking stream, passed Rose an indemnity form sign. She skimmed over the first part: *In case of getting lost and/or injury, rescue services will . . .*

She skipped to the part she was required to fill in: *Next-of-kin . . .* Hmmm. Whose name to put? In the end she left it blank, thinking – how sad. *Hiking destination . . .* She didn't have a clue.

'Where are we going? What's your village called?' she asked Happiness.

'Patilweng.'

The name rolled like thunder in Rose's ears.

Patilweng? Hadn't she just been reading about a Patilweng? Wasn't that the village mentioned by the mysterious lady traveller in the diary? Could it be the very same place that they were headed to now? Or was there more than one Patilweng in the area?

She passed the completed form across the desk and the officer took it from her.

'The office closes at 5.00. Then I lock the gates and go home,' he told her.

'Oh I'll be back long before that,' Rose answered breezily. She bought two bottled waters, for her and Happiness, and stowed them in her backpack; picked up a brochure from a pile on the counter and left the office with Happiness in tow.

The brochure featured a small hand-drawn map with hiking trails demarcated with dotted lines leading to points of interest: Eyrie Lookout; Devil's Drop; Sleeping Beauty Cave. There was a list of what not to do:

DO NOT remove vegetation
DO NOT litter
DO NOT light fires
DO NOT hike alone
DO NOT hike in the mist
DO NOT hike when it is dark
DO NOT hike when it is lightning
DO NOT tease the baboons

Rose put the brochure in a side pocket of her backpack and followed Happiness along a well-trodden riverine path. It thrust its way through growth dense with ferns and grasses, and trees with exposed roots that crossed their course like pale serpents. Some of the trees had been identified for the conscientious hiker, green tags tacked on the trunks denoting their names: Forest Num-Num; Bushman's Grape; Sneezewood; Hairy Turkeyberry. A variety of butterflies drifted about them – huge black shadows with iridescent blue stripes; bits of white confetti bobbing gaily in the air; floating hearts of purple and yellow.

The water in the river was a slow trickle – it hadn't rained for a while, and the men who usually waited with their tyres to carry desperate travellers across were nowhere in sight. In any case, Happiness needed no help. She was surprisingly agile as she leapt from rock to rock in her navy skirt and tan court shoes, carrying a large white handbag.

The path veered steeply up and away from the river and became a sandy trail that meandered for miles through grassy hills. Although the route was not nearly as taxing as the previous day's trail that Rose had hiked, her legs felt weary and heavy. She and Happiness walked mostly in silence. The sun beat down on them, its fierce rays glinting off the lenses of Rose's sunglasses. She felt the skin on her forehead tightening. Crap. A headache on the way. She didn't think she had any Panado with her, either.

After what felt like hours of walking, they came to a large open plain with a scraggly collection of wattle-and-daub rondavels squatting forlornly on it. Was this it? Patilweng? Somehow she'd been expecting a much larger settlement. The air was icy here and Rose shivered, despite the sun. The place looked so forsaken. Where was everybody?

They wove their way between the huts, avoiding the goats and chickens that wandered and scratched amidst patches of spinach and stunted mealies struggling to grow in the poor soil. A few children playing with stones in the dust looked at Rose with wide eyes as she passed. Happiness led her to a hut and ushered her in. The gloom was a relief after the sun's glare but the acrid smell of embers made her headache feel worse. She rubbed her temples.

Near the hearth, a girl lay on grass matting. Opening her eyes, she scowled at them then rose slowly to her feet.

'My daughter,' Happiness said. The girl looked about eighteen years old. When Happiness had told Rose that her child was sick, she'd been under the impression that the child was much younger. A baby. She had a sickness of the blood, the sangoma had said. Rose smiled in a friendly way but the girl didn't respond. She looked sullen and depressed.

Happiness gave instructions in Sesotho and the girl dragged herself out of the hut.

'She must tell sangoma that you are here. Then you go to sangoma. I will go with you because I translate.' Rose nodded. She sank onto the floor and sat cross-legged against the wall, her brain knocking relentlessly against her skull. When she was active and walking, her headache seemed to ebb but sitting here doing nothing brought it on with a vengeance.

Happiness poured water from a ewer into two tin mugs and gave one to Rose. She realised she was parched, probably dehydrated. She asked for more.

Happiness busied herself, lighting the fire, boiling water to make pap, soaking a bunch of spinach and other leaves in a bowl of water. Smoke filled the hut, its sharp smell intensifying the pain Rose felt behind her eyes. The daughter shuffled back into the hut. She said something to Happiness, who passed her a wooden spoon so that she could take over stirring the pot, to which Happiness had been adding mealie meal little by little.

Rose followed Happiness to the sangoma's hut. She was standing by the opening, waiting to guide them inside – a small, wizened woman, wearing black wellington boots below her brightly coloured dress and layers of beads around her neck. They shone incandescent white against her black skin.

She looked shrewdly at Rose with clear, bright eyes and spoke to Happiness. Rose felt quite apprehensive. What if the sangoma said something really bad – like a terrible disaster was about to befall her? She decided she would take it all with a pinch of salt.

'Here – she says you must take the chair.' Happiness indicated that Rose should sit on the white plastic stack chair placed opposite two green, drum-shaped stools; the two older women sat on these. Rose, sitting higher, cast a glance around the hut. The walls and floor were a beautiful rich ochre colour. Matting, the colour of the veld, was arranged to form a low screen that shielded a section of the hut from her gaze.

The sangoma lifted her arms and placed a double-stranded circle of beads around her head, similar to the ones she wore around her neck.

'She's going to pray now,' Happiness said.

Closing her eyes, the sangoma began intoning in a low voice. Presently, she opened her eyes again, then slowly lifted the beads from her head and placed them reverently on the floor. Next, she opened a bag made from woven grass and removed some objects. Holding them between her hands and intoning some more, she threw them on the floor. There was a large cowry shell; a few periwinkles; a pansy shell; a black flintstone; and some tiny bones, aged and yellow, whose origins Rose couldn't identify. The sangoma studied the objects then carefully, and with obvious veneration, she picked them up and handed them to Rose.

'She says you must do the same, you must throw the bones,' Happiness told her.

Holding her breath, Rose threw the objects. They fell with a muted clatter around the circle of beads. The sangoma studied them and began to speak.

'She says the white stranger is welcomed by her ancestors.'

Happiness waited. 'Your ancestors are here, watching over you.' Pause. 'Your health is good. Excellent. You will live a long and fruitful life.'

That's good, Rose thought. This headache's not a brain tumour; I'll live longer than my mother, then.'

The sangoma looked at her and smiled, revealing a missing upper tooth. Rose returned the smile.

'You are very lucky lady. You will have great riches. Your life will be very enriched.'

Well, that's true, it already is, thought Rose.

'You will travel very far – she sees many, many journeys. And you will touch many – she says you will touch many children – you must thank your ancestors for your good luck.'

There was a silence. Then the sangoma spoke again.

Happiness said: 'She wants to know if you have any questions.'

'I . . . I'll have children? M . . . many?' Rose's voice faltered. She lifted her hand to her aching forehead.

'Yes – you will touch many and they will thank you.'

What did that mean? And she did have other questions – like . . . about finding a life-partner, and finding out about her ancestors. Yes, she had plenty of other questions but she didn't have too much faith in the answers. And how did one thank one's ancestors? That was a question she had, too, but didn't want to ask. She needed to hold onto the sangoma's auspicious prophecy – and if thanking one's ancestors meant practices that completely overstepped the bounds of her belief systems, she feared the comfort offered by the prophesy would fly away like salt in the wind.

'I've got no questions,' she said. Her head was pounding again, worse than ever. She stood up: 'Thank you, thank you very much.'

She had brought some notes in her pocket but didn't have a clue how much she should give. Twenty rand? Fifty? A hundred? She gave the sangoma the hundred and Happiness the fifty and hoped it was enough.

Back in Happiness's hut, Rose went to sit against the wall again, her head bursting with pain. It was especially bad over one eye. And the nausea . . . a migraine? She pressed the heel of her hand into her eye. She wasn't normally prone to migraines. But it couldn't be anything too ominous – the sangoma had told her she would live a long and fruitful life; that was reassuring.

She doubted that Happiness would have any painkillers on hand but she asked anyway: 'You wouldn't happen to have a Panado or something, would you? I have a really bad headache.' Happiness shook her head. What should Rose do? Sleep it off? She couldn't – she needed to get back to her car before 5.00. Could she follow the path back by herself? She needed to check directions with Happiness. But it was difficult even to speak.

Happiness unfurled a grass mat on the floor and told Rose to lie down, covering her with a thick Basotho blanket. It was coloured a vivid yellow and decorated with a repeating pattern of mealie cobs woven into the textile. After a while, she brought Rose some hot liquid in a tin mug. It tasted disgusting but Rose gulped it down obediently.

25th October 1880

The sun sank and the moon rose. Soon, I was aware of the ceaseless throb of drums, from whence I did not know. Drawn to investigate, I pulled on my khaki trousers and veldskoene and slipped into the night. My way lit by the pale moon, I strode across the plain towards the orange glow that emanated from the cliffs. After a time, I came upon the source of the light, a towering fire that cast wild, dancing shadows on the rock face, illuminating the villagers who had gathered around the flames. The women sat clapping and singing as the men danced wildly about the circle, stamping their feet and moving their arms, the cowrie shell rattles around their ankles clattering noisily. Some waved fly switches in the air. Musicians sat at the edge of the circle beating their tom-toms and tapping their bows, their eyes closed as if spellbound by the strange haunting melodies they produced. I stopped warily in my tracks. The scene that played out before my eyes was so alien, strange and mysterious to my sensibilities that I was sure my foreign presence would not be welcomed.

I crept towards a rocky outcrop and crouched down behind its shield. Through the veils of smoke, I saw the dancing become wilder as the music's tempo quickened. Round and round the fire the men leapt and pranced until out of the billowing smoke, the medicine man materialised. Supported by two of the men, he staggered about, bent over as if in mortal agony, his arms held out behind him like wings. Then he collapsed out of my line of vision. Other men staggered about in similar fashion before collapsing in their turn. The women wailed and swooned around the fire. I watched for another fifteen minutes or so until cold and tiredness overtook me. Then I crept away and headed to my tent.

For many hours I lay awake, sleep evading me as the drumbeats, clapping and wailing continued unabated into the night.

It was dark in the hut when Rose awoke. She felt fragile and hung-over but her headache was gone. She reached for her backpack to look at her phone. Nearly nine o'clock! She clearly wasn't going anywhere tonight. Her car should be safe enough behind the locked gates. She checked her cell phone for signal: none. Her battery was running low, too. She wondered if anyone would worry about her, whether Brigit or Hank were even aware of her absence.

Freezing in her shorts and T-shirt, she rummaged in her backpack for her tracksuit pants and the windbreaker jacket she'd brought along. She became aware of the sound of drums, steadily beating. She was alone in the hut, Happiness and her daughter nowhere to be seen. She stood up on shaky legs and walked outside.

The huts were outlined in the light of the three-quarter moon hanging suspended in a starry sky. Could she see Orion from here? She searched but couldn't make out the constellation. Everywhere seemed deserted, the huts empty of all life. There was an orange glow in the distance, lighting up the dark night and a faint smell of smoke. It came from the direction of the mountain.

She started walking towards it, following a path whittled out by countless footsteps over countless years. The path led away from the village for about a kilometre, across a tract of level ground towards a towering cliff face. As Rose drew nearer, she could see the silhouettes of people thrown onto the rock face. A circle of women were gathered around the large fire that sent its flames to the stars. They sat singing and clapping their hands in time to the beat of the drums, their bodies swaying to and fro. Some had the mealie-patterned blankets draped around their shoulders. The men, dressed in hide aprons over black shorts, moved around the outer edges of the circle. They had decked themselves out with bracelets and anklets made from dried cocoons that rattled angrily as they jumped and leapt about in the firelight or veered off into the dark night and came staggering back again. Some wore caps with antelope ears sewn in and carried fly whisks that they flicked sharply at invisible perils that lay in their paths. Others wore leather thongs decorated with beads and shells, similar to the one Rose wore on her wrist – the one she had found in the box.

The musicians sat to one side of the circle, the drummers sweating as they beat on the stretched hide with their palms; others tapped with sticks against hunting bows cradled against their left shoulders, from which they wrung out music so strange and unearthly, so desolate and heart-rending, that it was as if all the lost souls of the Bushmen had gathered here to mourn.

Rose felt herself drawn irresistibly into the circle. Women shifted up for her and she sat down in the space they made, feeling far too visible in her white tracksuit and pale face. She clapped along with the others to the beat of the drums, scanning the circle for familiar faces; thought she caught sight of Happiness's stern black eyebrows in the flickering firelight but couldn't be sure. A bare-chested man threw a large bunch of grey-green herb onto the fire, causing it to rear up like a stallion and release clouds of spicy perfume into the night air.

The women's clapping increased in intensity and tempo and the men's dancing took on a frenzied fervour. They bent forward from the waist, bodies covered in sweat, their faces contorted, with arms stretched out behind them or hands clutching at their heads. Some cried out.

Some dropped to the ground, trembling violently. Others lay in a dead faint, blood pouring from their nostrils. Some of the women, too, were rocking and moaning as they sat, bleeding from their noses, collapsing into lifeless heaps.

Rose watched impassively, breathing in the scented smoke and clapping along in time to the drums. She had a sense that she had been here before; she felt oddly at peace with the world.

As bodies fell about her, she had an unimpeded view of the rock face, which now dissolved into a boat-shaped area of dark nothingness, its edges flickering like fish in a fast-flowing stream. Eland and other antelope emerged from the darkness, their bodies gleaming in the moonlight. Fleet-footed and with muscles rippling, they raced across the rock face, changing into men as they ran. And there was that Killarney woman again, blanket still wrapped around her waist, clapping her hands and swaying along with the rest; but then her body turned into a fish and she swam away into the night.

Rose recognised that she was at the sacred place of the gods. She rose slowly and waded into a pool. Rain began to fall, dimpling the water. She floated and held up her arm that bore the thong, watching as raindrops deflected off the beads. Now she knew that within each bead was held an ancient promise, red, green and gold. She broke the leather thong like an umbilical cord from the past and let it fall, watching as it sank slowly to the invisible bottom of the pool.

A flash of lightning zigzagged across the sky and the Victorian lady, the White Goddess of the painting, appeared before her. She wore a dress of purest white, its skirts full and the neck and sleeves edged with lace. Her arms were outstretched as if about to gather Rose up in an embrace.

'I will give you the gift of the universe,' she said. 'Raise your hands and take the stars as your tools.' So Rose flew to the stars, following a thread of silver that hung from the sky, and she received them and they became pebbles of light in her hands.

Ruby appeared, wearing an old faded T-shirt and sunglasses. 'When we recognise that we have lost our distant past, only then can we mourn for it and move on,' she told her daughter and disappeared, leaving the White Goddess behind her. But then she, too, faded away into the rock face, taking the eland and the antelope with her.

Everyone was quiet around the dying fire. Shivering under the bright moon, Rose dozed off.

26th October 1880

My curiosity much roused by the mysterious rites of the previous night, I was driven to explore the site where they had taken place. At the first stirrings of the sun I awoke, hoping that the camp would still be in stupor after the night's frenzied activities. Not wanting to rouse anyone, I trod stealthily across the fields to where the horses were tethered and silently mounted Dolly. Stillness was everywhere, not even a child playing in the dust.

Through the gauzy mist the cliffs towered like an impenetrable fortress at the edge of the plain. There was nary a sound save for Dolly's hoof beats and now and then, the lonely call of a bird or the distant bark of baboons—creatures I fear meeting at close quarters. I clutched my rifle close to me as we made our way towards the cliffs.

On reaching the cliff face, I distinguished a path that appeared to follow the tortuous bends of the mountainside. Lo and behold! As Dolly and I walked along this path, the mist lifted, rising like curtains at the start of a theatre performance and there, in a recess under overhanging ledges of rock, I beheld the exquisite paintings. They were astounding to see. Countless scenes of great complexity inscribed on the bare rock, beautifully rendered in polychromatic shadings that range from burnt ochre to tan, sienna, umber, orange and yellow. They display so fine a line, such delicate colouring and detailed representation, that I am hard pressed to believe they did not emanate from the finest talent at the Academy. Antelope of all types are represented—eland, reedbuck, small duikers and a host of others, depicted in a range of poses—lying, standing, rearing up, grazing tranquilly, running in fear of their lives or dying. The human figures have been less realistically rendered but nonetheless display a remarkable vigour as they walk, sit, stand or dance, singly and in groups. Frightening monsters appear too, half man, half beast, seeming to slip into or emerge from the natural cracks in the rock face. There are other more puzzling markings too—what look to be ladders and bridges, and a series of dots that run mysteriously along the rocks.

Dismounting from Dolly I walked as if hypnotised, barely daring to breathe for fear of disturbing the mystical aura that radiates from the art. Then suddenly I stopped, for there before me was a large and glorious eland. It was rendered in tans and browns, glowing with an almost magical shimmer and veritably pulsing with potency and godliness. A strange compulsion made me reach out to touch it.

I placed my palm gently over the animal and immediately gasped in fear and awe as I experienced the sense of indescribable strength and power that seemed to radiate from it. The mystical aura enveloped me completely, and I was thrust suddenly forwards in time, towards the stars, towards the future, towards a child of my child's child who reached out to me as I reached out to her in turn, granting her the power that had been given to me. I stood entranced until the image dissipated. Then, still in my state of godly reverence, I retraced my footsteps, remounted Dolly and rode slowly back to the village.

The rest of the day I spent in a state of thrall, unable to get the paintings out of my mind. I cannot help thinking, too, of the medicine man's words to me regarding their sacredness. Can it be true that by touching them I have profaned them? I am tempted to dismiss his warning as mere superstition. Nonetheless I have decided to tell no one about my illicit visit to the rocks. Perhaps in this way any ill consequences of my action will be averted—for my Bushmen friends and for me.

It was morning. Rose found herself sprawled on the floor of Happiness's hut, lying half-on, half-off the mat, a small pile of smooth, white pebbles next to her head. The blanket lay in a heap at her side and her body ached from cold and the hours she had spent on the hard floor. She rolled over, pulled the blanket over her and snuggled into its considerable folds, lying like that for a few minutes, looking up into the murky reaches of the thatched roof.

She felt her wrist; the thong was gone. Sitting up, she lifted the blanket and shook out its folds, looked here and there on the floor, searching the hut as far as the hearth. But the thong was nowhere. Scooping up the pebbles, she dropped them into a side pocket of her backpack. Then she poured herself a mugful of water from the ewer and drank deeply, pausing to catch her breath, then drinking again.

Her stomach ached from emptiness. She realised it was a long time since she had last eaten. She opened the lid of the pot that still sat on the hearth and broke off a piece of the cold pap. It tasted bland and sat heavily in her empty stomach, but she broke off another piece and another. What time was it? She had no idea. Anxious, she checked her phone; but it was dead. She wondered where Happiness and her daughter were. Was she expected to wait for them at the hut? Deciding to go in search of them, she picked up her backpack by the straps and walked out the door.

As before, the village looked deserted, except for the goats and chickens that picked amid a rubbish heap, and the children. There was a young girl of not more than eleven or twelve, carrying a baby on her hip. Rose walked up to the pair.

'Hello,' she said, stroking the baby's chubby arm, as smooth as chocolate liqueur. She wanted to ask where all the adults were but the baby started yelling. The girl and Rose looked into each other's eyes and smiled shyly. Rose said goodbye and walked away.

Judging by the height of the sun, it was somewhere round mid morning. As Rose gazed towards the mountain, a shadowy recollection of the strange night flitted, dream-like, across her mind. She remembered receiving something so valuable and important that it would change her life forever; but for the life of her she couldn't recall what it was. Slippery as a fish it eluded her and each time she tried to recover it, grew more distant, swimming further into the recesses of her memory.

She walked towards the cliff face, retracing her steps along the path from the night before. Now, in the light of day, she could see the desolation of the landscape, the cold and empty plain where no tree took root.

She wondered whether the adults of the village would still be at the fire, sleeping off their trance-induced stupors. But when she got there, there was no one; only a pale pile of ashes remaining to hint at the frenzied activities of the night before.

She walked on towards the rock face where she recalled having seen the paintings, following the path that now hugged the mountainside. She searched the rocks as she walked, full of expectation, remembering the vividness of the images she'd seen there – the running antelopes . . . the White Goddess . . . But all she found were a few disappointing scratchings, so faded she couldn't even be certain they were there at all; the passage of time had been cruel. She continued on along the cliff path for half a kilometre or more, hoping to find more paintings that were perhaps hidden behind outcrops or concealed in the facets of the rocks. But if they were there, she didn't discover them.

The night had left her feeling strange and disconnected from herself. She suddenly wanted to be gone from this place, felt an urgent need to get back to Oberon and feel its familiar ground beneath her feet. If she started now, there would be plenty of time to reach her car before the gates closed. She felt more confident this morning that she could find her way back without Happiness. It wasn't that far, a few hours at most. The path that had brought them to the village was just over there, on the other side of the donga. She could see it from where she stood.

Pushing her khaki cap firmly down on her head and her sunglasses up on her nose, she began walking towards the faint trail snaking away through the pale-green grass that covered the lonely contours of the earth.

27th October 1880

This morning, unable to restrain my longing, I again rode to the cliffs to relive my strange and mystical experience with the magical eland. But as I trod the now familiar path with Dolly and rounded the bend to the spot where the paintings began, I received the shock of my life.

There, at the place of the eland, a dreadful vandal had been at work. The painting's splendour was entirely spoilt, the whole of it now overlaid with a white figure so crude in execution that it looked as if a child had dipped his finger in a jar of white paint and rudely daubed the rock.

As I stood aghast, my mouth agape, a shock of recognition tremored through me—the white figure bore an uncanny resemblance to me! There was my bustle dress and my white bonnet with the wide curvy brim, that always sits upon my crown in these hot altitudes. It was I, no doubt about it—but in the throes of some ghastly spell. I appear to flail about, my arms outstretched, as if in mortal agony. Red and white lines, like blood and foam, stream from my nose. Above my likeness, at a higher aspect in the rock, are two more figures, rendered in the same crude strokes. Their heads are bowed, their bodies bent low and arms extended behind their backs, as if paying homage to the dying white lady. Who had done this terrible thing?

Just then, a hand appeared from out of nowhere to grab my wrist. I cried out and tried to free myself—but in vain. The medicine man held me in a grip of iron. "No, you don't!" he rasped at me. His loathsome fingers, freshly stained with white pigment, dug deep into my wrist. "You!" he cried in his broken English. "Witch! Spirit-of-the-dead! You who have shot your treacherous arrows where they should not go. Thief who has stolen my power! You have broken the string that connects us to the Great God. Because of you, we will be forced to leave this land forever. Destroyer! Evil monster! You . . . white thing!" His voice broke on a sob.

He let go of me suddenly and fell to his knees, rocking backwards and forwards, ranting in his own tongue as one possessed. I stumbled away and ran to Dolly, whereupon I mounted her and galloped swiftly away, my heart almost bursting through my ribcage.

I realise that I have to leave Patilweng urgently. It is no longer safe for me to remain here.

Rose followed the path that undulated through the landscape of grassy hills. At this high altitude the sun radiated harshly but the wind was chilly on her face. She had set up a brisk pace and swung her arms jauntily in time to the song that played in her head. She had never been one to sing aloud, but suddenly her voice emerged, soft and breathy.

Where had it come from, this verse of song? Where had she heard it before? She couldn't remember. But she couldn't get it out of her head: 'The Happy Wandering Song'. Over and over it played like a mantra as she headed for the horizon, towards the edge of the earth. The sun climbed higher and higher, warming the crown of her head through the cap and releasing balm-like smells from the grass. Soon she had to stop and take off her jacket. Stuffing it into her backpack, she noticed its grime, the smears of red dust and black soot from her adventures of the night before.

Disconnected images drifted through her head. She remembered the heat of the flames burning her cheeks, the silhouettes dancing around the fire, explosions of sparks released by the herbs . . . the feeling of flying . . . falling . . . floating. And then that fleeting moment of profound understanding and enlightenment, followed by overriding peace and calm. But what had been reality and what had been illusion and imagining? That, she couldn't determine.

And then this morning, the silence and emptiness of the village. Where had all the adults gone? And Happiness? Rose would have liked at least to have told her she was leaving and thank her for her hospitality.

The path led to the edge of a gulley. She remembered this from yesterday, when she had slithered down through the tangled growth to the river and then scrambled up the other side. Now she did it in reverse. She walked downstream, scrutinising the flat, pale boulders; the sandbanks where imagined crocodiles sunned themselves; the small, rocky rapids that fizzed like newly poured Tab; trying to recognise the spot where she and Happiness had crossed over the day before.

She walked on some more, feeling hesitant. It was taking too long. She didn't remember the crossing place being this far downstream. Now she'd reached a patch of marshy ground, like thick, black soup, with a smell that rose putrid and sulphurous from it. Rose stopped. So, okay, she'd gone too far. No problem. She'd retrace her footsteps and see if she could spot the path on the other side of the river, the one that she and Happiness had come along.

She turned around and walked back, feeling less and less certain. The topography looked so different from this direction. Had she actually come this way? There was a sandbank that stretched three quarters of the way across the water. She thought about crossing there but she couldn't remember the feature at all from yesterday's trek. She walked further upstream. And further still.

It felt like her best course would be to go back to the grassy section of path that had first led her down to the river, and start again. Or maybe it would be wiser to return all the way to Patilweng and wait for Happiness to accompany her back. But hang on . . . there – wasn't that the spot where they had crossed? She paused to make sure, then decided that it was and tripped effortlessly over the stones, the tension draining from her shoulders.

It seemed easier crossing today – or perhaps the river was lower than it had been yesterday. She remembered that on the way here, the path had led directly into the water but now, in reverse, she could find no path. She struggled up the embankment through brambles and bushes . . . and there it was again, the humus-rich track carved out of the slope. Relief flooded her. It was wonderful, this wandering along the mountain-side, now that she knew where she was going. The sun glittered harshly on the water but in the dappled shade of the path, the air was cool and gentle.

The path started climbing. On their way here, it hadn't seemed as steep as this but they'd been descending, then. Now, she had to stop often to catch her breath. Looking up through the trees to check her progress, she saw the harsh white light of the sun glaring through the branches. She still had a good few metres to ascend. Inhaling deeply, she resumed her way and climbed doggedly onwards and upwards.

The increasing burn in her thighs brought back the feelings of unease that she'd been trying so hard to suppress. A vision of Happiness's sturdy back flitted across her mind's eye. Why hadn't she waited? Why hadn't she looked for her more diligently? What was her rush anyway? To get to her car, was that it? She was worried about a material object? An assemblage of metal, rubber and plastic?

Her legs shaking from exertion, she finally crested the rise and emerged through the woodland to find a landscape that had changed dramatically. A grassy knoll rose gently to her right but on her left the terrain fell away sharply to a deep rift that curved, serpentine-like, into the earth before disappearing into the folds of the horizon. In front of her, across a huge swathe of undulating land, rose far-flung peaks, like the impenetrable walls of a forbidden city. Where was she? They definitely had not come this way yesterday, of that she was sure. There was nothing she recognised here, not a single feature that was familiar to her. Oh God! She couldn't deny it – she was completely lost, alone in these mountains with a dead phone and not a soul around to guide her through . . .

She pressed her hand over her mouth, panic rising in her throat. She had no idea how long she'd been walking but it felt like forever. She heard her breath emerge, shallow and jagged from her mouth. Calm down! she told herself sharply. She slowed her breathing deliberately. In. Out. She had the brochure with the map in her backpack. This path she was on must lead somewhere – could she find it on the map? But the map was too roughly sketched to be of any help. She turned it this way and that, trying to work out where north was, fighting her rising hysteria. At least she was on a path. People used paths. Someone was bound to come this way sooner or later. The sun was still high in the sky and there were plenty of daylight hours left. Carry on walking, she told herself. Just carry on. There's no stopping now.

31st October 1880

On my return to the camp, I found the whole village astir, talking excitedly among themselves. I dismounted and still trembling like a leaf, led Dolly to the pasture. It was there that I spied the red uniforms of two British cavalrymen, brilliant against the soft greens of the landscape. I was overwhelmed with relief as they told me they had been sent by Uncle to secure my safe return to Oberon. He had been warned of uprisings, even war, brewing against the colonial administration. With this whiff of rebellion in the air, he was taking no chances with my safety. Abel and the bearers had already started packing my effects. Although the day was still sunny, clouds had begun to gather and we needed to make haste.

It was under a brooding sky that the entire clan (only the medicine man notable by his absence) congregated to bid me farewell. Connie, Beth and Katy presented me with a beautiful leather thong to wear around my wrist. It is most skillfully crafted, adorned with green, red and gold glass beads. With the help of Abel to translate and through copious tears, I declared that with this keepsake the people of Patilweng shall remain forever in my heart, and I shall always remember my sojourn in their village with fondness. At this, the rain began to fall, spattering the dry earth with large heavy drops. I thought of the medicine man wreaking his magic on the rock and couldn't repress a shiver. The rain bull has returned; the medicine man's power is restored. He will doubtless be triumphant at my departure, imagining himself victorious.

20

The sun's great white heat beat down relentlessly on Rose's head, penetrating through her cap to her scalp. In the distance, a sinister black spot circled in the otherwise spotless sky. A vulture? Thirsty for blood. Hers. She was going to die. People died in these mountains. Thirsty. Suddenly she remembered the two bottles of water in her backpack. In her excitement to reach Patilweng yesterday she had forgotten all about them, neglecting to drink at all and becoming dehydrated in her stupidity. She reached into her pack, closed her hand around the smooth curve of a bottle. It felt warm to her touch and gave a little sigh as she unscrewed the lid. But the water tasted like nectar to her parched tongue. One step at a time, that's all you need, she told herself.

The landscape changed again. Huge boulders hulked on the donga-furrowed earth, weathered by aeons of wind and water into shapes weird and wonderful: giant Mexicans enjoying eternal siestas under huge sombreros; oversized balls balancing one atop the other; massive mushrooms thrusting up from the ground. She became aware of the great silence enveloping her. There was only the sound of her breathing, and her footsteps beating out a regular rhythm in her head.

Still she followed the path, struggling against the black hopelessness that threatened to descend over her like a shroud. She was going to die. Before her life had even really begun. No, she wasn't – she was going to make it. She was a survivor. She would wake up from this bad dream and live to tell the tale. She stopped, looking towards the peaks ahead, then backwards to gauge her progress. She allowed herself another small sip of water, trying to conserve it. So thirsty. Weary. Oh so weary, and she still had so far to go. This path had no end. And she could see by the position of the sun that day was running out. She needed to get to a more protected area, look for a cavern or rocky overhang where she could take shelter for the night if she had to; one of those hidden caves that had once been home to hunter-gatherers of old.

The sun was on its downward slide. Cumulus clouds were building up like giant cauliflowers to her left. Rose stumbled doggedly onwards, the path taking her down to a plain recently ravaged by fire, traversing a wasteland of blackened earth and scorched stalks that poked nastily into the thin rubber soles of her hiking shoes. Her eyes smarted from the acrid smell and she wiped them with the back of her hand, smudging soot like a bruise across her face. Her white tracksuit pants were filthy, her T-shirt equally so. She lacked the energy to wave away the flies that droned about her ears, their buzzing rising and falling like olden-day fighter planes. The first bottle of water now finished, she sipped slowly from the second. She must come upon a stream soon, surely? Wasn't the source of the country's water here, in these mountains? She watched anxiously the progress of the clouds. They had become grey and heavy and she could see flashes of lightning on the distant horizon. Were the clouds coming this way? Oh no, please not! 'More people die from lightning in these mountains than on the Highveld.'

The patch of scorched earth ended abruptly and she stood now on a barren plateau. Looking across its rocky surface, she saw four cairns like dwarf sentinels placed randomly about. She walked towards them, over the myriad fissures and cracks that told of the baking and freezing, the innumerable sunrises and sunsets over this lonely earth. She circled each cairn in turn, looking for a plaque, a sign that would indicate something – anything. But there was nothing. Who had so diligently collected the orange-stained rocks and coaxed them into balancing in these mini-towers? And why? Rose looked to see if she could find anything about them on the map. But no, they didn't feature. Their presence seemed to signify that humans had been here once, but they had since vanished, leaving only these mysterious markers behind.

At the edge of the plateau a donga dipped into the earth, its rough sides gouged out by rivulets of rainwater. Rose looked for a way across it. She found one further along and slid and slithered down to the rock-strewn bottom, clambering up the other side, where she picked up the path once again.

The banking clouds on her left had turned black and heavy, and flashed sporadically. It was raining somewhere. She looked anxiously at the sky. What would she do if the storm came this way? Where could she hide? Cold sweat pooled under her arms and in the hollow of her spine under the backpack. Her tired head bowed under the weight of her skull. She'd had nothing to eat all day but she was beyond hunger. Her face and arms throbbed where they had caught the sun.

DO NOT hike when it is lightning. She couldn't lose sight of the mountains, the cliffs of pale sandstone and black basalt towering ahead. UKhahlamba, Barrier of Spears.

She trudged along, hyper-aware of the diminishing patches of sunlight on the path. Night would be here before she knew it. She was going to be prey for jackals, carrion for vultures. She was going to die out here. From exposure, from lightning, from thirst and starvation. Who would ever find her in this endless maze of mountains that went on forever and ever? Her footsteps faltered and her chest heaved with hopeless sobs. She knew she couldn't carry on much longer.

But what about the sangoma's prophecy? She wanted to believe it with all her heart, to hang onto the promise of it; she was going to live a long and fruitful life; she was going to take many journeys, touch many children; she was a lucky, lucky lady. People did die in these mountains but she wasn't going to be one of them. She gave another sob. She wasn't going to die – she was *not* going to die. What had happened to the song in her heart?

How long had she been walking for? Six hours? Eight? As the shadows lengthened about her, she'd never tasted regret more bitter; she'd lived such a puny existence, accumulating neither good deeds nor bad. No debits, no credits. Her life was a balance sheet that lacked all entries. A mere waste of space.

Coming here to Patilweng, and then trying to get back on her own had been the biggest mistake of her life. What had she been thinking? Would Brigit and Hank send out the search parties? The Parks Board official wouldn't; he thought she was with Happiness. She felt so bereft, suddenly aware of the pathos of her situation. There was no one out there who would alert the authorities on her behalf, no one who would miss her, who would mourn her. Her loneliness was so profound that it was as if she could touch the very stuff of her soul, the essence of her humanity.

She trudged along on her leaden legs, tears streaming down her cheeks as she scanned her surroundings hopelessly, looking for a place where she could shelter for the night. There was nowhere. Just the grass-covered slopes. Endless undulations to traverse before she reached the distant crags. And even if she made it there before nightfall, what would she find but more of the same? Loneliness and exposure. There was nothing else out here. She wanted to just sink down to her knees, curl up, and go to sleep. She staggered to a stop. No! Keep going. Just make it up the next slope.

Then, halfway up the hill, she came to a fork in the path, marked by a large rock. There were two arrows in white paint and some crude lettering. She focused her eyes with difficulty and read slowly: 'Sleeping Beauty Cave'. 'Eyrie Lookout'. Hang on – she'd seen these features on the map, hadn't she? She drew the crumpled brochure from her backpack and smoothed it out with shaking hands. The map swam before her eyes. She blinked and refocused; yes, there was the fork and the cave and there was the lookout . . . Normally she hated caves – they made her claustrophobic with their dank, rank air and spooky darkness, their bats and dripping water. But now, in her state of extremis, she felt so grateful that if she'd had the energy she would have whooped. Better Sleeping Beauty Cave than Eyrie Lookout – where she definitely didn't want to go. To scale some barren, inaccessible cliff and risk confronting a nesting eagle . . . No thanks!

The shadows were merging into one big shadow. She had to get going if she wanted to reach the cave before darkness rolled in. How far was it? The map gave no help.

She set off once again, with renewed impetus, scrambling to the top of the hill. The path became more rugged, hugging the mountainside then entering a patch of dense forest, where huge ferns stretched their fronds among the tree trunks and poisonous excrescences grew in black hollows. The sounds of water burbled below her as she tore along, trying to make it to the cave before night came, losing her footing more than once as she scrambled over roots and fallen trunks slippery with moss.

The sky was a lurid green above the leaf canopy and she heard the ominous rumble of thunder. The air had turned chilly suddenly and the wind that rattled through the leaves carried the definite smell of rain. She dreaded its coming, the pelting of raindrops, the rocks under her feet turning to glass . . . falling to her death on the slippery surfaces. Gazing down into the ravine that lay far beneath her, she imagined poisonous roots and legions of deadly snakes slithering in rocky crevices so remote from the sun that they remained forever wet and putrid. Again she became tearful as she heard the bark of a baboon, a plaintive roar that echoed from the surrounding rocks.

And then, suddenly, the wind stopped and there was silence.

She emerged from the forest to find herself on top of the world, walking along a path bounded by masses of small-petalled flowers that stretched in tracts of yellow, white, pink and purple. The heavy clouds parted and patches of blue sky showed between them. Before her, a pool of water shone golden in the last rays of the sun. Rose couldn't believe what her eyes were seeing. In this magical place, she threw herself to the ground and scooped up handfuls of water to her mouth, until her thirst was slaked. She stripped her filthy clothes off and slid, gasping, into the icy depths of the water, slowly submerging herself until her feet came to rest on the pebbly floor, her head arched back to feel the current gently tugging at her hair. After a few minutes she was forced to emerge, her goose-pimpled body numb with cold.

As she was putting her clothes back on, her eye was caught by a streak of white on a rock nearby. Going closer, she saw a white-painted arrow pointing to the cliff ahead of her, where a jumble of massive rocks hid a furtive opening. Beside it was a stone plaque, with the words 'Sleeping Beauty Cave' painted on it. Relief swept over her, buckling her knees; she had made it! Ducking through the opening between the boulders, she found herself in her shelter for the night.

It was a cave but not quite a cave; a black envelope of rock where magma long ago had folded in on itself to form a large, boulder-strewn cavern. Beyond the gravelly shelf where she now stood, the rock sloped steeply down to unknown depths, then somersaulted back up again to form a ceiling lofty as a cathedral's. In the middle of the shelf there was a small pile of charred remains left behind by previous campers. She laid her backpack down and sat on top of it, studying the map, trying to get her bearings before the light faded completely. She thought briefly about venturing down the slope to explore what was there, but decided it was safer to stay right where she was. Too exhausted even to feel hunger, she slid down onto her back, rested her head on her backpack and closed her eyes. The rocky floor felt hard and cold beneath her and the sharp edges in her backpack dug into her head. But she was too tired to care.

There it was again – the bark of the baboon. Was she going to be sharing this place with a baboon? The thought terrified her. Maybe she should rather try and make her way back to the car park . . . But it was too late for that. It would be fully dark in no time. It warned right there on the pamphlet: *DO NOT hike alone. DO NOT hike in the dark.* Was she much better off here, though? When night came it would be pitch black in the cave – she wouldn't sleep a wink. Sleeping with baboons or hiking in the dark? What a choice!

Outside, she heard the rustling of leaves and the snapping of branches. What was out there? In the crepuscular light, a shadow loomed at the mouth of the cave. Rose jumped up, grabbing her backpack, wielding it in front of her chest like a weapon. Panic had turned her knees to water and her heart was pounding wildly in her chest.

The shadow had long legs and a lean frame. It paused for a moment, as if gathering itself, then entered the space. She recognised the doctor. Wim Metheus.

He didn't seem surprised to see her there. He merely nodded a greeting. 'Are you also camping here for the night?' he asked matter-of-factly.

Her knees still shaking, her voice tremulous, Rose replied: 'Er . . . yes.' She felt so stupid. Did you book this place? Should she offer to leave? She couldn't. She was just too weary and cold and footsore, too traumatised . . . and too relieved not to be alone any more. Where would she go in any case?

Wim had shrugged his backpack off his shoulders and was busy unpacking it. She watched as he unrolled a sponge mat, sleeping bag, blanket and provisions. He disappeared down the gravelly slope and returned with water in a pot; there must be a stream running through here.

Rose lay back on her pack again and closed her eyes, peeping through them every now and then to check what he was doing. The two white stripes down the sides of his tracksuit pants signalled his movements; which way he bent, which way he stretched. His presence was hugely comforting. Rather a human for company than a baboon! He looked so in control. She watched him light a fire with twigs and firelighters, his movements dexterous, his fingers long and tapering. There was a pungent smell and black smoke rose, hovered, then slithered out the opening of the cave. Sitting back on his haunches, he took out a little three-legged cooker and began to boil the water. In the meagre firelight, with the angles of his face deepened by shadow, he looked like an evil magician.

Rose was freezing. What was the camping etiquette here?

'Can I share your fire?' she asked, sitting up to shuffle closer to the heat of the flames.

'Ja. Ja. Where is your food to cook?'

'I don't have any . . . I just need the warmth . . . I'm sorry.' She sat on her knees, as close to the small fire as she could get, holding her palms up to the meagre heat. 'I've got nothing . . . I got lost . . . I didn't mean to . . . be intruding in your cave . . .' She found him so intimidating, couldn't string a coherent sentence together. And she couldn't stop shivering. She wanted to cry but managed a crooked smile instead.

'Here. You better eat some of these. Get your sugar levels up.'

'Thanks.' Koeksisters. Dripping with syrup. She must look such a fright with her tangled hair and filthy clothes but she didn't care because it was only her soul that he could see here.

'And take this.' He gave her the folded blanket.

She wrapped it round her gratefully. 'Thanks! I'm . . . Rose.' She thought she'd remind him.

'Yes, I remember. Rose. The flower.'

She had been ravenous, her stomach aching from hunger. Now she found she couldn't eat. She took a small bite of the koeksister, then held the remnant delicately between thumb and forefinger, unsure what to do with it. Surreptitiously she deposited it on the rock next to her backpack.

'What's the time?' she asked.

He stretched out his arm to expose a big, rugged watch. '6.40.'

6.40! They were about to spend hours and hours together – they couldn't spend them in silence. She had to make conversation. 'Do you know Patilweng?' she asked.

'Yes, I know it. I know these mountains well.'

'I've just come from there. How far is it from here?'

'Not so far. About eight, ten kilometres.'

'I . . . I got so terribly lost. I walked for hours. It felt like I . . . I was in this strange trance. I didn't know what I was doing. And . . . and . . .' And then she did the unthinkable – she broke down in front of him. She covered her face with her hands and sobbed and sobbed, her body heaving with the release of fear and emotion. She should have felt mortified to be crying in front of him but, strangely, she didn't; she'd earned the right to these tears.

Sniffing and wiping her face with her sleeve, she found herself telling him everything. '. . . And in the night, I had such a headache, and she gave me this potion . . . I was like . . . in some sort of drugged state. I just needed to get back to civilisation . . .'

He handed her a piece of kitchen towel. Was that a look of long-suffering on his face? But he would be used to women's tears.

She blew her nose and dabbed at her wet cheeks. The paper felt rough against her sunburnt skin. 'I truly thought I was going to die out here.'

He nodded sympathetically. 'You're very lucky. Lost people often walk round and round in circles and sometimes they do die.'

'And there was lightning. I thought I was following the path that we'd come along yesterday. But I must have gone wrong somewhere.'

He shook his head. 'You're very lucky,' he repeated, slowly feeding the fire with the packet of sticks he'd brought in his backpack.

There was quiet between them now. They sat in silence, watching the flames grow. Rose gathered her calm.

Wim got up and busied himself among his supplies. Using a sachet of instant coffee and sugar, and the water now boiling in the pot, he made a mug of coffee and passed it to her.

She held the steaming mug with both hands: 'Ah . . . thank you. This is great.' He nodded, unwrapping mealies from newspaper and adding them to the pot.

'These villagers from Patilweng, have you heard anything about them? Like those stories of them being the descendents of the San?' Rose said presently.

'Yes, I have heard something like that. But I don't think it's true.'

'Why not?'

He shrugged. 'It's just a silly romantic notion. There probably is San blood in many of the natives of this area. But in terms of a surviving culture, I sincerely doubt it. The San way of life must have died out generations ago.'

She wanted to tell him that she had taken part in a Great Dance and had fallen into a trance, had an out-of-body experience, followed a silver thread and floated up to the sky to meet her ancestral mothers. But instead, she said: 'Have you been to a lot of the rock-art sites that are around here?'

'Ja, I have.'

Rose couldn't think of anything more to say. They sat in silence again, listening to the bubbling of the water in the pot and watching the fire that he fed every now and then from his packet of sticks.

'You're not allowed to take firewood from outside? You have to bring your own?' she asked.

'Ja. Imagine if everyone used the wood from the mountains. Soon, there'd be nothing left. You can make fire here – because it's a camping place. But you're not allowed to in the other caves. It causes too much damage to the sandstone. And of course the rock art, if there's any.'

He has haunted eyes, Rose thought. There's a fanatical zeal that burns in them. What's his quest? In earlier times he would have been a missionary. Had he, too, lost his way? Or had he found it here, through his work and through hiking in these mountains? Maybe it was his foreignness that she couldn't relate to; he was a closed book. They didn't share the same frames of reference – their histories were too different.

Now he was squatting over the fire, holding a piece of meat clamped between braai tongs. It was very cosy, the two of them here. She watched closely as he concentrated on his cooking. The mountain man; self-sufficient, preferring his own company. She wondered about his family, his mother. Did it break her heart to see her son's defences building up, on his way to becoming this man's man? Or was she the type who could barely wait for her children to leave the nest?

The smell of meat was giving her an appetite.

High cheekbones. Slavic roots? He felt her eyes on him and looked up. Their gazes met.

'Biltong?' He passed her a paper bag.

Rose laughed. 'Koeksisters and biltong. You've really taken on South African cuisine. How long have you been here?'

His face softened in the orange glow of the firelight and he smiled a crooked smile.

'Koeksisters and biltong are good camping foods.' His face regained its serious expression.'When did I get here? About ten, twelve years ago. I first worked in a rural facility in KZN, running a hospital there. I was fired for dispensing free ARVs. It wasn't state policy at the time. So then I moved to Lesotho. The government there was just starting a roll-out programme . . . building Aids clinics. I wanted to do something for the ones that it's too late for. And I love Lesotho, the country. It's just a small thing I do. Maybe it grows.'

He stooped to extract an aluminium plate from his rucksack, and a set of cutlery that fitted neatly together. Cutting the steak into two, he doled out the mealies and then sat cross-legged beside her, their knees and elbows almost touching.

'Here. You eat with the knife and fork. I eat with my fingers.'

'No, I can't take your food, really.'

'You need to eat after such a trauma.'

She hesitated then capitulated, the blanket falling off her shoulders as she stretched for the cutlery.

On her previous encounters with him, he'd seemed austere and unapproachable, as if there were no room in his life for any human foible or weakness. Tonight he was the benevolent magician.

'Thank you. You're very kind. I'll have to buy you a meal in Oberon – to reciprocate. In the pub, where I first saw you.'

'I noticed you, too.'

Their eyes met again, for a split second.

'I think it's a great thing that you're doing,' Rose said, spearing meat. 'I find it really hard to confront all this poverty and suffering that's around us. But I don't contribute . . . or do anything . . . to alleviate it.'

He nodded. 'You feel bad because it disturbs your middle-class identity. To have it upfront like this. You don't know how to deal with it. It's – how can I say – out your comfort zone.'

'That's true. Except . . . I live with the discomfort every day – every day I'm accosted by beggars . . . poverty . . .'

He nodded. 'For me, I try to do something to make it better but I know, deep down, it's really to feel better about myself. And my guilt. I feel responsible, you know . . . guilty for what my ancestors did – they really screwed up in Africa.' He put a piece of meat in his mouth and chewed slowly, deliberately.

'Tell me about Tjhetjhella Morao. Did you choose to build it there, so far away from everything?'

'No, no. The building existed already and was vacant, so we moved in. But my dream is to build a haven in the valley. I'm trying to raise funds . . . there are about eight thousand people living there, so it makes more sense to have it there. Like this, it's very difficult.'

'And Aids orphans? Is there any project for them? An NGO that takes care of them?'

'No. Not here in the valley. There's great need but no projects. Some of the orphans are looked after by people in the community. But much more needs to be done for them.' He looked into the fire as he spoke.

Rose had had enough to eat. 'Take the knife and fork, I'm finished. I'll rinse them off in the pot for you.' She got up to do it, felt her stiff, sore limbs protesting. Passing him the utensils, she took up her position beside him again, wrapping the blanket round her shoulders.

'You know,' he continued, 'in other, bigger communities, things are even worse. On both sides of the border. There are many, many orphans . . . families headed by children. They're easy targets for criminals. These gangsters steal their welfare grants and the money their dead parents leave behind. They get abused . . . raped. The older children can't even go to school. They must stay at home to protect their things. And the worst thing is, the people in the community know who the criminals are. They're often related to the children! It's very bad.' He shook his head.

'Such a problem. There should be some sort of adoption drive – to encourage people to adopt these children.'

'There are so many needy children. Too many.'

'Then maybe someone needs to start something, like a safe haven, where they can be protected, fed and schooled.' Her eyelids were feeling very heavy.

'Yes, but to start a project on the South African side . . . it's difficult. It would be better to do it on this side . . . there's less bureaucracy in Lesotho. Michael would be a good person to help with this. He would make sure the community supports the project. Ja.'

They sat in silence, hypnotised by the glowing embers. Rose pulled her backpack towards her and lay down with her head resting on it, her body curled towards the fire.

'I'm sorry . . . I'm falling asleep,' she said drowsily. A cold draught blew onto her back and she shivered, despite the blanket.

'You must sleep in the sleeping bag otherwise you'll be too cold. The fire will go out and it will get very cold in here . . .'

'I can't, really . . . I . . . I've taken enough advantage . . . If I can use the blanket, I'll be fine . . .'

'Come – I'll unzip the bag. We'll both fit inside. I'll only come in when you are sleeping so you won't even know I'm there. It's going to be very cold tonight. The rain's coming back.'

Oh my God – sharing a sleeping bag with this stranger. He was right, though – she was already freezing. How would she sleep with him alongside her? It didn't matter. At least she'd be warm.

Swallowing her reserve, she took off her shoes and socks – they were filthy, covered with burrs and blackjacks – then her jacket, equally filthy, and slipped in under the sleeping bag, stretching out on the foam mat.

'If you need to go in the middle of the night, here's a torch.' He threw the blanket over the sleeping bag and placed the torch above her head. That's a comfort, Rose thought.

The man with the kaross draped over his shoulders led the cow he had just captured across the wide open veld. The animal's tail twitched as they walked. There was a Great Dance going on at the cliff – she could see the glow that lit up the sky and hear the rhythmic beat of the drums. The man slit the cow's throat with one deft stroke of a sharp stone. The animal sank onto its knees, gave a great bellow and died. Rain started to fall, splattering onto the dry earth. But it was not water that fell but blood and milk. They merged on the ground, generating great puddles of pink liquid . . .

Rose woke to the sound of the rain; a soft, soaking, feminine rain. She became aware of the male presence behind her and the heat generated by its closeness, the two of them curled like a double apostrophe in the sleeping bag. Her mind blanked out and she fell once more into the abyss of sleep.

Later, she became aware of Wim's hand slipping under her T-shirt, touching the warm, soft skin around her navel. He moved closer, pressing against her so that she could feel his body along the whole length of hers. He nuzzled the nape of her neck, then her shoulder, his hand moving to her breast, softly caressing, then slipping slowly down her torso, under the waistband of her pants. She desired him, lusted for sex. She rolled onto her back and together they peeled off their clothes. She felt his weight, heavy on her, his cheek rough and warm against hers, his taut back . . . a groan escaped from the back of her throat as he thrust into her and she surrendered so completely to her desire that she was aware of nothing else – except her body that had become a receptacle of pure pleasure. There was no shame in their sex, no inhibition; no shared history or common memories – no thing that complicated their connection. She felt him burst into her, a million stars filling her every crevice and fold. 'More,' she whispered, and he pleasured her until she cried out, shuddering. And again, until she was finally satiated.

Her full bladder woke her. Early-morning light crept into the cave and she heard the dawn chorus of a myriad birds. Taking care not to disturb Wim, she eased herself out from under the sleeping bag and stood up. A trickle of fluid rolled down her leg. In the twilight zone between sleep and wakefulness, she'd thought she might have imagined it all, but now she knew it had to be true.

The sky was clear and pale over the damp earth, raindrops quivering on the leaves as she made her way to a spot near the river. As she squatted, she could smell the distinctive post-coital smell, the mixing of bodily fluids.

Unprotected sex with a complete stranger. Was she mad? What had happened to her usual caution and common sense? And what about him? Where had he been – this lonely man living in the heartland of the plague? Was this kind of thing a habit for him? Surely he, of all people, knew the consequences of one incautious night of passion. Always wear a condom. No glove, no love. Tainted blood and bodily fluids . . . the fragility of mucous membranes, especially female. She was more at risk than he. But still – he was taking a chance, too. He knew as little about her as she knew about him. She needed at the very least to ask him his status; could she trust him to tell her the truth?

She walked back into the cave, her footsteps faltering as she neared the sleeping bag. She stood looking upon his sleeping frame . . . the bristly head, dark-blond eyelashes, sharp cheekbones . . . and her stomach lurched from the memory of her uninhibited desire. Shame woke in her and she felt too self-conscious for speech. She knew at that moment that she couldn't ask, couldn't discuss what had taken place. And there was the other thing, too; she couldn't quite remember where she was in her cycle. She'd have to get to a chemist sooner rather than later.

Quietly picking up her backpack, she stole out the cave and, map in hand, soon found the path that would lead her to her car.

21

It was just after seven o'clock by the time she got back to Oberon. In the main street, taxis disgorged domestic workers, cleaners, shop assistants, waitresses and cooks. It was too early to go to the chemist. How long did she have? Wasn't it twenty-four hours at least, for the morning-after pill? She'd have to get tested at some stage for the other thing, too. How long did you have to wait to test? And did you have to be on ARVs in the meantime? She should know these things, by her age. How unschooled she was in the ways of the sexual world. She passed the garage and turned onto the dirt road that took her down to the bridge, then up again on the other side, following the bends past the now familiar houses and farm buildings. The gate to The Chameleon stood open and she drove straight in.

Her cottage looked humble and welcoming in the rainwashed morning. She couldn't wait to soak in a bath and wash away the grime on her body and the damp that chafed between her legs. Opening her backpack, she poked around for the key. She delved deeper, rummaging in side pockets, feeling amongst the stones. Where had she put it? She hunted on the floor of her car and under the seats. To lose the key, now – of all times! She could either knock on Brigit's door or wait until breakfast at eight o'clock; she decided she couldn't wait that long.

Feeling weary to the bone, she dragged her feet across the dew-covered grass. A dark body hurtled down from a lofty branch of the pine tree and she ducked in alarm as the peacock landed at her feet; she hadn't realised they roosted so high. What a fright it gave her! Her heart jumped flabbily in her chest.

She went round to the Lieber's back door, smacking at her filthy pants and trying to smooth her messy hair. Neither car was there but Thuli had to be inside. Rose raised her hand to knock and froze on the threshold. The door was ajar, and through the gap she could see the breakfast area in disarray. Chairs had been flung around, drawers pulled open. From somewhere inside she heard the children crying.

Oh no! Oh God! She ran down the passage, looking into the lounge as she passed. There was an empty space on the unit where the TV normally stood. A bunch of coloured wires poked out from the wall where the set had been wrenched off roughly. She felt sick to her stomach. Where were they? The children? Brigit?

She rattled the door handles of the children's rooms. The doors were locked, the keys missing. The crying grew louder.

'Jamie, Jemma,' she cried. 'Are you okay? Where's mommy?'

She dashed to the main bedroom, dreading what she'd find, steeling herself before entering.

'Brigit!' she screamed, clapping her hand over her mouth. Brigit lay on the carpet, on her side. She swivelled her head to look up at Rose, her eyes weary and owlish without her glasses. Her hands and feet had been bound and she'd been tied to the leg of the bed. Duct tape was stuck down over her mouth. Greasy footprints marred the beige carpet and the duvet cover on the double bed was crumpled up. Please, not that!

Next to Brigit lay Thuli. She moaned when she saw Rose. Were they hurt? Get them untied. She ran to the kitchen to find a knife or scissors. When did this happen? Just as well the children weren't able to come out their rooms.

Rose felt like she was living in an old film reel, time moving in jerky frames. She cut the ties and tape and Brigit got slowly to her feet, rubbing the red welts on her wrists. Thuli sat up, looking dazed.

'Are you okay? What happened?' Rose's voice sounded strange, choked up. Tears rolled down her cheeks. Why was she crying? Brigit and Thuli should be the ones crying. She wiped her cheeks with the back of her hand.

Brigit sat on the edge of the bed for a few seconds then jumped up and bounded to the children's rooms. 'Children! Are you okay? Don't cry. Everything's fine. Mommy's fine. I'm finding the key now.' She ran down the passage and into the study. Rose followed her, body trembling, mouth dry, tears continuing to run down her cheeks. Was she the only one aware of the foetid smell of swamp that followed her? She hoped so.

'Shit. Computer's gone. Where are my glasses? And my cell phone?' Searching through drawers roughly, Brigit said: 'I'm a bit bruised, that's all. Nothing else. They knocked me around a bit. Thuli, too.' Her face softened. 'Shame. She told them not to hurt me. Ah – here they are.' Brigit hurried to the children's rooms with the keys.

Doors unlocked, she gathered the children to her and comforted them, hugging them tightly as Jamie and Jemma cried, more with anger than fear. 'Come, come,' she soothed. 'Everything's okay now. We're all fine. Look! Here I am.'

'Where's daddy?' Jamie sobbed.

'He'll be here soon. He's fine. Everything's fine. Let's go have breakfast.'

Where was Hank? Rose wondered. Bad time to be off chasing stock thieves.

'Mommy, Mommy.' Jamie had run down the passage into the lounge. 'Where's the TV?'

'Oh no! Is it gone?' Brigit shook her head in a dazed way.

They made their way to the breakfast room, Brigit carrying the tear-stained Jemma, groaning as she cast her eyes into each room. 'What else is missing? I'm scared to look. Is my car there?'

Rose shook her head, remembering the empty parking spots. Had the cottage been left intact? She hadn't seen any signs of forced entry, but then she hadn't really looked. What could they have stolen from her? Her computer. It was the only thing of value. She hoped it was still there.

Brigit told Rose: 'The children were asleep. I was busy in the study. I heard a noise, you know, but didn't think anything of it. The next thing, these two thugs burst into the room – or three, there might have been another one somewhere – and started pulling me to the bedroom. I was worrying about the children. Thuli was in her room and they dragged her over here, too. Why, I don't know. Thank goodness for Thuli. She was great . . . but we're fine, aren't we, Thuli?'

Thuli nodded, then hid her face in her hands. 'I was so scared – it was terrible! I thought they were going to kill us. They had guns. Youngsters. They took my cell phone, my handbag, all my papers . . . I'm going to have troubles now.'

'I'm making you both tea,' Rose announced. 'Or maybe I shouldn't, I don't know. Maybe we shouldn't disturb anything. Fingerprints. I'll call the police. Where's the number?' She opened cupboards, not sure what she was looking for. Tremors still surged through her body.

Brigit shook her head. 'It's just typical. Typical that Hank's not here,' she muttered. 'Call the Community Watch. The number's next to the phone. They'll know what to do.'

'S'cuse me Ma'am,' Thuli said in a soft voice, 'I'm going to dress.' She was in a pale-blue nylon nightie, her hair snarled and knotted around her face, which had taken on a dull grey cast from the shock. She went out the door.

'What happened, Mommy? Why did those men take our TV? Were they baddies?' Jamie asked, wide-eyed. Jemma sat in her high chair, cheerfully banging a spoon on the tray.

'That's right, Sweetie. And I'm furious! How dare they!' Brigit exclaimed, roughly throwing cereal into bowls and tea bags into mugs.

'The main thing is that you're all unhurt. Material things are nothing,' Rose soothed, dialling the Community Watch's number with her shaky hands.

'That's not the main thing! We shouldn't have to be subjected to this. It's not normal. We can't live always looking over our shoulders, always worrying about our safety.' Brigit banged the mugs down on the table, sloshing tea over the sides.

'The Community Watch said they'll be here now. They told me to call the police as well.'

'Waste of time. What are they going to do?' Brigit snapped.

The two women sat at the table, steam rising from the bright mugs.

'Ah – this tastes good. Ow. It's burning my lips. When I ripped off the duct tape skin came with it . . . Anyway, thank God you came when you did. Otherwise who knows how long we would have stayed like that . . .' Brigit looked suddenly at Rose. 'Where were you this weekend, Rose?' She hesitated, then said: 'I was quite worried when you didn't come back. I was getting ready to phone around when . . . this happened. You never know, in this day and age . . . a woman on her own . . .'

Would it have made any difference if Rose had been around? Could she have sounded the alarm? Probably not. Maybe she would have been tied up along with Brigit and Thuli. She shuddered, wondering how she would have coped with such an ordeal. Not as well as Brigit, she was sure.

'I thought I'd be gone only a few hours . . . I'm really sorry. I would have phoned to let you know but there was no signal. And then my phone went dead. And . . . look at me!' She laughed embarressedly, feeling a wave of guilt wash over her. 'I did this gruelling hike and got lost in the mountains . . . and spent the night in a cave and . . . look how filthy I am . . .'

She hadn't given Happiness a thought till now. Had she caused her anxiety as well by vanishing like that? Probably not.

'Oh God, Brigit. That reminds me. I seem to have lost the cottage key. Do you have a spare? Sorry! This is all you need now.'

As Brigit got up to give her the spare key, hanging from a hook behind the door, the Community Watch arrived – three burly men, abounding in the expected machismo, complete with boeps and bristling moustaches. They poked about, talking loudly on their two-way radios.

Finally, the police arrived and when they left, Rose did, too.

Back in her cottage, Rose sat on the edge of the bath, dipping her hand in to feel the temperature of the water. The police hadn't seemed hopeful about apprehending the criminals. They took no fingerprints nor even asked for descriptions of the men, simply instructed Brigit to make a list of stolen and damaged property for insurance purposes. Rose climbed into the bath, submerging herself, the water closing over her like a wave of melancholy. Crime had hit too close to home. She had only walked into the crime scene, experiencing it from the margins but even so she felt sullied by it, and so weary all of a sudden that she wondered how she would even manage to pull herself out of the water.

Collapsing onto her bed, she passed out, waking in the late afternoon, feeling dazed. Forlornly in need of company, she arranged to meet Petra and Ronald for a drink at The Olive Branch. It was too late now for the chemist; time was running out.

She told Petra and Ronald what had happened to Brigit. 'She was amazing . . . really strong. She picked herself up and brushed herself off and just got on with it . . . comforted the children, directed Thuli . . .'

'You never know how you're going to react in these situations,' Ronald observed.

'And she had to be strong for the children,' Petra said. 'You can't wallow in self-pity at times like that . . . the needs of the children take preference to your own.'

'This thing that happened has really upset me,' Rose told them. 'I need to get going . . . I'll probably leave tomorrow. Well, to be honest – it's not only to do with the break-in . . . I just . . . need to get home.

There are things waiting for me that I have to confront and I suddenly feel ready.'

'That's sad, that you're leaving. You must keep in touch. Let us know if you find out anything . . . about your parents,' Petra told her. 'Your story's really stirred our interest, you know, Rose. Ronald and I went to the rock-art museum today. I tried to get hold of you to ask if you wanted to come but your phone was off.'

'Battery,' Rose said. 'So? What did you think?'

'Well, Steve was right, it was kind of kitsch, but the film was well done,' Ronald answered. 'I knew nothing about San art, had never heard of the Great Dance. It was very interesting . . . but probably only hypothetical. The lives of those old Bushmen were so far removed, so remote from ours – how can anyone, even expert scientists, be sure what their world was all about?'

'And the portrayal of the San themselves – the film showed such an idealised version of their lives, if you know what I mean. But as you say, Ronald, how can any modern person know?' Petra added.

'What did you make of the White Goddess story at the end?' Rose asked eagerly, and without waiting for a reply, rushed on: 'When I saw the painting, I couldn't believe it. I'd just been reading that exact incident in the dairy, about the village shaman painting her picture on the rock. It was exactly as she'd described it. I'm convinced the writer of the diary is the same Victorian lady that was in the film – she just has to be! *And* she's the one in that painting of Sir Geoffrey's, too . . . the one I showed you, "The Bushmen pay homage to the White Goddess". The question is, who is this person and how is she connected to me?' Rose looked hopefully at Ronald and Petra in turn.

'You know what I think?' Petra said. 'I think that painting of Sir Geoffrey's might be your starting point. There must be a record somewhere of who he used as his model for it. And you say the diary was written anonymously, but the entries are dated, so it might be possible to trace her arrival in Durban on the ship's manifest . . . if that record still exists. There couldn't have been many single women travelling unaccompanied from England. Look,' she went on, 'I'm going to do some research on the painting when I get to London. I'm sure there'll be other sources of information there . . . books, journals, that sort of thing; the Internet has its limitations . . .'

Much later, they said their goodbyes; Rose felt sad as they exchanged fond hugs.

'I won't forget about your White Goddess,' Petra smiled. 'I promise I'll email you the minute I find anything . . .'

Rose watched them drive away, waiting until she couldn't see either of their cars. Then she did the short drive back to The Chameleon.

The light was still on in the Liebers' house when she got back. Opening the door a crack, she peeped in to see Hank sitting alone at the table, surrounded by an array of metal parts, spanners and screwdrivers.

'I came to see how Brigit's doing,' Rose told him.

'Ja – she's strong. She'll be fine.'

'And you?'

'Me?' He laughed but it sounded a little hollow to Rose's ears. 'I'm fine, too. Great. Just fixing this piece of tractor.'

'Hank – I'm leaving tomorrow. After breakfast.' She waited for some reaction but he just looked bemused. 'Remember those seeds I told you about?' she continued. 'Here they are. Will you plant them for me?' She passed him the packet.

He held it up to the light and nodded: 'It's worth a shot. You never know with seeds.'

He looked at her then, a serious expression on his face: 'I'll miss you, Goddess. Hey, come back and stay with us again.'

'You never know,' she smiled.

The next morning, her car packed and ready, she stepped through the shrubbery for the last time and across the courtyard to the Liebers' house. The peacock accompanied her as far as the back door.

Happiness was in the breakfast room. There were no sounds from the rest of the house and Brigit and the children were nowhere to be seen.

'Oh, Happiness . . . I'm so sorry,' Rose began, but then she stopped. Happiness was looking at her blankly, almost without recognition. Okay, Rose thought, let's play it like this, then; it's easier if we remain in the roles we know.

'Thanks for everything, Happiness,' she said, slipping a R100 note into her hand.

'Thank you, madam.' Happiness pocketed the money and went to stand in her spot against the wall, leaning on her hands.

Rose had planned to get the morning-after pill first thing, before she embarked on the long journey home. She decided to stop off at the chemist next to the Pick 'n Pay on the outskirts of town, since it was on her way; the parking would be easier there, too. Would they ask her for a script? She felt hot and prickly at the thought of having to confess her folly to the pharmacist. A one-night stand. And with no condom. God!

She got out her car and started towards the building, walking briskly, head down in contemplation. What if it was already too late? Strangely, the thought didn't alarm her nearly as much as it should. It wasn't the prospect of an unplanned pregnancy that bothered her; it was that other thing – the thing she couldn't even name to herself.

As she walked towards the shopping centre entrance, she saw a mob of workers emerge from the doors of Pick 'n Pay, like a swarm of dark-blue locusts in their uniforms. They carried placards that read:

Out with Fat Kat Bosses!
Wages below Bread-line = No Workers behind Tills
Better Wages + Better Working Conditions

They toyi-toyied towards her, ululating like banshees. Rose stood stock still, wondering whether to make a run for it. They were coming right at her. Before she knew it, she was enveloped in the sea of dark blue, swept off her feet, spun around and pulled along by the irresistible current. She found herself toyi-toyiing with the workers up the hill, her fist raised, sometimes hopping on one leg then changing to the other, stridently singing protest songs from the Struggle years; not knowing the words but joining in anyway.

They jogged along the national road that led out of Oberon, the sun beating angrily on their heads. Cars hooted and swerved sharply to avoid them, the drivers rolling down their windows to curse. Rose's was the only white face in the crowd. It was exhilarating, being part of this angry, militant mob. She threw her head back and laughed, turning to look at her neighbour, wanting to share her excitement. The woman smiled encouragingly at her.

'Hey!' Rose grabbed the woman's arm. She was so out of breath. 'Are you . . . aren't you . . .?' The woman looked at her questioningly. 'I know you! From Johannesburg . . . did you ever find your husband? And your son? Is he out of hospital?'

The woman grinned broadly at her then was swept away on a wave of toyi-toyiers rolling in from the back. Before Rose knew it, she'd been left behind. She walked back with a handful of stragglers heading towards Pick 'n Pay. She had to get a move on. She had a long road to travel and it was getting late.

It was only while filling up her car at Harrismith that she remembered that she still hadn't got the morning-after pill.

22

Whitecliff Court seemed part of another life. A few weeks after her return Rose was unlocking her flat when she heard a familiar voice at her shoulder.

'Hey neighbour, I haven't seen you in ages,' Abi said.

'I was in the Berg . . .' The Berg. Now she, too, could claim ownership and refer to it by its diminutive designation. 'Other than that I've been here. Where've you been?'

'I went home to Nigeria for the holidays. Just got back. I start college soon.'

'Aha! So you've been away, too. How's your uncle?' Rose asked.

Abi tossed her head, long braids whipping the air. 'He's back home – looking after his business interests. His managers were robbing him blind. So I'm in the flat by myself now.'

'Want to come in?' Rose invited.

'I'm just on my way to the mall. Later?'

'Sure. I've got something for you,' Rose smiled.

The plane tree outside the window looked tired, its leaves faded and wilting. It had been a hot, dry January. Rose wandered through the lounge, revelling in its new spaciousness. She'd done it – finally cleared the flat. Rid it of its clutter, made space for her life. The display cabinets were gone as well as some of the fussier items. She'd given away a lot – the Royal Doulton shepherdess, the Wedgwood Jasperware bowl, the Moorcroft jug . . . all gone to a charity shop. The Swarovski crystal hedgehog was waiting for Abi.

Rose looked at 'The Drakensberg Lady' still hanging in her place above the escritoire. She never had got round to buying Corrie's photos, the ones displayed on the walls of The Olive Branch. Perhaps there'd be another time.

Feeling all adrift since her work had ended, she sat down at the dining-room table and opened her computer, addicted to its blank screen. The email icon blinked. It was from Petra:

From: Petra Steyn
To: Rose Clemens
Re: White lady identified?

I think I've identified your white lady on the rocks. I'm here at the British Library, looking through diary journals of Victorian women travellers in Africa, and had an amazingly serendipitous find. Came across the transcript of a diary attributed to a Rosamund Swan who travelled to Natal in 1880, and then to the remote border village of Patilweng. There she encountered an encampment of the Bushmen and stayed with them for a few weeks, sketching them, studying their cultural practices, their rock paintings etc. How many white women could there be who travelled to the area at that time?

Rose read the email several times before her brain registered its meaning. Since her return from Oberon she had relegated her parentage quest to the backburner, but this startling information rekindled her interest. Rosamund Swan. Could she be the one? Rose imagined her swanning her way around Patilweng, walking regally amongst the goat droppings and naked children.

The ringtone of her cell phone pierced through the quiet in the flat.

'Hello Rose, it's Betty . . .'

Oh, remember her? Your former landlady from another life . . .

'We're back in town from Toronto. Harry said I must phone to see how you're doing. Come for tea on Saturday? I've invited Marion. And Glynnis. Do you know she's having trouble with her marriage? But don't say anything,' she warned. 'Marion told me in confidence.'

Poor Marion. There was no one more talented, more accomplished than her children and grandchildren. They were all so perfect. How would she deal with the failure of her daughter's marriage?

As for Betty . . . now she was a different kettle of fish. So what type of fish was she? Rose googled 'fish', and found: 'Boarfish, medusa fish, megamouth shark, old wife, red snapper, toothcarp'. Harry, clearly, was a 'grunt'; she chuckled.

At the appointed time on Saturday, Rose drove along Riviera Road, crossed Oxford Road into Saxonwold and sped down the hill past the zoo and into the quiet streets of Forest Town. The sun had settled on the head of the bronze Angel of Peace that sat atop the War Monument, and itchy balls from the plane trees formed golden eddies in the gutters as a harsh little wind, like a dry cough, blew in from the west.

It felt strange to be entering the property from the main entrance and not the cottage side, but when she spied her previous home through the hedges, it was as if she'd never lived there. Had Betty found a new tenant?

Glynnis stood next to the big pot filled with hydrangeas, no longer in bloom.

'Glynnis – it's been years!' Rose said, as they kissed each other. 'And . . . are these your children?' There was a little girl of about three clinging to Glynnis and mumbling into her leg that she wanted to go home, and a toddler who had pulled himself up onto the pot and was busy palming sand into his mouth.

'Oh, look at him,' Glynnis laughed, trying to wipe the sand away. The baby smiled up at her and screamed with delight. 'There's such a difference between girls and boys,' she said emphatically. 'And you, Rose – no marriage plans?'

‘No.’ Rose sat on the white wicker chair that faced out onto the garden. The giant old oaks threw long shadows onto the lawn, lush and verdant despite the absence of rain.

‘Maybe you’re better off. Look how great you look . . . and look at me.’

Glynnis had put on weight since Rose had seen her last. She looked worn out, heading towards middle age.

‘Well, come sit down.’ Betty bustled about.

‘You’ve got enough food here to feed an army, Betty,’ cried Marion.

Martha came onto the veranda carrying a tray laden with bone-china cups and saucers.

‘You can put it down here.’ Betty indicated an empty place on a server between a steaming urn, a large cheesecake, biscuits piled on a tiered stand and a platter of fruit. ‘I’ll put the fruit on the table.’

‘Hello, Martha,’ Rose said. ‘How are the children?’

‘You know Talita died?’ Betty said.

‘I’m so sorry,’ Rose said to Martha. It seemed an inadequate thing to say. ‘At least . . . her suffering is over now.’

‘Ja,’ Martha sighed. ‘But now I’ve got the problem with Pule.’ Shaking her head, she went back inside.

‘Rose, darling – how have you been?’ Marion paused in her adoring fussing over the children to blow a kiss to Rose. ‘I must say, you’re looking particularly well.’

‘Am I?’ Rose brought her hand up to touch her cheek lightly. ‘I’ve been away. Did me good.’

The baby had crawled over to the table and sunk his sandy fingers in a slice of melon. Glynnis whipped him away and he started to yell.

‘Darling, give him the melon. Here, give him to me. Have your tea then you can take him. Come, darling,’ Marion said to the little girl, ‘come with Granny. I want to show you how to make witch’s fingers.’ Baby on her hip, she held the little girl’s hand and led her to the wall adjoining the veranda. A big bignonia creeper grew there, heavy with flower. Putting the baby down on the ground, where he pulled at the tufts of grass, Marion picked a red trumpet bloom. 'Can you do this?' she asked, putting the bloom on the little girl's forefinger. 'I hope you don't mind me picking your flowers, Betty.' What a good granny, Rose thought.

'Marion's got a lot of energy,' Betty observed. 'You can't let them out of your sight for a second at their age. The pool's always a worry. With Pule here, we make sure the gate's kept closed . . . cheesecake, Glynnis?'

'I won't, thanks Betty,' Glynnis responded. 'I can't seem to shake this weight since the pregnancy.' To Rose, she said: 'Children are exhausting. You have to have help otherwise you can go mad.'

'I've got such a problem,' Betty informed them. 'Martha made me promise not to send Talita's child back to her family at her home when she dies. She says I must bring him up. Me! Bring him up! Rose, cheesecake?'

'Thanks. Looks delicious. I wouldn't worry too much. Who says she's going to die anytime soon?' Rose said, thinking that the situation at home must be really desperate if Martha thought Pule would be better off with Betty and Harry.

'Martha's old. She's got all types of problems. High blood pressure, water on the heart. I don't know what all.'

'Oh, I will have a piece of cheesecake, thanks. But just a little one,' Glynnis told Betty.

'Why can't she send him home? They all do it,' Marion retorted from the sidelines.

'She says she can't burden them with him. They're all just children themselves. There's no one looking after them there. They fend for themselves.'

'Well you can't take this on. Not at your stage of life,' Marion declared firmly.

'I can't. Not at any age. He's got Aids, you know,' she told them conspiratorially. 'Who's going to make sure he gets his medicine? He needs medicine every day. He gets sick often. No – even if he was healthy . . . I don't know what I'm going to do about it. I told Harry I want to emigrate. Run away from the problem. He tells me I'm mad but I can't help feeling guilty.'

Glynnis asked: 'Where is he now?'

'Playing golf.'

'Huh? No, the child – with Aids.'

'Oh,' Betty said breezily, 'he's around somewhere. In the back. With Martha.'

'Well, I don't want him near my children.'

'I feel like letting Martha go but she's the only breadwinner for all those children. Who's going to employ her at her age?' Betty forked a large piece of cheesecake into her mouth.

An image of the boy presented itself to Rose. She remembered the challenge in his eyes as he cast his spell on her. What he needed was nurturing, a stable home, decent education . . . a computer . . . cell phone . . . Sony Playstation . . . Would he get this in Martha's care under Betty's roof? More so than if he returned to his ancestral home. But still, it was far from ideal. What would happen when Martha died? She couldn't live forever. And Betty, too, wasn't that young.

'I'll take him. I'll adopt him,' Rose said, with a nonchalance that belied the utter astonishment she felt at her own words. Where had they come from? They seemed to have popped unbidden into her mouth.

'Who?' Glynnis said, her fork poised ready to deliver a large mouthful from a second helping of cake.

'Pule. I'll adopt him. And by the way, he hasn't got Aids. He's HIV positive – there's a difference. And it's being well managed, from what I can gather.' She was feeling more sure of herself now.

The three women stared at her, mouths open and forks frozen in mid-air.

Glynnis gave a mordant laugh. 'You are joking, hey? You can't mean it?' She'd taken over from Marion as childminder and was standing on the grass with the children, who sat in a pile of scarlet witch's fingers, shrieking as they threw them up into the air.

'I do mean it,' Rose said, very serious. They were right to be shocked; taking on a child like Pule wouldn't be problem-free, she knew that. Aside from the fact that he was HIV-positive, there would be issues about roots and culture and identity. She understood this better than most. And, because of that, she'd probably know how to deal with it better as well.

Marion, who had popped a strawberry into her mouth, said thickly: 'Do you know what you'd be taking on? Arnold was telling me the other day how much it costs to raise a child. Probably a million, in today's money.'

'But that's with private schooling,' asserted Betty. 'He wouldn't need to go to a private school. There are still some government schools that are . . . er . . . decent.' She didn't see the need to discourage Rose.

'But she's young. Why should she burden herself with this? And on her own? And on top of it all, this Aids or HIV or whatever – he's not a well child. When she does meet a man, it might put him off. You're ruining your chances, Rose – your life! What do you think Livvie would have advised you to do?' Marion looked serious.

Rose laughed dryly. 'Livvie? I know what she would have done. Anyway, Martha will be there to help. She may be old but she'll still be around for a while.'

'Well, I think it's a good idea,' Betty pronounced.

'I think you're mad!' Glynnis asserted.

'Maybe I am,' Rose said. 'But I mean it. Absolutely. I was thinking of moving out the flat anyway, letting it and going into a house. Maybe in Orchards or . . . I'll have to see where there are schools. I'll employ Martha. They can both come and live with me. We'll do it properly – I'll adopt him legally, and then when Martha dies, he'll just carry on living with me.'

‘Listen, don’t make any rash decisions. You need to think about this very carefully before you commit. Maybe talk to someone, a lawyer, or your therapist,’ Marion advised. ‘And remember, I’m there for you. You can always talk to me. I’ve got big ears!’ She smiled benignly, gently yanking at the large fake earrings clipped to her ear lobes.

The sky was streaked with orange and faded blue when Rose got into her car to leave. A Hadeda honked despondently overhead. Rose snorted derisively as she drove. She could just imagine what the women in the house were saying about her. They probably thought she was just being contrary, that she wouldn’t go through with it. But she was dead serious. She could give Pule a great life. And Martha would be there to help. Rose would employ someone else to assist with the housework.

She must remember to phone the lawyers first thing in the morning.

23

From: Petra Steyn
To: Rose Clemens
Re: White Goddess identified?

The White Goddess in the painting is *Rosamund Swan! The one and same woman who lived with the Bushmen and wrote the diary. For a 22-year-old of her era she was amazingly accomplished and self-assured. She apparently didn't die in the Drakensberg but returned to London towards the end of 1880.*

I looked in Debretts and similar sources for background info. She was born in 1858. Her family were minor members of society. Her father, Sir Edward Swan, was landed gentry. She was something of a celebrity, fêted by the arty set, in particular the artist Sir Philip Geoffrey. She was the model for both 'The Drakensberg Lady' and 'The White Goddess', which was probably a collaborative effort, the background detail being her own work, based on sketches and watercolours she made during her stay in Patilweng. It seems like she and Geoffrey were lovers for a time although both were married to other partners and he was much older than her. And the Bushmen paying homage . . . probably her take. Maybe a deliberate distortion of the far less flattering version done by the medicine man on the rocks. I can't find out where the White Goddess painting is now.

Early the following week, Rose was shown into Marshall Bleazard's office. The lawyer listened silently when she told him of her plan to adopt Pule. Contrary to her expectations, he didn't try to dissuade her, simply stared hard at her over his glasses, and then said: 'If you're sure that's what you want, I see no problem. I'll contact the adoption agency and set the process in motion.'

Jubilant at the ease with which her proposal had been accepted, Rose felt the need to celebrate. Drawn on a whim, she turned into Hyde Park Corner and, car safely parked, joined the throngs cruising through the mall. As she rounded the stairs that led to the first shopping level, she saw a Perspex stand full of posters, their slogans singing out phrases like: 'Own your piece of the Drakensberg'; 'Development of Distinction'; 'Freehold and fractional ownership'; 'Fully-stocked trout dams'; 'Flyfishers' Paradise'.

The salesman in charge of the stand had a distinctly bizarre appearance. He was oddly dressed, in a limp tartan kilt and tatty, ruffled shirt. On one leg he wore a thick, knee-high khaki sock, while the other, which looked like a prosthesis, was wrapped in a grubby white bandage. He thrust a pamphlet into Rose's chest and started to speak, but she couldn't hear a word over the noise of lunchtime shoppers and blaring muzak.

'Thanks,' she said, taking the pamphlet without slowing down. So she, too, could own a piece of the Berg, she thought, as she peered into shop windows filled with luxury goods that only people who felt entitled to own a piece of the Berg would buy. It made her sad, the Berg being sold off that way. Was this one of those dodgy enterprises where developers greased the Enviro official's palm and Bob's your aunty?

She passed the shop with the beautiful chiffon dress that had floated down over her head like a butterfly. On impulse she stopped, turned on her heel and entered. The saleslady behind the counter was not the friendly young girl from before but an older woman, with runny black lines around her eyes. She barely looked up as Rose entered.

Rose sifted through the designer wear on the rail. There was a large sign attached: 'Summer Sale – less 35%'. The dress was still there. It felt like a good omen. She fingered the midnight-blue chiffon, deciding she had to have it. She didn't care whether or not it was frivolous, whether or not there would be an occasion when she'd get to wear it. She took it over to the counter.

'Don't you want to try it on?' the lady with the raccoon eyes said, eyeing her curiously.

'Er . . . no . . . thanks. I already did.'

The saleslady wrapped the dress in tissue paper as carefully as if it were human tissue, gently stuck the parcel down with a sticker and placed it in a white carrier bag – which had to be the fanciest that Rose had ever carried. The shop's initials were embossed onto the thick cardboard and it had a black satin ribbon for a handle. Walking through the shopping centre, the bag knocking against her thigh, Rose felt she had joined the ranks of the Hyde Park cognoscenti.

Back at Whitecliff Court, she placed the package on the bed and slowly unwrapped it. The membranous dress fluttered in the barely there air currents as she picked it up and held it against her body. She gazed at her reflection in the mirror; it looked as if she'd immersed herself in the deep-blue Drakensberg sky. She threaded the dress through a hanger and hung it on the rail in her wardrobe, then stood back to admire the new addition – a midnight-blue butterfly coming to rest in a field of flax.

From: Petra Steyn
To: Rose Clemens
Re: Rosamund's daughters

I've been nosing around genealogical records and have made some really interesting discoveries about Rosamund's descendants. Rosamund married Cedric Grail not long after she got back from South Africa, in February, 1881. She had quite a few children, including a Regina who was born in 1890. Regina married James Room, and they had Rita who was born in 1924. It seems that the girls in (your?) family line all have names beginning with the letter 'R'. Rita, with her husband Simon Crystal, embarked on the Gloucester Castle for Durban, where they docked in 1946. (Saw ship's manifesto.) From here, I lose the trail.

My thought is that Rita Crystal is your mother's mother. But then, why is your mother's surname Le Grange and not Crystal? Did Rita get divorced from Simon Crystal and marry a Mr Le Grange? Was your mother perhaps married to a Le Grange? It's up to you to pick up the threads from here. You'd need to apply to Home Affairs for marriage, birth certificates etc. Maybe employ a genealogist. I'm not sure how you find a reputable one or how expensive it is. If you make the link, you could probably trace your ancestry back to Boadicea!

Rose rested her chin on her hand and stared at the words in front of her. Okay – let's say Rosamund Swan . . . Grail . . . is my third great grandmother, she thought. What difference would it make to my life? Would it change it in any way? I don't think so.

What was this human need to trace genetic ancestry? What drove people to untangle the branches of their family trees, even if they uncovered bad roots and rotten apples in the process? Was it purely about identity? Did people believe that by knowing where they came from, they would know themselves? Could you ever know yourself?

Or was it all just about ego and vanity? People wanted to discover greatness in their ancestors as evidence of the genius lurking in their own genes. Or maybe it had to with the need to feel part of an extended family, a connecting web of cousins, aunts, uncles, grandfathers and grandmothers; a network that grew wider and wider the further back you went . . . back and back, until there was the one Eve who spawned us all . . . all of us sharing her genes.

Rose didn't know the answers. She clicked the Internet icon and typed in 'Eve' and 'genetic ancestry' into the box. Good ol' Wikipedia delivered the following:

> *In the field of human genetics, Mitochondrial Eve refers to the ancestor from whom all living humans are descended. She is generally estimated to have lived around 200,000 years ago, most likely in East Africa, when Homo sapiens sapiens was developing as a species.*
>
> *Modern humans originated in Africa and spread from there . . .*

So; she didn't need to trace her ancestry back to Rosamund, who lived a hundred years ago – or back to Boadicea, who lived two thousand years ago. She, Rose, was descended from Mitochondrial Eve who lived two hundred thousand years ago. In Africa! Where every single person on the planet had originated . . . or so the current thinking went. Everyone had a claim, a stake in Africa. We are all Africans – what an irony. She laughed.

24

'How old did you say those seeds of yours were?' Hank had phoned Rose one evening as she lay flopped on the floral couch, watching TV with half an eye.

'Thirty years at least.' She sat up, placing her bare feet on the carpet and toyed with the rosewood box on the coffee table.

'Well, that's unbelievable – some of them have germinated. Must have been stored in ideal conditions. At first, I couldn't make out what they were – they were so strange – but then I realised they were part of Eric Vogel's experiments.'

'Eric Vogel?'

'He was a farmer from around here who used to do weird experiments with crops: lucerne, maize . . . he even had his own lab . . . a real mad scientist.'

'Where is he?'

'Long dead. But his widow's still alive. Lives here, in town. She has a small place down the road.'

'What type of man was he, this Eric Vogel?' Rose demanded breathlessly.

'He seemed decent. A family man . . . I dunno. What d'you mean, what type of man?'

'Hey, listen, I'm coming down there. I'll leave first thing tomorrow morning. Do you have accommodation for me?'

'I'll check the bookings. But even if the cottages are full I'm sure we can make a plan.'

'Thank you. And Hank – I need to get hold of . . . Dr Metheus.'

'Wim?' She heard his breathing for a moment. 'Should I be jealous? Are you planning a thingy with him?'

'Something like that.'

'Lucky sod. Try his cell. He's often out of range. The weekends are better – that's when he's usually in town. I'll get you the number.'

Hank was waiting on the veranda of the cottage as Rose drove into The Chameleon late in the afternoon of the following day. She almost didn't recognise the place, with the high electrified wall that now surrounded it and electronic gates.

'Rose!' Hank pressed her to his chest for a moment then held her away at arm's length: 'Wow! Look at you! Can it be possible that you're even more beautiful? What's changed?'

Certainly not your methods of seduction; sorry, Heartbreak Hank, but I can see right through you. 'I've put on weight,' she said.

'Suits you.'

'Thank you.' She looked around, gesturing at the new security measures. 'Feels like home from home,' she commented wryly.

Hank took her bags out of the car and deposited them on the veranda of her old cottage.

'So, don't keep me in suspense. What's the story with the seeds?' she said.

'Come look for yourself,' he grinned.

As he led her round the back of the carport, she noticed that Brigit's Volvo wasn't parked in its usual spot, then remembered that it had been taken in the robbery.

'Brigit not here? How's she doing?' she asked.

'Ja, better with the increased security. She's gone into town. She'll be back soon.' He stopped at a rusty iron frame supporting rough wooden shelves, where rows of seedlings grew in small plastic pots.

'Are those my seeds?' Rose asked.

He nodded, picking up one of the pots. 'Check this out. Amazing! See these maize leaves? They're crinkly. At first I thought something had attacked the seedlings, a virus or something. But then I saw . . . take a look at this lucerne plant; see the colour? It's purple. Lucerne's normally bright green.' He tapped the side of the pot. 'So then the penny dropped and I realised that these must be some of Eric Vogel's mutant plants.'

'So this was what Eric Vogel was busy doing? How was he doing it?'

Hank shrugged. 'He told everyone he was taking bits of genetic stuff . . . genes . . . from one plant, and even bits from goggas and things, and sticking them into other plants. In his shed. But that was back then and no one believed him. Now, they're doing that sort of thing all the time.'

'Thirty years ago would have been early 80s. He was a pioneer of genetic engineering?'

'Ja, I suppose you could put it like that. You know, he committed suicide. No one believed him, about his work. He was this big failure. Everyone round here thought he was loony tunes. Where did you get these seeds from, Rose? Remind me.'

The Dragon's Tooth loomed gun-metal grey in her windscreen as Rose drove towards the widow's home on the outskirts of town. It was Saturday, just after lunch. She'd struggled with the information Hank had given her, thought just to ignore it; but her curiosity had won out.

Hello, Mrs Vogel – I might be your husband's love child. Do you know of any affair he had? Did he tell you that he might have a love child? Can I come over and see you? Maybe you can identify him in a picture I found, or maybe you can spot the resemblance between us . . .

Rose didn't know what she would say. When she finally phoned Mrs Vogel, she merely asked if she could visit, saying that she was interested in her late husband's work.

The house was a small bungalow that stood on a flat patch of neatly mown lawn, encircled by wire-mesh fencing. There was no other vegetation on the property; no flowering bushes, no annuals or perennials, not even a pot filled with aging chrysanthemums on the slastoed apron that surrounded the house. Was Mrs Vogel another Livvie, who didn't like looking after living things? Rose leant her forehead against the wooden door for a moment before ringing the bell. Her mouth felt bone dry from anxiety. She had told herself that just because Eric Vogel's experimental seeds were in the box along with the other objects, that didn't mean he was her father. The connection was as flimsy as her new dress. With no hard evidence, she wasn't intending to drop a bombshell on the poor widow. What was she going to say, then?

Mrs Vogel opened the door, a shrunken slip of a woman wearing a faded yellow housecoat, shabby Jiffy slippers and false teeth that clattered slightly when she spoke. She had a strong South African accent, augmented by a sibilance from the teeth. Her hair was grey and wispy, like the fur of the dog she carried in her arms.

'Thanks for coming. I get lonely these days. I like to have visitors. Dusty here's my only company now. I need to pick him up when the doorbell rings otherwise he piddles on the carpet. He's very nervous,' she told Rose, who tickled the dog's bony head.

The house was dark and smelt musty, as if there had once been a chain-smoker living there. Rose followed the woman into the lounge off the entrance hall and sat down on an old, faded sofa with crocheted antimacassars on the arms and back. There were dusty ornaments in the room and paintings on the walls of the mountains, and mountain lakes, and moonlight in all seasons, the dark, denatured oils murky and moody.

Rose cleared her throat: 'Mrs Vogel, thanks very much for seeing me.'

'Would you like some tea?' She peered short-sightedly at Rose from across the room. The dog lay stretched out at her feet atop the faded roses patterning the old carpet, his belly rising and falling rapidly.

'Er . . . no thanks . . .' Rose felt herself wilting in the room, the air of it heavy with unknowable secrets. Her confidence waning, she drew a deep breath: 'Mrs Vogel, I'm interested in your husband's work. It seems . . . he was a real pioneer in genetic engineering. Did you know what he was doing?'

'No, my dear. I'm afraid I never understood his work. He never discussed it with me. He spent all his time in his workroom, in the shed or outside. I was looking after the house, busy with the children. There was the farm but that was never very successful. He was too busy with his seeds. It was his father's, the farm, but he wasn't interested in it. I used to tell him, "Eric" – I used to say – "we've got mouths to feed". He used to read a lot, get magazines from all over the world. Cost a fortune. He spent years and years on his work.' She shook her head. 'And he was so talented. He had a brilliant mind, you know. Such a waste. He . . . he took his own life, you know.'

Rose nodded. How? she wanted to ask. 'Yes, I heard. Terrible. When was that?'

'It was in 1984,' the woman sighed.

I was two at the time, Rose thought. Ruby was already dead.

'Time flies. It's a lifetime ago. Left us in a terrible way, me and the children. Never got over seeing him like that. That sight has stayed with me always.' She shook her head. 'I never told the children how he died until they were all grown up, you know. Maybe that was a mistake – I don't know. Nowadays, they have other ideas but in those days things got swept under the carpet. You never discussed anything out in the open.'

'How many children do you have?'

'Five. Ja.' She beamed, showing lots of teeth and gum. 'They're all grown up now, with their own children. None of them live here anymore. It's just me. They were all quite young at the time. It was very hard. I tried keeping the farm on my own but I had to sell eventually. It was too hard for a woman to manage the workers. Zulus – you know. They don't like being told what to do by a woman. There were terrible debts. I had no one to turn to. No skills, no certificates. We struggled and scraped. I baked, helped in the home industry, knitted little animals and what not. Things like that. But the children have all done well. They're all educated, they all live nicely. They got their father's brains, not mine,' she chuckled. She proceeded to tell Rose in detail about the five children, their qualifications, their spouses' qualifications and the quantity, gender and ages of their children.

Rose nodded along, thinking that she could be hearing about her half siblings, nieces and nephews. A whole new clan.

'He could have made millions with his discoveries . . . I don't know,' Mrs Vogel said dejectedly.

'He was doing really ground-breaking stuff. Do you have any photos of him?' Rose asked.

'Ja, I do.' She stood up. 'Come with me.' She picked up the dog. 'Are you sure you won't have something cold to drink?'

Rose shook her head and followed her hostess down the dark passage, stealing a look into each room as they passed. The woman led her to a small bedroom with faded floral curtains and matching bedcover. On the bedside table, alongside a *You* magazine and a pair of reading glasses, was a framed wedding photo of the young Mr and Mrs Vogel. Black and white. Rose's hand trembled as she took the picture from Mrs Vogel's hand.

How long did it take before your husband strayed? 'What year was this taken?' she asked her.

Mrs Vogel responded without hesitation. '1974.'

'You were so pretty. And the groom so handsome.' He was blondish, wavy-haired, maybe blue-eyed . . . or grey. Moustache. Smiling. Nice straight teeth; at least he complied in this one respect with her picture of an ideal father.

This was how they had started out, the Vogels, in a world that held such promise for them. What had happened to the pretty girl with the Stork-margarine skin? This poor old woman didn't need to know about her husband's affair . . . if indeed it was him; the man in the Polaroid. *Oberon, Sept. 1981*. Rose would never know. She wasn't going to ask the woman to take a look, to confirm whether that could have been her husband, relieving his seven-year itch with Rose's mother, Ruby, who was having her own moment of madness under the sun . . . or was it in a cave? And she wasn't going to contact any of the children, either – all grown-up now with children of their own; at least, not until Mrs Vogel had passed on. And even then . . . would she do it? It would open such a can of worms.

Rose Vogel. It had a certain ring to it, but she preferred Clemens. All these potential relatives – she laughed silently; they'd be banging on her door if they knew her worth!

'I've got some photo albums, too. Do you want to see them?' Mrs Vogel asked eagerly.

'I'd love to.' She was burning to see if within them were any photos of a brawny man with a droopy moustache, wearing a cowboy hat pushed low on his forehead. But she fretted about how long it would take to page through the albums. She had an urgent phone call to make. An assignation that wouldn't wait. She could feel her anxiety levels rising as she pored over page after page of family snaps, to the accompaniment of Mrs Vogel's running commentary. There were not many in which Eric Vogel appeared. And none of those she saw featured him wearing a cowboy hat. He may have been the man in the Polaroid . . . or not. She couldn't tell for sure.

But she was interested in the Vogel children, too. Four were tall and blond. The Oberon look? Sporty-looking, always laughing . . . they had their father's teeth. One was small and dark with soulful eyes, taking after her mother. And then the pictures of weddings, and the spouses, and the next generation. She could see the facial features passed down from father to son, mother to daughter. Did any of her features bear a similarity to theirs? She was dying to ask Mrs Vogel . . . but didn't, couldn't. And she was just too close to be able to see it for herself.

She left at last. It seemed as if the musty smell of the Vogel house had penetrated her clothes and coated her hair. She lifted a lock to her nose and sniffed distastefully. Returning to the cottage, she showered and washed her hair, then sat in front of the mirror at the dressing table. Her hair dripped onto her breasts, which were full and heavy, blue-veined and milky white. She put her hand over her belly and closed her eyes; the secret that was in there. She loved the thought. No, not just a thought – a state, a condition.

She and Wim had arranged to meet in the late afternoon, when the sun sank into the peaks and the day lost its burnt brittleness. They met at Lakeview Farm – Rose's suggestion. She stood for a moment, observing him as he stood at the water's edge, looking into the lake. Sensing her eyes, he turned around suddenly. She walked hesitantly down the hill towards him, the blue of her dress floating around her like a piece of Drakensberg sky. She was very aware of him watching her. Who was this man? What did she know about him?

'Do you want to walk?' he asked her.

She nodded and they paced in silence around the lake, their shoulders a breath apart, until they reached their starting point again.

'Come, we sit.' He directed her to a bench at the water's edge, overlooking the velvet of bulrushes interspersed with yellow water irises, their petals like crinkle paper.

She could feel his gaze on her, expectant and eager; but she kept her eyes on the shimmering water. A pair of ducks sailed together in the shallows and water striders skated across the reflective surface – a magical membrane that separated the light and the air from the dark and unknowable depths below.

It was a time for words, for truths. She had to speak out – it was now or never.

'Wim, I'm pregnant . . .'

She saw his body tense at her words, heard the intake of his breath.

'Please . . .' she whispered, holding up her hand. 'Don't say anything.' She swallowed hard. 'I'm not asking for support. I don't need anything. There's no problem with . . . finances.' Again he made as if to speak and again she silenced him. 'It was my choice to have this child but . . . but I had to tell you . . . it's your child as well. There's always a . . . a paternity test, if you want . . . but it is yours . . . In case anything happens to me, I've made a will . . . lodged your name with a lawyer. It would be your choice whether you wanted to take it on or not.'

She kept her eyes on the water, not daring to look at his face.

'I wanted to at least give you the opportunity to know your child, to be the father . . . It's your right. I'd like this child to know her biological father . . . for your child to know you. If you want that. It is a girl, by the way. I'm going to name her Reverie . . .' At that point Rose broke off, unable to speak any longer. Her eyes had filled with tears and she knew that if one escaped, she would begin to weep, and once she started, the lake would overflow with her tears. It was like that in pregnancy; you blamed it on hormones.

Wim's hand came up and with the lightest of touches, stroked her cheek.

They sat silently side by side, looking out over the water that reflected the darkening sky. Rose began to compose a letter in her mind:

Dear . . . Marshall,
I would like to fund a facility for vulnerable children in the Gabriel's Gate valley in Lesotho. In John and Livvie's name. No – in the name of Ruby. Or . . . maybe the community should name the project. I think I'll come and live in the Berg for a while. In Oberon. Or in the Gabriel's Gate valley. For a while. While the project's getting off the ground. Or until there are decisions to be made about schools. Pule can meet his siblings, his family, get to know them . . . And – Wim can get to know his child. And me. Oh, and by the way – in the really unlikely event of my death, the project will be taken up by him, Dr Wim Metheus, co-executor and biological father of my unborn daughter.

The sun had begun to sink into the water. She watched the sparkling path it made on the calm surface and felt as if she'd emerged from secret depths into the light, arms upraised to greet the world. She was suddenly awed by the wonder and miracle of her existence; the existence of her unborn child; and the strength of her foremothers, each of whom had survived to bear the next generation . . . and the next . . . and the next. On and on. She could envisage the straight line that led from her original mother to herself, from the beginning of time to the present . . . and then further forward, on to the next generation.

A heron hovered overhead, with a fish in its bill, then swooped towards the water where it flew, skating along the surface, until it disappeared from view.

Glossary

AA	Affirmative Action
Allele	Genetic material transmitted from parent to offspring. Each gene is comprised of two alleles, one from each parent
Babalaas	Hangover
Bakkie	Pick-up truck
BEE	Black Economic Empowerment
Biltong	Meat salted and dried into strips
Boerboel	Large, mastiff-like South African dog bred for its strength and protective qualities; a popular choice with farmers, hence its name, which means 'farmer's dog'
Boerewors	South African sausage
Braai	Barbecue
Doek	Headscarf
Donga	Ravine
Dorp	Town
Gogga	Insect
Haai	Exclamation of surprise or displeasure

Homeless Talk	A fundraising magazine sold by homeless people on the streets of Johannesburg
Ja-nee	Afrikaans speech mannerism; literally, 'yes-no'
Khakibos	A pungent-smelling weed
Klaar	Afrikaans for 'finished'
Koeksister	A twisted doughnut, deep fried and dipped in syrup
Koppie	Small hill
Kraal	Traditional homestead or cattle pen
Kugel	Slang for a spoilt, wealthy, materialistic woman
KZN	KwaZulu-Natal
Laat lammetjie	'Late lamb', referring to the last-born child, implying something of an afterthought
Lala ngoxolo	Rest in peace
Larney	Slang for 'smart' or 'stuck-up'
Mealie	Maize
Muti	Traditional medicine
Ninjani	How are you?
Okes	Colloquialism for 'boys'
Pap	Porridge made of maize meal
Platteland	The 'flat' regions of South Africa, particularly the Free State, traditionally the Afrikaner stronghold

Randlord	One of the wealthy Johannesburg mining magnates of the early twentieth-century
Sakabula	Colloquial name for the Long-tailed Widow Bird
Sangoma	Diviner
Sanibonani, mkhulu	Greetings, grandfather
Saphila	I am well
Sawubona	A greeting addressed to one person
Shweshwe	Ethnic-print fabric
Slap chips	Fried potato chips, crisp on the outside, soft on the inside
Sluk	Swig or gulp down
Tata wethu	Our father
Toyi-toyi	Stylised dance-step used on protest marches
Tsotsi	Gangster
Umlungu	White person
Veldskoene	Supple walking shoes made of animal hide
Verkykerskop, Jakkalskop, Leeukop	Lookout Hill, Jackals Hill, Lion Hill
Voetstoets	Just as it is
Wits	University of the Witwatersrand